BY THE BROODING TYCOON

BY

LUCY GORDON

AND

FIXED UP WITH MR RIGHT?

BY

MARIE FERRARELLA

MILLS & BOON

Dear Reader,

Years ago "family" suggested a gathering of relatives living in or near the same place, certainly the same country. But as travel speeded up, the world grew smaller, and a family could be spread over a great distance.

This has been useful to Amos Falcon, a man who believes in doing what suits himself. Starting poor, he's pursued his dream of wealth through many counties, fathering sons wherever he goes: England, America, France and Russia.

In his eyes they are all his property. With a great fortune to distribute in his will, he's studied them, wanting to see in each one a reflection of himself.

In a sense he's right. They all have their father's determination, skill, money-making ability, and, when necessary, ruthlessness. But they also have qualities their father lacks. Some are gentle, generous, some have charm, and all of them are waiting for the woman who can bring out their true nature.

Darius, the eldest, seems most like his forbidding father, but his startling encounter with Harriet, an impudent young woman, turns his world upside down. Unlike most people she isn't afraid of him, and when she saves his life it's the harbinger of another rescue—when she will save his heart and soul, and keep him safe for ever.

On their wedding day Darius' brothers gather, knowing that if they too are lucky the same day will dawn for them. Their stories have yet to be told.

I don't think I've ever liked one of my own heroines better than Harriet. Right to the end I was cheering her on, hoping that Darius would turn out to be good enough for her. But she thinks he is, and that's what really matters.

Lucy

RESCUED BY THE BROODING TYCOON

BY
LUCY GORDON

First published in Great Britain 2011
by Mills & Boon, an imprint of Harlequin (UK) Limited,
Eton House, 18-24 Paradise Road, Richmond, Surrey TW9 1SR

© Lucy Gordon 2011

ISBN: 978 0 263 88902 4

23-0811

Harlequin (UK) policy is to use papers that are natural, renewable and recyclable products and made from wood grown in sustainable forests. The logging and manufacturing processes conform to the legal environmental regulations of the country of origin.

Printed and bound in Spain
by Blackprint CPI, Barcelona

Lucy Gordon cut her writing teeth on magazine journalism, interviewing many of the world's most interesting men, including Warren Beatty, Charlton Heston and Sir Roger Moore. She also camped out with lions in Africa and had many other unusual experiences which have often provided the background for her books. Several years ago, while staying Venice, she met a Venetian who proposed in two days. They have been married ever since. Naturally this has affected her writing, where romantic Italian men tend to feature strongly.

Two of her books have won the Romance Writers of America RITA® award.

You can visit her website at www.lucy-gordon.com

I should like to dedicate this book to the Royal National Lifeboat Institution, without whose help my heroine could never have been as spunky as she is.

CHAPTER ONE

IT WAS the burst of beauty that caught Darius unaware.
He didn't regard himself as a man vulnerable to beauty.
Efficiency, ruthlessness, financial acumen, these things
could be counted on.

He'd been driven to hire a helicopter on the English
mainland and fly five miles across the sea to the little
island of Herringdean. Since it was now his property, it
made good sense to inspect it briefly on his way to an even
more important meeting.

Good sense. Cling to that, since everything else had
failed him.

But the sudden vision of sunlit sea, the waves glittering
as they broke against the sand, stunned him and made him
press closer to the window.

'Go lower,' he commanded, and watched as the helicopter descended, sweeping along the coast of Herringdean
Island. From here he could study the place with a critical
eye.

Or so he believed. But there was no criticism in the
glance he turned on the lush green cliffs, the golden
beaches; only astonished pleasure.

The cliffs were sinking until they were only a few feet
higher than the beach. He could see a large house that
must once have been elegant, but was now fast falling into

disrepair. In front of it stretched a garden leading to a plain lawn, close to the sand.

In the far distance were buildings that must be Ellarick, the largest town on the island: population twenty thousand.

'Land here,' he said, 'on that lawn.'

'I thought you wanted to fly over the town,' the pilot protested.

But suddenly he yearned to avoid towns, cars, crowds. The beach seemed to call to him. It was an unfamiliar sensation for a man who wasn't normally impulsive. In the financial world impulsiveness could be dangerous, yet now he yielded with pleasure to the need to explore below.

'Go lower,' he repeated urgently.

Slowly the machine sank onto the lawn. Darius leapt out, a lithe figure whose fitness and agility belied the desk-bound businessman he usually was, and hurried down to the beach. The sand was slightly damp, but smooth and hard, presenting little threat to his expensive appearance.

That appearance had been carefully calculated to inform the world that here was a successful man who could afford to pay top prices for his clothes. A few grains of sand might linger on his handmade shoes but they could be easily brushed off, and it was a small price to pay for what the beach offered him.

Peace.

After the devastating events that had buffeted him recently there was nothing more blessed than to stand here in the sunlight, throw his head back, close his eyes, feel the soft breeze on his face, and relish the silence.

So many years spent fighting, conspiring, manoeuvring, while all the time this simple perfection had been waiting, and he hadn't realised.

Outwardly, Darius seemed too young for such thoughts;

in his mid-thirties, tall, strong, attractive, ready to take on the world. Inwardly, he knew otherwise. He had already taken on the world, won some battles, lost others, and was weary to his depths.

But here there could be a chance to regain strength for the struggles that lay ahead. He breathed in slowly, yielding himself to the quiet, longing for it to last.

Then it ended.

A shriek of laughter tore the silence, destroying the peace. With a groan he opened his eyes and saw two figures in the sea, heading for the shore. As they emerged from the water he realised that one of them was a large dog. The other was a young woman in her late twenties with a lean, athletic build, not voluptuous but dashingly slender, with long elegant legs. Her costume was a modest black one-piece, functional rather than enticing, and her brown hair was pinned severely back out of the way.

As a man much pursued by women, Darius knew they commonly used swimming as a chance to parade their beauty. But if this girl was sending out any message to men it was, *I wear what's useful, so don't kid yourself that I'm flaunting my body to attract you.*

'Can I help you?' she cried merrily as she bounced up the beach.

'I'm just looking round, getting the feel of the place.'

'Yes, it's wonderful, isn't it? Sometimes I think if I ever get to heaven it'll be just like this. Not that I expect to go to heaven. They slam the gates on characters like me.'

Although he would have died before admitting it, the reference to heaven so exactly echoed his own thoughts that now he found he could forgive her for interrupting him.

'Characters like what?' he asked.

'Awkward,' she said cheerfully. 'Lots of other things too, but chiefly awkward. That's what my friends say.'

'Those friends who haven't been driven away by your awkwardness?'

'Right.'

He indicated the house behind him. 'I believe that belongs to Morgan Rancing.'

'Yes, but if you've come to see him you've had a wasted journey. Nobody knows where he is.'

Rancing was on the far side of the world, hiding from his creditors, including himself, but Darius saw no need to mention that.

She stepped back to survey him, a curious look in her eyes. Then it vanished as though an idea had occurred to her, only to be dismissed as impossible.

'You're lucky Rancing isn't here,' she observed. 'He'd hit the roof at you bringing down your machine on his land. Nobody's allowed on his property.'

'Does that include this beach?' he asked, regarding the fences that enclosed the stretch of sand.

'It certainly does.' She gave a chuckle. 'Be a sport. If you see him, don't say you caught me on his private beach. He disapproves of my swimming here.'

'But you do it anyway,' he observed wryly.

'It's so lovely that I can't resist. The other beaches are full of holidaymakers but here you can have it all to yourself; just you and the sun and the sky.' She flung out her arms in a dramatic gesture, smiling up at him. 'The world is yours.'

Darius nodded, feeling a curious sense of ease at the way her thoughts chimed with his own, and looked at her with renewed interest. Despite her boyish air, she wasn't lacking in feminine charm. There was real beauty in her eyes, that were large and deep blue, full of life, seeming to invite him into a teasing conspiracy.

'That's very true,' he said.

'So you won't tell him that you saw me on his private beach?'

'Actually, it's my private beach.'

Her smile vanished. 'What do you mean?'

'This island is mine now.'

'Rancing sold it to you?' she gasped.

Without knowing it, she'd said the fatal word. Rancing hadn't sold him the island, he'd tricked him into it. In a flash, his goodwill towards her vanished, and a stubborn expression overtook his face. 'I told you it's mine,' he said harshly. 'That's all that matters. My name is Darius Falcon.'

She drew a quick breath. 'I thought I'd seen your face before, in the newspaper. Weren't you the guy who—?'

'Never mind that,' he interrupted curtly. He knew his life, both private and business, had been all over the papers, and he didn't like being reminded of it. 'Perhaps now you'll tell me who you are.'

'Harriet Connor,' she said. 'I have an antique shop in Ellarick.'

'I shouldn't think you get much trade in this place,' he said, looking around at the isolation.

'On the contrary, Herringdean attracts a lot of tourists. Surely you knew that?'

The question, *How could you buy it without knowing about it?* hung in the air. Since he wasn't prepared to discuss the ignominious way he'd been fooled, he merely shrugged.

From behind Harriet came a loud yelp. The dog was charging up the beach, spraying water everywhere, heading straight for Darius.

'Steady, Phantom,' she called, trying to block his way.

'Keep him off me,' Darius snapped.

But it was too late. Gleeful at the sight of a stranger to

investigate, the dog hurled himself the last few feet, reared up on his hind legs and slammed his wet, sandy paws down on Darius's shoulders. He was a mighty beast, able to meet a tall man face to face, and lick him enthusiastically.

'Get him off me. He's soaking.'

'Phantom, get down!' Harriet cried.

He did so but only briefly, hurling himself at Darius again, this time with a force that took them both down to the ground. As he lay helplessly on the sand, Phantom loomed over him, licking his face and generally trying to show friendliness. He looked aggrieved as his mistress hauled him off.

'Bad dog! I'm very cross with you.'

Darius got to his feet, cursing at the wreck of his suit.

'He wasn't attacking you,' Harriet said in a pleading voice. 'He just likes people.'

'Whatever his intentions, he's made a mess,' Darius said in an icy voice.

'I'll pay to have your suit cleaned.'

'Cleaned?' he snapped. 'I'll send you a bill for a new one. Keep away from me, you crazy animal.'

He put up his arm to ward off another encounter, but Harriet threw her arms protectively around the dog.

'You'd better go,' she said in a voice that was now as icy as his own. 'I can't hold him for ever.'

'You should know better than to let a creature that size run free.'

'And you should know better than to wear a suit like that on the beach,' she cried.

The undeniable truth of this soured his temper further, leaving him no choice but to storm off in the direction of the helicopter. He guessed his pilot had seen everything, but the man was too wise to comment.

As they lifted off, Darius looked down and saw Harriet

gazing at the machine, one hand shielding her eyes. Then Phantom reared up again, enclosing her in his great paws, and at once she forgot the helicopter to cuddle the dog, while he licked her face. So much for being cross with that stupid mutt, Darius thought furiously. Clearly, he was all she cared about.

He thought of how he'd stood on the beach, alone, peaceful for the first time in months, and how clumsily she had destroyed that moment. He wouldn't forgive her for that.

From this high point on the hill overlooking Monte Carlo, Amos Falcon could see the bay but, unlike his son, he failed to notice the beauty of the sea. His attention was all for the buildings on the slope, tall, magnificent, speaking of money, though none spoke so loudly as his own house, a sprawling, three-storey edifice, bought because it dominated its surroundings.

It was money and the need to protect it that had first brought him to this tax haven years ago. He'd started life poor in a rundown mining town in the north of England, and got out fast. Working night and day, he'd built up a fortune of his own, helped by marrying a woman with wealth, and he'd left England for a more friendly tax regimen as soon as he could, determined that no government would be allowed to rob him of his gains.

'Where the devil is he?' he muttered crossly. 'It's not like Darius to be late. He knows I want him here before the others.'

Janine, his third wife, a well-preserved woman in her fifties with a kind face and a gentle manner, laid a hand on his arm.

'He's a busy man,' she said. 'His company is in trouble—'

'Everyone's company is in trouble,' Amos growled. 'He should be able to deal with it. I've taught him well.'

'Perhaps you spent too much time teaching him,' she suggested. 'He's your son, not just a business associate to be instructed.'

'He's no business associate of mine,' Amos said. 'I said I'd taught him well, but he never quite learned how to take the final, necessary step.'

'Because he has a conscience,' she suggested. 'He can be ruthless, but only up to a point.'

'Exactly. I could never quite make him see… Ah, well, maybe his recent troubles will have taught him a lesson.'

'You mean his wife leaving him?'

'I mean that damn fool divorce settlement he gave her. Much too generous. He just let her have whatever she demanded.'

Janine sighed. She'd heard him ranting on this subject so often, and there was no end to it.

'He did it for the children's sake,' she pointed out.

'He could have got his children back if he'd played hard, but he wouldn't do it.'

'Good for him,' Janine murmured.

Amos scowled. He could forgive her sentimental view of life. After all, she was a woman. But sometimes it exasperated him.

'That's all very well,' he growled, 'but then the world imploded.'

'Only the financial world,' she ventured.

His caustic look questioned whether there was any other kind, but he didn't rise to the bait.

'And suddenly he had a pittance compared to what he'd had before,' he continued. 'So he had to go back to that woman and try to persuade her to accept less. Naturally, she refused, and since the money had already been transferred to her he couldn't touch it.'

'You'd never have made that mistake,' Janine observed

wryly, perhaps thinking of the pre-nuptial agreement she'd had to sign before their wedding five years earlier. 'Never give anything you can't take back, that's your motto.'

'I never said that.'

'No, you've never actually said it,' she agreed quietly.

'Where the devil is he?'

'Don't upset yourself,' she pleaded. 'It's bad for you to get agitated after your heart attack.'

'I'm over that,' he growled.

'Until the next time. And don't say there won't be a next time because the doctor said a massive attack like that is always a warning.'

'I'm not an invalid,' he said firmly. 'Look at me. Do I look frail?'

He rose and stood against the backdrop of the sky, challenging her with his pose and his expression, and she had to concede the point. Amos was a big man, over six foot, broad-shouldered and heavy. All his life he'd been fiercely attractive, luring any woman he wanted, moving from marriage to affairs and on to marriage as the mood took him. Along the way, he'd fathered five sons by four mothers in different countries, thus spreading his tentacles across the world.

Recently, there had been an unexpected family reunion. Struck down by a heart attack, he'd lain close to death while his sons gathered at his bedside. But, against all the odds, he'd survived, and at last they had returned to their different countries.

Now he had summoned them back for a reason. Amos was making plans for the future. He'd regained much of his strength, although less than he claimed.

To the casual eye, he was a fine, healthy specimen, still handsome beneath a head of thick white hair. Only two people knew of the breathless attacks that followed exertion. One of them was Janine, his wife, who regarded him with a mixture of love and exasperation.

The other was Freya, Janine's daughter by an earlier marriage. A trained nurse, she'd recently come to stay at her mother's request.

'He doesn't want a nurse there in case it makes him look weak,' Janine pleaded, 'but if I invite my daughter he can't refuse.'

'But he knows I'm a nurse,' Freya had pointed out.

'Yes, but we don't have to talk about it, and you can keep an eye on him discreetly. It helps that you don't look like a nurse.'

This was an understatement. Freya was delicately built with elegant movements, a pretty face and a cheeky demeanour. She might have been a dancer, a nightclub hostess, or anything except a medical expert with an impressive list of letters after her name.

An adventurous spirit had made her leave her last job in response to her mother's request.

'I was getting bored,' she said. 'Same thing day after day.'

'You certainly won't get that with Amos,' Janine had remarked.

She was right. After only a few days Freya remarked, 'It's like dealing with a spoilt child. Don't worry. I can do what's necessary.'

Luckily, Amos liked his stepdaughter and under her care his health improved. It was she who now came bouncing out onto the balcony and said, 'Time for your nap.'

'Not for another ten minutes,' he growled.

She smiled. 'No, it's now. No argument.'

He grinned. 'You're a bully, you know that?'

'Of course I know that. I work at it. Get going.'

He shrugged, resigned and good-natured, and let her

escort him as far as his bedroom door. Janine would have gone in with him, but he waved her away.

'I can manage without supervision. Just keep your eyes open for Darius. I can't think what's keeping him.' He closed the door.

'What's going on?' Freya asked as the two women walked away.

'Goodness knows. He was supposed to arrive this morning but he called to say there'd been an unexpected delay.'

'And then all the other sons, Leonid, Marcel, Travis, Jackson, just a few days apart. Why is Amos suddenly doing this?'

'I can only guess,' Janine said sadly. 'He puts on this big act of being fully recovered, but he had a scare. He's seen that his life could end at any time, and he's…getting things sorted out, is how he puts it, starting with changes to his will.'

'Funny, he's so organised that you'd think he'd have fixed that ages ago.'

'He did, but I believe he's taking another look at all of his lads and deciding—I don't know—which one will manage best—'

'Which one is most like him,' Freya said shrewdly.

'You're very hard on him,' Janine protested.

'No more than he deserves. Of all the arrogant—'

'But he's very fond of you. You're the daughter he never had and he'd love you to be really part of the family.' She paused delicately.

'You mean he wants me to be his daughter-in-law?' Freya demanded, aghast. 'The cheeky crook.'

'Don't call him a crook,' Janine protested.

'Why not? No man builds up the kind of fortune he did by honest means. And he's taught his sons to be the same.

Anything for money, that's how they all think. So if one of them can talk me into marriage he'll cop the lot. Was Amos mad when he thought of that? Nothing on this earth would persuade me—there isn't one of them I'd ever dream of—ye gods and little fishes!'

'Don't tell him I told you,' Janine begged.

'Don't worry. Not a word.' Suddenly her temper faded, replaced by wicked mischief. 'But I might enjoy a good laugh. Yes, I think it deserves that.'

As she hurried away her mother heard the laughter echoing back, and sighed. She couldn't blame Freya one bit. She, of all people, knew what madness it was to marry into this family.

Darius arrived the next day, apologising with a fictional tale of business dealings. Not for the world would he have admitted that he'd been forced to leave Herringdean, return to the mainland and check into a hotel to put on a fresh suit. Normally, no power on earth could force him to change his plans and he resented it. Another thing for which Harriet Connor was to blame.

He found her mysteriously disturbing because she seemed to haunt him as two people. There was the girl who'd briefly charmed him with her instinctive empathy for his feelings about the isolated place. And there was the other one who'd interfered with his plans, destroyed his dignity with her stupid hound, and committed the unforgivable crime of seeing him at a disadvantage. He had dismissed her from his mind but she seemed unaware of that fact and popped up repeatedly in one guise or another.

A fanciful man might have defined her two aspects as the Good Fairy and the Bad Fairy. Darius, who wasn't fanciful, simply called her 'that wretched female'.

His father greeted him in typical fashion. 'So there you are at last. About time too.'

'An unexpected matter that required my attention.'

Amos grunted. 'As long as you sorted it out to your advantage.'

'Naturally,' Darius said, brushing aside the memory of lying on the sand. 'Then I got here as soon as I could. I'm glad to see you looking better, Father.'

'I *am* better. I keep saying so but my womenfolk won't believe me. I suppose Freya talked a lot when she collected you from the airport.'

'I asked her questions and, like a good nurse, she answered them.'

'Nurse be damned. She's here as my stepdaughter.'

'If you say so.'

'What do you think of her?'

'She seems a nice girl, what little I've seen of her.'

'She cheers the place up. And she's a good cook. Better than that so-called professional I employ. She's doing supper for us tonight. You'll enjoy it.'

He did enjoy it. Freya produced excellent food, and could crack jokes that lightened the atmosphere. She was pleasant to have around, and Darius found himself wondering why more women couldn't be like her instead of invading other people's private property with their sharp remarks and their dangerous dogs.

Awkward. She'd said it herself, and that was exactly right.

After supper, in his father's study, the two men confronted each other.

'I gather things aren't too good?' Amos grunted.

'Not for me or anyone else,' Darius retorted. 'There's a global crisis, hadn't you heard?'

'Yes, and some are weathering it better than others. That

contract you had the big fight over, I warned you how to word the get-out clause, and if you'd listened to me you could have told them where to stuff their legal action.'

'But they're decent people,' Darius protested. 'They knew very little about business—'

'All the better. You could have done as you liked and they wouldn't have found out until too late. You're soft, that's your trouble.'

Darius grimaced. In the financial world, his reputation was far from soft. Cold, unyielding, power-hungry, that was what people said of him. But he drew the line at taking advantage of helpless innocence, and he'd paid the price for it; a price his father would never have paid.

'But it's not too late,' Amos conceded in a milder tone. 'Now you're here there are ways I can help.'

'That's what I hoped,' Darius said quietly.

'You haven't always taken my advice, but perhaps you've got the sense to take it now. And the first problem is how you're going to deal with Morgan Rancing.'

'I must tell you—'

'I've heard disturbing rumours about some island he owns off the south coast of England. They say he'll try to use it to cover his debts, and I'm warning you to have no truck with that. Don't give it a thought. What you must do—'

'It's too late,' Darius growled. 'Herringdean is already mine.'

'What? You agreed to take it?'

'No, I wasn't given the chance,' Darius snapped. 'Rancing has vanished. Next thing, I received papers that transferred ownership of Herringdean to me. His cellphone is dead, his house is empty. Nobody knows where he is, or if they do they're not talking. I can either accept the island or go without anything.'

'But it'll be more trouble than it's worth,' Amos spluttered.

'I'm inclined to agree with you,' Darius murmured.

'So you know something about it?'

'A little. I need to go back and inspect it further.'

'And you're counting on it to pay your debts?'

'I don't know. But in the meantime I could do with an investor to make a one-time injection of cash and help me out.'

'Meaning me?'

'Well, as you're always telling me, you've survived the credit crunch better than anyone.'

'Yes, because I knew how to treat money.'

'Like a prisoner who's always trying to escape,' Darius recalled.

'Exactly. That's why I came to live here.'

He pushed open the door that led out onto the balcony overlooking the view over the bay that now glittered with lights against the darkness.

'I talked to a journalist once,' Amos recalled. 'She asked me all sorts of tom-fool questions. Why had I chosen to live in Monte Carlo? Was it just the tax relief or was there something else? I brought her out here and became lyrical about the view.'

'That I would have loved to hear,' Darius said.

Amos grinned. 'Yeah, you'd have been proud of me. The silly woman swallowed it hook, line and sinker. Then she wrote some trash about my being a man who appreciated peace and beauty. As though I gave a damn about that stuff.'

'Some people think it has value,' Darius murmured.

'Some people are fools,' Amos said firmly. 'I'd be sorry to think you were one of them. You've got yourself into a mess and you need me to get you out.'

'Two firms I did business with went bankrupt, owing me money,' Darius said grimly. 'I hardly created the mess myself.'

'But you made it worse by giving Mary everything she asked for in the divorce settlement.'

'That was before the crisis. I could afford it then.'

'But you didn't leave yourself any room for manoeuvre, no way to claw any of it back. You forgot every lesson I ever taught you. Now you want me to pour good money after bad.'

'So you won't help me?'

'I didn't say that, but we need to talk further. Not now. Later.'

Darius spoke through gritted teeth. 'Will my father invest in me, or will he not?'

'Don't rush me.'

'I have to. I need to make my decisions quickly.'

'All right, here's a way forward for you to consider. A rich wife, that's what you need, one who'll bring you a thumping great dowry.'

'What the hell are you talking about?'

'Freya. She's already my stepdaughter, and I want her properly in the family as my daughter-in-law.'

Darius stared. His ears were buzzing, and somewhere there was the memory of Freya, on the drive from the airport, saying, 'Your father's got some really mad ideas. Someone needs to tell him to forget them.'

She'd refused to elaborate, but now he understood.

'Why not?' Amos asked genially. 'You like the girl, you were laughing together at dinner—'

'Yes, I like her—far too much to do her such an injury, even if she'd agree, which she wouldn't, thank goodness. Do you really think you could make me crawl to do your bidding? If I have one thing left it's my independence, and I won't part with that.'

'Then you'll buy it at a high price. Don't blame me when you go bankrupt.'

Darius gave a cold smile. 'I'll remember.'

He turned and walked away, resisting the temptation to slam the door. Within an hour he'd left the house.

CHAPTER TWO

THE storm that swept over Herringdean had been violent, and nobody was surprised when the lifeboat was called out to an emergency. A small crowd had watched the boat plunge down the slipway into the sea, and a larger one gathered to see it return later that night.

Soon the rescued victims had been taken ashore into the waiting ambulance and the crew were free to exhale with relief and remove their life jackets.

Harriet took out her cellphone, dialled and spoke quickly. 'Is he all right? Good. I'll be home soon.'

When they had all finished making their report she slipped away and was followed by Walter and Simon, fellow crew members and friends.

'Hey, Harry,' Walter called. 'You sounded worried on the phone. Is someone ill?'

'No, I was just checking on Phantom. I left my neighbour looking after him. She promised to keep him safe.'

'Safe? Why suddenly? You never worried before.'

'I never had cause before. But now I worry. He's a very powerful man.'

'Who?'

From her pocket she took a newspaper cutting with a photograph and passed it to Walter.

'"Darius Falcon,"' he read. '"Giant of commerce, skilled

manipulator, the financial world is agog to know if he will avert disaster—'" He lowered the paper. 'How does a big shot come to know Phantom?'

'Because he's bought the island,' she said. 'Rancing had money troubles and he solved them by selling this place.'

Simon swore. 'And not a word to the people who live here, of course.'

'Of course. What do we matter to men like that, up there on their lofty perch? If you could have seen him as I did, arrogant and sure of himself—'

'You've met him?' Simon demanded.

'He came here a couple of days ago and I saw him on the beach. Phantom made a mess of his suit and he got mad, said he'd make me pay for a new one, and Phantom shouldn't be allowed out. So tonight, I asked my neighbour to watch over him while I was away, in case…well, just in case.'

'Hell!' Walter said. 'But is he really as bad as you say? If you two had a dust-up he probably just got a bit peeved—'

'You didn't see his face. He was more than a bit peeved. Now, I must get home.'

She hurried away, leaving the two men gazing after her, frowning with concern.

'Surely she's overreacting?' Simon mused. 'A bodyguard for a dog? A bit melodramatic, surely?'

'She's been that way for the last year,' Walter sighed. 'Ever since her husband died. Remember how good she and Brad were together? The perfect marriage. Now all she has left is his dog.'

'Hmm,' Simon grunted. 'Personally, I never liked Brad.'

'You say that because you fancied her rotten.'

'Sure, me and every other man on the island. Let's go for a drink.'

* * *

Harriet's car made quick time from the harbour to Ellarick, then to the little shop that she owned, and above which she lived. As she looked up the window opened and Phantom's head appeared, followed by that of a cheerful middle-aged woman. A moment later she was climbing the stairs to throw her arms about the dog.

'Mmm,' she cooed, and he responded with a throaty growl that sounded much the same.

'No problems?' she asked Mrs Bates, the neighbour who'd kept watch in her home.

'No sign of anyone.'

'Let me make you a cup of tea,' Harriet offered gratefully.

But Mrs Bates refused and departed. She was a kindly soul and she knew Harriet wanted to be alone with Phantom, although how she could bear the loneliness of the apartment Mrs Bates couldn't imagine.

But to Harriet it would never be lonely while Phantom was there. She hugged him fiercely before saying, 'Come on, let's take a walk. You need space to go mad in.'

They slipped out together into the darkness and walked down through the streets of the town, heading for the shore.

'But not "the ogre's" private beach,' she said. 'From now on, that's out of bounds.'

They found a place on the public sands where they could chase each other up and down in the moonlight.

'That's enough,' she gasped at last. 'Yes, I know you could go on till morning, but I'm out of puff.'

She threw herself down on the sand and stretched out on her back. Phantom immediately put a heavy paw on her chest, looking down into her face while she ruffled his fur.

'That's better,' she sighed. 'How could he not like you

when you were trying so hard to be friendly? Being hurled to the ground by you is a real privilege. You don't do it for everyone.' She gave a soft grunt of laughter. 'Just people with expensive clothes. If he really does send me the bill you'll be on plain rations for a long time. So will I, come to think of it.'

He woofed.

'The funny thing is, when I first saw him…he seemed decent, as if he really loved the sun and the fresh air; like someone who'd found himself in heaven. But when I discovered who he was he looked different. And then he was so rotten to you—'

Suddenly she sat up and threw her arms around the dog.

'You must be careful,' she said fiercely. 'You must, you *must*! If anything happened to you I couldn't bear it.'

Harriet buried her face against him. Phantom made a gentle sound, but he didn't try to move. This often happened, and he knew what he must do: keep still, stay warm and gentle, just be there for her. Instinct told him what she needed, and his heart told him how to give it.

'They think I'm crazy,' she whispered, 'getting paranoid over your safety. Well, perhaps I really am crazy, but you're all I've got—without you, there's no love or happiness in the world…only you…'

She kissed him and gave a shaky laugh.

'I expect you think I'm crazy too. Poor old boy. Come on, let's get home and you can have something special to eat.'

They left the beach, climbing the gently sloping road that led to the town. Suddenly she stopped. Far away, she could just make out the house where Rancing had lived before he fled, and where 'the ogre' would soon appear. It went by the grandiose name of Giant's Beacon, which might have been justified in its great days, but seemed rather over-the-top now that it was in a state of disrepair. At this distance it was tiny, but it stood out against the moonlit sky, and she could just make out that lights were coming on.

'He's here,' she breathed. 'Oh, heavens, let's get home, fast.'

They ran all the way, and as soon as they were safely inside Harriet locked the door.

Within hours of Darius's arrival the news had spread throughout the island. Kate, who'd kept house for Rancing, had a ready audience in the pub that evening.

'You should see the computers he's brought,' she said. 'Dozens of 'em. One for this and one for that, and something he calls "video links" so he can talk to people on the other side of the world, and there they are on the screen, large as life. It's like magic.'

The others grinned. Kate had never quite come to terms with the dot-com revolution, and most modern communications struck her as magic. She had little idea that behind its sweet, traditional image Herringdean was a more modern place than it looked.

Darius was also making the discovery, and was delighted with it. For a while he would be able to run his main business and his many subsidiary businesses, controlling everything from the centre of the web. It would be enough until he was ready to turn this place to his financial advantage.

Checking through the figures, he discovered that it was larger than he'd thought, about a hundred square miles with a population of a hundred and twenty thousand. Sheep and dairy farming flourished, so did fishing, and there were several industries, notably boat building and brewing.

Ellarick was not only a flourishing town, but a port with its own annual regatta.

One source of prosperity was tourism. Now summer was coming, the hotels were filling up as visitors began to flood the island, seeking tranquillity in the country lanes or excitement in the boats.

Ellarick also contained an elderly accountant called James Henly, who had dealt with Rancing's business. An early visit from him pleased Darius with the news that the rent paid to him by the other inhabitants was considerable, but also displeased him with the discovery that he was the victim of yet another piece of sharp practice.

'Mr Rancing persuaded several of his larger tenants, like the breweries, to pay him several months' rent in advance,' Henly explained in his dry voice. 'Apparently, he convinced them that there would be tax advantages. I need hardly say that I knew nothing about this. I was away and he took advantage of my absence to act on his own account. When I returned and found out, it was too late. He'd pocketed the money, and within a few days he'd vanished.'

'Meaning that it will be some time before I can collect rent from these establishments again,' Darius said in a mild manner that revealed nothing.

'I'm afraid so. Of course, what he's done is legally open to question since he made over everything to you, so technically it was your money he took. You could always try to get it back.'

His tone made it clear that he didn't attach much hope to that idea. Darius, who attached none at all, controlled his temper. It wasn't his way to display emotion to employees.

'How much are we talking about?' he said with a shrug.

He felt less like shrugging when he saw the figures.

Rancing had staged a spectacular theft and there was nothing he could do about it. But at all costs Henly mustn't be allowed to suspect his dismay.

'No problem,' Darius said as indifferently as he could manage. 'The tourism season is just starting. I shan't let a detail get me down.'

Henly's eyes widened at the idea of such a financial blow being a mere detail. He began to think the stories of Mr Falcon's impending ruin were untrue after all.

Darius, who'd intended him to think exactly that, asked casually, 'Did he leave owing you any money?'

'I'm afraid he did—'

'All right, just send me a detailed bill. That's all for now.'

For several days he remained in the house, rising early to link up with business contacts on one side of the world, eating whatever Kate brought him and barely taking his eyes from the computer screen. As the hours wore on, he turned to the other side of the world where he had business contacts whose day was just beginning. Day and night ceased to exist; all he knew was what he needed to do to survive.

On a whim, he searched the local phone directory until he found Harriet Connor, living in Bayton Street in Ellarick. A map showed him that it was in the centre of the town.

Then he put away the papers quickly. What did he care where she lived?

Thinking back to his work, at last he felt he'd put things on a firmer footing and could dare to hope. Perhaps it was time to venture outside. He'd hired a car but so far not used it. Now he drove into Ellarick, parked in a side street and got out to walk.

No doubt it was pure chance that made him walk down Bayton Street. He reckoned that must have been the reason because he'd forgotten her address. Now he found himself in a place of expensive shops and hotels that looked even more expensive. The tourist trade must be good. No doubt she did well out of the hotels.

There was her shop, on the corner, and through the open door he could just see her with a female customer. There was a child there too, and Harriet was talking to the little boy, giving him all his attention, as though nobody else mattered. He was clutching a large model boat, and Darius saw him turn to the woman and say, 'Please, Mum. *Please.*'

He could just make out her reply, 'No, darling, it's too expensive.'

For a moment the child looked rebellious, but then he sniffed and handed the boat to Harriet. She took it thoughtfully, then suddenly said, 'I could always make a discount.'

The mother gasped, and gasped again when she saw the piece of paper on which Harriet had written the price. 'Are you sure?'

'Quite sure. It ought to go to someone who'll really appreciate it.'

Darius moved quickly back into a doorway as the woman paid up and hurried away with the child. The last thing he wanted was for Harriet to realise that he'd witnessed this scene. Instinct told him that she wouldn't be pleased at knowing he'd seen her kindly side any more than he would be at knowing she'd seen his. Not that he admitted to having a kindly side.

He waited until she put up the shutters before hurrying back to the car.

The following night he was out walking again, much later this time. Darkness had fallen as he headed for the harbour. At last he came to a public house and went inside, only to find the place too crowded for his mood.

'It's nice outside,' the barman suggested. 'Plenty of space there.'

He led Darius to the garden, where a few tables were laid out. From one of them came laughter.

'We're near the lifeboat station,' the barman explained, 'so the crew members tend to come in here to relax after a call out. That's them, just there.'

He pointed to where two women and four men were sitting around a table, laughing and talking. They were well lit, but then the lights faded into darkness, tempting Darius to slip in among the trees, hoping to remain unseen. From here he could catch a distant glimpse of the sea, that mysteriously always had the power to make him feel better.

A cheer rose from the table, making him back away, but not before he'd seen who was sitting there, surrounded by laughing admirers.

It was her. The Bad Fairy. Or was she now the Good Fairy? He wished she'd let him make up his mind.

The man beside her put a friendly hand on her shoulder, roaring, 'Harry, you're a fraud.'

'Of course I'm a fraud, Walter,' she teased back. 'That's the only fun thing to be.'

Harriet, he remembered. Harry.

Was there no escape from the pesky woman? Why here and now, spoiling his quiet contemplation? And why was she wearing a polo shirt that proclaimed her a member of the lifeboat crew?

Phantom was at her feet, and Darius had a chance to study him. Before, he'd sensed only a very large dog of no particular breed. Now he could see that Phantom's ancestry included a German Shepherd, a St Bernard, and possibly a bloodhound. He was a handsome animal with a benign air that at any other time Darius would have appreciated. Now he only remembered the heavy creature pinning him to the ground and making a fool of him.

The crowd around the table were still chattering cheerfully.

'So what are we going to do about this guy who thinks he owns the place?' Walter asked.

'Actually, he really does own the place,' Harriet sighed. 'And there's nothing we can do. We're stuck with him, I'm sorry to say.'

A groan went up, and someone added, 'Apparently, he's spending money like there's no tomorrow, yet according to the newspapers he's a poor man now. Go figure.'

'Hah!' Harriet said cynically. 'What we call poor and what Darius Falcon calls poor would be a million miles apart.'

Now Darius was even more glad of the trees hiding him, so that they couldn't see his reaction to the contemptuous way she spoke his name.

'It's a big act,' she went on. 'He has to splash it around to prove he can afford to, but actually he's a fraud.'

'Gee, you really took against him!' said the other woman sitting at the same table. 'Just because he got mad at Phantom for ruining his suit. I adore Phantom, but let's face it, he's got form for that kind of thing.'

Amid the general laughter, Harriet made a face.

'It wasn't just that,' she said. 'It's also the way I first saw him, with his head thrown back, drinking in the sun.'

'Perhaps he just likes nature,' Walter suggested.

'That's what I thought. I even liked him for it, but then I didn't know who he was. Now I see. He was standing there like a king come into his birthright. He owns the land and he owns us, that's how he sees it.'

'He told you that?'

'He didn't need to. It was all there in his attitude.' She assumed a declamatory pose. 'I'm the boss here and you'd better watch out.'

'Now that I'd like to see,' said Walter. 'The last man who tried to boss you about was me, and you made me regret it.'

More cheers and laughter. Someone cracked a joke about Darius, someone else cracked another, while their victim stood in the shadows, fuming. This was another new experience and one Darius could have done without. Awe, respect, even fear, these he was used to. But derision? That was an insult.

Walter leaned towards her confidentially. 'Hey, Harry, make a note never to rescue him. If you find him in the water, do the world a favour and look the other way.'

Roars of laughter. She raised her glass, chuckling, 'I'll remember.'

That was it. Time for her to be taught a lesson.

Emerging from the trees, he approached the table and stood, watching her sardonically, until the others noticed him and became curious. At last Harriet's attention was caught and she turned. He heard her draw a sharp breath, and registered her look of dismay with grim satisfaction.

'You'd better remind yourself of my face,' he said, 'so that you'll know who to abandon.'

She couldn't speak. Only her expression betrayed her horror and embarrassment.

He should then have turned on his heel and departed without giving her a chance to reply. But Phantom had to spoil it. Recognising his new friend, he rose from where he was nestled beneath Harriet's seat and reared up, barking with delight.

'Phantom, no!' she cried.

'Leave him,' Darius told her, rubbing Phantom's head.

'You daft mutt! Is this how you get your fun? Luckily, I'm in casuals tonight. Now, get down, there's a good fellow.'

After Harriet's dire warnings, his relaxed tone took everyone by surprise and he noticed that puzzled frowns were directed at her. Fine. If she wanted battle, she could have it. He nodded to them all and departed.

When he reached the road he heard footsteps hurrying behind him and turned, half fearing another canine embrace. But it was her.

'That thing about leaving you in the sea—it was just a silly joke. Of course we'd never leave *anyone* to drown.'

'Not anyone,' he echoed. 'Meaning not even a monster like me.'

'Look—'

'Don't give it another thought. The chance of my ever needing to rely on you is non-existent—as you'll discover.'

'Oh, really!' she said, cross again. 'Let's hope you're right. You never know what life has in store next, do you? Let's make sure.'

Grabbing him, she yanked him under a street lamp and studied his face, frowning.

'You look different from last time,' she said. 'It must be the darkness. OK, I've got you fixed. Hey, what are you doing?'

'The same to you as you did to me,' he said, holding her with one hand while the other lifted her chin to give him the best view of her face.

Harriet resisted the temptation to fight him off, suspecting that he would enjoy that too much. Plus she guessed he wouldn't be easy to fight. There was an unyielding strength in his grasp that could reduce her to nothing. So she stayed completely still, outwardly calm but inwardly smouldering.

If only he would stop smiling like that, as though something about her both amused and pleased him. There was a gleam in his eyes that almost made her want to respond. Almost. If she was that foolish. She drew a long breath, trying not to tremble.

At last he nodded, saying in a thoughtful voice, 'Hmm. Yes, I think I'll remember you—if I try really hard.'

'*Cheek!*' she exploded.

He released her. 'All right, you can go now.'

Darius walked away without looking back. He didn't need to. He knew she was looking daggers at him.

At home in Giant's Beacon, he sat in darkness at the window of his room with a drink, trying to understand what had so disturbed him that night. It wasn't the hostility, something he was used to. Nor was it really the laughter, which had annoyed him, but only briefly. It was something about Harriet—something…

He exhaled a long breath as the answer came to him. She'd spoken of seeing him on the beach, 'standing there like a king come into his birthright.'

That hadn't been her first reaction. She'd even said she'd liked him, but only briefly, until she'd discovered who he was. Then she'd seen only arrogance and harshness, a conqueror taking possession.

But wasn't that partly his own choice? For years he'd assumed various masks—cool, unperturbed, cunning, superior or charming when the occasion warranted it. Some had been passed on to him by a father whose skill in manipulation was second to none. Others he'd created for himself.

Only one person had seen a different side of him—loving, passionate. For twelve years he'd enjoyed what he'd thought of as a happy marriage, until his wife had left him for another man. Since then he'd tried to keep the vulnerable face well hidden, but evidently he should try harder.

He snatched up the phone and dialled his ex-wife's number in London.

'Mary?'

'Do you have to ring me at this hour? I was just going to bed.'

'I suppose *he's* with you?'

'That's no longer any concern of yours, since we're divorced.'

'Are Mark and Frankie there?'

'Yes, but they're asleep and I'm not waking them. Why don't you call during the day, *if you can make time?* I never liked having to wait until you'd finished everything else, and they don't like it either.'

'Tell them I'll call tomorrow.'

'Not during the day. It's a family outing.'

'When you say "family" I take it you mean—'

'Ken, too. You shouldn't be surprised. We'll be married soon, and he'll be their father.'

'The hell he will! I'll call tomorrow evening. Tell them to expect me.' He slammed down the phone.

Darius had a fight on his hands there, he knew it. Mary had been a good wife and mother, but she'd never really understood the heavy demands of his work. And now, if he wasn't careful, she would cut his children off from him.

How his enemies would rejoice at his troubles. Enemies. In the good times they had been called opponents, rivals, competitors. But the bad times had changed all that, bringing out much bile and bitterness that had previously been hidden for tactical reasons.

As so often, Harriet was hovering on the edge of his mind, an enemy who was at least open about her hostility. Tonight he'd had the satisfaction of confronting her head-on, a rare pleasure in his world. He could see her now, cheeky and challenging, but not beautiful, except for her eyes, and with skin that was as soft as rose petals; something that he'd discovered when he'd held her face prisoner between his fingers.

This was how he'd always fought the battles, gaining information denied to others. But now it was different. Instead of triumph, he felt only confusion.

After watching the darkness for a long time he went to bed.

CHAPTER THREE

HARRIET prided herself on her common sense. She needed to. There had been times in her recent past when it had been all that saved her from despair. Even now, the dark depths sometimes beckoned and she clung fiercely to her 'boring side' as she called it, because nothing else helped. And even that didn't make the sadness go away. It simply made it possible to cling on until her courage returned.

She knew that people had always envied her. Married at eighteen to an astonishingly handsome young man, living in apparently perfect harmony until his death eight years later. As far as the world knew, the only thing that blighted their happiness was the need for him to be away so often. His work in the tourist industry had necessitated many absences from home, but when he returned their reunions were legendary.

'A perfect couple,' people said. But they didn't know.

Brad had been a philanderer who had spent his trips away sleeping around, and expected her not to mind. It only happened while he was out of sight, so what was she complaining about? It was the unkindness of his attitude that hurt her as much as his infidelity.

She'd clung on, deluding herself with the hope that in time he would change, presenting a bright face to the world so that her island neighbours never suspected. Finally Brad had left her, dying in a car crash in America before the divorce could come through, and the last of her hope was destroyed.

To the outside world the myth of her perfect marriage persisted. Nobody knew the truth, and nobody ever would, she was determined on that.

All she had left was Phantom, who had been Brad's dog and who'd comforted her night after night when he was away. Phantom alone knew the truth; that behind the cheerful, sturdy exterior was a woman who had lost faith in men and life. His warmth brought joy to what would otherwise have been a desert.

It was the thought of her beloved dog that made her set out one morning in the direction of Giant's Beacon. There was still a chance to improve relations with Darius Falcon, and for Phantom's sake she must take it.

'I suppose I'm getting paranoid about this,' she told herself. 'I don't think he'd really do anything against Phantom, but he's the most powerful man on the island and I can't take chances.'

She recalled that at their last meeting he'd actually spoken to him in a kindly tone, calling him 'You daft mutt' and 'a good fellow', thus proving he wasn't really a monster. He probably had a nicer side if she could only find it. She would apologise, engage him in a friendly chat and all would be well.

The road to Giant's Beacon led around the side of the house, and over the garden hedge she could see that the French windows were open. From inside came the sound of a man's voice.

'All right. Call me again when you know. Goodbye.'

Excellent, she would slip inside quickly while he was free. But as she approached the open door she heard him again,'There you are. I know you've been avoiding my calls—did you really think I'd let you go that easily?—I know what you've been doing and I'm telling you it's got to stop.'

Harriet stood deadly still, stunned by his cold, bullying tone. She must leave at once. Slowly, she flattened herself back against the wall and began to edge away.

'It's too late for that,' Darius continued. 'I've set things in motion and it's too late to change it, even if I wanted to. The deal's done, and you can tell your friend with the suspicious credentials that if he crosses me again he'll be sorry—what? Yes, that's exactly what I mean. There'll be no mercy.'

No mercy, she thought, moving slowly along the wall. That just about said it all. And she'd kidded herself that he had a nicer side.

No mercy.

Quietly, she vanished.

'There'll be no mercy.'

Darius repeated the line once more. He knew that these days he said it too often, too obsessively. So many foes had shown him no mercy that now it was the mantra he clung to in self-defence.

At last he slammed down the phone and threw himself back in his chair, hoping he'd said enough to have the desired impact. Possibly. Or then again, maybe not. Once he wouldn't have doubted it, but since his fortunes had begun to collapse he had a permanent fear that the person on the other end immediately turned to a companion and jeered, 'He fell for it.'

As he himself had often done in what now felt like another life.

That was one of the hardest things to cope with— the suspicion of being laughed at behind his back; the knowledge that people who'd once scuttled to please him now shrugged.

The other thing, even harder, was the end of his family life, the distance that seemed to stretch between himself and his children. It was easy to say that he'd given too much of himself to business and not enough to being a father, but at the time he'd felt he was working for them.

Mary, his wife, had been scathing at the idea.

'That's just your excuse for putting them second. You say making money is all for them, but they don't want a great fortune, they want *you* there, taking an interest.'

He'd sacrificed so much for financial success, and now that too was fading. Lying awake at night, he often tried to look ahead to decide which path to take, but in truth there was no choice. Only one path stretched forward, leading either to greater failure or success at too great a cost. They seemed much the same.

He rubbed his eyes, trying to shake off the mood, and turned on the radio to hear the local news. One item made him suddenly alert.

'Much concern is being expressed at the suggestion of problems with the Herringdean Wind Farm. Work has only recently started, yet—'

'Kate,' he said, coming downstairs, 'what do you know about a wind farm?'

'Not much,' she said, speaking as she would have done about an alien planet. 'It's been on and off for ages and we thought it was all forgotten but they finally started work. It'll be some way out in the channel where we don't have to look at the horrid great thing.'

'Show me,' he said, pulling out a map of the island.

The site was located about eight miles out at sea, within

England's territorial waters. As these were owned by the Crown, he would gain nothing. He could even lose, since the island might be less appealing to potential buyers.

'They've actually started putting up the turbines?' he said.

'A few, I believe, but it'll be some time before it's finished.'

He groaned. If he'd bought this place in the normal way, there would have been inspections, he would have discovered the disadvantages and negotiated a lower price. Instead, it had been dumped on him, and he was beginning to realise that he'd walked into a trap.

Fool! *Fool!*

At all costs that must remain his secret. Kate was too naïve for him to worry about, and nobody else would be allowed near.

'Shall I start supper?' Kate asked.

'No, thank you. There's something I've got to see.'

Darius had just enough time to get out there before the light faded. When he'd inspected the turbines he could decide if they were a problem.

For this he would need the motorboat that was also now his property, and that was lodged in a boating shed at the end of a small creek that ran in from the shore. He found it without trouble, opened the door of the shed and started up the engine.

He was expecting problems. The engine might not work, or would at least be complicated to operate. But it sprang to life at once, everything was easy to operate, and since the fuel gauge registered 'full' he reckoned that luck was on his side, just for once.

Briefly he glanced around for a life jacket but, not seeing one, shrugged and forgot about it. A breeze was getting up as he emerged from the creek and set out across the channel. Glancing back, he could see the beach where he'd had his first ill-fated meeting with Harriet. Then he turned determinedly away and headed for the horizon.

At last he saw it—a dozen turbines rearing out of the water, seventy metres high, and, nearby, the cargo ships bearing the loads that would become more turbines. He got as close as he could, trying to think only of the benefit to the island of this source of electricity. But the new self, who'd come to life on the beach, whispered that they spoiled the beauty of the sea.

Functional and efficient, that was what mattered. Concentrate on that.

Now the light was fading fast and the wind was mounting, making the water rough, and it was time to go. He turned the boat, realising that he'd been unwise to come out here. He wasn't an experienced sailor, but the need to know had been compelling. Now he had just enough time to get to shore before matters became unpleasant.

Almost at once he discovered his mistake. The waves mounted fast, tossing his little boat from side to side. Rain began to fall more heavily every moment, lashing the angry water, lashing himself, soaking through his clothes, which weren't waterproof. The sooner he drove on the better.

But without warning the engine died. Nothing he could do would start it again. Frantically, he peered at the fuel gauge and saw, with horror, that it still showed 'Full'.

But that was impossible after the distance he'd already travelled. The reading was wrong, and must have been wrong from the start. He'd set out without enough fuel, and now he was trapped out here in the storm.

He groaned. It went against the grain to admit that he needed help, but there was no alternative. He would have to call Kate and ask her to notify the rescue service. Then it would be all over the island. He could almost hear the laughter. Especially *hers*. But it couldn't be helped.

Taking out his cellphone, he began to dial, trying to steady himself with his feet as he needed both hands for the phone. That was when the biggest wave came, rearing up at the side of the boat, forcing him to cling on with both hands. With despair, he saw the phone go flying into the water. He made a dive for it but another swell hoisted the boat high, twisting it so that he went overboard into the sea.

Floundering madly, he tried to reach the boat, but the waves had already carried it away. Farther and farther away it went, beyond his strength to pursue, until it was out of sight.

Now his own body seemed to be turning against him. The shock of being plunged into cold water had caused his heart to race dangerously, making him gasp and inhale water. His limbs froze, and he could barely move them. He wondered whether he would die of cold before he drowned.

Time passed, tormenting him, then vanishing into eternity until time itself no longer existed. Perhaps it had never existed. There was only darkness on earth and the moon and stars high above.

His wretchedness was increased by the thought of his children, waiting in vain for his call tonight. They would think he'd forgotten them, and only the news of his death would tell them otherwise. Then it would no longer matter.

Darius wanted to cry aloud to them, saying he loved them and they must believe that, for he would never be able to tell them again. But the distance stretched into infinity, and then another infinity that he feared because so much was left undone in his life—so many wrongs not righted, so many chances not taken, so many words not spoken… and now…never…never…

Why was he even bothering to tread water? Why not just let go and accept the inevitable?

But giving in had never been his way. He must fight to the end, no matter how much harder it was.

In his dizzy state he seemed to lose consciousness. Or was he going mad? That might make it easier. But doing things the easy way wasn't his style either.

Yet the madness was already creeping over him, giving him the illusion of lights in the distance. It was impossible but he saw them, streaming out over the water, turning this way and that as though searching. Then the beam fell on him, blinding him, and a cry split the darkness.

'There he is!'

The universe seemed to whirl. Vaguely, he sensed the boat approaching, ploughing through the waves. Another few seconds—

But it seemed that a malign fate was intent on destroying him even now. A wave, bigger than the others, reared up, sweeping him with it, up—then down back into the abyss—up—down—then away from the boat to a place where he would never be found. A yell of fear and rage broke from him at being defeated at the last moment.

Then he felt a hand clasp his, the fingers tightening with fierce determination, drawing him closer. The waves fought back but the hand refused to yield to them. Suddenly he realised that two men were in the water with him, and were loading him onto a stretcher. Gradually the stretcher began to rise, taking him clear of the sea, lifting him to safety.

From somewhere a man's voice said, 'OK, I've got him. You can let go, Harry.'

And a woman replied, "No way. This one's mine.'

Harry! That voice—

Shocked, he opened his eyes and saw Harriet's face.

'You,' he whispered hoarsely.

Harriet was there, leaning close to ask, 'Was there anyone else with you—anyone we still need to look for?'

'No,' he gasped. 'I was alone.'

'Good. Then we can go back. There'll be an ambulance to take you to hospital.'

'No, I must go home—my children—I've got to call them. Wait—' he grasped her '—my cellphone went into the water. Let me use yours.'

'I don't have it here.'

'Then I must call them from home.'

'But the hospital will have—'

'Not the hospital,' he said stubbornly.

'Gee, you're an infuriating man!' she exclaimed.

'Yes, well, you should have left me in the water, shouldn't you?' he choked. 'You had the right idea the first time.'

A coughing fit overtook him. Between them, Harriet and Walter got him under cover, and she stayed with him for the rest of the journey. He slumped in the seat, his eyes closed, on the verge of collapse. Watching him, Harriet was glad she hadn't needed to answer his last remark. She wouldn't have known how.

At the lifeboat station she helped him ashore, and there was another argument.

'No hospital,' he insisted. 'I'm going home.'

'Then I'll take you,' she said. 'Walter—'

'Don't worry, I'll do the report. You keep him safe.'

Darius was about to say that he would drive himself when he remembered that his car was a mile away. Besides, there was no arguing with this bossy woman.

Somehow, he stumbled into her car and sat with his eyes closed for the journey.

'How did you manage to find me?' he murmured. 'I thought I was a goner.'

'Kate raised the alarm. She said you left suddenly after you talked about the wind farm. Later, she went out and bumped into an old man she knows who works on the shore. He said he'd seen you leaving in your motorboat. When you didn't return she tried to call you on your cellphone, but it was dead so she alerted the lifeboat station.'

Kate was waiting at the door when they arrived. Darius managed to stand up long enough to hug her.

'Thank you,' he said hoarsely. 'I owe you my life.'

'As long as you're safe,' Kate insisted. 'Just come in and get warm.'

In the hall, he made straight for the phone.

'Get changed,' Harriet said urgently. 'You're soaking.'

'No, I've got to call them first. They'll be waiting.' He'd been dialling as he spoke and now he said, 'Mary? Yes, I know it's late. I'm sorry, I got held up.'

From where she was standing, Harriet could hear a woman's sharp voice on the other end, faint but clear.

'You always get held up. The children went to bed crying because you didn't keep your word, and that's it. Enough is enough.'

'Mary, listen—'

'I'm not going to let you hurt them by putting them last again—'

'It's not like that—*don't hang up*—'

Harriet couldn't stand it any more. She snatched the phone from his hand and spoke loudly. 'Mrs Falcon, please listen to me.'

'Oh, you're the girlfriend, I suppose?'

'No, I'm not Mr Falcon's girlfriend. I'm a member of the lifeboat crew that's just taken him from the sea, barely in time to save his life.'

'Oh, please, do you expect me to believe that?'

Harriet exploded with rage. 'Yes, I do expect you to believe it because it's true. If we'd got there just a few minutes later it would have been too late. You're lucky he's here and not at the bottom of the ocean.' She handed the phone to Darius, who was staring as though he'd just seen an apparition. 'Tell her,' she commanded.

Dazed, he took the receiver and spoke into it. 'Mary? Are you still there?—yes, it's true what she said.'

A sense of propriety made Harriet back away in the direction of the kitchen but an overwhelming curiosity made her leave the door open just enough to eavesdrop.

'Please fetch them,' she heard him say. 'Oh, they've come downstairs? Let me talk to them. Frankie—is that you? I'm sorry about the delay—I fell in the water but they pulled me out—I'm fine now. Put Mark on, let me try and talk to both of you at once.'

His tone had changed, becoming warm and caressing in a way Harriet wouldn't have believed possible. Now she backed into the kitchen and shut the door, gratefully accepting a cup of tea from Kate.

'He'll go down with pneumonia if he doesn't get changed soon,' Kate observed worriedly.

'Then we'll have to be very firm with him,' Harriet said.

'Like you were just now.' Kate's tone was admiring. 'He didn't know what had hit him.'

'I suppose he'll be cross with me, but it can't be helped.'

'As long as we keep him safe,' Kate agreed.

Harriet look at her curiously. 'You sound as though you really care. But he can't be very easy to work for.'

'I'll take him rather than the last fellow any day. Rancing

just vanished, leaving me here for weeks. He never got in touch, never paid me—'

'Didn't pay you?' Harriet echoed, aghast. 'The lousy so-and-so. How did you live?'

'I had a little saved, but I had to spend it all. I couldn't contact him. Nothing. Then Mr Falcon walked in and said the place was his. I was still living here because I've got nowhere else to go. I thought he'd throw me out and bring in an army of posh servants, but he said he wanted me to stay and he paid me for all the weeks after Rancing left.'

'He—paid you? But—'

'I know. He didn't have to. He didn't owe me and I couldn't believe it when he handed me the cash.'

Harriet stared, feeling as though the world had suddenly turned upside down. This couldn't be true. Darius was a villain. That had been a settled fact in her mind. Until tonight—

'Why didn't you tell anyone?' she asked.

'Because he said not to. He'd be good and mad if he knew I'd told you now, so you'll keep quiet, won't you?'

'Of course. I'm not even quite convinced.'

'No, he said you wouldn't be.'

'He said what?'

'Not at the time, but last night when I was making his supper, I mentioned it, asked if I could tell people, and he said that you especially must never know because you enjoyed seeing him as the devil and he didn't want to spoil your fun.'

'Oh, *did* he?'

There were no words for the unfamiliar sensation that shook her. Darius had looked into her mind and read it with a precision that was alarming. Or exciting. She wasn't sure. One thing was certain. Everything she'd thought she knew about him was now in question. And the truth about his real nature was an even bigger question. The world had gone mad, taking her with it.

And what a journey that might be!

She recovered enough to say, 'But if people knew he could be as generous as this they'd see him differently.'

'Perhaps he doesn't want them to,' Kate said wisely.

That silenced Harriet. This was too much to take in all in one go. She needed space and solitude.

It was time to see how he was managing. Opening the door, they looked out into the hall and saw Darius sitting so still that they thought the call was ended, but then he said, 'All right,' in a hard voice.

After a pause he added, 'You'd better go back to bed now—yes, all right. Goodbye.'

He set the phone down and leaned back against the wood, eyes closed, face exhausted. Something told Harriet the call hadn't gone well.

'Time for bed,' Kate told him. 'Shall we help you up the stairs?'

'Thank you, but there's no need,' he growled.

He hauled himself slowly to his feet and began the weary trek, stair by stair, but waving the two women away if they seemed to get too close. They contented themselves with keeping a respectful distance, following him up and into his room, where he sat heavily on the bed.

'It's all right,' he said. 'I can manage.'

'No, you can't,' Harriet firmly. 'If we leave now you'll just stretch out and go to sleep in your freezing wet clothes. Next stop, pneumonia.'

'Now, look—'

'No, you look. I didn't give up my evening to come out to sea and fetch you to have you throw your life away through carelessness. You're going to take off those wet clothes and put on dry ones.'

Darius looked warily from one to the other, and seemed to decide against argument. His eyes closed and Harriet thought for a moment he would lose consciousness. But when he opened them again an incredible change seemed to come over him.

Astonished, Harriet saw a faint grin that might almost have been good-natured, or at least resigned. Then he shrugged.

'I'm in your hands, ladies.'

He unbuttoned his own shirt and shrugged it off, then unzipped his trousers and stood while they removed them. Kate fetched towels and a bathrobe that Harriet helped him put on. He tried to draw the edges together before removing his underpants, but his grip was weak and they fell open at the crucial moment.

Harriet quickly averted her eyes, but not before she'd seen his nakedness. Just a brief glimpse, but it told her what she didn't want to know, that his personal magnificence measured up to his reputation in business.

Hastily, she began opening drawers, asking, 'Where are your pyjamas?'

'I don't have any. Sleeping in the nude is more comfortable.' He raised an eyebrow at her. 'Don't you find that?'

'I really wouldn't know,' she said primly. It was incredible to her that he'd chosen this moment to tease her. He was half dead, for pity's sake! Did nothing crush him?

'I'm making you a hot tea,' she declared, 'and when I come back I expect to find you in bed.'

'Yes, ma'am,' he said meekly.

Now Harriet was sure she could see a gleam of humour far back in his eyes, but she couldn't be sure.

'I'll leave you in Kate's capable hands.' Some defensive instinct made her add, 'Don't stand any nonsense from him, Kate.'

'Don't you worry,' Kate said significantly.

'Harriet!' She turned at the door in response to Darius's voice. 'Thank you,' he said quietly.

'Don't mention it.'

She departed hurriedly. Downstairs, she made the tea but only took it halfway up the stairs before calling Kate and handing it to her. Suddenly it was important to escape him, above all to escape his knowing look that said he would tease her if he wanted to, and what was she going to do about it?

There was nothing to be done, except get back home—a place of safety, where she knew what was what.

When she got there safety greeted her in the form of Phantom. As they snuggled down under the covers she discussed the matter with him, as she discussed everything.

'What a night! Him of all people. And it seems he's not like... Well, I don't know what he's like any more. He was nice to Kate, I'll admit that. Maybe we were wrong about him. No, not we. Just me. You always liked him, didn't you?

'If you could have seen him getting undressed tonight. It was an honest accident—at least, I think it was. But what I saw was impressive and maybe he meant me to see and maybe he didn't.

'He ticks the boxes—great thighs, narrow hips and the rest—well, never mind. But Brad also ticked the boxes, and he *knew* he ticked them. A man like that wasn't going to confine himself to me, was he? And he didn't. So if His Majesty Falcon is expecting me to be impressed he can just think again.

'You agree with me, don't you? Well, you do if you want that new stuff I bought for your breakfast tomorrow. Yes—yes—that's a lovely lick. Can I have another? Thank you. Now, let's go to sleep. And move over. Give me some room.'

CHAPTER FOUR

HARRIET spent the next morning at her shop, which was doing well. She'd recently taken on a new assistant who was good at the job, something she was glad of when Kate rang, sounding frantic. 'Darius is driving me crazy wanting to do all sorts of daft things.'

'Hah! Surprise me.'

'He's got a nasty cold, but he insists on getting up. He says he's got to go out and buy another cellphone. He's ordered a fancy one online but it'll take a few days to arrive so he's determined to get something basic to fill in. And then he wants to come and see you.'

'All right, I'm on my way. Don't let him out. Tie him to the bed if you have to.'

Distantly, she heard Kate say, 'She says I'm to tie you to the bed,' followed by a sound that might have been a snort of laughter, followed by coughing.

'You hear that?' Kate demanded into the phone. 'If you—'

Her voice vanished, replaced by a loud burr. Harriet hung up, very thoughtful.

Before leaving, she took out an object that until then she'd kept hidden away and looked at it for a long time. At last she sighed and replaced it. But then, heading for the door, she stopped, returned and retrieved it from its hiding place. Again, she gazed at it for several moments, a yearning expression haunting her eyes. Her hand tightened on it and for a moment she seemed resolute. But then she returned it firmly to its hiding place, ran out of the room and downstairs, where she got into her car and began the journey to Giant's Beacon.

Halfway there she stopped, turned the car and swiftly headed back to streak up the stairs, snatch the precious object, ram it into her pocket and flee.

She'd done it now, the thing she'd vowed never to do, and that was that. She told herself it was time to be sensible, but she made the journey with her face set as though resisting pain

Kate was waiting for her on the doorstep, calling, 'Thank goodness you're here!'

'Kate, is that her?' cried a hoarse voice from the back of the house.

'I'm coming,' she called, hurrying into the room he'd turned into an office.

At first she was bewildered by the array of machinery, all of it obviously state-of-the-art. Kate had spoken of wonderful things, but still the variety and magnificence came as a surprise. And one man could control all this?

Darius, in his dressing gown, was sitting at a large screen, his fingers hovering over a keyboard.

'Don't come near me,' he croaked. 'I'm full of germs.'

'You shouldn't be up at all,' she scolded him, sitting down at a distance. 'And Kate says you want to go out. That's madness. It's far too cold.'

'I thought summer was supposed to be coming. Is it always like this in May?'

'The weather can be a bit temperamental. It's been colder than usual the last few days. It'll warm up soon, and then we'll be flooded with tourists. In the meantime, take care.'

'I just need a new cellphone to replace the one I lost last night. I have a thousand calls to make, and the house phone keeps going dead.'

'Yes, the line's faulty and they don't seem able to repair it. You were lucky it held out last night when you were calling your children. All right, you need one to tide you over. Try this.'

Reaching into her pocket, she handed over the object that had given her such anguish earlier.

'You're lending me yours?' he asked.

'No, it's not mine, it…belonged to my husband.'

He took it from her left hand, realising for the first time that she wore a wedding ring.

'Husband?' he echoed.

'He died a year ago. He hadn't used this for some time because he'd replaced it with a better one. But it might get you through the next few days.'

He seemed uncertain what to say.

'That's very kind of you,' he murmured at last. 'But—are you sure?'

'Quite sure. You'll find it blank. I've wiped off every trace of him.'

Something in her voice made him glance at her quickly, but she was looking out of the window.

'I appreciate this,' he said. 'Now I can call my children again. I'll be in touch as soon as I'm a bit more normal. I still have to thank you properly for saving me. Perhaps we could have dinner.'

'You don't need to thank me. I was just doing what I do and I wasn't alone. What about all the others on the lifeboat?'

'I'll show my gratitude by making a donation. But I

think you can tell me a lot about Herringdean that I need to know, so I'd appreciate it if you'd agree to dinner.'

'All right, I'll look forward to it.'

'By the way,' he added as she reached the door, 'how's my ghostly friend?'

'Who?'

'His name is Phantom, isn't it?'

She gave an uncertain laugh. 'You call him your friend?'

'You assured me he was only being friendly. Tell him I look forward to our next meeting. What kind of bones does he like?'

'Any kind.'

'I'll remember.'

As she left the house Harriet was saying to herself, 'I don't believe it. I imagined that conversation. I must have done.'

That evening she poured out her thoughts again to the one friend she knew she could always trust.

'I don't know what to think any more. He's different— well, all right, he nearly died and that changes people— but they change back. In a few days he'll be talking about showing no mercy again. Hey, don't do that! Phantom, *put that down!*—oh, all right, just this once.'

Three days later she looked up from serving in the shop to find Darius standing there.

'It's a nice day so I managed to escape,' he said with a smile. 'I wanted to bring you this.' He held out the phone. 'I've got my new one now, but this was invaluable. Thank you. There seems no end to what I owe you.'

'Did you manage to call your sons?'

'My son and daughter, yes.'

'Oh, I thought—Mark and Frank.'

'Frankie. Her name's Francesca, but we call her Frankie. It's a bit like calling you Harry.'

She laughed. 'Yes, I suppose it is.'

'And there's also this,' he said, reaching into a bag and drawing out a huge bone. 'This is for Phantom, by the way, not you.'

Her lips twitched. 'I'm glad you explained that.'

'About our dinner. Kate's set her heart on cooking it for us.'

'Good idea. She's a great cook, and it would be better for you.'

'If you say I need to stay indoors for a few more days I shall do something desperate,' he warned. 'You two mother hens are driving me crazy.'

'No, I was only going to say that anywhere else you'll get stared at. I'll come to Giant's Beacon.'

'You and Phantom.'

'He's included?'

'It wouldn't be the same without him. Friday evening.'

'I look forward to it. *We'll* look forward to it.'

He thanked her and departed. Outside the shop, he hesitated a moment, then headed for the harbour and the lifeboat station, but after a moment his attention was claimed by a man watching him from across the road with an air of nervousness. Enlightenment dawned, and he crossed over.

'I know you, don't I? You were part of the team that saved me from drowning.'

'I'm glad you remember that,' Walter said, 'and not the other thing.'

'You mean when you advised Harriet to let me drown?' Darius said, grinning.

'Ah, yes—'

'It's in the past,' Darius assured him. 'Look, do you have a moment? There's a pub over there.'

When they were settled with glasses of ale, Darius said, 'I want to show my gratitude in a practical way, with a donation to the lifeboat.' He took out his chequebook. 'Who do I make it out to?'

Walter told him, then looked, wide-eyed, at the amount. 'That's very generous.'

'It's not too much for my life. Will you make sure this reaches the right part of your organisation?'

'It'll be a pleasure. It's good to see you on your feet again. Harry said you were in a bad way.'

'All that time in the cold water. I reckon I was bound to go down with something. But Harriet got me home and took wonderful care of me.'

'She's a great girl, isn't she? Sometimes I wonder how she survived after what she's been through.'

'Been through?'

'Losing her husband. Oh, I know she's not the only widow in the world, but they had a fantastic marriage. Everyone who gets married hopes they're going to have what those two had. We all envied them. When he died we thought she might die too, she was so crushed. But she came back fighting. I don't reckon she'll ever really get over him, though.'

'But she's a young woman, with plenty of time to find someone else.'

'Yes, if she really wants to. But you only get something as good as that once in your life. It wouldn't surprise me if she stayed single now.' He drained his glass. 'Got to be going. Nice to meet you.'

They parted on good terms.

* * *

On Friday Darius came in the late afternoon to collect both his guests. Phantom leapt into the back seat of the car as though being chauffeured was no more than his right.

'Don't worry, I've washed him,' Harriet said.

Darius grinned over his shoulder at his four-pawed guest, who nuzzled his ear.

'Wait,' Harriet said suddenly, bouncing out of the car. 'I'll be back.'

He watched as she ran into her home, then out again a moment later, clutching a small black box.

'My pager,' she said, settling into the front seat. 'It has to go with me everywhere in case the lifeboat gets called out.'

'You're on call tonight?'

'Lifeboat volunteers are always on call. The only time that's not true is if we're ill, or have to leave the island for some reason. Then we give them notice of the dates and report back as soon as we return. But normally we take the pager everywhere and have to be ready to drop everything.'

'Everything? You mean…even if…suppose you were…?'

'At work or in the bath,' she supplied innocently. 'Yes, even then.'

That wasn't quite what he'd meant, and her mischievous look showed that she understood perfectly. For a moment another memory danced between them, when the edges of his robe had fallen open just long enough to be tantalising. By mutual consent they decided to leave it there.

'What made you want to be a lifeboat volunteer?' he asked as he started the car.

'My father. My mother died when I was very young and Dad raised me alone. When he went out on a call I used to love watching the boat go down the slipway into the water. All that spray coming up seemed so thrilling. He was a fisherman and I often went out with him. He taught me to be a sailor and bought me my first boat. My happiest times were spent on the water with him, and it was natural to follow him onto the lifeboats.'

'A fisherman? You mean herring?'

She laughed, 'Yes. There have always been shoals of herring in the water around here. Other fish too, but that's how the island got its name.'

'You've never wanted to leave it behind and move to the mainland?'

She made a face. 'Never! There's nowhere better in the world.'

'You sound very sure? As simple as that?'

'As simple as that. It's the best place on earth, and it always will be; unless something happens to spoil it.'

Darius didn't need to ask what she meant. He had the power to do the damage she mentioned, and they both knew it. But this wasn't the right moment.

The drive ran along the shoreline, from where they could see the sun beginning to set.

'I'd never seen anything like that before I came here,' he said.

'Never seen a sunset?'

'Not like a Herringdean sunset. I haven't been much by the sea. It's usually something I see looking down on from a plane.'

'Stop the car,' she urged.

He did as she asked and the three of them walked to the edge of the beach and stood watching as the water turned crimson, glittering as tiny waves broke softly. None of them made a sound. There was no need. Harriet glanced at Darius and saw on his face a look akin to the one she'd first seen when they met—absorbed, ecstatic. At last he gave a regretful sigh.

'We'd better go.'

'You can see it from the house,' she reassured him.

'In a way. But somehow it's different when you're out here with it.'

As they walked back to the car he glanced appreciatively at her appearance. Her soft blue dress wasn't expensive nor glamorous, but neither did it send out the warning he'd sensed from her functional bathing gear. Her light brown shoulder length hair flowed freely in soft waves. She looked relaxed and ready to enjoy herself and he found himself relaxing in turn.

The evening stretched ahead of him, warm and inviting. Another new experience. When had he last whiled away the hours with a friend?

Two friends, he realised, feeling Phantom nuzzle his hand.

'Just wait until we get home,' he said. 'Kate's got something really special for you.'

'I'm looking forward to it,' Harriet declared.

Man and dog stared at her, then at each other. Darius gave a shrug of resignation, and Harriet could almost have sworn that Phantom returned the gesture.

'You have to explain things carefully to women,' Darius told him.

Woof!

'You meant that remark about something special for Phantom?' Harriet demanded.

'Who else? Kate's taken a lot of trouble with his supper. I told her he was the guest of honour.'

Harriet chuckled. 'I guess you're learning.'

Kate was waiting at the door, beaming a welcome. For Phantom there was the dog equivalent of a banquet, which he tucked into with due appreciation. Her mind at ease, Harriet left him to it and followed Darius into the large dining room at the back where a table for two had been set up by the French windows. From here the lawn stretched out until it shaded into the stretch of private beach where they had first met.

'Remember?' he asked, filling her wine glass.

'I remember, and I shouldn't think you'll ever forget,' she said. 'You never did send me the bill for that suit.'

'Well, maybe I'm not the monster you think me to be,' he said.

'Thought, not think. I wouldn't dare think badly of someone who treats Phantom so well.'

'Ah, you've noticed that I'm grovelling to him. I'm so glad. I knew I had no chance of getting on your right side unless I got on his first.'

Harriet seemed to give this serious consideration. 'I see. And it's important to get on my right side?'

'Well, I can't let you go on being my enemy. It wouldn't be practical.'

'And at all costs we must be practical,' she agreed. 'But I have to say, Mr Falcon, that I'm disappointed at how badly you've misread the situation. I'd expected more efficiency from "the most fearsome man in London."'

'Please,' he protested. 'None of that. It was enough of an embarrassment when I could make a pretence of living up to it. Now—' He shuddered. 'But how did I misread the situation?'

'I was never your enemy.'

'Really? You expect me to believe that when you got a bodyguard for Phantom? Oh, yes, I heard. And then you despised me so much that you made jokes about leaving me to drown.'

'Well, you got your own back by walking in on me right after, didn't you? And I didn't leave you to drown—' She checked herself, alerted by his teasing look. 'Oh, ha ha! Well, I guess you're entitled to make fun of me.'

'Yes, I think I am as well,' he said, smiling and raising his glass. 'Truce?'

She regarded him with her head on one side. 'Armed?'

He nodded. 'Safer that way for both of us.'

'It's a deal.'

She raised her own glass and they clinked as Kate entered with the first dish.

'Just in time to save me from your terrible vengeance,' Darius said.

'Don't fool yourself,' she told him. 'When I wreak terrible vengeance on you, nothing and nobody will be able to save you.'

'Then I'd better have my supper quickly,' he said, leading her to the table.

Kate gave them a strange look and departed, making Harriet say in a quivering voice, trying not to laugh, 'She thinks we're both potty.'

'She's very observant.'

For a few moments they didn't speak, concentrating on the food, which was Kate's best, plain but delicious. Harriet wondered how it tasted to Darius, who must be used to more sophisticated fare, but he seemed happy to devour every mouthful.

'If I had "enemy" thoughts, so did you,' she observed. 'When you came upon us in the garden of the pub you seemed to hate me.'

She thought he wasn't going to reply, but then he nodded.

'I did. I heard you talking about how I looked on the beach, "standing there like a king come into his birthright" according to you.'

'That'll teach me to jump to conclusions,' she sighed. 'You weren't really feeling anything like that, were you?'

'No, I was feeling what a glorious place it was. It took me completely by surprise and I just stood there, stunned, trying to believe such beauty existed.'

'That was what I sensed when I first saw you,' she admitted. 'It was only later that I thought—oh, dear, I'm sorry. I guess I got it all wrong.'

'We both got a lot of things wrong, but this is the moment when we put it all behind us and become friends.'

'Friends…' She considered the word for a moment before saying, 'I must warn you, friends claim the right to ask each other questions.'

'Fire away.'

'Why did you go out to sea at all? It was madness.'

'I needed to see the wind farm, and learn all I could.'

'But surely you did an in-depth investigation before you bought the island?' Something in his wry expression made her say, 'You did, surely?'

'The first I heard about it was when Kate told me.'

She stared. 'I can't believe a smart operator like you bought this place without checking every detail first.'

He shrugged.

'You didn't?' she breathed. 'But why?'

'Perhaps I'm not quite as smart as I like people to think. Look, if I tell you, you've got to promise not to breathe a word to another soul.'

'I promise.'

'Seriously. Swear it on what you hold most dear.'

'I swear it on Phantom's life,' she said, holding up her hand. 'Now, tell, tell! The curiosity's driving me crazy.'

'I didn't buy Herringdean. Rancing owed me money, couldn't pay it, so he assigned the place to me, sent me the papers and vanished.'

'*What?*'

'My lawyer says everything's in order, I'm the legal

owner. But I had no chance to study the place, negoti-
ate, refuse the deal, anything. Whatever I learn about the
island comes as a surprise. My "investigation" consisted
of looking Herringdean up online. What I found wasn't
informative—fishing, beautiful countryside, but no mention
of a wind farm.'

'Probably because it had only just got under way and
they hadn't updated the site,' she mused.

'Exactly. So you see I've approached everything like a
dimwit. All right, all right,' he added as she choked with
laughter. 'Have your fun.'

'I'm sorry,' she gasped. 'I didn't mean to but—he fooled
you—'

'Yes, he fooled me,' Darius said, managing to be faintly
amused through his chagrin. 'And I'll tell you something
else. Before he left, he got a lot of the bigger tenants to
pay him several months' rent in advance, then he pocketed
the money and ran. So it'll be a while before they pay me
anything.'

He knew he was crazy to have told her such damaging
things. If she betrayed his trust she could make him look
like an idiot all over the island.

But she wouldn't betray him. Instinctively, he knew that
he was safe with her.

Harriet was making confused gestures, trying to get her
head around what she'd just heard.

'But the papers always say—you know, the mighty en-
trepreneur, all that stuff—'

'Been checking up on me, huh?' he said wryly.

'Of course. Be fair. Since you control our lives, I had to
find out what I could.'

'Control your lives? Oh, sure, it looks like it. I arrive
knowing nothing, nearly die finding out, get snatched from

the jaws of death by you and the others. Some control! So I suppose you know all there is to know about me?'

Harriet shook her head. 'Only basics. Your father is Amos Falcon—*the* Amos Falcon. Empire builder, financial mogul—all right, all right.' She backed off hastily, seeing his expression. 'And you have lots of brothers. It must be nice coming from a large family. I'm an only child and it can be lonely.'

'So can being in a large family,' Darius said.

'Really? I can't imagine that. Tell me more.'

But suddenly his mouth closed in a firm line. It was as though something had brought him to the edge of a cliff, Harriet thought, and he'd backed away in alarm. She could almost see him retreating further and further.

'What is it?' she asked.

He rose and walked away to the window. She had a strange feeling that he was trying to put a distance between them, as though she was some kind of threat. After a moment's hesitation she followed him and laid a tentative hand on his arm.

'I'm sorry,' she said. 'Of course it's none of my business. I'm always sticking my nose into other people's affairs. Just ignore me.'

With anyone else he would have seized this offer with relief, but with her things were mysteriously different. In his mind he saw again the defining moment of their relationship, the moment when she had reached out to him, offering rescue, offering life. The moment had passed, yet it lived in him still and, he guessed, would always do so.

The need to accept her friendship, trust it, rely on it, was so strong that it sent warning signals. Nothing would ever be the same again. But there was no turning back now.

'I don't think I'll ignore you,' he said softly, taking her hand. 'You're not a woman that's easy to ignore.'

'I'll just vanish if you like.'

'No,' he said, his hand tightening on hers so suddenly that she gasped. 'Stay. I want you to stay.'

'All right,' she said. 'I'll stay.'

He led her back to the table and poured her a glass of wine.

'People always think big families are charming,' he said after a while. 'But it can be an illusion. Most of us didn't grow up together. My father's family was very poor and he had a hard life, which he was determined to escape at all costs. Some of the things he did don't look very sympathetic, but maybe if you have to live as he did—' He made an expressive gesture with his hands.

'Was he very—?' She paused delicately.

'Yes, very. Still is, for that matter. His family were miners, and he was expected to go down the pit. But his father had died down there and hell would freeze over before he went the same way. He did well at school, got top marks in practical subjects like maths. Not literature, or "the soft stuff" as he calls it. He reckons that's for fools. But with figures there's nothing he can't do.

'So he ran away and managed to start up his own business, just a little market stall, but it grew into a big one, and then bigger, until he got a shop.'

'He made enough profit to rent a shop? Wow!'

'Not rent. Buy. By that time he'd married my mother. She came from a rich family and they met when he made deliveries to their house. Her relatives did everything they could to stop the wedding. They believed all he really wanted was her money.'

'But they gave in at last?'

'No way. He simply ran off with her. "If you want something, go after it by the shortest route." That's his motto.

She gave him every penny she had. I know that because I've heard her father complaining about it.'

'But he probably loved her, and you. Surely everything in his life wasn't about money? It couldn't be, could it? There's always something else.'

'Is there?' he murmured. 'Is there?'

His face had changed. Now it wore a look of pain that made her take his hand in hers in a gesture of comfort.

'Don't say any more,' she said. 'Not if it hurts too much.'

He didn't answer. His gaze was fixed on the hand holding his, as it had once before. Then it had offered survival, now it offered another kind of life, one he couldn't describe. He had no talent for words, only figures. She'd spoken of it hurting him too much to talk, but now he knew that the real pain lay in not talking about things that had been shrouded in silence for too long. Somehow the words must come. But only with her.

CHAPTER FIVE

'I'LL tell you something,' Darius said at last. 'Falcon isn't my father's real name. He chose it for effect.'

'He wanted to be named after a bird?'

'No, he discovered that it has connections with a Roman consul and two princes.'

'You're kidding me.'

'Do you mean you've never heard of Pompeyo Falco?' Darius demanded with mock surprise. 'He was a very powerful Roman. The princes were Spanish, and there's even supposed to be a saint in the background. Not that he's ever made too much of that one. Nobody could keep a straight face.'

'I guess your father isn't much like a saint.'

'That's putting it mildly. He called me Darius because it means "wealthy". It was his way of signalling what he expected of me.'

Harriet dropped her face into her hands. 'I can hardly believe it,' she said at last. 'It's like something out of a mad fantasy.'

'That's just what it is. I grew up knowing what I had to do to please my father—or else! Luckily, I'd inherited his head for figures, so I was able to live up to at least some of his expectations.'

'Only some?'

'He's not pleased with me at the moment, losing so much money and letting things crumble under me.'

'But that's happened to a lot of people.'

'Doesn't matter. It shouldn't have happened to a Falcon. He's currently considering whether I, or one of my brothers, does him the most credit. At the moment I think I'm bottom of the list.'

Harriet frowned. 'I think I read somewhere that your brothers come from different parts of the world,' she said carefully.

'If you mean that my father spread himself thinly, yes, that's right. As the business built up he did a lot of travelling, first in England, then abroad. I don't think he was ever faithful to my mother for five minutes; that's how, in addition to a full brother, I come to have a half-brother from Russia, one from France, and one from America.

'In the end my mother couldn't stand it any more and she left, taking my brother Jackson and me with her. But she died after a few years and my father reclaimed us. By that time he had a new wife and a new son. We entered their house as strangers, and that was how we felt for a long time. Jackson coped better, although even he had a tough time with our stepmother.'

'She was furious that we were there at all because that meant that her boy, Marcel, wasn't the eldest. When she caught my father playing around she left him and went back to France. Marcel turned up a few years ago and, oddly enough, we all get on well. Our father has helped him start up in business in Paris, and I understand he's a real chip off the old block.'

'More than you?' she asked shrewdly.

He hesitated before saying, 'Who can say?'

Greatly daring, she ventured to ask, 'Is that what you want? To be like him?'

'I don't know,' he said. 'It's all become confused. When I was growing up my one thought was to follow in his footsteps and be a power in the land. People were awed by him, they hurried to please him, and that seemed wonderful to me. But I was immature and, as you grow up, things happen to you—'

He grew silent. After a while he repeated softly, 'I simply don't know.'

A noise made him look up quickly, smiling as if everything was normal. Nobody, Harriet thought, could guess that the moment of insight had taken him by surprise. Now she felt he was trying to forget it.

'Ah, here's Kate with the next course,' he said cheerfully. 'And not only Kate.'

Phantom had slipped in and came to curl up near the table.

'Have you had enough?' Harriet asked, caressing his ears. 'Has the guest of honour been properly cared for?'

A soft woof was the reply.

'How did Phantom happen to be with you and the rest of the crew that night?' Darius asked when they were alone again. 'I gather you'd been out on a shout. Don't tell me he comes too?'

She laughed. 'No, I left him with my neighbour—'

'To protect him from me?'

'Please.'

'All right, I won't say it again.'

'She was out walking him when she saw the boat coming home across the water, so she waited, then came and joined us.'

'How old is he?'

'Fourteen, maybe. He belonged to Brad, my husband, before we married, and he'd got him from a home for abandoned dogs, so he wasn't sure of his age. I know he's getting on a bit but he's still full of beans.'

There was a hint of defiance in her voice that warned Darius to go carefully. Fourteen was old for a dog, especially a large one, but not for the world would he have voiced his conviction that she would soon lose her beloved companion.

'Talking of being full of beans, are you really better?' she asked.

'I'm fine now. I've spent some time in bed—why that cynical look?'

'I'm getting to understand you now. All that time in bed, I'll bet you weren't alone.'

'No, I haven't seduced any willing ladies—'

'I meant you had your laptop computer with you.'

'Ah…yes…I see.' He met her teasing eyes and grinned sheepishly. 'I fell right into that one, didn't I? Yes, I did have it with me now and then. But not always. I got a lot of sleep and I have to admit you and Kate were right. It was what I needed. And, as well as rest, I've been taking exercise. I go swimming from my private beach. I keep looking out for you, but you're never there.'

Her eyes widened in theatrical innocence. 'But how can I be? I don't have the permission of the owner. He's a terrible man. When he found me there once before he was very annoyed.'

'No, you just imagined that.' He grinned. 'In future you go there whenever you like. And take Phantom too.'

A soft noise from under the table told him that this was appreciated.

'And I'm not glued to the computer all the time,' he continued.

'No, I'm sure you read the *Financial Times* and *The Wall Street Journal*—'

'I've been reading up about Herringdean and its history. It's fascinating.'

'You'll find that this island is two places,' she said. 'We're not behind the times. There's plenty of dot-com. But it's the wildness that makes Herringdean stand out, and draws people.'

'Have you always lived on the island?'

'Yes, I was born here.'

'And your husband?'

'No, he came over because he worked for a tourist firm, and they were setting up a branch.'

'And you met, fell in love and married quickly?'

'A couple of months.'

'Wow! A decisive lady! How long were you married?'

'Nearly eight years.'

'Any children?'

'No,' she said quietly.

'And he died quite recently?'

'Last year.' Suddenly she became animated. 'You know, this coffee is really delicious. Kate is a wonderful cook.'

He was silent. Walter was there in his mind, talking about Harriet's husband, saying, 'When he died we thought she might die too, she was so crushed…I don't reckon she'll ever really get over him…'

Now the way she'd swerved off the subject seemed to suggest that Walter was right. It was a warning to him to be cautious.

'What about your children?' Harriet asked. 'Have you managed to call them again?'

'Yes, several times. There's a dangerous situation building up. Mary's going to remarry soon, and if I'm not careful I could be elbowed aside.'

'But you won't let that happen.'

'No, I won't. I had time to do a lot of thinking while

I was resting. It's incredible how being half-awake, half-asleep can make things clear to you.'

Harriet nodded, and for a moment there was a faraway look in her eyes that roused his curiosity. But it vanished before he could speak, and now he thought he understood. Beneath her cheeky schoolgirl charm lurked a woman who kept her true feelings, and even her true self, safely hidden away. In fact, she was mysteriously like himself.

'So what conclusions have you come to?' she asked.

'Not to let myself be sidelined. I try to call them every day.'

'I'm sure they're glad of that.'

He made a face. 'They're not. I made a hash of it the night of the accident and things haven't really improved.'

'Well, you weren't at ease on the phone, I could hear that, but surely they understood what a state you were in.'

'Maybe, but I'm seldom much better than I was then. I don't know what to talk about. It was easier when we were living in the same house, but I'm not really part of their lives any more. Perhaps I never really was. Mary accused me of never putting them first.'

She nodded. 'Children really do like to feel that they have all your attention,' she mused.

Suddenly he saw her as she'd been that day in the shop, talking to the little boy as though only he existed in the entire world. And the child had responded with delight. When had he seen such a look on the faces of his own children?

'You've got a fight on your hands,' she said, 'but you've got to go about it the right way. Do you want some advice from a friend?'

'If the friend is you, yes.'

'That night when you called them after the accident I heard her voice on the other end. I couldn't make out every word but I heard enough to show me an unhappy situation. You told her you'd been "held up" and she said, "You always get held up. The children went to bed crying because you didn't keep your word."

'And then she said, "I'm not going to let you hurt them by putting them last again."'

She waited to see if he would say anything, but he only clasped his hands on the table and stared at them.

'Again?' she asked.

'Yes, I can't deny it. I would plan to spend time with them, but a crisis would come up, someone I urgently needed to meet would be passing through London for just a few hours.'

'Oh, you idiot!' she breathed.

'I guess I am, but I didn't see it then. I always thought there was time to put things right.'

'Yes, we always think that,' she murmured. 'There never is.'

'You sound as though you really know.'

'I guess we all know one way or another.'

'Sure, but the way you said it sounded as though—'

'The thing is—' she interrupted him quickly '—that you have to find a new way to put things right. Concentrate on that.'

'All right,' he said, retreating before the warning she was sending out. 'But how? One minute I thought I was in control. The next minute they were all gone, and if I was a hopeless father before I'm even worse now. When we talk on the phone I can sense them trying to get away. I'm becoming an irrelevance to them.'

'Then do something about it,' she said urgently. 'Put a stop to it now. Never forget that cunning is better than aggression. Above all, don't lose heart, don't even think of giving in. Remember, you're a match for anyone.'

'If you're going to start on that "mighty man of business" stuff again I'm out of here.'

'Don't worry,' she said wryly. 'I can't take it seriously any more.'

'Thanks. That about says it all.'

'Friends have to be frank with each other,' she reminded him.

'I know.' He suddenly became more urgent. 'Harriet, I wish I could make you understand how much I need your friendship. From the moment I stepped onto that beach I knew I was in a different world, and now I know that it's your world. All the vital things that have happened to me since I came here are connected with you.'

'You never know what fate has in store.'

'Yes, after we got off to such a bad start, who could have guessed that you'd be the one who'd save me?'

'Be fair. It was Kate who really saved you, not just by raising the alarm, but by explaining that you'd probably gone to the wind farm, so that we knew where to look.'

'I know that, and I've shown her my gratitude.'

Harriet nodded. Kate had told her about the huge bonus he'd given her.

'And I didn't pull you out of the water on my own. There were a few hefty fellers there, doing the heavy work.'

'I know. But yours was the hand that stretched out to me first, the hand that I clasped, and when I think of that moment that's what I see.'

It was also what he felt in the night, feeling a firm, reassuring grip on his hand, knowing it was her in the last moment before he awoke to find himself alone. Only a dream, yet his hand still seemed to tingle.

'I've just become a sort of symbol, that's all,' she told him.

'If you say so.'

'But if you want a friend, you've got one in me.'

'Promise?'

'Promise. Call on me any time.'

As long as you're here, she thought. But how long will that be? Are we a financial asset to you, or a financial disaster? And won't it be the same in the long run?

It would have been sensible to say this outright and remind him of the reality of the situation, yet something held her silent. There was an intensity in his eyes that she'd never seen before in any man—not the passionate intensity of a lover, but the desperate yearning for help of a man who needed friendship. It had been her hand he'd first seized in the water and that had set matters between them for all time.

'You may regret saying that,' he said. 'I'll call on you more often than you think.'

'I'll never regret saying it. I'm here for you.'

'Shake on it?'

She took the hand he offered, and felt her own hand engulfed. She could sense the power, as she'd sensed it that other time when he'd held her against her will to study her face. But now she also felt the gentleness deep within him, knowing instinctively that few people were ever allowed to know about it.

He touched her heart—not as a lover, she assured herself. That part of her life had died a year ago. But his need spoke to her, making it impossible for her to turn her back on him.

'Shake,' she said.

A couple of days later she resumed bathing on his beach. After splashing around with Phantom for half an hour she gasped, 'All right, boy. Time we were going.'

But as she turned towards the shore she was halted by

the sight of Darius, striding onto the beach wearing a dark blue towel bathrobe, which he stripped off, showing his black bathing gear beneath.

Instead of tight-fitting trunks he wore shorts, looser and less revealing, leaving many of her questions still unanswered. Even so, she could see that he was more powerfully built than a mere businessman had any right to be. If there was any justice in the world he would be scrawny, not taut and lean, with long muscular arms and legs.

He saw her and waved. Next moment he was running into the water and powering towards her. She laughed and swam away, swerving this way and that until he caught up, reaching out his hands. She seized them and he immediately began to back-pedal, drawing her with him. As they reached the shore she slipped away, laughing, and he chased her up the beach to where he'd dropped his bathrobe next to her towel.

Phantom galloped after them, delighted at the prospect of a rematch, but this time Darius was ready for him, dropping to one knee, greeting his 'opponent' with outstretched arms and rolling on the sand with him.

'I reckon that's about even,' he said, getting up at last.

'Now you really are a mess,' she said, regarding the sand that covered him.

'Yes, I am, aren't I?' he agreed with something that sounded suspiciously like satisfaction. 'All right, play's over. Time for the serious stuff. See you tomorrow.'

So it went on for several days—pleasant, undemanding friendship with almost the innocence of childhood. It seemed strange to think of this man in such a light, but when she saw him fooling with Phantom it was hard to remember his harsh reputation, and the power he held over them all.

Then he vanished.

'He just took off without a word,' Kate said when they bumped into each other while shopping. 'He was sitting at the computer when I took in his morning coffee. I don't know what he saw there but it made him say a very rude word. Then he made a phone call. I got out fast but I could hear a lot more rude words.'

Walter, who also happened to be there, said, 'Only rude words?'

'I heard him say, "I don't care; it mustn't be allowed to happen," and "Do you realise what this would mean if—?" and "When I get my hands on him I'll—" and then more rude words.'

'Sounds like a disaster,' Walter observed.

'Nah,' Kate said. 'Not him. He's too big for disaster. You mark my words, they can't touch him.'

'That's not what the papers say,' Walter insisted. 'This "credit crunch" thing has hit all the big shots. Next thing you know he'll have to sell this place and we'll have someone new to worry about.'

'Oh, stop panicking!' Harriet said, trying to sound amused and not quite succeeding. 'He's better than Rancing. The furniture shops love him now he's started kitting out Giant's Beacon, and he's given quite a bit to charity.'

'Yes, I heard about that donation to the animal shelter,' Walter said. 'I wondered how he knew about it—unless you told him.'

'I may have mentioned it. He likes to be told about things.'

'Yes, everyone's talking about how you and he swim together in the mornings. You're a clever lass, getting on his right side.' He added significantly, 'You probably know more than anyone.'

'I know he looks fantastic in swimming gear,' she agreed.

'That's not what I meant.'

Yes, she thought, she knew what he meant. This was the moment a less loyal friend would tell how he'd been tricked by Rancing, exposing him to ridicule. For the first time she appreciated how vulnerable Darius had left himself by confiding in her.

'We don't discuss business,' she said. 'I wouldn't understand it if we did. I've no idea where he's gone, why he's gone or when he'll be back.'

Or if he'll ever be back, she thought sadly.

She didn't doubt that another financial calamity had befallen him, and that he'd gone to try to head off trouble. It must be urgent because, despite their friendship, he hadn't left her a word. Still she was sure he would call her.

But he didn't. Days passed without a word. Wryly, she decided that this was a lesson in reality. When his real world called she simply ceased to exist, that was something to remember in the future.

If there was a future.

Harriet tried to follow the financial news and learned of the sudden collapse of a property company with global tentacles, but she could only guess whether he had had an interest there.

Then, just when she'd decided that he'd gone for good, Darius turned her world upside down yet again. As she and Phantom headed for their morning swim he suddenly gave a bark of joy and charged onto the beach to where a figure lay stretched out on the sand. Fending off the dog, who was trying to lick him to death, Darius rose on one elbow and watched her approach.

'Hello, stranger,' she said when she could speak through her emotion.

'I hoped you'd be here,' he said as she dropped beside him. 'I got back at three in the morning and came out here so as not to miss you. I dozed off for a while, but I knew someone would wake me. All right, Phantom, cool it, there's a good fellow.'

'Did things go as you'd hoped?' she asked.

'More or less. I averted disaster—until next time.'

'You mean we're safe—here on the island?'

'You're safe. This is the last place in the world that I'd give up. Now, I need to ask a huge favour from you, an act of friendship. It's very important to me.'

'Then consider it done.'

'I told you Mary left me for another man, and they were planning marriage. Well, the date has been set, and I've been invited.'

'To your ex-wife's wedding?'

'Yes, it took a bit of manoeuvring, but I managed it. I told her we should seem friendly for the sake of the children. They'll be there so we'll get some time together and they'll know their parents are on good terms. You see, I really took your advice.'

'*I* advised this?'

'You said cunning was better than aggression, and it took all my cunning to manipulate myself an invitation. Mary finished by saying she completely agreed with me and she praised me for thinking of it. She even said I must be improving.' He gave a self-deprecating grin. 'And I owe it all to you.'

He spread his hands in a gesture of finality, his expression radiating such cheerful triumph that she chuckled and said, 'You're telling me that *I* instructed *you* in cunning?'

'There's cunning and cunning,' he said. 'Some kinds I'm better at than others. Manipulating share prices is easy, but—'

'But a child's heart is more complicated than a share price,' she supplied.

'You see how right I was to listen to you. The best friend and adviser I have.'

'Stop buttering me up,' she said severely, 'and tell me what you want me to do.'

'Come with me to the wedding, of course. How can I turn up alone when my ex-wife is marrying another guy? I'd look like a prat.'

'And we can't have that,' she said in mock horror. 'If the markets got to hear—'

'All right, make fun of me. I wouldn't put up with it from anyone else, but with you I guess it's the price of friendship. OK, I'll pay it.

'And there's another thing. I told you about my father and how he likes to control everyone's life. His latest mad idea is to marry me off to Freya, my stepsister. Either me or one of my brothers, but at the moment it's my head he's trying to put on the block.

'Luckily, Freya's no more keen than I am. We get on all right, but that's all. If I can convince my father that it's not going to happen then he'll turn his attention to one of the others.'

'Poor Freya.'

'That's what I think. You'll like her.'

'But will she be at the wedding? And your father? Isn't he furious with Mary for leaving you?'

'Yes, he is. He's even more furious because she managed to get a decent divorce settlement out of me, but he'll want to see his grandchildren. They're Falcons, which means that in his mind they're his property. He doesn't have much contact with them because they live in London and he can't leave Monte Carlo very often.'

'For tax reasons?' she hazarded.

'That's right. He's only allowed to be in England for ninety-one days. Any more and he'd be counted as an

English resident and liable for English tax. He's nearly used up his allowance for this year so he has to dash to London for the wedding, and get back very quickly.'

How casually he spoke, she realised. How normal he seemed to consider this. It was a reminder that his life was centred around money, just in case she was in danger of forgetting.

'And your brothers?' she asked. 'Will they be there?'

'As many as can manage it. They all like Mary, rather more than they like me, actually. And the kids are fascinated by them coming from so many different countries. To them it's like a circus. So we're all going to bury our differences, but you won't send me into the lion's den alone, will you?'

Harriet regarded him sardonically. 'You really don't feel you can face it without me?'

'Definitely not. I'm shaking in my shoes at the prospect.'

There it was in his eyes, the teasing humour that linked with her own mind in a contact sweeter than she had ever known.

'In that case, I'll just have to come along and protect you,' she sighed. 'It's a dreadful responsibility, but I guess I'll manage.'

'I knew you wouldn't fail me. The wedding's in London in two weeks' time. It'll be a civil ceremony held at the Gloriana Hotel, and that's where the reception will be too, so I'll book us in there. You'll be my guest, of course, but we'll have separate rooms, so don't worry. Every propriety will be observed.'

Propriety. There was that word again. How often it cropped up in her mind with regard to this man, always implying the opposite.

Don't go, said a warning voice in her mind. *To him this is a matter of friendship, but can you keep it as mere friendship? You don't even know the answer, and oh, how you wish you did! Stay here, keep yourself safe.*

'I'd love to come,' she said.

CHAPTER SIX

OVER the next few days Harriet made her preparations, arranging extra hours for her assistant, notifying the lifeboat station that she would be away so that they could arrange a substitute to be on call. Her neighbour would look after Phantom, and she explained her coming absence to him with many caresses. He accepted these politely but seemed far more interested in the box of bones that had been delivered from Giant's Beacon.

On the last day before their departure Harriet and Darius went for a final swim, frolicking like children, splashing each other, laughing fit to bust.

Harriet knew that at the back of her mind there was an unfamiliar aspect to her happiness. Part of her had been so sure that their friendship was over, but then he'd drawn her back in, seeking her help and her warmth again, and it was like a balm to her spirit. Suddenly all she wanted to do was laugh and dance.

As they raced up the beach she stopped suddenly and looked around.

'My towel's vanished. Where—? *Phantom.*'

In the distance they could see him tearing along the sand, her towel in his jaws, deaf to her cries.

'He'll be back in his own good time,' Darius said.

'But what do I do in the meantime?'

'Let me dry you.' In a moment he'd flung his towel around her, drawing it close in front, and began to rub her down. She shrieked with laughter and tried to wriggle away but he held her a prisoner while his hands moved over her.

'You wretch,' she cried, pummelling him. 'Let me go.'

But it was no use. He had ten times her strength, as she was beginning to understand. And there was something else she understood. She'd been mad to engage in this struggle that drew her near-naked body so close to his. The pleasure that was pervading her now was more than laughter with a dear friend. His flesh against hers, his face close to her own, the meeting of their eyes; she should have avoided these things like the plague. Except that he hadn't given her the chance.

Caution, she'd promised herself, but where was caution now? And did she really care?

'Let me go,' she repeated.

But now his arms had enfolded her completely, allowing no movement.

'Make me,' he challenged.

She made a half-hearted attempt to kick him but only ended up with her leg trapped between his.

'Do you call that making me?' he demanded.

'Will you stop this?'

'Nope.'

It shocked her to realise how disappointed she would have been if his answer had been any different.

'What do you think you're doing?' she cried.

'I just thought it was time you learned who was boss around here.'

'OK, you're boss. Now let me go.'

'Only if you pay the ransom.'

'And what's that?'

'This,' he said, dropping his head.

It wasn't a major kiss, no big deal, she told herself, trying not to respond to the gentle pressure of his lips. But it was precisely that light touch that was her undoing, making her want to lean forward, demanding that he kiss her more deeply, and more deeply still, threatening her with her own desires. And with that threat came fear.

'No,' she whispered. 'No.'

'I wonder if you really mean that.'

She too wondered, but now she gathered all her strength together and said more firmly, *'No!'*

He drew back a little, frowning.

'You promised this wouldn't happen,' she reminded him.

'I didn't exactly—'

'Every propriety observed, you said.'

'Does that mean I can't even kiss you?'

'It means you can't kiss me now, just when we're about to embark on this idea of yours, pretending to be together when we aren't really.'

Slowly he released her and she took the chance to step back.

'Isn't this something we have to work out as we go along?' he asked.

'You're a businessman, Darius. I'm sure you know that when exploring new territory it's wise to have a plan.'

'And is that your plan?' he demanded. 'To turn away from all human desire?'

'I have to. Can't you try to understand? I'm not sure that I can ever…I don't know, *I don't know.'*

'But how long? For the rest of your life? Was he really that perfect?'

She took a step back and her face was distraught. 'Leave me alone. Just leave me alone.'

He sighed. 'Yes, all right. I'm sorry, Harriet. I should have known better. You have to pick your own time. I can't pick it for you. I shouldn't have—it's just that I've wanted to do that for some time and…well, I guess you don't want to know that.'

'I'd rather not,' she agreed.

'Just try to forgive me, please.'

'There's nothing to forgive,' she said calmly. 'It didn't happen. Now, I think it's time we went and started to get ready. We have a long day tomorrow.'

Harriet left him without a backward glance, followed by Phantom, dragging her towel.

After a moment Darius walked after them, cursing himself for clumsiness.

The trip to London was like nothing Harriet had ever known before. Darius had chartered a helicopter that collected them from the lawn and swept them up and over the channel. Looking down, she drew in her breath.

'Herringdean looks so different, and the sea—nothing is the way I know it below.'

'Yes, they're different worlds,' he agreed, looking down with her. 'And it can be hard to know which one is the place you belong.'

'I suppose it wouldn't be possible to belong in the world up here,' she said thoughtfully. 'You could never stay up that long.'

'True. Sooner or later you have to come down to earth,' he said in a voice that had a touch of regret.

In London, they landed at an airport where a car was waiting, ready to sweep them into the West End, the place of theatres, expensive shops and even more expensive hotels.

The sight of the Gloriana Hotel rearing up eight floors

startled Harriet. She'd guessed that it would be luxurious, but the reality took her by surprise. Again, she wondered if she'd been wise to come here, but it was too late. The chauffeur was carrying their bags to the door. Darius had drawn her arm through his and for his sake she must steel herself. He'd asked this as an act of friendship—and from now on she had only one function; to do him credit so that he could hold up his head.

It needed all her resolution when she saw the inside of the hotel with its marble floor and columns. As Darius had promised, they had separate accommodation but they were next door to each other. When he'd left her alone she studied her surroundings. The bedroom was the largest she had ever seen, and the bathroom was an elegant dream of white porcelain and silver taps. She knew she should have been in heaven, but such luxury intimidated her even more.

Ah, well, she thought resolutely. Best dress forward!

But unpacking was a dismal experience. Suddenly none of her dresses seemed 'best' as it would be understood in the Gloriana.

Then she recalled seeing a gown shop in the reception area. A moment to check that she'd brought her credit cards and she was out of the door, hurrying to the elevator.

The shop exceeded her wildest expectations. The clothes were glorious. So, too, were the prices but she decided to worry about that later. Anything was better than looking like a little brown mouse in the kind of elegant company that Darius regarded as normal.

Two dresses held her undecided for a while, but at last—

'I'll take this one,' she said.

'And the other one,' said Darius's voice behind her. 'They both suit you.'

She whirled to face him. 'How did you—?'

'When I found your room empty I asked the desk and they told me you were here. You should have brought me with you so we could make the decision together. Mind you, I like your choices.' To the assistant he said, 'We'll take both of these, please.'

'No,' she muttered urgently. 'I can't afford them both.'

'You?' He regarded her with quizzically raised eyebrows. 'What has this got to do with you?'

'Evidently, nothing,' she said.

'I invited you here to do me a favour. I don't expect you to buy your own clothes as well.'

Light dawned.

'When you say clothes you mean props, don't you? I'm playing a part and the director chooses the costumes?'

'Got it in one.'

'Next thing, you'll be telling me I'm tax deductible.'

'Now there's a thought! Come on, let's get to work. What have you chosen for the wedding?'

'I thought that one,' she said, indicating her first choice.

'No, something a little more formal.' He turned away to murmur to the assistant, and another flow of gowns was produced.

'Try that on,' Darius said, pointing to a matching dress and jacket.

Turning this way and that before the mirror, she saw it looked stunning on her. As Darius said, it was only right that he should pay the expenses, and when would she get the chance to dress like this again? She fought temptation for the briefest moment before yielding happily. It would take more stern virtue than she could manage to reject this.

While the dress was being packed up Darius said, 'Now, about jewellery.' As if anticipating her protest, he hurried on, 'I'm afraid this will only be hired. Take a look at these.'

If they hadn't been on hire she knew she couldn't have accepted the gold, silver and diamonds that were displayed before her. As it was, she was able to make her choice with a clear conscience.

Before they returned to their rooms Darius led her to the back of the hotel, where a huge ballroom was being decorated.

'This is where they'll hold the party tonight,' he said. 'And tomorrow night the wedding reception will be here.'

More size. This place had been created to hold a thousand. So why was she on edge? she wondered. She was at ease with the much greater size of the ocean. But that was natural, not created artificially to be impressive and profitable. She could never be at ease in an environment like this.

But she smiled, said the right things and tried to look as if she belonged here.

'I've got to go and make phone calls,' Darius said as they reached her room. 'I'll have something delivered for you to eat, then why don't you put your feet up until your attendants get here?'

'Attendants?'

'Hairstyle, make-up. Just leave it to them. You don't need to worry about a thing.'

In other words, she thought, let them array her in her stage costume and make her up for the performance.

'All right,' she said good-humouredly. 'I promise not to interfere with my own appearance.'

'That's my girl! Bye.'

He dropped the briefest kiss on her cheek and was gone, leaving Harriet alone and thoughtful. A mirror on the wall of the corridor showed her a neat, efficient young woman, pleasant but not dynamic.

Still, I've never had much chance to be dynamic, she thought. *And who knows—?*

Her reflection challenged her, sending the message, *Don't kid yourself.*

But why not? she thought. *If I want to kid myself, that's my business. Hey, I forgot to ask him—*

Approaching his door, she raised her hand to knock, then stopped as she heard Darius's voice.

'Mary? So you've arrived at last. Are the kids with you?—Fine, I'm on my way.'

Harriet heard the phone being replaced, and moved fast. By the time Darius emerged, the corridor was empty.

Lying on the bed, she tried to rest as Darius had advised, but her mind was too full of questions. What was happening now between him and his ex-wife, between him and his children? Would the wedding be dramatically called off at the last minute because of a reconciliation?

And why should she care? She'd had her chance and turned it down.

The chance wouldn't come again. She must force herself to remember that.

But after only half an hour she heard him return, walking quickly along the corridor until he entered his room and slammed the door like a man who was really annoyed.

After that she dozed until there was a knock at her door.

Even though Darius had told her about the attendants, what happened next was a shock. They simply took her over, allowing no room for argument, and proceeded to turn her into someone else. She yielded chiefly out of curiosity. She was fascinated to discover her new self.

If she'd been fanciful—which she prided herself on never

being—she might have thought of Cinderella. The fairy godmother, or godmothers since there were two of them, waved their wands and the skivvy was transformed into a princess.

Or at least a passable imitation of one, she thought. How well she could carry it off was yet to be seen.

When she was alone again she surveyed herself in the mirror, wondering who was this glamorous creature with the elegant swept-up hair, wearing the dark red glittering cocktail dress. She had always regarded herself as a tad too thin, but only a woman with her shape could have dared to wear this tight-fitting gown that left no doubt about her tiny waist and long legs, while revealing her bosom as slightly fuller than she had imagined.

A princess, she thought. Princess Harry? Not sure about that.

Even she, self-critical though she was, could see how the expert make-up emphasised the size of her blue eyes, which seemed to have acquired a new sparkle, and the width of her shapely mouth.

From nowhere came the memory of her husband, whose work in tourism had often taken him away on trips.

'I could get jealous of all those expensively dressed women you meet,' she'd teased him once.

'Forget it,' he'd told her. 'You don't need that fancy stuff. You're better as you are.'

'A country bumpkin?' she'd chuckled.

'*My* country bumpkin,' he'd insisted, silencing her in the traditional way, making her so happy that she'd believed him and wasn't jealous. Only to discover at last that she should have been.

And if he'd ever seen her looking like this? Would anything have been different?

Suddenly she wanted very badly to find Darius, see the

expression in his eyes when he first glimpsed her. Then she would know—

Know what?

If she only knew that, she would know everything. And it was time to find out.

A few moments later, she was knocking on Darius's door. As soon as he opened it he grew still. Then he nodded slowly.

'Yes,' he said. *'Yes.'*

'Will I do?'

'You cheeky little devil; I've already given you the answer to that.'

He drew her into the room and stood back to look at her, then made a twirling movement with his hand. She turned slowly, giving him time to appreciate every detail, then back again, displaying herself to full advantage. After all, she reasoned, he was entitled to know that his money had been well spent.

'As long as I do you credit.'

'I'll be the envy of every man there.'

And that, she thought, was what he chiefly cared about, apart from his children. She was there to be useful, and it would be wise to remember that. But it was hard when the excitement was growing in her.

Darius put his hands on her shoulders, holding her just a few inches away, his eyes fixed on her face.

'Beautiful,' he said. 'Just as I hoped. Just as I imagined. Just as—'

'Am I interrupting anything?' said a voice from the doorway.

Darius beamed at the young man standing there. 'Marcel!' he exclaimed.

Next moment, he was embracing the newcomer, thumping him on the back and being thumped in return.

Marcel, Harriet thought. The half brother from Paris.

'I'm sorry to come in without knocking,' he said, 'but the door was open.'

His eyes fell on Harriet, and the pleasurable shock in them was very satisfying.

'You've been keeping this lady a big secret,' he said, speaking with the barest trace of a French accent. 'And I understand why. If she were mine I would also hide her away from the world. Introduce me. I insist.'

'This is Harriet,' Darius replied, moving beside her.

'Harriet,' Marcel echoed. 'Harriet. It is a beautiful name.'

She couldn't resist saying cheekily, 'Actually, my friends call me Harry.'

'Harry?' He seemed aghast, muttering something in French that might have been a curse. 'That is a monstrosity, to give a man's name to such a beautiful lady. And this fellow allows them to treat you like this? You should be rid of him at once.'

'Cut it out!' Darius said, grinning, which seemed to amuse Marcel even more.

'Just thought I'd get in the mood now the circus has come to town,' he said.

'Circus is right,' Darius agreed. 'I've warned Harriet.'

'Harriet? You mean *you* don't call her Harry? But of course, you're not a friend; you are—' He made a vague but significant gesture.

'Hey,' she said and he turned his merry gaze on her. 'Don't jump to conclusions,' she told him impishly.

'Ah, yes, I see. How wise.'

'Can we drop this?' Darius asked.

'Certainly. So, Harriet, Darius has warned you, and you know we're a load of oddities.'

'I'll bet you're no odder than me,' she riposted.

'I'll take you up on that. Promise me a dance tonight.'

'She declines,' Darius said firmly.

'Oh, do I?'

'Definitely.'

Marcel chuckled and murmured in Harriet's ear, 'We'll meet again later.'

'Are any of the others here?' Darius asked.

'Jackson. Travis isn't coming. He can't leave America—some television series he's working on. Leonid tried to get here but an urgent meeting came up at the last minute. And our honourable father arrived an hour ago, but I expect you already know that.'

'No, he hasn't been in touch. I'm in his black books at the moment. Anyone with him?'

'Janine and Freya.'

Harriet's teasing impulse got the better of her again and made her say, 'Ah, yes, she's the one you're supposed to be marrying, isn't she?'

'You can stop that kind of talk,' Darius said, while Marcel grinned.

'A lady with a sense of humour,' he said. 'That's what I like. Believe me, you're going to need it. I said before that it was a circus, and Papa is the ringmaster. He cracks the whip and we jump through hoops—or at least we pretend to.'

'Yes,' Darius growled.

'I gather you're not playing his game,' Marcel said, his eyes on Harriet again.

'Right, and so I've told him. Let's hope he believes me.'

'You realise that means he'll set his sights on Jackson or me next,' Marcel complained. 'Luckily, Freya finds me irritating.'

Darius grinned. 'I can't think why.'

'Neither can I. Right, I'll be off. I'll see you at the reception.'

He blew Harriet a kiss and hurried away.

'I like your brother,' she said when the door had closed.

'Most women do,' Darius observed wryly.

'No, I mean he looks fun.'

'Most women say that too.'

'Which is why you find him irritating?'

'He's a good fellow. We get on most of the time. It may have crossed my mind that he sometimes has it too easy in certain areas. Mary used to accuse me of being jealous of his charm, and perhaps she was right. Charm isn't one of my virtues.' He gave her a wry look. 'As you've found out.'

As he spoke he reached for her hand, and some impulse made her enfold his in both of hers, squeezing comfortingly.

'Charm isn't always a virtue,' she said. 'A man can have too much of it.'

'Well, nobody's ever accused me of that.'

'Good. Just honesty—'

'I hope so.'

'And upright virtue.'

'Nobody's ever accused me of that either,' he said with an air of alarm that made her chuckle. 'You teasing little shrew. What are you trying to do to me?'

'Cheer you up,' she said. 'You really need it.'

'Yes, I do. And I might have guessed you'd be the one to see it. Come on. Let's face them together.'

On the way down in the elevator he said, 'Mary's here. I saw her this afternoon.'

'And the children?'

'Briefly. None of us knew what to say, but that was because *he* was there.'

'He?'

'Ken, the guy who thinks he's going to replace me as their father. They're all in the same suite, a "family", Mary says.'

'How do they get on with Ken?'

'They seem to like him,' Darius sighed.

'Good.'

For a moment he scowled, but then sighed and said, 'All right, say it.'

'If they get on with their stepfather they'll be happier. And I know you won't spoil that because you love them too much.'

A faint ironic smile touched his lips. 'All right, teacher. I've taken the lesson on board.'

'Just make sure that you pay attention,' she commanded him severely.

His eyes swept over her glamorous appearance. 'I am paying attention,' he assured her. 'But that wasn't what you meant, was it?'

'No, it wasn't. Bad boy. Go to the back of the class.'

'Fine, I'll get an even better view of you from there.'

'Behave!'

'Aren't I allowed to say that you're beautiful and gorgeous and—?'

'No, you are *not* allowed to say it.'

'All right. I'll just think it.'

She'd done what she'd set out to do, put him in a cheerful mood for the evening. And nothing else mattered. She had to remember that!

As they emerged from the elevator downstairs they could see people already streaming towards the great room where the reception was to be held.

As soon as they entered Harriet saw their hosts on a slightly raised dais at the far end. There was Mary, smiling, greeting her guests. Beside her stood Ken, the man she was about to marry, and on the other side were the children, dressed up in formal clothes and looking uncomfortable.

Harriet was alive with curiosity to meet the woman Darius had loved and married, who had borne him two children, then preferred another man. An incredible decision, whispered the voice that she tried vainly to silence.

'Ready?' Darius murmured in her ear.

'Ready for anything.'

'Then forward into battle.'

She was aware of heads turned in curiosity as Mary's ex-husband advanced with another woman on his arm, and now she was glad he'd arrayed her in fine clothes so that she could do him proud.

Mary was a tall, elegant woman, with a beauty Harriet could only envy. But she also had a down-to-earth manner and an air of kindness that Harriet hadn't expected from the woman who'd spoken to her sharply on the phone.

'Mary, this is Harriet,' Darius said. 'Harriet, this is Mary, who was my wife until she decided she couldn't stand me any longer.'

There was real warmth in Mary's embrace, and her declaration, 'It's a pleasure to meet you.' But the way she then stood back and regarded Harriet was disconcerting. It was the look of someone who'd heard a lot and was intensely curious. It might have been Harriet's imagination that Mary then gave a little nod.

Ken, her fiancé, was quiet, conventional, pleasant-looking but unremarkable. He greeted Harriet in friendly fashion, acknowledged Darius and escaped as soon as possible.

'We've spoken on the telephone,' Mary said to Harriet. 'I recognise your voice.'

'Yes, Harriet was part of the lifeboat crew that saved me,' Darius said.

'Then she's my friend.' Suddenly Mary's eyes twinkled. 'And I was right about something else, wasn't I? You denied that you were his girlfriend but I knew.'

'Have a heart, Mary,' Darius growled.

'All right, I'll say no more. I don't want to embarrass either of you.'

But Darius was already uncomfortable, Harriet could tell. At the sight of his children his face lit up with relief and he opened his arms so that they could hug him.

She knew that Frankie was ten years old and Mark nine. Both were lively, attractive children with nice manners.

'Here she is, guys,' Darius said. 'This is the lifeboat lady that I told you about.'

Both of them stared.

'You work on a lifeboat?' Mark asked, awed.

'Not work. I'm on call if they need me.'

'But how often do you have to go out saving people?'

'It varies. Sometimes once a month, sometimes twice a day.'

'It must be ever so exciting,' Frankie breathed.

'Hey, she doesn't do it for fun,' Darius protested. 'I didn't find it exciting to be stuck in the water, wondering if I'd ever get out.'

'But Dad, she *saved* you,' Mark pointed out.

'Yes,' he agreed quietly. 'She saved me.'

He might have said more, but something he saw over their shoulders made him straighten up, tense.

'Hello, Father,' he said.

So that was Amos Falcon, Harriet thought. Research had made her familiar with his face, but the reality was startling. This was a fierce, uncompromising man with dark eyes shadowed by heavy brows. His mouth might once have been merely firm, but now it looked as though a lifetime of setting it in resolute lines had left it incapable of anything gentler. This was a giant, to be feared. And she did fear him, instinctively.

More troubling still was the astonishing resemblance between him and Darius. They were the same height and with broad shoulders, features that were similar, even handsome. They were undoubtedly father and son.

In how many ways? she wondered. Was Darius doomed to grow into a replica of a man everyone called awesome? Or was there still time for him to seek another path?

Darius drew her forward for introductions, and she was surprised to see that Amos studied her intently. Of course, he was naturally concerned to know about his son's companion. But she sensed there was more. His eyes, boring into her, seemed to combine knowledge, curiosity and harsh suspicion in equal measure. It was unnerving

He made a polite speech of gratitude for Darius's life, then introduced his wife, Janine, who smiled and also spoke of gratitude. She struck Harriet as a modest, retiring woman, which probably suited Amos.

'And this is my daughter, Freya,' she said, indicating a tall young woman beside her.

This was the wife the powerful Amos had chosen for Darius. She didn't look like the kind of female who would shrink back and let herself be a pawn. She was tall, fair, well, but not extravagantly dressed, with an air of self-possession. She shook Harriet's hand vigorously and said all the polite things before hailing Darius with an unmistakable air of sisterly derision. Harriet discovered that she liked Freya a lot.

There were more arrivals, people approaching the dais

to be greeted, and the crowd moved on and shifted her with it. When Darius began to lead her around the room, introducing her to people, she couldn't resist looking back and found Amos staring after her.

Glancing about her, Harriet was more than ever glad that she was dressed in style. This was a gathering of the rich and mighty, and at least she looked as though she belonged amongst them, however fake it might be.

It was clear that Darius really did belong in this gathering. Many of them knew him and spoke respectfully. They knew he'd taken a hit, but so had they, and his fortunes could yet recover, so they addressed him as they had always done, crossing their fingers.

Harriet found herself remembering the day she'd overheard him on the phone vowing, 'no mercy!' How long ago that seemed now that she'd discovered his other side. But these people had never discovered it, and wouldn't have believed it if she'd told them.

And nor, she realised, would Darius want them to believe it. Much of his power depended on a ruthless image.

'What's the matter?' he asked suddenly.

'Matter? Nothing?'

'Why are you giving me that curious look?'

'I didn't know I was.'

'What's going on in that mind of yours?'

'Nothing. My mind is a pure blank.'

He grinned. 'You're a very annoying woman, you know that?'

'Have you only just found that out?'

'I guess I'm still learning. Come on, let's have a good time.'

CHAPTER SEVEN

SUDDENLY Darius's face lit up at something he'd seen over Harriet's shoulder. '*Jackson, you young devil*. Where have you been?'

The young man approaching them was sufficiently like Darius to be his brother, yet better looking. His features were more regular, less interesting, she thought. Most women would have called him handsome.

He greeted Darius with a friendly thump on the shoulder and stood back to survey him with pleasure.

'I've been abroad,' he said. 'I just got back yesterday to find that nobody had seen hide nor hair of you for ages. Where did you vanish to?'

'Herringdean. I'm the unexpected owner of an island off the south coast. This lady—' he drew Harriet forward '—lives there and has been kind enough to be my guide and friend.'

Jackson beamed and engulfed her hand in his. 'I don't know how you put up with him,' he said.

'Neither do I,' she said, liking him immensely.

'Did I hear right? Herringdean? *The* Herringdean?'

'I don't know of any other,' she said.

Delight broke over his face. 'You've got fulmars there, haven't you?'

'Yes, plenty of them. They're beautiful.' Light dawned. 'Hey, I've seen you before, haven't I? On television?'

'I've done a programme or two,' he agreed. 'But never one about fulmars. Could you and I have a talk some time soon?'

'Of course we can.'

'Then you can really have a deep discussion about fulmars,' Darius observed. 'I don't know how you can bear the suspense.'

Laughing, the other two turned on him.

'They're birds,' Harriet said. 'Very big and lovely. They look like gulls but they're really petrels.'

'Fascinating!' said Darius, who wouldn't have known a gull from a petrel if they'd attacked him together.

'They nest high up on cliffs,' Harriet continued, 'and they're one of the beauties of Herringdean.'

Darius regarded her with comic irony. 'And I've owned these fabulous creatures all this time and you didn't tell me?'

'Nobody owns fulmars,' Harriet said. 'It's they who own the world, especially that bit of it called Herringdean.'

Jackson looked at her with appreciation. 'I see you're an expert,' he said. 'Don't waste yourself on this fellow. Let's go and have that talk now.'

'Yes, be off while I make some duty calls,' Darius said.

She was briefly afraid that the exchange might have offended him, but he kissed her cheek, saying, 'Take care of her, Jackson.'

Now she remembered Darius saying that his brother was a naturalist. 'Not an academic. He just works a lot with animals and charities. Does TV a bit, goes off on expeditions. You'd find him interesting.'

And she did. Jackson knew his stuff, and as she also

knew hers they plunged into a knowledgeable discussion that pleased them both.

Darius did his duty, going from acquaintance to acquaintance, saying the right things, avoiding the wrong things, smiling mechanically, performing as expected. Nothing in his demeanour revealed that he was intensely conscious of Harriet and Jackson sitting at a side table, their heads close together, each so absorbed that they seemed to have forgotten the rest of the world.

Gradually, he managed to get near enough to eavesdrop but what he heard brought him no comfort. He couldn't discern every word, but Jackson clearly said, 'It depends whether you're talking about northern fulmars or southern fulmars…'

His last words were drowned out, but then Harriet said, 'It's a pity that…any old rubbish…almost makes you want to…'

Jackson asked a question and she replied eagerly, 'That's always the way with *Procellariidae*, don't you think?'

'*What?*'

Jackson looked up and grinned. 'Here's my brother. Perhaps you'd better return to him before he goes out of his mind.'

He touched Darius on the shoulder and departed. Darius drew Harriet's arm through his, saying, 'I hardly dare ask what you were talking about. What the blue blazes are procellar—whatever?'

'*Procellariidae*. It's just the name of the family that fulmars belong to, just like crows and magpies are *Corvids*—'

'Are they really? You'll be telling me next that wrens are dinosaurs.'

'Oh, no, wrens are *Troglodytidae*.' Her lips twitched.

'There, and you thought of me as a silly little creature who didn't know any long words.'

'Well, if I was foolish enough to think that you've made me sorry. I feel as if I've been walked over by hobnailed boots.'

'Good,' she teased. 'Serve you right.'

She was looking up at him with gleaming eyes, and he couldn't have stopped himself responding, however much he wanted to. But he didn't want to. He wanted to take her hand and follow her into the world where only she could take him—the world of laughter and good fellowship that had been closed to him before but now seemed to open invitingly whenever she was there.

A few yards away Jackson watched them, unnoticed, a curious expression on his face. After a while he smiled as though he'd seen something that satisfied him.

Harriet had tried to prepare herself to cope among Darius's family. She told herself that she was ready for Mary, for Freya, even for Amos. But it was the children who surprised her. After doing their social duty, Frankie and Mark effectively took her prisoner, corralling her into a corner and sitting one each side, lest she have ideas of escape. Like all the best hostage-takers, they provided her with excellent food and drink, but there was no doubt they meant business.

First she had to tell the story of Darius's rescue, suitably edited for their childish ears. Then they wanted to hear about other rescue trips, listening in awed silence, until Mark said breathlessly, 'But aren't you scared?'

She thought for a moment. 'Not really.'

'Not even when it's terribly dangerous?' Frankie persisted.

'There isn't time to be scared. There's always so much to do.'

Frankie looked around before leaning forward and whispering, 'It's more fun when it's dangerous, isn't it?'

Harriet hesitated, aware of a yawning pit at her feet. She must be careful what she said to children. Especially these two. Frankie's gleaming eyes showed that she already had her own opinion of the joys of danger.

'No,' Harriet said, trying to sound firm. 'And that is a very irresponsible point of view. Danger has to be taken seriously.'

'Yes, Mrs Connor,' Frankie said, straight-faced.

'Harry. My friends call me Harry, like yours call you Frankie.'

United by the bond, they shook hands.

She liked them both enormously, but with Frankie she also had the connection of like recognising like. As a child, she too had felt that danger could be fun. Truth to tell, she still often found it so, as long as it was only her own. Other people's peril had to be taken seriously, but there was a 'ping' about fighting for one's own survival that most people wouldn't understand, and certainly not sympathise with.

Her father had lectured her about being sensible. Now she had passed on the lecture to the next generation, just as she would have done with a child of her own, she thought wistfully.

But she had no children and probably never would have. Darius's offspring would have to be her consolation.

'Go on about Herringdean,' Mark begged. 'Why did you join the lifeboats?'

'I followed my father. He taught me to love being on the water. I've got a little yacht that I sail whenever I can. Every year Herringdean has a regatta, and I compete in a lot of the races. I win some too.' She added proudly, 'I've got all sorts of trophies.'

'Tell, tell,' they demanded.

They were as sailing-crazy as she was herself but, living in London, had fewer chances to indulge their passion.

'Mum takes us on holiday to the seaside,' Frankie said, 'and she gets someone to take us out in a boat, but then we have to come home.'

'What about your father?' Harriet asked. 'Does he go out in the boat with you?'

'He's never been there,' Frankie said. 'He was always too busy to come on holiday.'

'That's very sad,' Harriet said, meaning it. 'He misses so much.'

'He nearly came once,' Mark recalled. 'We were going to have a wonderful time together, but at the last minute he got a call and said he had to stay at home. I overheard him on the phone—he was trying to stop some deal from falling apart. He said he'd join us as soon as he could, but he never did. It was soon after that he and Mum split up. Now we don't go at all.'

Frankie took a deep breath. 'Harry, do you think—?'

'Ah, there you are, you two,' came Mary's voice from nearby. 'I've got someone for you to meet.'

They groaned but got up obediently. Harriet felt a pang of dismay, wondering if Mary had deliberately sought to separate her from the children. And had she heard Frankie call her Harry? If so, was she resentful at their instant bond?

But the smile Mary gave her before hurrying away was unreadable.

Socially, she knew she was a success. Janine and Freya spoke to her pleasantly, Marcel and Jackson claimed her company, while Amos looked on. When he did address her, his manner was courteous but distant, as though he was reserving judgement.

None of the other men there reserved judgement. Admiring glances followed her everywhere and when the dancing started she had her pick of partners. Jackson was at the head of the queue, finally yielding to Marcel.

'Whatever is Darius thinking of to leave you alone?' Marcel asked as they hot-footed it around the floor.

'Darius has urgent things to attend to,' she said primly. 'I don't get in his way.'

'*Sacre bleu!* You talk like that?' he demanded, aghast.

'Sometimes I do,' she said mischievously. 'Sometimes I don't.'

'You keep him guessing?'

'Definitely.'

'So you believe in ill-treating him?'

'It has its uses.'

'Well, then, you must do this. In the end he will rebel, the two of you will quarrel, and it will be my turn.'

Harriet couldn't have said what made her choose her next words. She'd never been a flirt or a tease, but a delightfully wicked impulse made her say, 'Oh, you're going to wait your turn?'

'If I have to. Does brother Darius know you tease other men?'

'Darius knows exactly what I want him to know.'

'I see. I must remember that. I wonder what he did to be such a lucky man.'

She seemed to consider. 'I think he's still wondering that too. Some day I'll tell him.'

That made him roar with laughter. She joined in, relishing the experience of flirting on the edge of indiscretion, a pleasure she'd never known before. Suddenly the world was full of new delights, and she felt herself becoming slightly dizzy.

No doubt it was coincidence that made Darius appear

at that moment. Marcel made a resigned face and yielded, kissing her hand before he departed.

'Until the next time,' he said.

'Do I get a little of your company at last?' Darius asked. 'I seem to be the only person you're not spending time with.'

'Just trying to do you credit,' she said. 'You wouldn't want to be known as the man who accompanied a little brown mouse, would you?'

'I don't think there's much fear of that,' he said. 'I'm beginning to think I've never really known you.'

'Is that so surprising?' she asked. 'We met only a few weeks ago. Neither of us really knows anything about the other.'

'No, we don't,' he said slowly. 'You've taken me by surprise so many times… You'd think I'd realise by now…'

'Maybe we never realise,' she whispered.

The evening was drawing to a close. The bride- and groom-to-be embraced each other for the last waltz, and other dancers joined in. Darius took her hand and held it gently for a moment.

'My turn,' he said. 'Unless you object.'

'No,' she murmured. 'I don't object.'

No words could express how much she didn't object to dancing with Darius as he took her into his arms. Suddenly the most vibrant sensation she'd ever known was the light touch of his hand on her back, drawing her close but not as close as she would have liked. His hand holding hers seemed to whisper of that other time when he'd clung to her in a gesture that had transformed the world.

And then it had been transformed again, and yet again, with how many more to come? Once she would have wished she knew the answer to that, but now she was content to let the path lead where it might, as long as it ultimately led to him. In the enchanted atmosphere of tonight that didn't seem as crazily impossible as it normally would.

There was warm affection in his smile, but was it real or only part of tonight's performance? Or could she make it real? Was Cinderella's power great enough for that?

The music was coming to an end. The ball was over.

But there would be another ball tomorrow, and Prince Charming might yet fit the glass slipper on her foot.

Darius? she thought. Prince Charming?

Well, it took all sorts.

'Is everything all right?' he asked, searching her face.

'Yes,' she said contentedly. 'Everything's all right.'

As they went upstairs he said, 'You were wonderful. Everything I hoped.'

'I floundered a bit.'

'No, you didn't. My kids love you, even Mary thinks you're terrific. You're a star.'

'So I really have helped you?' she asked hopefully.

'More than you'll ever know. And tomorrow's going to be even better.'

'Would you like to come in and talk about it?' Harriet ventured to suggest. 'You can give me my instructions for tomorrow.'

For a moment she thought he would agree, but then a wry look came over his face.

'I'd love to but…things to do. You know how it is.'

'Yes,' she said a touch sadly, 'I know how it is.'

'And besides, you don't need any instructions from me. You've got it all sussed. Now, go and have a good sleep.'

She smiled up at him. 'Goodnight.'

He didn't reply at first, just stood looking down at her with an expression more gentle than she had ever seen before and the faintest smile on his lips. But then the smile faded, became tight and constrained.

'Goodnight,' he said, and moved away.

For a moment Harriet was too dazed to know where she was or what was happening to her. Hearing her door close, she realised that she had entered her room without even being aware of it. As if from a great distance, she heard his own door being closed.

He'd been about to kiss her. She knew it beyond a shadow of doubt. It had been there in his face, until he changed his mind, probably remembering that other time on the beach when she'd told him to back off. How could she have known then that by now she would feel so differently?

So much had changed tonight. She'd been practically the belle of the ball, surrounded by admirers, seeing herself through their eyes but trapped inside her ivory tower. But it was she who, only yesterday, had slammed shut the door of that tower, and she could blame nobody but herself.

Not so much Cinderella as the Sleeping Beauty.

'Except that nobody could consider me a beauty,' she mused wryly.

But Darius had thought so, perhaps only for a brief moment but a little feminine strategy might have transformed that moment into long-lasting joy. Had retreating into the tower, protecting her safety at the expense of life's joy, really been the right thing to do?

'Curses!' she muttered. 'Why did this have to happen now?'

Brooding thus, she snuggled down in the huge bed, wishing it was smaller. Its size seemed to demand two people and she was attacked by a feeling of loneliness.

It was still dark when she awoke. The illuminated clock showed that three hours had passed since they had parted and she had the feeling that something strange was happening. After a moment she realised that a phone was ringing.

It seemed to come from the other side of the wall, so surely Darius would answer it soon. But it went on and on. Nobody was going to answer it.

Perhaps the sound came from somewhere else? She slipped out of bed, threw on her wrap and went out into the dark corridor. Now there was no doubt. It was Darius's phone and there was nobody to answer it.

He wasn't there. He was spending the night with someone else. And she was a fool not to have realised that it was bound to happen. In London there would be a hundred women he could turn to. Returning to her own room, she had to stop herself slamming the door. She had no right to feel insulted or neglected, but that didn't help.

So, who? Freya? Perhaps he really needed his father's money that much. Or one of the numerous females who'd made eyes at him that evening?

She threw herself back down onto the bed but sleep was impossible, and now she wondered how she could get through tomorrow. How could she look at him without an accusation in her eyes, however illogical?

Restlessly, she jumped up and began to pace the room. From the street outside came the sound of a car and she drew aside the curtain to look down.

Then she grew still as she saw the passenger get out. It was Darius, and he was weighed down with baggage. Three large suitcases were offloaded onto the pavement and collected by the porter, then they disappeared into the hotel.

Harriet scurried to her door, listening. She heard the elevator arrive, the doors open and the sound of a trolley being wheeled across the floor, stopping outside the room next to hers. Only then did she look out.

Darius was opening his door, indicating for the porter to

take the luggage in. When the man had departed he seemed to notice Harriet.

'Sorry if the racket disturbed you.'

'It didn't. I happened to see you arrive downstairs. You look worn out.'

'I've been to my apartment to collect a few things. At least, it was meant to be a few things, but once I started I couldn't stop.'

'You mean—that's where you've been all this time?' she breathed.

'Yes, I decided I couldn't be in London without going home for a few hours. I've had someone going in to collect any mail that arrived, but there was still plenty of stuff on the mat. I didn't mean to stay so long but things built up. What's the matter? What's funny?'

'Nothing,' she said in a trembling voice.

'Then why are you laughing?'

'I'm not—not really.'

'Yes, you are. What's so funny at this hour?'

'You wouldn't understand. Go to bed quickly. I'll see you in the morning.'

She escaped before she could give herself away any more. It was vital to be alone to throw herself on her bed, to laugh and cry, and marvel at where the path was leading her.

Now for the big one.

That was her thought as she sat before the mirror next morning, watching as her make-up was again applied by an expert.

Today her clothes were less ostentatiously glamorous, although no less costly, a matching dress and jacket in light grey heavy silk. Around her neck she wore the diamond pendant.

Now the attendants had gone and there was just time for one last important job. Quickly, she dialled her neighbour's number.

'Hi, Jenny, is everything all right?—Lovely—he's not off his food, is he?— Oh, good, they're his favourite bones but I was afraid he might pine—oh, please fetch him.'

Marcel and Jackson, knocking on their brother's door, found it opened promptly.

'I'm honoured,' he said ironically.

'Not you, her,' Jackson informed him. 'Do you think we're going to miss the chance to be seen with the most gorgeous girl since—? Is this her door? Good.'

All three of them raised their hands, but before they could knock they heard Harriet's voice inside.

'Oh, darling, do you miss me? I miss you so much. I'll be home soon. I love you more than anyone in the world.'

Jackson and Marcel stared at their brother.

'A *ménage à trois*?' Marcel demanded, aghast. 'You?'

'Not in a million years,' Darius declared. 'I leave those kind of shenanigans to you.'

'But she was talking to the one she loves *more than anyone in the world*.'

'She was talking to her dog,' Darius said, grinning. 'She does that a lot. She left him with a friend and she called him as soon as we arrived.'

Jackson nodded. 'She's probably had him since she was a child.'

'No, he belonged to her husband who died a year ago.'

'Ah!' Enlightenment settled over Marcel. 'Then perhaps it is the dead husband whom she loves more than—'

'Shall we be going?' Darius interrupted him, knocking. 'Harriet, are you ready in there?'

'Coming!' She opened the door and stood basking in their looks of admiration.

Instantly, Marcel and Jackson extended their hands to her, but Darius stayed firm.

'Back off, you two,' he said, drawing her hand into the crook of his elbow. 'She's mine.'

And Harriet thought she detected a note of pride in his voice, if only she could allow herself to believe it.

Heads held high, they went downstairs to where the ceremony would take place. It would be a civil ceremony, but the venue had been done up to emulate the grandeur of a church. There were flowers everywhere and chairs laid out in rows, while at the far end a choir was assembling.

It was almost time to begin. Ken took his place and stood waiting, his eyes fixed on the door through which his bride would come.

At last Mary appeared and began to walk slowly towards him. She was magnificently dressed in a long gown of saffron coloured satin, a diamond tiara on her head. Behind her walked Frankie and Mark.

What would Darius be feeling now, she wondered, as his one-time beloved married another man and his children became part of another family? He was between her and the procession, so that his face was turned away, and she could only wonder about his expression. But she guessed it would reveal nothing.

As the children passed she saw that Frankie wore a frilly bridesmaid dress and Mark had a page's costume, also frilly. How he would hate that, she thought.

As if to confirm it, he glanced up at her and made a face of helpless resignation. She made a face back, conveying sympathy. By chance, Darius happened to turn his head in time to see them both.

'Poor Mark,' she murmured.

The procession was slowing down, bringing Mark to a brief halt. Just a couple of seconds but it was enough for

Darius to put his hand on his son's shoulder and grunt, 'Don't give up, lad.'

Then they were on their way again, with only the memory of Mark's look of amazed gratitude at his father.

Slowly, the ceremony advanced until the moment when the bride took her groom's hand, looking up into his face and saying fervently, 'You are mine, and I am yours. We will be together for always, and no other man will ever live in my heart.'

Conventional words for a wedding, but how did they sound to the man who had once been her husband? Carefully, Harriet turned her head, hoping to catch a sideways glimpse of his face, only to find it turned towards her. He wasn't looking at the couple swearing their love. His gaze was fixed on her, and something in it made her turn quickly away.

A few feet away, Amos and his family were seated, their chairs at an angle that enabled Amos to see Darius and Harriet clearly. His eyes narrowed, an expression that Jackson recognised with a sigh and that made him exchange a glance with Marcel.

They knew that look on their father's face, and it didn't bode well.

CHAPTER EIGHT

As they walked out afterwards Amos fell into step beside Jackson, speaking in a low voice. 'What do you know about her?'

'Only that she's delightful, and a very good influence on Darius.'

'And just what does that mean?'

'I've been watching them together.' Jackson fell silent.

'And?' Amos demanded. *'And?'*

'He was laughing.'

'What are you talking about?'

'It's true. Darius was laughing.'

'I've seen that too,' Marcel put in. 'And you know what makes him laugh? She makes fun of him.'

'She makes fun of him? And he likes it? Rubbish.'

'They share jokes,' Jackson agreed. 'I've seen them and heard some of the things they say. Daft remarks tossed back and forth, things that wouldn't make any sense to other people, but understand each other, and they laugh together. I've never seen that in Darius before. She's transformed him.'

Amos didn't answer this, but he strode on ahead and waited for Darius to appear. He nodded briefly at Harriet and jerked his head for his son to follow him.

'What is it, Father?' Darius asked.

'We need to talk.'

'Right now? They're just starting the reception.'

'It won't take long.'

He walked away without stopping until they'd both entered a little side room and closed the door. Then Amos turned on him.

'I gather things are getting worse.'

Darius hesitated a moment before saying, 'Financially, they're not going well but in other ways—'

Amos brushed this disclaimer aside. 'I was speaking financially.'

'Of course,' Darius murmured.

'You can't raise the loans you need, and when you put property up for sale it won't raise the asking price.'

'May I ask how you know these details?' Darius said grimly.

'You don't imagine there are any secrets, do you?'

'Not from you.'

'You ought to be here in London, working things out. Instead, you waste time on that island that can hardly be worth—well, what *is* it worth?'

'You mean in money terms?' Darius asked in a strange voice.

'Don't play games with me. Of course I mean money. How much could you raise from it?'

'I have no idea.'

'But you've been living there for weeks; you must have investigated.'

'In a sort of way,' he said carefully. 'But it's too soon to form conclusions. I don't want to rush things.'

'I suppose that's the influence of the young woman you brought with you. I hope you're not taking her too seriously.'

'As seriously as a man takes a woman who saved his life.'

'Don't make too much of that. It means nothing to her. It's just her job.'

'But it's not,' Darius said fiercely. 'She isn't employed by the Lifeboat Institution, she's a volunteer. She has an ordinary job, but night and day she's ready to drop everything for the people who need her, even if their cries for help come at awkward moments. She doesn't think of herself, she thinks of them.'

'All right, all right, spare me the speech,' Amos said in a bored voice. 'I get the point. Naturally, I expressed my gratitude and of course you've shown your own gratitude by bringing her here. I hope she enjoys herself. But let it end there. She's no real use to you. She doesn't have a penny and she won't understand your way of life.'

'And how do you know what she has and hasn't?' Darius demanded harshly. 'Have you been having her watched, because if you've dared—'

'No need to be melodramatic. I've merely made a few enquiries. She seems a decent sort, lives a quiet life.'

'As you'd expect from a widow grieving for the husband she loved, and who loved her.'

Amos's smile was coldly self-satisfied. 'Ah, so you don't know. I wondered.'

'Know about what? What the hell are you talking about?'

'Did she ever take you to see her husband's grave?'

'Of course not. Naturally, she prefers to keep it private.'

'Have you known her visit that grave at all?'

'How could I know?'

'How could you indeed since she takes such care to hide the truth? But you'll find the answer here.' He thrust a sheet of paper in Darius's hand. 'Read it and find out just how cunningly she's been keeping her secrets. Then see how much of a heroine she looks.'

Darius took the paper and read its contents. Then he grew very still, trying to control his mounting outrage.

His eyes were hard as he looked up at his father, then down again at the paper in his hand. 'Los Angeles,' he murmured.

'Brad Connor died in a car crash in Los Angeles, and he's buried out there,' Amos said.

'And you read something into that? He was in the tourist industry, so he probably travelled a lot.'

'He wasn't there to work; he was living with the woman he planned to marry as soon as his divorce came through.'

'You can't know that,' Darius declared. But he knew as he spoke that Amos could find out anything he liked. It had always been one of the things that inspired admiration for his business abilities, but now Darius could feel only a horror that he'd never known before.

'Of course I know,' Amos snapped. 'I know everything that's been happening to you on that island.'

'You've dared to plant spies?'

'I've taken steps to assess the situation. That's always been my way and you know it. You should be grateful. Do you think I'd stand back and see you run into danger without doing anything?'

'I'm not in any danger.'

'You're in danger of becoming sentimental, and that's one thing you can't afford. I'd hoped by now you'd be seeing things more sensibly but, since you're not, let me spell it out. This young woman has deceived you, presenting a picture of her life that's far from the truth.'

'She has not deceived me,' Darius snapped. 'She's kept

things to herself, but why shouldn't she? Her personal trag-edy is none of my business. If she can't bear to talk about it, that's up to her.'

His eyes were full of fury and for the first time it dawned on Amos that he'd miscalculated. His son was every bit as enraged as he'd wanted him to be, but his anger was di-rected not against Harriet, but against the man who sought to damage her. Amos decided that it was time to change tack. Reasoning might work better.

'I understand that,' he said, 'but it doesn't change the fact that she's holding things back while pretending to be open. You don't know her as well as you thought you did. What other secrets is she concealing?'

'Whatever they are, she'll confide in me in her own good time, *if she wants to.*'

'Just stop and think what's going on in her head. One husband let her down, so next time she's going to make certain that she scores. She's out to marry you with her eyes on the divorce settlement she'll eventually claim.'

Darius gave a harsh laugh. 'Out to marry me? You know nothing. She's here as my companion, no more. I had to promise to stick to her rules or she wouldn't have come.'

Amos groaned and abandoned reasoning as useless. 'How can any son of mine be so naïve? That's the oldest trick in the book.'

'She doesn't go in for tricks,' Darius said. 'She's as honest as the day is long. You have no idea.'

'You've really got it bad, haven't you?' Amos said in a voice that verged on contempt.

'If you mean that I'm in love with her, you're wrong. Harriet and I are friends. With her I've found a kind of friendship I didn't know existed. I can talk to her with-out wondering if she'll make use of the information. She gives far more than she takes, and that's something I never thought to find in anyone. Try to understand. She's a revelation. I didn't know women like her existed, and I'm not going to do anything to spoil it.'

Amos regarded him with pity. 'A revelation—unlike any other woman,' he echoed. 'Well, I'll say this for her. She's more skilled and astute than I gave her credit for. All right, maybe she's not out to marry you. Perhaps she's just stringing you along for the sake of her island friends. After all, you're the power there. It would pay her to get on your right side.'

'Stop it!' Darius raged. 'If you know what's good for you, stop it *now*!'

'Or what? Is my son threatening me? I really did underestimate her, didn't I? All right, we'll say no more. I tried to warn you but there's no helping a fool.'

'Maybe I am a fool,' Darius said. 'And maybe I'm happy to settle for that.'

'That makes you an even bigger fool.'

'If you dare make yourself unpleasant to Harriet—'

'I've no intention of doing so. Now, it's time we were getting back to the party.'

He strode out. As he walked through the door Darius saw him position a smile on his face, so that he appeared to the assembled company wearing the proper mask.

Suddenly Darius felt sick.

It was an effort to get his own mask in place and he knew he was less successful than his father, managing only an air of calm that covered the turmoil within. Harriet was sitting with her arm across the empty seat beside her, looking around worriedly. Someone spoke to her and she answered briefly before returning to her troubled search. It was as though the world had stopped in its tracks until she found what she was looking for.

Then she saw Darius and he drew in his breath at the

transformation. Suddenly it was as though she was illuminated from inside, radiant, joyful.

'I'm sorry,' he said, going to sit beside her. 'I got waylaid. Forgive my bad manners.'

'Is everything all right?'

'Everything's fine.' He laid his hand over hers. 'Nothing for you to worry about.'

A waiter poured champagne for them both.

'Now, let's forget everything else and enjoy ourselves,' Darius said, raising his glass to clink hers.

Around the various tables, his family observed them. His brothers grinned. His stepsister smiled with relief. His children rubbed their hands. His father scowled.

It was time for the speeches. The best man spoke, the bride and groom talked eloquently. Various other guests proposed toasts. Darius was barely aware of it. He was conscious only of Harriet beside him, wondering if she was remembering the joy of her own wedding, and the marriage that had ended in tragedy. But he could detect nothing in her manner that gave him a clue. Her barriers were in place.

He'd meant it when he'd told his father that he didn't feel deceived that she had kept her secrets. It was yet more proof of their special friendship that he made no claims on her, demanded no rights.

But he knew a faint sadness that she hadn't felt able to confide in him.

Your fault, he told himself. *If you'd shut up talking about yourself for five minutes she might get a word in edgeways.*

That eased his mind briefly, but he could remember a couple of times when the talk had strayed to her husband and she'd diverted it to something else. The truth was she didn't want to open up to him. That was her right. He'd said so and he believed it. But it hurt.

Nor could he entirely escape the suspicion that if she hadn't warned him off he would have sought more than friendship. She was beautiful, not conventionally, like other women, but with a mysterious enchantment that came from within and that beckoned him on.

He'd made promises about keeping his distance but, with a woman like this, how could a real man keep such insane promises?

Now waiters were clearing away for the dancing. The bridal couple took the floor and were soon joined by the rest of the crowd.

'This time I'm seizing you first,' Darius said firmly. 'Before I get trampled in the rush.'

'Nonsense,' she said tenderly.

'It isn't nonsense. Of course it's nice when the lady on your arm turns out to be the belle of the ball, but it has its troublesome moments too. I don't like sharing.'

'Neither do I, but we both have to do our social duty.'

'Ah, I see. You've gone into teasing mode.'

'Why not? I enjoy new experiences and, after all, you brought me here to help stage a performance. Think of me as a piece of stage scenery. Under this dress I'm just wood and plaster. Hey, what are you doing?'

'Just checking the stage scenery,' he said, letting his hand drift around her waist until it sank immodestly over her hips. 'It doesn't feel like any wood and plaster I've ever known.'

It was shocking and she knew she should tell him to move his hand from where it lay over the smooth grey silk, softly caressing the movements against his fingers. But a little pulse was beating in her throat and she couldn't get the words out. And probably nobody could see it in the crowd, she reassured herself.

She was suffused by a warmth and sweetness so intense that it made her dizzy. She wanted to dance like this for ever, his arms around her, his body close to hers, and never have to think of anything else again.

The music was slowing, couples were pulling apart. Marcel presented himself expectantly.

'Go to blazes,' Darius told him pleasantly.

'Certainly,' Marcel said, and vanished.

Harriet was barely aware of Marcel, or any of their surroundings. Lost in a dream, she let herself drift into a new world, refusing to heed the warnings of danger, although she knew that danger would intrude in the end. But let it, she thought. First she would have her moment, and cherish its memory to see her through the dark times.

With a sigh, she felt his movements slow as this dance too came to an end, and she knew that he would not claim her again. The moment had come and gone until, perhaps, another time.

Harriet wondered if it could possibly have been the same for him, but when she looked into his face she saw that it was troubled.

'What's on your mind?' she asked. 'Something's worrying you. I know it. Tell me.'

For a moment he hesitated on the verge of telling her about his father and what he'd learned, but then he backed off, unable to risk hurting her.

'Can't you tell your friend what's wrong?' she asked gently.

Once, younger and more careless, he'd joked that at all costs a man should avoid a woman who understood him too well. How often had he avoided Mary's piercing mental gaze! Yet with this woman he only felt a renewed sense of comfort, as though her hand had once again stretched out to offer safety.

'No,' he said softly. 'Nothing is wrong.' And at that moment he meant it.

It was just like his brothers to barge in, he thought, finally yielding to Marcel. But there was always later. Patience would bring him everything.

After that they both concentrated on their social duty. Harriet was never short of partners, until finally she glanced up to find Amos approaching, the very picture of geniality.

'I've been hoping to dance with you but there were so many men ahead of me.' He held out his hand. 'Please say I'm not too late.'

'Of course not,' she said, smiling and taking his hand.

Heads turned as he led her onto the floor, the crowd parted for them, and there was a smattering of applause as he drew her into the dance. Darius, passing the time with Freya, turned his head casually, then grew tense.

'What the devil—?' he breathed.

'He seems quite charmed with Harriet,' Freya said. 'Look at the way he's smiling, practically welcoming her into the family.' She gave Darius an amused look. 'I should be grateful to her, really. It helps take the pressure off me, *brother, dear.*'

'Look at them,' he said distractedly. 'Why is he laughing like that?'

'She's laughing too,' Freya pointed out. 'Obviously they're getting on well. He can be so grim, it's nice to see him putting himself out to be nice to her.'

But for Darius, who knew what really lay behind Amos's 'charm', every moment was torment. He was trying to lure Harriet into a trap, hoping she would say something he could use against her. Darius had often seen him wear a pleasant mask as long as it could be useful, and had thought little of it.

But this was different. This was Harriet—great-hearted, innocent, vulnerable—and he was filled with desire to protect her at all costs.

'Dance with me,' he said, taking Freya's hand.

She was too astute to mistake his motive, especially when she realised how determinedly he steered her in the direction of the other couple.

'Is this near enough for you?' she asked.

'Only just. Can you hear what he's saying?'

'Something about a shop on Herringdean—an antique shop—since when was he interested in antiques?'

'Since he found out she owned one,' Darius growled.

'Now he's talking money—how much is the shop worth?'

'Damn him!'

'Don't act surprised. That's always his first thought. Hey, he's watching us. Let's teach him a lesson.'

'How?'

'Look deep into my eyes, then he'll think what a good son you're being. You never know, he might solve all your problems with one cheque.'

'Yes, but he'd post-date it so that I'd have to marry you first.'

'Never fear. I'll avoid that catastrophe with my last breath.'

'So will I,' he assured her cheerfully.

They finished the dance with no hard feelings on either side.

When Amos had bid her farewell and departed, Harriet went to quench her thirst with an orange juice. Standing beside a large potted plant, she was only vaguely aware of movement from the other side until she heard Mary's voice say, 'Wherever did you find that marvellous girl?'

And Darius's eager reply. 'Harriet is marvellous, isn't she? I'm glad you like her.'

'Are you surprised? Did you think I'd be jealous? On the contrary, she's doing me a great favour. If you've got her, I don't have to feel guilty about leaving you. And the children like her, so I can send them to stay with you with an easy mind.'

'Do you really mean that?' Darius demanded urgently.

'I know you thought I was trying to separate you from them, but I wasn't. It's just that you hurt them so often with your stupidity.'

'There was a lot I didn't understand, but now—'

'But now things are beginning to change, and they'll go on changing as long as you stick with her. She's good for you, Darius. You've become almost human.'

'I never thought to hear you say that, Mary.'

'I never thought to be able to say it. That's why Mark and Frankie will be going to my mother while Ken and I are on honeymoon. They'd much rather have come to you in Herringdean, but I honestly didn't think you'd cope on your own. Now it's different.'

'Too late to send them to me?'

'My mother is so looking forward to having them. I can't disappoint her now. But there's plenty of time in the future. Keep up the good work. The kids are really happy about Harriet.'

'I know, and I can't tell you how much that means to me.'

'Well, make sure you keep her for good. You're a clever man and, believe me, that's the clever thing to do.'

They moved away, leaving Harriet deep in thought.

The evening was drawing to a close. Bride and groom

withdrew and reappeared in outdoor clothes. Cars were at the door. Mark and Frankie said their farewells to Darius and Harriet before being scooped up by their grandmother and swept off to her home on the other side of London.

'Are you tired?' Darius asked Harriet, who was yawning.

'Mmm, a bit sleepy. You did say we're going early to-morrow, didn't you?'

'That's right. Time for bed.'

On the way up in the elevator he slipped his arm around her. 'Did you enjoy it?'

'Oh, yes, it was lovely. Everyone was so nice to me, especially your father.'

'Yes, I saw the two of you dancing.'

'I couldn't believe it when he asked me, but he was ter-ribly gallant and charming.'

'You should beware my father's charm,' Darius said wryly.

'Oh, I know he was just being polite but…I don't know… he was nice. He asked me about my antique shop, said he understood antiques were very profitable these days. I had to admit that it's as much of a souvenir shop for tourists as an antique shop. He laughed and said that was life and nothing was really the way it seemed, was it? Hey, careful. Don't squash me.'

'Sorry,' he said, relaxing the arm that he'd tightened sharply about her. Listening to her innocent pleasure when he knew how misguided it was brought a return of the rage that had attacked him earlier. But now it was a million times more intense, nearly blinding him with the desire to lash out against her enemy.

From the start he'd known of her strength, her defiance, her ability to cope, essential in a lifesaver. Suddenly he was discovering her other side, the one that could be slightly naïve, that believed the best of people, the side she hid behind cheerful masks.

But the face she turned up to him now wore no mask. It was defenceless, the mouth soft, the eyes wide and trusting. He knew it would be a sin to betray that trust by kissing her, no matter how much he longed to. So he contented himself with brushing her cheek with his fingertips, and felt her relax against him.

What he might have done next he never knew, for the elevator reached their floor, the doors opened and the world rushed in on them again.

Now she was smiling brightly in a way that set him once more at a distance.

'Sleep tight,' he told her at her door. 'We have to be up with the dawn.'

'I'll be there,' she promised. 'Goodnight.'

He thought she would give him a final look so that the sweet connection they had established might live again. But he was facing a closed door.

Inside her room, Harriet stood in darkness, listening as his footsteps moved away to his own door.

Her heart was heavy. Midnight had struck and Cinders had been forced to leave, not running away and leaving a shoe, but escorted by the Prince who'd been tempted only briefly before his common sense had rescued him.

It's over. All over. Finished. Done with. Get undressed, go to bed, and stop indulging in fantasies. Didn't you learn anything from last time?

Switching on the bedside lamp, she stripped off her beautiful attire with ruthless fingers and replaced it with plain cotton pyjamas. Her packing was done at top speed, and then she was ready for bed. Defiantly, she got under the duvet and switched out the light.

There was a knock at the door.

'Who is it?' she asked without opening.

'It's me.'

CHAPTER NINE

HARRIET opened the door a crack and saw him. He'd removed his jacket and bow tie and his shirt was torn open at the throat.

'Can I talk to you?'

She stood back as he went past her. She would have turned on the bedside lamp but he stayed her hand.

'Better just let me talk. I owe you an apology for my behaviour tonight.'

'Do you? You didn't offend me.'

'That's very sweet of you, but I got a bit possessive in a way that I promised not to. Just friends we said but I didn't really stick to that, did I? I hadn't expected you to look so beautiful—'

'Thanks,' she said wryly.

'No, I didn't mean that,' he said hastily. 'Oh, heavens, I'm making a mess of this. I only wanted to say that you were a hundred times more wonderful than I'd dared to hope and...*Harriet!*'

Then his arms were around her, pulling her tightly against him, and all the sensible restraint drained out of her as she received the kiss she'd been longing for, never completely admitting her own desire. Now there was no chance of denying it to herself or him. She felt herself soften and fall against him, reaching out so that he was enfolded in her arms as she was enfolded in his.

Her hands were exploring him, the fingers weaving into his hair before drifting down to his face. He raised his head from hers, looking down with a question in his eyes, as though wondering if he only imagined her passionate response.

'Harriet,' he whispered, 'why have we…?'

'Shh!' She silenced him with her fingertips over his mouth. 'Don't speak. Words are dangerous. They mean nothing.'

She was right, he realised with a sense of relief. Words were nothing when he had her body against his. He could feel the cheap cotton against his hands and wondered how any woman could feel so lusciously desirable in those almost masculine pyjamas. They taunted him, hiding her beautiful body while suggesting just enough of it to strain his self-control.

Harriet felt as though she had lived this moment before, earlier that evening when he'd allowed his hand to drift indiscreetly behind her dress, but then been forced by propriety to restrain himself. She hadn't wanted restraint either in him or herself, but she'd had no choice.

But she had choice now. She could choose to be warm, intimate, seductive, enticing, passionate. Anything but restrained. Her breathing came fast as he kissed her again and again, little swift kisses covering her face, her forehead, her nose, her eyes, mouth, then sliding lower to her neck.

He was so skilled, she thought in delirious delight. They might have been one person, so sensitively did he know the right way to rouse her—to make her want him—want him more—

'Make sure you keep her for good…'

Without warning, the words screamed at her. Fran-

tically, she fought them off but they danced in her consciousness.

'You're a clever man…'

She'd known that but never thought what it meant—until
now—

*'Keep her for good…the clever thing to do…the clever
thing to do…'*

'Kiss me,' he whispered. 'Kiss me as I kiss you…
please…'

The clever thing to do. The words went through her like
ice, quenching the storm within her.

'Kiss me…'

'Darius, wait…please wait…'

'I don't want to wait any more—Harriet, let me…'

She drew back to meet his eyes, and what he saw in her
cooled his ardour as mere words could never have done.

'This wasn't part of the bargain,' she said calmly.
'Friends, remember?'

'The bargain,' he said slowly. 'Ah, yes, the bargain. How
could I have forgotten?'

'Exactly. You, of all people, should know about bar-
gains.' As she said it she even managed a faint smile. 'Let's
not complicate things by breaking ours.'

She could feel him shaking but he brought himself under
control and stepped away.

'You're right, of course. I'll say goodnight…er…sleep
well. I'll see you tomorrow.'

The door closed behind him, too quietly to hear, and
then there was only darkness.

It was a long night. Darius spent it trying to order his
thoughts, dismayed that they were suddenly rebellious,
going their own way instead of obeying him as in the
past.

Now he was alone he could admit that he was troubled by

what he'd learned that night. How painful Harriet's secrets must be for her to conceal them so determinedly. How sad must be her inner life. And he'd imagined that he knew her.

She had come into his arms, physically and, he'd hoped, emotionally, only for that hope to be dashed when she'd hastily retreated. The message was clear. Briefly she'd weakened, but then her husband's ghost had waked and that was the end. As, perhaps, it would always be.

He opened his window and stood listening to faint noises from next door. Her movements sounded restless, but what was she thinking? And would she ever tell him?

After a while he heard her window close, and then there was nothing to do but go to bed.

Harriet arose next morning with her mind made up. Cool, calm and collected, that was it. But also with a touch of their usual humour, to emphasise that nothing had changed.

In contrast to her glamour of last night, she donned a pair of functional jeans and a plain blouse. Her reflection stared back at her, asking if she really wanted this no-nonsense look when she could have something more enjoyable?

But I can't! It's a trap. No-nonsense suits me fine!

Not any longer. Never mind, it would have to do.

A waiter served breakfast in her room, and as he retreated Darius appeared at the door with a bread roll in one hand and a coffee in the other.

'Glad to see you up,' he said cheerfully. 'I was afraid the evening might have tired you too much.'

'I'm always up with the lark,' she assured him. 'Sit down. I'll be ready in a moment. I've packed up the jewellery ready to go back,' she said, indicating the box. 'Perhaps you'd better check it.'

Looking intent, Darius fingered the contents of the box until he came to the diamond pendant, which he lifted out.

'Not this,' he said. 'It's yours.'

'But it can't be. You hired this stuff.'

'Everything else, yes, but—oh, dear, did I forget to mention that I bought this one?'

'You certainly did.'

'Well, it's done now. Put it away safely.'

His expression was too innocent to be convincing, and she stared at him, open-mouthed with disbelief.

'Who do you think you're kidding?' she demanded.

His face was full of wicked delight. 'Not you, obviously.'

'You deceived me.'

'Yes, and I made a pretty good job of it too,' he said, defiantly unrepentant.

'You know I wouldn't have let you buy me anything as expensive as this.'

'Ah, well, I'm not used to people telling me what they'll let me do. It doesn't suit my autocratic, overbearing nature. I just do what I want and they have to put up with it. So there you are.' He assumed a grim expression. 'Put up with it.'

'You…you…'

He sighed. 'I know it's a great burden, but you'll learn to endure it.'

'It's…it's so beautiful,' she sighed. 'But you shouldn't have done it.'

'Don't tell me what I should and shouldn't do.'

'Yes, but—'

'Stop arguing. That's an order.'

It might be an order but it was delivered with a grin that made her heart turn over.

'Stop bullying me,' she demanded.

His grin broadened. 'I shall bully you if I want to. Now, put it away safely and don't lose it, otherwise I shall have to bully you even more by buying another.'

She ducked her head quickly so that he shouldn't see she was on the verge of tears.

Darius drank his coffee and went downstairs to pay the bill, congratulating himself on having tricked her into accepting his gift without risking the emotion that would have made her reject it.

When he returned she was on the phone to Phantom.

'I'm coming home, darling—see you later today—'

But by now Darius had himself in hand and could cope.

A car took them to the airport, where they boarded the helicopter and were soon soaring to the south and over the ocean, where the brilliant sun made the little waves sparkle.

'I love this time of year,' Harriet said, looking down to where Herringdean was just coming into view. 'The island is at its best.'

'I don't suppose you get called out on the lifeboat so often,' Darius observed.

'It depends. There aren't so many storms, but the fine weather tempts more people out in boats, so things still happen.'

Now they were crossing the coastline, covering the island until they reached the far side, and there below was the beach where they had first met.

'Look who I can see,' Darius said.

'Phantom!' she cried joyfully.

They could just make out the dog racing madly along the beach in pursuit of a ball thrown by a middle-aged woman, bringing it back to her, begging for it to be thrown again, which it always was.

'That's my neighbour, Jenny Bates,' Harriet said. 'She's wonderful with him. Hey, what's he doing now?'

Suddenly Phantom had changed course and raced into the sea. Mrs Bates ran to the water's edge and called him but he took no notice.

'Oh, no!' Harriet wailed.

'He'll be all right,' Darius said. 'He's swum often enough.'

'Yes, when I was with him. But without me he'll do something idiotic like going too far. Oh, look how far out he is! *Come back, you stupid dog!*'

'Land as close to the beach as you can,' Darius told the pilot quickly.

Down they went, finishing in almost the same place as on that first day, a lifetime ago, leaping out and running down onto the beach where Mrs Bates was wailing, 'I can't swim, I'm sorry—he's never done that before—'

'No problem,' Darius said. 'I'll go and—'

He'd been about to say that he would go after Phantom, but Harriet was way ahead of him, powering her way through the waves, calling Phantom urgently. He heard her and looked around, woofed in delight and began to paddle back to her. They met in deep water, greeting each other ecstatically with much crying and barking.

Darius remained where he was, knowing he wasn't needed.

As they emerged from the water Phantom recognised him, yelped joyfully and began to charge up the beach, spraying water everywhere. Quick as a flash, Harriet hurled herself onto the hound, taking him down to the sand.

'Oh, no, you don't,' she said breathlessly. 'Let the poor man have at least one suit that you don't ruin.' She looked up at Darius. 'You'd better run for it. I can't hold him much longer. Hurry up! Go quickly. Thank you for a lovely time, but go before he gets away from me. *Go!*'

There was nothing for it but to do as she said, so he returned to the helicopter. As it took off he looked down and discovered that history was repeating itself in that she was totally absorbed in Phantom, without even a glance to spare for himself.

It was only when he reached home he discovered that he still had her luggage. Briefly, he considered returning it in person, but settled for sending it in a taxi. He knew if he took it himself she would greet him politely while longing for him to be gone so that she could be alone with the one she really cared about.

And he couldn't face that. He could have dealt with her hostility, but her cool politeness would flatten him.

Coward, he thought wryly.

Amos would be ashamed of him.

But Amos could go and jump in the lake.

For a while things seemed peaceful. Harriet slipped back into her old routine, bathing in the mornings, sometimes seeing Darius on the beach for a few minutes, chatting about nothing much, cracking a few jokes before saying a polite goodbye.

One evening, while she was working late in her shop, a knock at the door made her look up and see him through the glass. She unlocked the door.

'Sorry, sir, we're closed for business,' she said cheekily.

'Thanks for the welcome. Hiya, Phantom. Careful not to knock any of these antiques around.'

'He doesn't need you to tell him to behave perfectly,' she said indignantly. 'He's always perfect.'

'Sure, that's why you pinned him to the ground when we landed.'

'Oh, well, that was different. What brings you here at this hour?'

'I'll be honest; I have an ulterior motive. And don't say it.'

'Say what?' she asked innocently.

'That I never do anything without an ulterior motive.'

'I wasn't going to say that.'

'No, but you were thinking it.'

'Very perceptive of you. All right, what's the ulterior motive?'

He held up his mobile phone.

'The kids call me every evening and they always ask to talk to you. I have to invent excuses why you're not there.'

'But surely they don't think we're living together?'

'Well…no, but they're surprised that you're never around.'

'But when they call tonight I will be around?' she hazarded.

'Exactly.'

'Unless I make a run for it.'

'You're too good a friend to do that.'

Before she could answer, the phone rang. Darius answered and his face lit up.

'Frankie, lovely to hear from you, darling. What have you been doing today?'

Harriet studied his face, taking in its warmth and pleasure. Her resolution to keep him at a polite distance was fading with every moment.

'What's that?' Darius asked. 'Harriet? Well…I'm not sure if…' He looked at her with pleading eyes. 'I'll see if she's here,' he said. 'I'm just going looking now.'

Silently, he mouthed, *Please*. Harriet relented and took the phone.

'Hi, Frankie! Boy, am I glad you called and gave me a chance to sit down! Your dad and I are working our socks off. I've just had a delivery at my shop and he's helping me unpack and put things away—he's doing very well.'

From the other end of the phone Darius could hear his little girl chuckling. He grinned.

'Yes, I'm really making him work,' Harriet said. 'He's surprisingly good. Let's face it, he looks like a wimp—oh, dear, I shouldn't have said that. If you could see how he's glaring at me—'

'I'm not,' Darius said indignantly.

'Anyway, he's not as much of a wimp as he looks. He can manage heavy weights—much to my surprise—'

Darius's indignation had faded and he was looking at her with resigned amusement. She laughed back at him, sending a silent message. *That'll teach you!* And receiving his message in return. *Just you wait!*

Harriet rattled away for a while, enjoying the sound of Frankie's delight. Then Mark took over, wanting to know if she'd been sailing. She'd taken her little yacht out only that morning and had plenty to tell him. It was a happy conversation.

At last she handed the phone back to Darius.

'It's a conspiracy,' he told his son. 'She's as bad as you are, or you're as bad as she is. I'm not sure which.'

Sounding relaxed and happy, he bid his children good-night, then turned to her, laughing and exasperated in equal measure.

'Harriet, you little wretch! What are you trying to do to me? Wimp, indeed!'

'Shame!' she soothed him. 'All those hours spent in the gym, for nothing.'

'All right, enjoy your laugh. I suppose I asked for it.

And thank you. You did far more than I hoped for.' He looked around at the large boxes. 'You really have just had a delivery, haven't you?'

'Yes, a big one. Hey, what are you doing?'

'Well, I've got to prove I'm not a wimp, haven't I?' he said, beginning to unpack. 'Call it my gratitude.'

He wouldn't let her refuse, but worked for two hours fetching, carrying, lifting weights, finally breathing out hard and saying, 'I'm ready for a drink. Come on.'

The glass of ale in the pub that followed was in the same spirit of cheerful friendliness, and when they finally said goodnight she was able to feel confident that she'd successfully returned their relationship to safe territory.

She was to discover her mistake.

It was three days before she saw him again, racing towards her on the beach as she and Phantom emerged from the water, seizing her shoulders as soon as he reached her.

'You've got to help me,' he said. 'I know you won't want to but—'

'Why wouldn't I want to?'

'Well, I never stop asking for things, do I? It's always you giving and me taking—'

'Darius, calm down and tell me what it is.'

'Mary called me. The kids can't stay with their gran; she's gone down with a bug. It's not serious but they have to leave, and they want to come here.'

'Of course they want to be with you.'

'Yes, but Mary will only agree if you're part of the deal. I reckon it's really you they want to see rather than me.'

'Nonsense, you're their father.'

'Yes, but I'm still learning. Mary relies on you. If you don't say yes, *she* won't say yes. Please, Harriet.'

It was unfair of him, she thought, to look at her like that. How could she be sensible in the face of that imploring gaze, reminding her of his nicer side—the one that brought her dangerously close to falling in love?

'Of course I'll help you,' she said, 'as long as we agree beforehand what we're going to—'

She stopped as his cellphone had rung.

'Mary?' he said urgently. 'Yes, I've asked her and she's agreeable. It's going to be all right—what's that?—she's right here.' He handed her the phone.

'Harriet?' said Mary's urgent voice. 'Oh, thank heavens. We've got a disaster on our hands but I know you can take care of it.'

'Calm down; I'll be glad to help, and I'm sure they'll love the island.'

'Oh, yes, if you could have heard them talking after you spoke to them the other day. All I need to know is that you'll be there.'

'And I will.'

'They're well-behaved children. You won't have any trouble making them go to bed at the right time, and they're not picky eaters—'

'Mary, hang on, I didn't mean—'

But it was too late. With mounting dismay, Harriet realised that Mary had assumed that she was living with Darius and would be there for the children all the time.

'You don't understand,' she said frantically. 'I'm not actually—'

But she was watching Darius, and what she saw checked her. He'd followed her thoughts and was silently begging her not to destroy his hope.

'Not what?' Mary asked.

'I'm not—' She could tell that he was holding his breath. 'Not…not a very good cook,' she floundered.

'That's all right,' Mary assured her cheerfully. 'He says Kate's a terrific cook. All I'm asking you to do is be nice to them, and I know you will because—'

Harriet barely heard the rest. Dismayed, she realised that she'd committed herself to moving in with him, living close to him day and night, unable to escape the attraction that threatened to overwhelm her.

She'd been caught unawares, but now it was done and it was too late to undo. She could never bring herself to kill the blazing hope she could see in him. Dazed, she bid Mary farewell, handed over the phone and wandered to the water's edge.

What have I done? she whispered to herself. *Whatever have I done?*

Then she heard him calling her name, and turned to see him following her. The next moment he'd flung his arms around her.

'Thank you!' he said. *'Thank you!'*

He didn't try to kiss her, just held her with hands that gripped so tight it was almost painful. But she didn't even think of escape. There was a sweetness in his passionate gratitude that made her heart beat faster.

He drew back and she almost gasped at the sight of his face, lined with emotion, confusion, anguish and a kind of fierce joy that he himself didn't truly believe existed.

'Thank you,' he whispered again. 'Thank you, thank you.'

Now she knew what she'd done, and nothing in the world would ever make her regret it.

'I'm going to collect them in London tomorrow,' he said. 'Will you come with me?'

'If I can. I'll have to call the lifeboat station so that they've got a replacement on call. I'll do it now.'

At the station she was assured that there was no problem. There were plenty of volunteers to fill her place.

'It doesn't give you much time to move in,' Darius said, 'but I'll help you. And don't worry about anything. I know you didn't mean to live there but you can make everything just as you like it. Your word will be law, and you can choose your room. I won't trouble you, my word on it, and if you—'

'Stop, stop!' she said, laughing and touching his lips gently. 'You're babbling.'

He removed her fingers, but not before laying the lightest possible kiss on them, just enough to be felt, not enough for offence.

'I can't help it,' he said humbly. 'It matters so much, I can't risk anything going wrong.'

'Nothing's going to go wrong,' she promised. 'Now, we have a lot of work to do.'

'Yes, let's make a start. And you.' This last was addressed to Phantom, who'd nudged his hand.

'He's included?' Harriet asked eagerly.

'You don't think I'd leave him out, do you? The kids will love him. Now I come to think of it, he's almost more essential than you are.'

She chuckled. 'I think so too. Let's go.'

As they walked home his business side reasserted itself.

'What about your shop? You'll hardly have any time there for the next few weeks.'

'My assistant is reliable, and there's a temporary worker I sometimes use. She's very good.'

'Fine, hire her full-time at my expense. I pay her wages, is that clear? No argument.'

'I wasn't going to give you one,' she said. 'You're not the only one who can do business.'

She danced ahead of him, whistling.

CHAPTER TEN

HARRIET arranged the extra worker as soon as she got home, while Darius called Kate to alert her about Harriet's arrival.

They spent the rest of the day moving her things into Giant's Beacon. Kate ceremoniously showed her round the four available bedrooms, promising to get to work on whichever Harriet chose.

'You'll probably prefer the one at the end of the corridor,' Darius suggested, bland-faced.

It was certainly the most 'proper' room, being furthest from his, and having a lock on the door. It was also extremely ugly.

The nicest room was at the front of the house, just above the front door. There were two bay windows, a thick, newly laid carpet and a large comfortable-looking bed.

It was also directly opposite Darius's room.

'I wouldn't choose this if I were you,' Darius said. 'It's much too close to that fellow, and I've heard he's a bad character. Give him a wide berth.'

'And you'd know him better than anyone else, I suppose,' she riposted.

'Definitely. You shouldn't even have been shown this room, even though it's the most comfortable, and lovely in the mornings when the sun comes in.'

'Yes, I noticed it was facing the dawn.'

'But it doesn't have a lock on the door,' he pointed out.

'Ah, but he's promised not to trouble me. If he keeps his word, why would I need a lock?'

'That's very true.'

'And if he doesn't—I'll set Phantom on him.'

'There's a threat to frighten a man.'

'So I think—' She threw herself onto the soft mattress, and Phantom jumped up beside her. 'Yes, I think we'll have this one.' She turned to her companion. 'Do you agree?'

Woof!

'Then if everyone's satisfied,' Darius said, 'we'll call it a day, and be ready to leave early tomorrow.'

The helicopter was there on the dot, sweeping them off to the airport near London. From there a car took them to the house where the children were staying. Mark and Frankie were watching from the window, and yelled with delight when they saw them.

'Dad! You came!' Frankie cried.

'But of course I came. I said I would.'

They didn't reply, but Harriet wondered how often in the past he hadn't been there when he said he would.

The housekeeper appeared, saying that their hostess wouldn't come downstairs because of her illness, but she sent her thanks and best wishes. Darius returned a message of condolence, and they were ready to go.

As they left the house Harriet happened to notice the children exchanging glances, and was almost certain that she heard Mark whisper, 'I told you she'd come.'

On the journey home they made her talk about Herringdean, yearning for the moment when they could look down at it from high in the air. When that moment finally came they were speechless, gazing open-mouthed at so much beauty. Darius, watching them, understood.

'That's what I thought when I first saw it,' he said. 'The loveliest place in the world.'

They nodded agreement, but Harriet detected a slight bafflement in their manner. Their father had actually said that? Who was he trying to kid?

At last it was time to land and make their way to Giant's Beacon. As she had expected, their first meeting with Phantom was joyful. Since he asked nothing better than to be the centre of attention all the time and they had lots of attention to give, they forged an instant three-way friendship.

After supper she and Kate saw them to bed with the promise of plenty of action next day. They were already yawning and climbed into bed without argument.

Downstairs, Darius poured her a glass of wine and raised his own glass in salute.

'To you,' he said. 'Without you, none of this would be happening.'

'But it is happening. Now it's up to you to make the best of it.'

'Did you see their faces when I told them I felt the same as they when I first saw Herringdean? They didn't really believe I could feel that way.' He added wryly, 'Any more than you did.'

'I wish you'd stop brooding about that. It was a lifetime ago. You're not the same man.'

'Maybe not,' he murmured. 'But who am I now?'

'You'll find that out with them.'

'And you?'

'No. This is you and them. I'm not really a part of it.'

'That's not true and you know it,' he said quietly.

Suddenly she was faced with a dilemma. His words offered her the chance to turn the conversation in a direction that tempted her. Try as she might to stop her heart inclining towards him, it seemed to have a life of its own, beating more intensely when he was near, bringing her alive in his presence in a way that wasn't true at any other time. A little cleverness, a little scheming, and she could secure him. It would be so easy, if only—

If only she could bring herself to settle for second best, for a marriage in which she gave love in return only for gratitude.

'Why did you sigh?' he asked. 'Did I offend you by saying that?'

'No, of course not.'

'I really forced you here against your will, didn't I? I'm sorry.'

'There's nothing to be sorry for. Stop being so gloomy. Now, I'm going to take Phantom out for a walk before I go to bed.'

'I'll come with you.'

'Better not,' she said quickly. 'He wants me to himself for a while. Goodnight.'

She slipped away before he could say any more, escaping from the danger that always hovered in his presence these days, hurrying out of the house, signalling Phantom to follow her. Darius watched them run away in the moonlight, and only when they were out of sight did he climb the stairs to find two little faces looking down at him.

'Dad, *Dad!*'

'What are you two doing up? You should be asleep.'

'Harry's gone,' Frankie wailed. 'She took Phantom with her.'

'Don't panic. They've just gone for a walk. They'll be back.'

'Promise!' she demanded.

'Word of honour. And if she doesn't I'll go and fetch them. Now, back to bed.'

They vanished obediently and he, being naïve, assumed they had obeyed him. It was only later, as he strolled in the garden watching for Harriet's return, that he realised they were looking out of the window over his head.

'Is she coming yet?' Mark called.

Darius was about to admonish them when he had the strangest sensation that Harriet was there, reading his mind, shaking her head in disapproval. Enlightenment dawned.

'Come on down and we'll wait together,' he called back.

They darted away, appearing in the garden a moment later. Kate brought out milkshakes and they sat around a small table, chatting to pass the time. Darius described his first encounter with Phantom. Once, the thought of anyone, even—or especially—his own children—knowing about that undignified incident would have filled him with horror. Now, he found himself describing it in detail, relishing their shrieks of laughter.

Harriet would have been proud of him, he felt.

'Perhaps we should go with her next time,' Frankie suggested.

'You don't have to keep guard over her,' Darius said. 'She's not going to run away.'

'Really? She'll stay with us for ever and ever?'

'That's for her to say,' Darius said quietly.

A mysterious understanding was creeping over him. Like himself, they had seen Harriet in a light that set her apart from everyone else, as though she possessed a special power that acted like a shield against all the evil of the world. Those she defended were safe. Those she loved were fortunate beyond their dreams.

The difference between them was that they had seen at once what he had taken time to understand. And that delay might be his undoing. But for now he must profit by her influence to find the right words for his children's questions. He crossed his fingers, hoping against hope for wisdom.

But before he could speak Harriet again intervened to save him.

'Here she is,' Frankie cried, bounding up and pointing to two figures emerging from the trees.

She and Mark made off at top speed and in the riot of noisy delight nobody noticed Darius closing his eyes and thanking a merciful fate. When he was calm again he strolled towards her, calling, 'Nice to see you back.'

Harriet smiled at him. 'Nice to be back,' she said.

His eyes held hers. 'Really?'

'Yes, really. Right, you kids. Bed.'

When that job was done she leaned against the wall, yawning. 'I'm nodding off right here.'

'Go and get some sleep, because you're going to need it.'

'You too. Goodnight.'

Harriet slept until the early hours, then got up and glanced out of the window. From here she could just see a glow of light that she knew came from Darius's office.

Throwing on her dressing gown, she slipped downstairs. From behind the door she could hear him on the phone.

'I accessed the website half an hour ago and there's no doubt—I know how to fight this—I've already put things in place that'll make them think twice—don't worry, I've got it in hand.'

He sounded almost like the man she'd heard before vowing, 'No mercy', but she sensed something different. The cruelty had gone from his voice and only the determination remained.

As he hung up she opened the door and found him staring at the screen. He looked round and smiled wanly.

'Don't you ever sleep?' she asked.

'I'm trying to catch up at night so that I can be free during the day. There are things I still have to do.'

'You poor soul. Can I do anything to help?'

'I'd be glad of a coffee.'

She disappeared into the kitchen, returning with a full mug a few minutes later, only to find him dozing. She set down the mug and laid a gentle hand on his shoulder, so that he awoke at once, looking up at her with a faint smile. She had never seen him so vulnerable, never been so dangerously close to loving him.

'I'm going to do it,' he said. 'You'll be proud of me, teacher.'

'I was proud of you tonight,' she said. 'When I saw you sitting outside with them, cracking jokes. You must have been telling them a great story to make them laugh like that.'

'Yes, they really enjoyed hearing how their dad looked like a total prat.'

'I don't believe you said anything like that.' When Darius simply grinned she said, 'Well, go on, I can't stand the curiosity. Tell, tell!'

'It was about our first meeting—the way Phantom flattened me on the sand. I thought they'd enjoy it, and they did.'

'You actually managed to tell *that* story?' she breathed in astonishment and admiration. 'How come?'

'You told me to,' he said simply.

'I never—' She stopped. 'When did I?'

'There and then.'

'But I wasn't there.'

'Yes, you were. You were right there with me. You always are. Even when you're not there, you *are* there. Didn't you know?'

'No,' she murmured.

His gaze intensified. 'I guess there are a lot of things you don't know.'

'I guess there are.'

'I'm glad I'm not the only one who's confused.'

Everything was in a whirl. He was telling her something she longed with all her heart to hear, to believe; telling her not with words but with his eyes, with his hesitant tone, with his uncertainty that seemed to say everything was in her hands.

Playing for time, she said lightly, 'The great financier is never confused.'

'That's what *he* used to think,' he agreed. 'So when the confusion came he didn't know how to cope with it.'

A soft buzz came from the screen.

'You've got an email,' she said. 'I'm going back to bed. So should you. Get some sleep.'

She slipped away and ran back to her room, telling herself that she was glad of the interruption that had saved her from saying and doing things that she would regret.

If she tried really hard she might even manage to believe that.

Mark and Frankie were instinctively happy outdoors. Town life bored them, and escaping to the island lifted them to seventh heaven. They revelled in the visit to Harriet's little yacht, and the trip out to sea, gaining particular pleasure from their father's ignorance, even greater than their own, and the way he addressed Harriet as 'Captain'. Several times Harriet caught them exchanging knowing glances.

At home she took charge, banishing Darius to the office to catch up with his work while she and Kate saw to supper.

'Isn't Dad having supper with us?' Mark asked.

'The poor man's got to do a little work,' Harriet said. 'Last night he worked late so that he could spend the day with you. Now, I'll take his supper in to him.'

'Are you and Dad going to get married?' Frankie asked.

'It's much too soon to think of anything like that,' Harriet said quickly. 'We're just friends for now, and we're not rushing it. Don't mention it to him.'

Frankie nodded wisely. Harriet was left staring at Darius's office door. He'd been closing it when Frankie asked her question, and although Harriet tried to believe that he couldn't have heard anything she'd noticed the way the door was suddenly still for a moment, before being shut.

At the end of the evening he emerged to join them for a walk with Phantom, and perhaps only Harriet noticed that he was unusually quiet. Later, when the children had gone to bed and the house was quiet, it wasn't a surprise when he knocked on her bedroom door.

'I just wanted to say I'm sorry that Frankie embarrassed you,' he said, coming in. 'She's too young to understand that…well, things have to happen slowly.'

'You're right,' she said. 'Going slowly can save you from a lot of mistakes.'

'Does that mean anything special?' he asked, almost daring to hope.

'I guess it does.' She fell silent.

'Harriet,' he whispered, 'don't shut me out. Not any more.'

She sighed. 'I rushed into marriage with Brad…I was so young…ah, well…'

'Don't stop there,' he begged. 'Talk to me. You keep everything bolted and barred, and you shouldn't.'

'I know. I don't mean to but I've hidden the truth for so

long that it's hard to change now. My neighbours think we were the perfect couple, and that's what I wanted them to think. I'd have been ashamed for them to know the truth. I loved Brad so much but he…well, he just took my love for granted and did as he liked.'

'Go on,' he said gently. 'Harriet, please tell me everything. You know so much about me, but you hide from me and keep me on the outside.'

She drew away suddenly and went to the window, throwing back her head, breathing harshly. She felt as though she were being torn in two directions. It had taken her so long to reach this point and now her courage was failing her. She saw Darius watching her closely, with an expression so gentle that she reached out to him without even realising.

At once he went to her. 'Tell me,' he said again. 'Don't shut me out. If only I could make you understand how important it is.'

'Why?' she whispered.

He answered by laying his lips tenderly on hers, leaving them for just a moment.

'Can you understand now?' he asked.

She searched his face. 'I'm not sure. I'm so confused.'

'Trust me, Harriet. That's all I ask.'

She rested her head against him. 'Our marriage was a mistake. I rushed into love, and when it went wrong I wouldn't admit to myself that he wasn't the man I'd thought. I don't think he was ever really faithful to me, but nobody else knew because he was away so often.

'In the end he left me for a woman he'd met in America. He went to live with her over there, and they died together in a car crash. I still have the last letter he wrote me, demanding a quick divorce because his lover was pregnant. That really hurt because I'd always wanted children and he was the one who insisted on waiting.

'It's strange, but after what he did to me, the thing I'll really never be able to forgive him for is the way he abandoned Phantom. That poor dog adored him. When Brad was away he'd sit at the window, watching and watching until he returned. Then he'd go mad with happiness.

'I loved Phantom too, but I always knew I was second best to him. And when Brad said he was leaving him behind—I couldn't believe he could be so cruel. It was *her* fault. She didn't want him, so Brad simply tossed him out of his life.'

Darius uttered one word, vulgar and full of feeling.

'That's what I said,' Harriet agreed.

'I'll never forget the day he left. Phantom watched him loading his things into the car. He began to wail, then to howl, and he ran after Brad and tried to get between him and the front door. I'll swear he knew what was happening, and was begging not to be left behind.

'Brad pushed him aside and shouted at him. Then he went out and got into the car. Phantom followed, but suddenly everything seemed to drain out of him, and he just sat there in the road while the car vanished. I hated Brad at that moment. I could forgive him for leaving me, but not for breaking that poor creature's heart.

'After that, Phantom sat at the window every day, waiting for his return. Then one day he didn't go to the window, but just lay there staring into space. He knew it was final.

'I've tried to make it up to him. I tell him how much I love him, and I promise that I'll never, never desert him or let him down in any way.'

'Harriet, you're talking about him as though he was a person.'

'I suppose that's how I think of him, except that he's more loyal and loving than any human being. I think he's happy with me now, but I wonder if he still mourns Brad.'

'Perhaps that depends on you,' Darius said carefully. 'If he can tell that *you* still mourn Brad—'

'But I don't,' she said, a little too quickly, he thought. 'He's a part of my life that's over. I love Phantom for his own sake. How could I not love him when he's so lovable?'

'And when he reminds you of Brad,' Darius said. 'Are you sure you aren't hiding from the truth, just a little? Are you really over him?'

'That was another life, another world. It doesn't even feel like me any more.'

That was a clever reply, he thought wryly, because it sounded like a denial without actually being one.

'What about this world?' he asked, choosing his words carefully.

'This is the one that matters. I know that. It's just so hard to know where I belong in it. Sometimes I feel I never will know.' She searched his face.

'I can help you there,' he said, laying his mouth over hers and murmuring through the kiss. 'This is where you belong, in my arms, in my heart.'

She silenced him with the soft pressure of her own mouth, reaching up to caress his face before sliding one hand behind his head. She'd fought so hard to cling onto caution, but now she banished it without another thought. Whatever pain the future might hold, she would risk it in return for the beauty of this moment.

When she felt him drawing her to the bed she went willingly. Now everything in her wanted what was about to happen. Fear and mistrust were set aside as she felt a new self coming to life within her, and knew that this was the self that was always meant to be, a self that could yield joyfully to passion, but for whom tenderness mattered as much, or even more.

For, dazzling as was the physical pleasure, it was the look in his eyes that made her sigh with happiness as he brought her to the moment they both longed for. And afterwards it was the strength of his arms around her that carried her safely back to earth.

Now, at last, she knew where she belonged.

CHAPTER ELEVEN

HARRIET need not have been worried about the visit. It was blessed from the start by the fact that both children were instinctively at home in the country. Sailing, bathing on the beach, running through fields and trees with Phantom, trips around the island to small villages and communities—all this was their idea of heaven.

In only one respect was the holiday less than perfect. It lacked what they most longed for, and that was to see Harriet called out on a lifeboat rescue.

She'd obtained permission for them to visit the station where her friends greeted them jovially, and showed them around, including a moored lifeboat. But no emergency turned up, and the excitement they longed for failed to materialise.

It was time for the Ellarick Regatta. For the last week the hotels had been filling up, the island was full of visitors and the port was brilliant with flags. Mark and Frankie each had a copy of the programme, which never left them.

'How many races are you in?' Mark had demanded, studying the lists although he knew them by heart.

'It depends,' Harriet said. 'If I get eliminated in an early heat I won't go on to the next, but if I finish in the first three I'll go on to the next heat, and the next and maybe even the final.'

'And then you'll win the small boat trophy,' Frankie said triumphantly. 'Like before.'

'How did you know?'

'It's listed here,' Mark said, showing her. 'You've won once, and come second three times. Did you get a big prize?'

'I got a trophy. I keep it in the shop.'

'Then it's time we all saw it,' Darius announced.

They had a jolly expedition to the shop that, as Harriet had said, sold as many gifts as antiques, and at this time of year was full of souvenirs of the regatta. Darius kitted them out with T-shirts, plus anything else that took their fancy, and they ended the day in an ice cream bar.

That night Harriet went to bed early as she had to be up in the early hours. The children bid her a formal goodnight and blew her kisses before retreating. Darius saw her to her door.

'Aren't you coming in to tuck me up?' she asked innocently.

'You need to be at your best tomorrow. Go to bed, get some sleep,' he commanded.

'If you say so. Just one goodnight kiss—'

She took possession of his mouth before he could protest, kissing him softly, then with more vigour, then fiercely.

'Harriet, you're not being fair,' he murmured desperately.

'So who's fair?' she whispered back.

'I'm trying to protect you from distractions—'

'When I need your protection I'll ask for it. Now, come inside and stop arguing.'

This was another new person, one who could shamelessly demand a man's attentions while equally shamelessly offering her own. No, not offer her own, insist on her own, for he was trying to be virtuous and resist her, and she wasn't going to have that.

It was a week since they had found each other, and she had spent every moment of that week wanting to enjoy him again, that might have embarrassed her if she hadn't known he felt exactly the same. They'd been careful. The need to put the children first had meant there were fewer chances than they might have hoped. But tonight was a chance she was determined to seize—whatever nonsense he might talk.

When at last they lay dozing together, he murmured, 'Now you must go out and win.'

'But I did win,' she whispered. 'Just now. Didn't you notice?'

'I kind of thought I was the winner.'

'We'll call it a tie.' Her lips twitched. 'But I'm not sharing the trophy.'

'That's all right. We'll compete for another one in the next round.' He kissed her. 'And now I'm leaving—'

'Are you?' she said, moving her hand.

'Yes, you little wretch—Harriet, don't do that, it isn't fair—'

'I'm not trying to be fair—'

'I know what you're trying to do—*Harriet!*'

After that there was silence for a long time. Then he gathered his energy enough to say, 'Now I really am going so that you can go to sleep. You have to be at your best tomorrow. You've got to triumph in that race and go into the next round and win there, and we're all going to be there when you get the trophy. I'll be cheering and the kids will be cheering—'

'Ah, yes, the children,' she sighed. 'It's all for them. Don't let's forget that.'

Rejoicing in the pleasure of this wonderful time, she

often forgot the conversation she'd overheard, suggesting that Darius had another motive for securing her. Not only the passion they shared, but also the sense of being close in heart and mind, rescued her from fear. All would be well, she was increasingly sure of it.

From the door he blew her a kiss and was gone.

In the early hours of next morning she was up with the lark, finding the taxi waiting at the door. By mutual agreement, Darius was remaining at home with the children rather than driving her.

Then the port came in sight, and she forgot everything but the excitement of the regatta. She got to work on her yacht, making sure everything was ready, then settled in, feeling herself become one with it.

Forty yachts were entered for the race, but only ten could compete at any one time, so it began with heats. Some of the crowd watched from the shore, but the view was better from the large ferries that had positioned themselves out at sea, and Harriet knew that the three of them would be on one of these, eagerly watching for her.

They were off. She managed to keep ahead of most of the other boats, without actually getting into the lead. Halfway through the race she saw Darius and the children leaning over the railing of a ferry, cheering her. Inspired, she redoubled her efforts and managed to arrive second.

'That's it,' Darius said as they welcomed her ashore. 'You're in the next heat.'

'And next time you'll be first,' Mark said loyally.

'You'll show 'em,' Frankie cried.

And she did. Whether it was the sense of a loyal family rooting for her, or whether it was simply her time, she won the next heat, came second in the next, and won the final race. When she came ashore the band was playing as she went up to the dais to receive the trophy. There were photographs to be taken, herself holding up her prize, with Frankie and Mark one each side, then Frankie and Mark holding the prize. Darius was in some of the pictures too, but usually in the background, rather to her disappointment.

The day ended in a restaurant, being ecstatically toasted not only by the family but by her many friends. Then home to be toasted again.

Darius ended the evening, as he always did, at the computer, catching up with the work he'd been unable to do during the day. He looked worn out, she realised. With every day he seemed to get less and less sleep. She crept away and left him.

He came to her two hours later. 'I was afraid you might have gone to sleep by now,' he said, closing the door behind him.

'I'm just about to.' She yawned theatrically. 'I simply can't keep awake.'

Laughing, he took her into his arms. 'Let's see if I can help you find sweet dreams.'

She slipped her arms about his neck. 'Hmm, let me think about that.'

'Don't think too hard,' he murmured, dropping his head so that his lips were against her neck.

'You're a wicked man, you know that?'

'Would you like me to go away?'

'I'm not sure. Do that again and I'll decide.'

Their first love-making had been full of tender emotion, and because of that it had been perfect. Over the next few days, a new pleasure had revealed itself, love and laughter at the same time, and she discovered that its joy could be as great as any other. She hadn't known before that she could be a tease, but she was learning it now and revelling in the lesson.

He caressed her, watching her expression intently.

'Are you any closer to making your mind up?' he wanted to know.

'I'm not sure. Some things take longer to decide than others.' She stretched out luxuriously. 'But we have plenty of time.'

'Yes, all the time in the world,' he said with relish.

As he spoke he was drawing his fingers down her, touching lightly so she took a long breath as her desire rose.

'I've thought about nothing but this since last time,' he murmured. 'And the time before.'

'Neither have I. You're here now, and I'm going to enjoy every moment.'

'I intend to make sure you do—*what the blazes is that?*'

A shrill noise had rent the air, then again, and again and again.

'Oh, no,' Harriet groaned. 'That's my pager. I'm needed on the lifeboat. I've got to dash.'

'You're going to run away *now*?'

'I don't have any choice,' she cried, shoving him aside and making a grab for her clothes.

For a moment he was too stunned to speak, but lay on the bed, his heart pounding as he fought to bring himself under control. This couldn't be happening. It mustn't happen. To have the prize snatched from him as the climax mounted—to be defeated at the last moment and told to put up with it. His head was spinning.

'Bye,' she cried and headed for the door.

'Wait!' he cried, getting command of himself at the last minute, 'I'll drive you there.'

'I can't wait for you. I'm on my way.'

She was gone. A moment later, he heard her car start up.

Dazed, he wrenched on his clothes and went out into the corridor, to find his children already there.

'Dad, what's happened?' Mark demanded. 'There was a funny noise and Harry dashed off. She hasn't been called, has she?'

'That's right, she's on her way to the lifeboat station now.'

'Oh, wow!' Both children began to leap about. 'Let's go too, please, Dad.'

'They won't let us in. They're doing a serious job and we'd be in the way.'

'But we can watch from the shore and see the boat go out. Please, Dad, please, please, *please*.'

They were bouncing up and down, looking up at him beseechingly.

'All right,' he said, relenting. 'Get dressed fast.'

In ten minutes they were sweeping out of the drive. On the journey he switched on the car radio, tuned to the local station, that was carrying news about a small party out on a jaunt who'd sent a frantic radio message that their boat had sprung a leak.

By the time they arrived they were several minutes behind Harriet, who had completely vanished, but the station was buzzing with life. A crowd had gathered just outside, and they quickly joined it. A cheer rose as the lifeboat went down the slipway, hitting the water so that spray rose up high.

'Was it like this for you, Dad?' Mark breathed.

'I don't exactly know,' he said wryly. 'I wasn't here. I was a few miles out, going down for the third time.'

That was roughly how he felt right now. His mind told him that she'd had no choice but to leave and save others as she had saved him. He had no reasonable complaint.

But that was only his mind. The rest of him was complaining bitterly at losing the prize at the crucial moment.

She had laid in his arms, tender and sweet, giving him the look he loved, the one that said he could bring her a pleasure and happiness she'd never dreamed of before. That look had the power to open his heart, inviting her to reach out to him, as he reached out to her more with every day that passed.

Until now he'd shown his growing feelings through touch, waiting until he was sure of the right words. Since the night she'd confided in him he'd felt his defences collapse. The barrier of her husband's memory, once looming so high between them, no longer existed. She'd trusted and confided in a way he hadn't expected, filling him with happiness but also with a slight sense of guilt that he hadn't matched her openness with his own.

Honesty demanded that he admit he already knew the secret she was finally revealing, but he hadn't been able to bring himself to do it. It would involve telling her about his father's spies, and in her anger and dismay she might have laid some of the blame on himself. Not for the world would he risk damaging the bond between them. At least, not yet.

Soon he would be able to tell her of his feelings. It might even have been that night. But then—

He groaned. There were two Harriets—the passionate loving one, and the brave efficient one who put duty before everything. Tonight, the second one had taken over, leaving him stranded. Life with her would be more complex than he'd ever dreamed. Also more intriguing . That suggested an interesting future.

But tonight he was aching with frustration and thwarted feelings.

Hours passed. Occasionally someone would come out of

the station to brief the watchers on how things were going. So they knew that the lifeboat had reached its destination, rescued everyone safely, and was on its way back.

At last it appeared on the horizon, just visible in the faint gleam of the dawn. The children watched, thrilled, as it came closer and was hauled back up the slipway. When Harriet appeared they ran to greet her and be introduced to the rest of the crew. They were in seventh heaven.

'Gosh,' Mark exclaimed. 'Wasn't that the most wonderful thing that ever happened?'

'Oh, yes,' Darius said wryly. 'Wonderful.'

But his personal feelings vanished when he saw Harriet on the edge of total exhaustion.

'Let's get you home fast,' he said. 'Leave your car here; you're too tired to drive. I'll fetch it later. Let her have the back seat, kids, so that she can stretch out.'

She did manage to stretch out, falling asleep almost at once, and waking to find her head resting in Frankie's arms.

'We're home now,' the little girl said kindly. 'I'll help you to bed.'

With Kate's assistance, she did, finally emerging to where Mark and her father were waiting in the corridor.

'All right for me to go in?' Darius asked.

'Just for a moment,' she told him sternly. 'She needs to sleep.'

Darius gave her a comic salute. 'Yes, ma'am. Anything you say, ma'am.'

He vanished into Harriet's room too quickly to see his children stare at each other with an unmistakable message; Dad said *that?*

Going quietly to the bed, Darius whispered, 'Hello.'

Silence.

Leaning closer, he heard her faint breathing and realised that she was asleep.

'I guess Frankie was right to protect you,' he murmured. 'You need it sometimes. It's a pity about tonight because I was going to say…all sorts of things. Now they'll have to wait until the time is right.' He touched her face with gentle fingers. 'Let's hope that day comes soon.'

He kissed her softly, and left the room without her knowing that he'd been there.

The last few days of the holiday built on the success of the first week. Darius's relationship with his children was becoming everything he had hoped, and his manner towards Harriet was full of affection and gratitude.

'Without you, this would never work,' he told her. 'However much I want to, I can't spend all my time with them. I have to keep an eye on what's happening out there.'

'I know. You were up almost until dawn last night,' she said. 'I don't know how you manage to stay awake.'

'I don't always,' he said ruefully. 'Thank goodness for you distracting them. I swear if I nod off they barely notice.'

The end of the holiday was near. The four of them would fly to London, where the children would be reunited with Mary. After that, she hoped she and Darius would have a little time together before returning to Herringdean.

But the day before they were due to leave the financial world began to call to Darius more urgently. Hardly a minute passed without a text, an email or a call on his cellphone.

'Is it bad news?' she asked him urgently.

'Not bad, just interesting. It could go either way, depending on how I handle it. I think we need to change our plans.

It's best if you don't come to London after all. I'll have to stay there a few days, sort some things out. So I'll take the kids back to Mary and stay out of your hair for a while.' He grinned. 'You'll be glad to have a rest from me.'

'Of course I will,' she said in a dead voice. 'Who could think otherwise?'

The children complained bitterly about her not coming with them.

'I've got work to do,' she said cheerfully. 'It's time I took over the shop and I have to go to training sessions for the lifeboat.'

'But we will see you again?' Frankie urged.

'I'm sure you will. Who knows what's around the corner?'

She spoke brightly, but she couldn't help being glad Darius wasn't there to hear. She couldn't have helped watching for his reaction, and now something in her was warning her to expect the worst.

On the day she saw them off and stood looking up into the sky as the helicopter rose higher and higher, then swung away until it disappeared completely and the sky was empty but for a few seagulls.

How lonely it was now. After the pleasures of the last week, the quiet and emptiness were almost unbearable. Worse still was the fear that what had gone was gone for ever. He had said the news could be good, depending on how he handled it, and she guessed he would handle it with skill, perhaps ruthlessness. The 'no mercy' side of him would rise and take over again.

He would leave Herringdean, having no further use for it, or for her. He'd learned how to reach out to his children and he could carry those lessons forward without her help. He'd settle back in London, find a wife who suited him better, sell Herringdean and forget she existed.

And I should have known it would happen, she thought. *All this time the truth has been staring me in the face, but I wouldn't let myself see it.*

It was time to be sensible. She was good at that, she reminded herself. She had a shop to see to, and Phantom to look after. He was showing signs of depression now his two adoring young friends had gone.

'People always go off and leave you, don't they?' she said, caressing him. 'Well, not me. I'll always be here for you. That's a promise.'

Moving back into her home, she filled up the time by cleaning it. More time was occupied at the lifeboat station, but mostly in training sessions. For some reason, very few boats got into trouble.

Now she began to understand Mark and Frankie's frustration at the lack of action. Why couldn't people obligingly get into danger so that she could have the satisfaction of saving them? Not that she wanted anyone to suffer. She just wanted to feel needed, and that was becoming hard.

For the first few days Darius called her regularly, but the calls were always brief. Then they were replaced by texts, friendly, cheerful but unrevealing. Exactly the kind of message a man might send if he was easing his way out of a relationship.

One evening she and Phantom went out for a long walk. As she strolled back home a car passed her going in the other direction, and slowed down. It was Walter.

'I just drove past your place,' he called, 'and there's a fellow standing there.'

'Did you see who it was?' she asked eagerly.

'No, I wasn't that close, but he looked as if he was waiting for you.'

'Thanks, Walter.'

Her heart soaring, she sped away, racing Phantom until

her shop came in sight and she dashed around the corner, to where a man was walking impatiently up and down.

It was Amos Falcon.

CHAPTER TWELVE

'GOOD evening, Mrs Connor.'

Harriet wondered if she'd only imagined that he stressed 'Mrs' very slightly.

'Good evening, Mr Falcon. What a surprise. You didn't tell me you were coming.'

'It was a sudden decision. Aren't you going to invite me in?'

'Of course.'

She led him up to her apartment over the shop, keeping her hand on Phantom's collar, dreading that he might give one of his displays of friendliness. But she need not have feared. When they were inside, Phantom moved as far away from Amos as possible and sat huddled in a corner, eyeing him distrustfully.

When the door had shut, Harriet said, 'If you were hoping to see Darius—'

'I wasn't. I know he's in London. I've seen him several times in the last few days.' He was watching her face carefully, easily seeing that this disconcerted her. 'Did he not tell you that? Strange.'

On first finding him there she had remembered how pleasantly he'd spoken to her when they danced at the wedding. But now she saw that his smile was cold, and she remembered how Darius had described his father—ruthless, scheming, implacable; a man who was determined to make others do his will. She recalled too that Amos had chosen a wife for his son, and wondered uneasily what had brought him such a distance to see her.

'So you don't know what's been happening to him?' Amos said in a genial voice that struck a false note to her ears.

'I don't ask Darius about his business,' Harriet said. 'I doubt if I'd understand it, anyway.'

'Possibly, but when a man is taking hold of his problems and dealing with them successfully it's not hard to understand. Anyway, never mind that. You and I have things to discuss.'

'Coffee?' she asked politely.

'Thank you, I will. You know, I really took to you when we met before. You're an admirable young woman, not just because you helped save my son's life, but also because of the way you've built up this shop. It's worth a lot more than you'd think by just looking at the outside.'

'How do you know what it's worth?' she asked.

He shrugged. 'That kind of information isn't hard to come by. It belonged to your husband but he had very little time for it so the running of it fell to you. It was you who arranged the loans and made sure they were paid on time.'

'So you've been looking at my bank records?' she asked in outrage.

She knew that a man like this, who stood at the summit of the financial universe, would have no difficulty in accessing any figures that he wanted, yet the discovery that he'd had her investigated was a nasty shock that made her seethe.

'And I've been very impressed by what I found. You've turned this place into twice what it was before. I'm prepared to pay a high price for it.'

'It's not for sale.'

He gave a harsh chuckle. 'Of course it isn't. That's exactly what I expected you to say.'

'And I meant it.'

'Naturally. But you and I don't need to waste any time. We both know what the score is. You've gained a real influence over my son, but now that he's returning to his old life I don't want him harking back to you. The fight isn't over yet and he's going to need all his faculties to come out on top.'

Then Harriet did something that she did very rarely. She lost her temper, turning on him with such a look that he nearly backed away.

'Understand me,' she said. 'I will not discuss Darius with you. If he wants to consign me to the past then he can tell me himself, and I'll open my hands and let him go. I will not try to keep a stranglehold on him, and you don't have to buy me off. Is that clear?'

Amos Falcon's response was a genial smile that made her want to murder him.

'Perfectly clear and I respect your strength of mind, but you should allow me to show that respect by purchasing your shop at twice its value. You won't get such an offer again.'

'You're crazy,' she breathed. 'You think everyone's for sale.'

'No, I simply think you should be considering the long-term implications. After the appalling way your husband treated you, you should be protecting yourself.'

His words were like a douche of ice.

'The appalling way—? Darius told you about that?'

'Not at all. I told him.'

Suddenly the world had turned into a nightmare through which she could only stumble.

'You told—? When?'

'At the wedding. I discovered I knew rather more about you than he did, so I brought him up to date.'

Now she couldn't speak at all, only look at him from wide, horrified eyes.

'He was very chivalrous,' Amos went on. 'He said it was entirely a matter for you if you wanted to keep your secrets, which, of course, is right. But I think he was a little disturbed to discover that you'd been holding him off while pretending to be close to him.'

Harriet's head swam. There in her mind was the sweet moment when she'd confided in Darius what she'd told nobody else, meaning in this way to prove her trust in him.

But he'd known all the time, and never told her.

'Get out,' she breathed. 'Get out now, if you know what's good for you.'

'He doesn't,' said a voice from the door. 'He's never known what was good for him.'

Shocked, they both turned to see Darius standing there, a look of dark fury on his face.

'You heard her,' he told his father. 'Get out. Get off this island and don't ever come back.'

'What are you doing here?' Amos shouted.

'When I found out where you'd gone I came after you as fast as I could. I knew you'd try something like this. Luckily, I arrived in time to spike your guns.'

'I was only trying to do my best for you,' Amos growled. 'You've done so well these past few days.'

'Yes, I've put a lot of things right, not everything but enough to survive. And now I'm coming back here to stay. For good. I'm moving my centre of operations here permanently. From now on I'll operate out of Giant's Beacon, with the help of my wife.'

'Your wife!' Amos snapped. 'You mean you've asked her? Of all the damn fool—'

'No, I haven't asked her,' Darius said with a glance at Harriet. 'And after what you've told her I wouldn't give much for my chances. But I'm a man who doesn't give up. When I want something I keep on and on until I get it. *You* taught me that, and I was never more glad of a lesson in my life.

'It won't be easy. Why should any woman in her right mind want to marry into this family? But I'll keep going until she forgives me for keeping that little matter of her husband to myself, and understands that I can't live without her. Then, perhaps she'll take pity on me.'

Harriet tried to speak but she couldn't. Her eyes were blinded with tears and something was almost choking her.

'Now go,' Darius said quietly.

Amos knew when he was beaten. With a scowl at them both, he stormed out of the door and they heard his footsteps thundering on the stairs.

'I meant every word of it,' Darius said, coming to stand before her. 'I love you. I want to have you with me always. That's why I went to London, to set up the arrangements that would make it possible for me to move here permanently. I suppose I ought to have told you first—*asked* you first—but that's not my way. I fix things to suit myself, and then other people just have to fit in. Once I knew I wanted to marry you, you never had a choice.

'Harriet, Harriet, don't cry. I don't mean it. I'll do anything to marry you. You'll just have to be a little patient with me. Don't cry, my darling, please.'

But she couldn't stop crying. Tears of joy, of hope, of released tension, they all came flooding out, making it impossible for her to speak. Mysteriously, he also found that words had deserted him, so he abandoned them altogether, carried her into the bedroom and revealed his love in other ways. She responded with heartfelt tenderness, and they found that their mutual understanding was once more perfect.

'I can't believe the way you stood up to my father,' he murmured as they lay together afterwards. 'The world is littered with strong men he crushed beneath his feet, but he didn't stand a chance against you.'

'He tried to turn me against you,' she said. 'How dare he!'

'I heard him tell you that he and I had had several meetings while I was in London, but he didn't tell you what those meetings were about. He tried again to get me to marry Freya, offered me money, all useless. Freya was cheering me on, and actually drove me to the airport. The last thing she said to me was, "Go for it. Don't let her escape!"'

'Mary said much the same thing. There'll be a huge cheer when I tell them that we're engaged.' Suddenly, he sounded uncertain. 'Harriet, we are engaged, aren't we?'

'I thought you weren't going to take no for an answer.'

'I'm not.'

'And neither am I.' She drew him close.

'That old man thought he was being clever when he found out about your husband,' Darius said, 'but it just made me angry with him. It only affected me in that I longed for you to confide in me willingly, and when you did—I wanted to tell you that I already knew, but I was afraid to spoil what was happening between us. Say you forgive me.'

'There's nothing to forgive,' she whispered.

'And we'll marry as soon as possible?'

'I want to, of course I do. I love you. I thought I'd never love another man, but you're different from them all. But

can you really give up your old life to come and live here?
Aren't we being unrealistic?'

'I shan't have to give it up completely. I'm going to have
to downsize, but that suits me. My London home is up for
sale and I'll be selling quite a few other properties. I'll pay
off some debts, reschedule others, and what's left can be
controlled just as easily from here as from London.'

'But can you do it all alone?'

'I won't have to. I have staff who are willing to move
here permanently. I couldn't ask them before because I
didn't know where I'd be myself, but now it can all be arranged. I've got plans to create a little village for them.'

'And they won't mind leaving London for such a quiet
place?'

'Mind? They were falling over themselves to volunteer.
This will be a whole new life for a lot of people. It isn't
going to be the "great financial empire" I once had. It'll be
about a third of the size, but that's fine with me. Then I'll
have more time to spend with my wife and our children.'

'Our children?'

'If that's what you'd like.' He was silenced suddenly as
she took him into a fierce embrace.

'That's what I'd like,' she whispered at last. 'Oh, yes,
that's what I'd like, as soon as possible.'

'Then we'll have a dozen children, and I'll spend my
time pottering about the house, and sometimes helping you
in the shop.'

'Now you're getting carried away,' she warned.

'So what's wrong with being carried away?'

'Nothing,' she sighed blissfully. 'Nothing at all.'

'And I'm going to do my best to make Herringdean glad
I'm here. There must be things I can do for the community.
I expect they'll come and suggest them to you soon, and
you can tell me. I'm going to have a good look at that wind

farm. There may be some arrangement I can make to get a good electricity price for the island.'

'Do you really think you can?'

'I don't know.' His voice rose to a note of exhilaration. 'I simply don't know.'

'Darling, you're sounding a bit mad. Anyone would think not knowing was the best thing in the world.'

'Maybe it is. Maybe it's better to have things that you know you don't know, that you've got to learn about, because that's all part of having a new life. There's so much I don't know, and I'm going to have a great time finding out.'

'*We'll* have a great time finding out,' she suggested.

'Maybe. The trouble is that you already know so much more than me. I'm going to have to learn from you—teacher.'

She regarded him tenderly. She wasn't crazy enough to take all of this too seriously. Darius was caught in the exhilaration of their love and their new life, and he was celebrating with wild dreams. But he hadn't completely changed character, no matter how he sounded. Part of him would always be the fierce, dynamic man who'd first arrived on Herringdean weeks ago.

But she knew also that part of him would be this new man coming to life in her arms. And just how the mixture settled would be up to her in the years ahead. He'd put himself in her hands and she was eager for the challenge.

'You make it sound so wonderful,' she said. 'Oh, yes, everything is going to be perfect. No, no, it's perfect now.'

'Not quite,' he said. 'There's still one thing I want, although I don't suppose I'll ever have it.'

'Whatever can that be?'

'You've done so much for me. Saving my life was just the start of it. There are so many other ways in which you've saved me, I couldn't begin to count them. If only there was something I could do for you that would mean as much.'

'But it's enough that you love me.'

'Not for me. I want to give you something so precious that it's like a jewel, but I don't know that I can. I can't make it happen—it just has to happen, and maybe it never will.'

'Stop fretting,' she told him. 'We'll just have to be patient. It may take a long time to happen.'

But it happened before anyone could have expected, and in a way that nobody could have foreseen in a million years.

Preparations for the wedding started at once, with Harriet moving out of her tiny apartment and into Giant's Beacon, where she could take immediate charge of the renovations.

'Is Phantom pleased with his accommodation?' Darius enquired after the first day.

'Yes, he's asked me to express his approval of your efforts on his behalf. Putting him in the room next door to ours was pure genius.'

'Next thing, he'll have to meet the family. We'll start this afternoon.'

'What?'

'It's simple. We go into the computer room, switch on the video link—' he was doing so as he spoke '—and the family will appear.'

It was her first encounter with video link and it took her breath away. Jackson connected from his computer in London, and Marcel appeared from Paris. Then there was Mary and Ken, raising their glasses to her, and Frankie and Mark, bouncing with happiness.

Like Darius, she was discovering the joys of new experiences and they were exhilarating.

'It's all working out,' she told Phantom, stroking him as he settled for the night. 'We're going to have such a wonderful life, my darling—Phantom—are you all right? *Darius.*'

In a moment he was there, dropping to his knees beside the dog, who was heaving violently.

'Call the vet quickly,' he said.

The vet lived nearby. He was soon there, listened to Phantom's heart and shook his head.

'He's very old, and his heart's worn out,' he said. 'This was bound to happen soon. I think you should prepare yourself for the worst. Would you like me to put him to sleep now?'

'No,' Harriet said fiercely. 'I want him until the last possible moment.' She scooped Phantom up in her arms. 'There, darling, we'll stay together and you'll feel my arms around you all the time.'

Darius watched her wretchedly, torn apart by her grief.

'We'll stay with him together,' he said, touching her face gently.

But then the worst thing possible happened. A sound split the air, making them both start up in horror.

'My pager,' she gasped. 'No—no—I can't. I can't leave him to die alone.'

'Harriet, you've got to go,' Darius said urgently. 'Not for their sake but for your own. You swore to do your duty and put it above all personal considerations. If you fail now, you'll never forgive yourself as long as you live.'

Her wild eyes showed that she knew he was right, and tears streamed down her face as she fought between her duty and her feelings for her beloved dog.

'How can I leave him alone?' she whispered.

'He won't be alone. I'll stay with him until the last minute. He'll be in my arms, just as he would have been in yours. He'll know that he's loved, I promise you. Trust me, Harriet. *Trust me!*'

'Yes—' she gasped. 'Yes—' She caressed Phantom's head. 'Goodbye, my darling—goodbye—'

Darius never forgot the look on her face as she backed out of the room. Or the look on Phantom's face as he took the dog into his arms.

'She'd have stayed if she could,' he told him. 'We both know that, because she loves you more than anyone in the world. And I'm not even jealous.'

Incredibly, he felt the great furry body in his arms relax. Phantom's eyes closed, but he was still alive for a moment later they opened again.

'It's time we had a good long talk,' Darius murmured. 'We both love her so much, we had to get together sooner or later.'

He talked on, only faintly aware of the passage of time. He wondered where Harriet was now. Had she reached the station yet? He knew she was suffering, thinking of Phantom dying without her. But he had made her a promise, and he would keep it at all costs.

The hours passed. Daylight faded. He knew he was repeating himself, but that didn't matter. What counted was the love in his voice, reaching out to the dog as Harriet herself would have reached out to him.

At first he listened for her step on the stairs, but gradually he ceased to be aware of anything but the living animal dying softly in his arms. It might be madness but he had no doubt that Phantom could understand every word, just as he would have done from Harriet.

And then the truth came to him as a revelation. This was

the sign he'd longed for, the proof that he and Harriet were one. Phantom's eyes on him were full of trust.

Harriet, slipping into the house downstairs, listened to the silence, knowing what it meant. Phantom had died when she wasn't there to care for him. And however much she tried to believe that Darius had helped him, he would know that she herself had abandoned him when he needed her most. Tears streamed down her face as she climbed the stairs.

And then, halfway up, she stopped, holding herself tense against the incredible sound that reached her. Surely that was Darius's voice? He was talking to someone, that meant—?

Hardly daring to believe it, she sped up the rest of the way, pausing outside the door, then moving quietly into the room. There she stood just outside of Darius's vision, listening, entranced, to his words.

'I'm not sure she really understands even now how much I love her,' he was saying. 'I've tried to show it but I'm clumsy. I never knew anyone like her existed and I'm afraid that she'll leave me. That's why I'm hurrying her into our marriage before she has a chance to think. But she's turning me into someone else. This other guy, he doesn't do any of the things I'm used to, so I'm having to get to know him from scratch.

'I wish I could be more like you. You were never lost for what to do next, were you? Toss them to the ground and jump up and down on them, that's your way.

'I used to be jealous of you. How about that? I thought she loved you because she still loved Brad, but it's got nothing to do with him. I know that now. You're lovable and precious, and you've got to be here for us a while yet.

'Hey, you're restless. That's good. Hold on there, boy.

Don't give up now. She'll be home soon—just a little longer.
Harriet!'

She dropped down beside him, her hands caressing
Phantom, but her eyes turned up to him in a passion of
love and gratitude.

'You did it,' she whispered. 'You kept him alive for me.
Thank you, thank you—oh, if only you knew—'

'I think perhaps I do,' he murmured, his eyes meeting
hers in a moment of total understanding that was normal
with them now.

'I reckon he's got a little longer yet,' Darius said.

As if to prove it, Phantom shifted in his arms and leaned
forward to lick Harriet's face.

'You've got to live a bit longer, you hear that?' she said.
'I want you there at our wedding. Promise me.'

Woof!

They were married three weeks later, on the beach. Of
Darius's family, only Amos and his wife were missing;
but his brothers and Freya all said they wouldn't miss it
for the world. Mary and Ken said the same thing, watching
with satisfaction as Darius laid claim to the most valuable
property of his life.

Frankie walked behind the bride, pretty in frills
and flowers. And beside her walked Mark, his hand on
Phantom's collar, guiding him to a place at the front where
he could curl up and watch the ceremony.

The vet had expressed astonishment at his survival,
but Harriet wasn't surprised. Darius had done what he
longed to do—given her something so precious that it
was like a jewel. If she had doubted his love before, she
could doubt it no longer. She knew now that the jewel
would shine for ever.

* * * * *

FIXED UP
WITH MR RIGHT?

BY
MARIE FERRARELLA

First published in Great Britain 2011
by Mills & Boon, an imprint of Harlequin (UK) Limited,
Eton House, 18-24 Paradise Road, Richmond, Surrey TW9 1SR

© Marie Rydzynski-Ferrarella 2010

ISBN: 978 0 263 88902 4

23-0811

Harlequin (UK) policy is to use papers that are natural, renewable and
recyclable products and made from wood grown in sustainable forests. The
logging and manufacturing processes conform to the legal environmental
regulations of the country of origin.

Printed and bound in Spain
by Blackprint CPI, Barcelona

Dear Reader,

Here we are with the second installment of Matchmaking Mamas. This time it's soft spoken Theresa Manetti who is trying to find a mate for her workaholic daughter. Kate has only ventured out onto the dating field a handful of times. The last time was not the charm inasmuch as she became engaged to a high profile criminal lawyer who enjoyed more than his share of "undercover" work, the undercover in this case being sheets. After that disaster, Kate dedicated herself to building up her career and completely ignoring her personal life.

Until she meets district bank manager Jackson Wainwright. After building up a successful career, Jackson finds himself coming back to his roots because of his older brother, Jonah, a charming man with a seriously addictive personality. Assuming the role of his brother's keeper, Jackson finds himself in need of a family lawyer, which leads him to Kate. The rest is history.

I hope you enjoy this newest installment. From the bottom of my heart, I wish you someone to love who loves you back.

All the best,

Marie Ferrarella

To
Persis Choksy,
Operations Supervisor
At Wells Fargo,
For kindly answering all my questions

USA TODAY bestselling and RITA® Award-winning author **Marie Ferrarella** has written almost two hundred novels, some under the name Marie Nicole. Her romances are beloved by fans worldwide. Visit her website at www.marieferrarella.com.

Chapter One

"**Y**ou're kidding."

When her cell phone began to ring, Katherine Colleen Manetti, K. Manetti according to the silver scripted initials on her office door, had debated letting the call go to voice mail. She was almost too busy to breathe.

When she saw that the call was from Nikki Connors, one of her two oldest, dearest friends, she'd decided to give herself a quick, unscheduled break before she headed off to court. Talking to Nikki—or to Jewel Parnell, her other best friend—reminded her that there was a life outside of the prestigious family law firm where she seemed to spend most of her waking hours.

"Talk quick." Kate popped out a small mirror from

the middle drawer of her desk to make sure that every silken, shoulder-length, midnight black hair was in place. It saved her a trip to the ladies' room. "I've got to fly out of the office in less than five minutes."

"Kate, I don't have a date yet, but I need you to be my maid of honor. You and Jewel. You don't mind splitting the position with Jewel, do you? Because I really can't choose between you."

"Hold it. Why do you need a maid of honor?"

Kate knew the logical answer, but it just didn't fit. All three of them were too busy forging their careers to date, much less date long enough to create the need to utter vows before a saintly looking priest.

"Because I'm getting married."

Kate couldn't remember Nikki *ever* sounding this happy, not even when she graduated medical school near the top of her class. "Married?" she echoed in complete stunned disbelief. Light blue eyes narrowed as the twenty-nine-year-old attorney tried to wrap her head around the concept. "As in ''til death do us part'?"

It took Nikki a second to answer. Kate had strong suspicions that her friend was almost too happy to talk. What was *that* like? she wondered. She'd been engaged once a couple of years ago, but that had blown up in her face when Matthew McBain, the tall, dark and gorgeous criminal lawyer who'd taken custody of her heart turned out to be more interested in carving notches into his headboard then being faithful to her.

That was when she'd admitted that she had been

living the reverse of that old adage about kissing a lot of frogs to find a prince. In her case, she kissed a lot of princes only to discover that they were really frogs. And none had been a bigger frog than Matthew. That was when she'd decided to give her career center stage in her life. Careers, at least, gave back what you put into them. They didn't sleep around.

"Yes," Nikki assured her. "That kind of married."

"To a man?"

"Yes," Nikki said, laughing.

And then Kate remembered. At their last quickie get-together, Nikki had mentioned that she was seeing someone. To be honest, she hadn't paid all that much attention. But she was paying attention now.

"The guy with the kid?" Kate recalled.

"Yes, the guy with the kid." She could *hear* the smile in Nikki's voice. "I'm getting two for the price of one."

That was when Kate had blurted out, "You're kidding." The next moment, she remembered the way Nikki had met this supposed Prince Charming and his offspring. "The one your mother set you up with?" There was barely veiled horror in Kate's voice, not to mention apprehension.

"Technically, my mother didn't actually set me up with him, Kate. She sold Lucas a house and, because he was new to the area, he asked if she knew the name of a good pediatrician. She gave him my name *only* because he asked."

That wasn't the way Kate saw it.

"Po-tay-to, po-tah-to. It was a setup, Nik. You know it was a setup. *I* know it was a setup. And you know what else?"

"What else, Kate?"

"Now that your mother's had this success, that just empowers the rest of them to go crazy and *really* meddle in our lives—mine and Jewel's," she clarified. "Oh God, Nik, can't you just live with him in sin? Do it for Jewel and me. Otherwise, we're doomed."

"Kate, it's not that bad," Nikki assured her, amused.

"Did all that happiness I hear in your voice give you amnesia? Don't you remember what it was like when we were in college, constantly dodging all those men our mothers kept throwing in our path?" Kate shivered, remembering. "You know what they're like. A tiny taste of success keeps them going for months. I'd be surprised if there isn't some guy on my doorstep all wrapped up in a red ribbon by the time I get home tonight."

"Are you through?"

Kate sighed. "For now."

"Okay. Back to the reason I called. Can I count on you to stand up for me?"

Resigned, Kate said, "Yes, you can count on me to stand up for you. But make the wedding soon, okay? I'm going to have to get out of town, at least until this blows over. There'll be no living with my mother after this."

"You don't live with your mother," Nikki pointed out. "You hardly see your mother."

"There's a reason for that." It wasn't that she didn't

love her mother, she did. A great deal. And in order for that love to continue, there needed to be space between them. At times *lots* of space. "Mom's old-fashioned. She doesn't think a woman's complete without a man." There was a knock on her door and then it opened. Her brother, Kullen, stuck his head in. "Or that a man's complete without a woman, for that matter," she added.

Coming in, Kullen took hold of her wrist and turned it so that he could see who she was on the phone with. He recognized Nikki's number. "Very true," he agreed. "And the more women he has, the more complete that man is." He grinned broadly. Unlike his sister, he had a very full social life. Their mother would have argued that it was *too* full. Kullen never allowed himself to linger with anyone long enough to even remotely become serious. "C'mon, Kate, it's getting late. We've gotta go," he urged.

On the other end of the call, Nikki said, "Me, too. Say hi to Kullen for me," she requested cheerfully.

"Right. I'll talk to you later, Nik." After terminating the call, Kate tucked the cell phone into her pocket. As she rose to her feet, she saw the unspoken question in her older brother's eyes. "Nikki's getting married."

Kullen's mouth dropped open. "You're kidding."

"That was my reaction, too," Kate told him, "and no, I'm not."

Kullen held the door open for her. He and his sister were both heading for the courthouse on Jamboree. His sports car was in the shop—again—and he was getting a ride from Kate who admittedly drove a far more reliable car than his. But his was by far the more attractive one.

Reaching the elevator first, Kullen pressed the down button. "So who's the lucky guy?"

God, this was going to be awful, Kate thought. She could feel it in her bones. She'd just begun enjoying the fact that her mother had stopped trying to work her dating life—or lack thereof—into every conversation they had.

"Some guy that her mother set her up with."

Kullen looked surprised. "I thought Nikki was against that kind of thing."

"She is. Her mother was underhanded about it." Kate frowned. "You know what this means, don't you?"

Amusement highlighted Kullen's face. "We start screening our calls?"

"Not funny, Kullen. In the past year Mom's finally slacked off. What this means is that she's going to go back to her old ways."

The elevator arrived. Getting on, they had the elevator to themselves for once. Kullen laughed. "You make it sound like a war."

Kate tossed her head. Jet-black hair strained against an army of pins. She always wore it up when she went to court. "That's because that's exactly what it is."

And they both knew it.

"I have to hand it to you, Maizie." Admiration fairly vibrated in Theresa Manetti's voice. "When you first started pushing this idea of using our businesses as a starting point for finding husbands for our girls, I really had my doubts."

Theresa looked at the woman she had known since the third grade. There were cards in her hand, but the weekly poker game she, Maizie and Cecilia were supposedly engaged in wasn't remotely holding her attention. Maizie had just announced that her daughter, Nikki, was engaged. Maizie had done it. She'd found a suitable man for her daughter just as she'd set out to do. It was a goal they all aspired to.

"But you did it," Theresa declared with unabashed admiration. "You found a man for Nikki *and* the two of you are still on speaking terms. That's quite a feat in my book. Can you find one of those for me?" When she saw Cecilia looking at her with a puzzled expression, Theresa realized she hadn't made herself clear. "I mean find a man for Kate." With a sigh, she said for the umpteenth time what they all knew was true. "Ever since that horrid Matthew made mincemeat out of her heart, she keeps saying she has no intentions of getting married. That her career is enough for her."

Maizie listened with a sympathetic ear. "What she needs is a good man to make her reassess her stand." There was unwavering confidence in her eyes as she assured her friend, "Between the three of us, we'll find someone."

"The three of us?" Cecilia repeated. There was a skeptical note in her voice.

This was never meant to be a solo operation. Maizie firmly believed that there was strength in numbers.

"Sure. I sell houses, you have a cleaning service that goes into some of the best residential homes in Orange County and *you*—" Maizie shifted her sharp blue eyes in Theresa's direction "—cater affairs. We come in close contact with a lot more people than the average person. I *know* we can find two decent men in that pool."

It wasn't that Theresa didn't want to help, it was just that she knew her weaknesses as well as her strengths. Her strengths were love and cooking. Under weaknesses she could list social relationships. "You're so much better than I am at this sort of thing," Theresa told her friends.

"Don't sell yourself short, Theresa. You are probably the sweetest person I know." She glanced at Cecilia. "No offense, Cecilia."

Cecilia looked completely unfazed. "None taken," she assured Maizie. "Everyone knows what a sweetheart Theresa is."

"Don't worry, Theresa. We have three times the playing field, three times the possibilities. Just stay alert and who knows?" She winked. "This time next year, we might all be shopping for baby clothes."

"From your mouth to God's ear," Theresa murmured.

"Exactly," Maizie agreed with a huge, amused grin.

Maizie's words were still ringing in her ears the next day when Theresa made her way into Republic National Bank's corporate office to meet with Jackson Wainwright, a prospective client. When a very efficient assistant brought her in to meet with the man who required her services, those words were replaced by two: breath-takingly gorgeous.

If Theresa could have drawn a picture of the man she knew would make her daughter sit up and take notice, this was the man she would have drawn.

Tall, almost incredibly handsome, Jackson Wain-wright brought the word *dashing* to mind. Granted it was an old-fashioned description, but looking at the raven-haired man with his chiseled profile, his magnetic blue eyes and his broad shoulders brought the heroes she'd grown up watching and worshipping on the silver screen to mind.

At the moment, the man was on the phone—and not happily so. Nodding a silent greeting, he tried to wrap up the call as he gestured for her to sit down in the chair before his desk.

It was obvious that the person on the other end of the line was a source of irritation to him, even though he kept his voice low.

"I don't have time to argue with you, Jonah. The answer is no, I'm not going to lend you any more money. You need money, come in and we'll see about getting you a job."

Theresa watched as he pressed his lips together and replaced the receiver without another word. The man on the other end of the line had obviously hung up.

The apologetic smile her client-to-be flashed her instantly lit up the room. "I'm sorry."

"There's no reason to apologize, Mr. Wainwright.

I'm the one who walked in on you." She knew she should just let the matter drop, but she wouldn't have been Theresa if she hadn't asked, "Family trouble?"

The fact that the woman asked—and guessed correctly—took him aback. Strained, his guard momentarily down, he heard himself asking, "How can you tell?"

Theresa nodded at his right hand. "Your knuckles turned white on the receiver." And then she smiled understandingly. "I've found that family can get to us the way no one else can. I love my two children more than life itself, but there are times I could strangle them."

Jackson wasn't secretive by nature, but neither did he bare his soul to the first stranger he encountered. Yet there was something warm and understanding about this woman—and he was on overload. A great deal of that was because of Jonah.

He'd expressly taken this transfer from San Francisco back to his old hometown because it was impossible to keep tabs on Jonah from over four hundred miles away. Lately, Jonah seemed even keener than usual to head down a path of self-destruction. He'd been in town less than a week and he was already at odds with his older brother. It had gotten to the point where it was a case of either talking about it, or exploding.

Jackson talked.

"I can certainly relate to that," he told the woman with the sweet, heart-shaped face. "My brother Jonah is a big, overgrown kid who just never grew up."

"Younger brother?" she guessed.

"Older," he told her, shaking his head. "That's the funny part. Jonah was supposed to be the wiser one."

"Not necessarily," she said kindly. "A person's temperament, not the order of his birth, has a great deal to do with the way he—or she—reacts to responsibility."

About to comment, Jackson stopped himself. "I'm sorry, I didn't ask you to come here to listen to me complain."

Theresa smiled at him. "That's one of the fringe benefits of doing business with Theresa's Catering. I'm Theresa." She leaned forward, extending her hand to him.

Jackson felt himself responding to the woman's guileless warmth immediately. "I'm very pleased to meet you, Theresa."

He had a good, strong handshake, Theresa noted. Her father had always maintained that you could tell a lot about a man by his handshake. Jackson's said he was a man who was not afraid to take charge and who had the courage of his convictions. She liked that.

"Have you been your brother's keeper for long?" she asked with sincere interest.

The question made him laugh. He hadn't thought of himself in those terms, but this soft-voiced woman had hit the nail right on the head.

"Ever since my parents died," he told her. Right now, it felt like an eternity ago.

This transfer that he had initiated came with its own baggage, which only added to the weight pressing down on his shoulders. On top of that, the family lawyer,

Morton Bloom, the official juggler of all the balls, hadn't woken up last Monday morning. Seemingly healthy and robust, the sixty-eight-year-old man had died in his sleep. He had no partners, no one to step into his shoes.

This just when he'd made up his mind to have Mort change the way Jonah's trust fund had been worded.

Feeling vulnerable and strangely connected to this woman who was so easy to talk to, Jackson, half kidding, asked, "You wouldn't happen to know the name of a good lawyer, would you?"

He hadn't really expected an answer, but he got one. "I know several, Mr. Wainwright. What kind of a lawyer are you looking for?"

"A patient one." Instantly, he flashed that smile Theresa was fairly certain Kate would find bone-melting. She knew that if she was twenty-nine years young, she would have. "Sorry," he apologized for the second time in five minutes, "that was flippant, although the lawyer I need would *have* to be patient because part of his job would be to deal with my brother. I need a family lawyer," he specified. Jackson sighed. "It's been a rough few days, Mrs. Manetti. Now, about the party—"

As a rule, Theresa never interrupted a client. But this could be the only opening that would allow her to introduce Jackson to her daughter. So she broke her own rule and cut in. "I know two excellent family lawyers."

Jackson stopped, surprised. And then he shrugged. What did he have to lose? "Why don't you give me their names when we finish?"

Theresa had a better idea. "Why don't I give them to you now and get that out of the way?" she countered. "Then we're free to concentrate on the details of the party."

"All right," he said agreeably. "Give me their names and numbers."

Theresa wrote both names down, and just this once, she decided to go along with Kate's initial insistence on using her initials to hide her gender in an attempt to gain a foothold in what still was a male-dominated world.

Jackson took the paper from her when she finished writing. The neat, careful lettering impressed him. You didn't see handwriting like that anymore, he thought. And then he noted the names. *K. C. Manetti and Kullen Manetti.*

"Manetti?" he repeated. Amused, he asked, "Any relation?"

Theresa returned his smile. "Those children I sometimes want to strangle?" she said, recalling her initial reference. "Those are their names. They also happen to be excellent lawyers," she said proudly, adding, "They take after their late father."

"I'll give them a call," he told her, pocketing the paper.

Theresa drew in a deep breath, mentally crossing her fingers. She'd done all she could—for now. "Why don't you tell me what you had in mind."

Jackson blinked. "Excuse me?"

"For the party," Theresa prompted.

"Right. Sorry." What was that, his third apology to

this woman? Yet somehow, he felt that she understood. Her eyes were sympathetic. "I'm just a bit on overload right now."

"If this is a bad time," Theresa began.

She was perfectly willing to postpone any further discussion until it was more convenient for Jackson. As far as she was concerned, she'd already accomplished far more than she ever thought she could. The sooner she left, the sooner she would be able to drive to St Anne's and light a few candles. Never hurt to have backup.

"Between you and me, Mrs. Manetti, I've got a feeling that there's not going to be a better time," Jackson confided. "At least not for a while." He settled back at his desk. "Let me tell you what I had in mind...."

There was a quick rap on Kate's door and then Kullen poked his head in. "Hey, Kate, I need a favor."

Impatient because she was trying to finish something, Kate spared him a fleeting look.

"I'm not going to call another one of your five-night stands and tell her you've been called out of town. You want to break up with somebody? You're a big boy, you can do it yourself."

"First of all, she's not a five-night stand. I've been seeing Allison for two weeks now—"

"Alert the media," Kate deadpanned.

He pretended not to hear. "And two, it's nothing like that. I didn't realize that I'm due in Tustin in half an hour. Sheila accidentally scheduled a new client to come in at twelve-thirty. Do me a favor and take him for me."

She stopped typing and leaned back in her chair to look at her brother. He sounded entirely too innocent. "What's the catch?"

Kullen spread his hands wide, giving her his best innocent look. "No catch. Jackson Wainwright's a new client. His family lawyer suddenly died on him just as Wainwright needed to have some business straightened out. I gather it has to do with a trust fund." Kullen cocked his head as he looked at Kate. "You're up to that, aren't you?" He knew that nothing got his sister going faster than a challenge to her abilities. "Just start the ball rolling for me. We've got the same last name. He'll think you're me."

"Only if the man's legally blind," she pointed out.

"I am the prettier one," Kullen agreed, then ducked, laughing, as Kate threw a crumpled sheet of paper at him. She missed hitting him by a good two feet. "You throw like a girl," he crowed.

"There's a reason for that." Kate glanced at her desk calendar. "I can give this Wainwright guy half an hour, no more. After that, I've got to go to the courthouse to file Mrs. Greenfield's name change."

Kullen glanced at his watch. "Gotta run."

"You owe me one," Kate called after his retreating back.

"I'm good for it." Kullen smiled to himself as he made his way down the hall.

* * *

Kate was so immersed in what she was doing, she didn't hear the knock on her door until it came again, a little louder this time. Kate blew out a breath. *Now what?*

Her life was measured out in fifteen-minute increments. It was twelve-twenty. She had ten more minutes before Kullen's new client showed up.

"Come in, Sheila," she called out without bothering to look up. Not wanting to lose her place, she continued typing. "I'll be with you in a minute. I just need to finish this before my brother's castoff comes in." Kate heard the door open and close. "Whatever you're bringing, just drop it on my desk." She typed in the final line. "There, done!" she declared triumphantly.

Looking up, Kate was startled to see an incredibly handsome man in a custom tailored suit. Moreover, he was sitting in front of her desk, smiling at her. How— and when—had that happened?

"Hello," she said a little uncertainly.

"Hi."

When he didn't say anything else, she asked, "And you are?"

The smile on his lips deepened just a touch. "Your brother's castoff, I believe."

Oh God, why hadn't she looked up when she heard the knock? And what was Sheila doing, allowing clients to wander around by themselves? The woman was practically a fixture in the office ever since her father had hired her, but that was no excuse to let a client just walk in.

"Jackson Wainwright?" she guessed.

The man inclined his head. "The very same."

Damage control. She cleared her throat. "Of course I meant castoff in the best possible sense of the word."

There was a hint of amusement in his eyes. "I didn't realize that there *was* a best possible sense of the word regarding castoffs."

"I'm so sorry, I—" Kate could feel the rush of color coming up to her cheeks. Blushing was one of the things her father used to upbraid her for, telling her she'd never make a good lawyer as long as she had that flaw. She'd thought that she'd conquered it.

Obviously she was having a relapse.

Kate rose to her feet. "Excuse me," she said to Jackson as she passed him, striding out of her office. From the corner of her eye, she saw that her brother's twelve-thirty appointment rose to his feet. To leave, as well?

But when she opened the door again a beat later, Jackson Wainwright was still standing right where she'd left him, looking somewhat bewildered as he stared at the door.

With a purposeful, confident stride, Kate reentered the office, walked up to Kullen's client and extended her hand to him. "Hello, I'm Katherine Manetti." She saw the uncertain expression on the man's handsome face deepen. She could almost guess what he was thinking. Smiling serenely—she said, "This is called, 'first impression, take two.'"

For a moment, she thought he was going to walk out.

The sound of Jackson Wainwright's deep, resonant laughter told Kate that he'd decided to stay. Which meant she'd just gotten that second chance she was after.

Kate released the breath she hadn't realized until now that she'd been holding.

Chapter Two

Sitting up a little straighter in her chair, Kate discreetly took another breath, smiled and asked, "So, what is it that can I do for you, Mr. Wainwright?"

Several things came to mind, entirely unbidden, surprising him as much as they would have her, if he'd said them aloud. Luckily, he'd learned long ago to keep his own counsel and hold his tongue. But just for the moment, because the last two weeks had been unbelievably hectic and stressful, what with tying up all the loose ends where he'd worked, packing up all his belongings and dealing with his brother far more than he was accustomed to, Jackson allowed himself a single quick flight of fancy.

It coaxed an entirely different sort of smile from his lips.

His audience of one caught her breath again. This had to be the most seductive, sexy smile she had seen in a very long time. Lucky thing that she was immune to sexy. She had Matthew to thank for that. Matthew and the string of good-looking, soulless men who'd come before him.

A full five seconds of silence lapsed before Jackson finally spoke. "I'm new in town." Realizing that wasn't actually a true statement, he corrected himself. "Well, old-new."

"Excuse me?"

"I grew up in Bedford," he explained.

"But then you spread your wings and flew?"

He smiled again. "I flew."

His eyes crinkled when he smiled, she noted. The next moment, she upbraided herself for even noticing. But at least he didn't take themselves too seriously, and that was a good thing. "And how long has it been since you've 'flown'?"

Now that he was back, it seemed like only yesterday that he'd left home. But it wasn't. "A dozen years—if you count college."

"College counts," she affirmed. Because she saw no reason to curtail her curiosity and the information might prove useful to know down the line, she asked, "What brought you back?"

"A promotion—and family business," he finally said after a thoughtful pause.

"Which has the greater weight?" She kept her eyes on his, fairly certain that she would be able to tell if he was just paying lip service, or if he ultimately meant what he said. She'd become very good at spotting liars, also thanks to Matthew. Mining some good out of the experience was the only way she could forgive herself for being such a fool.

There was another pause on his part. And then he said, "I'm not sure yet."

Actually, Jackson thought, that was a lie. He knew damn well which of the two carried the greater weight for him. Knew, too, that he resented it for that reason. It had been drummed into his soul that family always came first. And if that wasn't enough, his mother's deathbed request was that he "look out for Jonah." Because he'd loved her, he'd promised.

And now, if not for his promise, he would have been content to spend the rest of his life living and working in the Bay area. San Francisco was an exciting city. There was always something going on, something to entertain a man, or to challenge him. The restaurants weren't too shabby, either. He considered himself a cosmopolitan kind of man and San Francisco suited his purposes just fine, thank you.

But despite the lure of the city, he couldn't very well turn his back on Jonah, especially since he was all Jonah had—whether Jonah acknowledged that little fact or not. Moreover, he was just possibly all that stood between Jonah and absolute self-destruction.

Kate nodded, digesting his answer. "At least you're honest."

He flashed a smile. "I have to be. It's written into my contract." The puzzled look returned to her eyes. Jackson elaborated. "I'm a district manager at Republic National Bank," he explained. "People like their bank executives honest."

She thought of the current economic climate. Kate had no doubt that it would continue in its present venue for a while to come. She was, at bottom—when the matter didn't involve romance—too optimistic a person to entertain the idea that it would ultimately collapse. This was what made her her mother's daughter rather than her father's. Anthony Manetti had been a born pessimist.

"These days," she replied, "they just like them to be solvent—and to refrain from recklessly spending the share holders' assets."

This time, the smile on his lips held no humor behind it. "Sadly, that's my brother's department. Which brings us back to why I'm here. Our longtime family lawyer, Morton Bloom, died somewhere in the night between last Sunday and Monday."

Kate realized that she was being "auditioned" for the position of his new family lawyer. She tried to look properly sympathetic. "I'm sorry to hear that."

What he heard in her voice—sincerity mixed with compassion—caught him off guard. He could think of only one explanation. "You knew him?"

"No." She'd never met the man. After that fiasco

with Matt—which included mistaking him for a decent human being—Kullen was the only lawyer she socialized with these days. "But you did. I imagine that when someone you've known for a long time dies, it does shake you up to a degree."

Until she said that, he wasn't sure how he felt one way or another about Mort's death, other than being annoyed because it was an inconvenience. Now, instead of coming down for the week to conduct his business with the lawyer, he had to move down here, watch out for Jonah and search for a new lawyer, all while familiarizing himself with an entirely new set of people and terrain in the district he was taking on.

He supposed his attitude toward Mort could be viewed as rather callous. He wasn't a callous person by nature. He liked to think of himself as compassionate. But anything that had to do with Jonah instantly had his back going up.

It was a far cry from when he was a boy and he'd idolized his brother. Sunny, gregarious, with a knack of making people forgive him, Jonah had been the center of everyone's universe—until he and his parents realized just how weak a character Jonah had.

Jackson could still remember accidentally coming across his mother sitting alone in the dark in her room, her fingers all but knotted together. She was softly crying to herself. It was the first time Jonah had been taken to the hospital. He'd been ten and Jonah had been fourteen. He'd thought his brother was sick. In a way, he supposed he'd been right. Drug addiction was a sickness and Jonah had overdosed.

That was when the crown that he had placed on his brother's head first began to slip. He'd always been fiercely protective of his mother and anything that hurt her instantly earned his fury. He remembered wanting to punch Jonah out despite the fact that his brother was twice his size.

"After a while you get used to it," he continued when he realized that too much silence had gone by. That had to sound cold and distant to the woman. He wasn't exactly sure why, but he wasn't comfortable with her thinking of him in that light. "My parents died in a car accident," he explained. "And there was a girl when I was in college…"

Jackson punctuated his sentence with a shrug. He wasn't about to go there right now. Wasn't about to revisit the way he'd felt when his college roommate had shaken him awake to tell him that Rachel had been struck by a drunk driver who'd lost his way and somehow had wound up on the campus. The man was going ninety on the twilight-darkened streets when he hit her. The driver wouldn't have stopped except that he wound up plowing his brand-new Ferrari into a tree. Rachel had been making her way through the crosswalk, on her way to her dorm when he ran her down. Both she and the drunken bastard were dead before the ambulance arrived.

Kate could almost literally feel the emotions vibrating around Wainwright. Was he telling her the truth, or was this something he was just saying for effect? From her experience, handsome men liked to cast themselves in a good light early on.

"I'm sorry," she said quietly.

"Thank you," Jackson answered stiffly. "But I'm here about the living." He thought of how reckless Jonah was becoming and what he'd gotten himself into this time. "Although I'm not sure just how much longer that's going to be true."

"You're going to have to explain that."

Yes, he supposed he should. "My brother has an addictive personality." All the signs had been there from the beginning, but no one wanted to admit it. "Every time he cleans up his act in one department, he latches onto something else, another crutch to help him stand upright—or reasonably so." Jackson paused to recall the correct order. "He has, by turns, been a drug addict, an alcoholic, a religious zealot, a food addict and—this is his latest craze—a gambling addict."

Being his brother had to be a heavy burden, Kate thought, suddenly very grateful that all Kullen did was collect lightweight girlfriends who had the IQ of a shoelace. "I'm sorry to hear that."

He laughed shortly. "If he didn't have an addictive personality, I wouldn't be here, so for you this might be a good thing."

That was rather a cynical remark, despite the fact that he punctuated it with a smile. "You do plan to explain that, too, right?"

Regarding her for a moment, Jackson made a decision. "I do, but not on an empty stomach. Do you have any plans for lunch?"

That caught her off guard. "Other than eating it, no. But I do have to file some papers at the courthouse this afternoon."

He had to get back to the office himself, but that wasn't for a couple of hours. Would she be leaving before then? "Is there a set time?"

Although she'd planned to get there in another half hour or so, in actuality she just had to get there before they closed for the day. "Before five."

He nodded. "Good. We'll be done with phase one by then."

The man definitely talked in riddles. "Phase one?"

"Getting to know each other."

A red light went off in her head. Was this a business meeting, or was it all a sham? Her eyes narrowed. "I'm afraid I don't follow."

"You won't be following. You'll be in my car. Parking will be easier that way." He was already rising to his feet.

Kate put up her hand like a traffic cop. "Wait, hold it," she ordered. He needed to clear this up for her. If he was a client, she'd cut him a little slack. But if he was trying to come on to her, there was no way she was going to go along with this. She didn't need another good-looking man creating havoc in her life. "Just why do we need to get to know each other?"

"Well, it doesn't have to be reciprocal if you choose not to ask any questions, but I for one need to get to know you." His eyes held hers as he made his point. "You don't expect me to just entrust the family fortune to you without knowing who I'm dealing with."

Maybe being in a crowded restaurant with this man wasn't such a bad idea. Although they were speaking mostly in generalities, there was this undercurrent of intimacy she found impossible to shake—or to understand. And when he looked at her like that, she caught herself thinking things that weren't entirely professional even though her guard was up.

"I'm assuming that you're here on someone's recommendation," she speculated. A recommendation should count for something with this man.

Sitting down again, Jackson smiled and she found that, just for a split second, she needed to remind herself to breathe. Alarms started going off in her head—but she couldn't very well just walk away from a client. The head of the firm, Harrison Rothchild, her father's successor, wasn't a very understanding or forgiving man.

"I am, actually," he told her, "but the recommendation was hardly unbiased."

She could see how that would happen. All of her clients as well as Kullen's were completely satisfied with their work. They were on retainer with a good many clients, something that actually *did* please Rothchild no end.

"Most of our clients tend to be quite sold on us after

they make use of our services." She did her best to go the extra mile for her clients and *none* of them remotely looked as good or seemed as charming as Jackson Wainwright.

Damn it, where had that come from?

His smile only widened, as if he was privy to some private joke he wasn't quite ready to share. "That might be true, but this recommendation, I suspect, started out biased."

"Forgive me, Mr. Wainwright, but I have to ask. Do most banking executives talk in some kind of code the way you do?"

All too often, he was given to beginning sentences in his head and voicing them out loud only when he came to the middle, so he took no offense.

"All right, let me be plain."

"Please." Although she truly doubted that was possible. Men who looked like Jackson Wainwright didn't even have a nodding acquaintance with the word *plain*. She was fairly certain that Jackson Wainwright was accustomed to women falling all over themselves to garner his favor.

"Your mother recommended you. Well, she recommended both of you, although she didn't mention that K. C. Manetti was actually her daughter. What she did say was that K. C. Manetti and Kullen Manetti were her children."

Her mind had temporarily frozen the moment he'd uttered the word *mother*. Her eyes were on his as she repeated, "My mother."

"Yes." Then, to keep her from asking if perhaps he'd

made a mistake, Jackson described the woman in question to her. "Petite, well-dressed lady. Lively eyes, trim figure, a smile that's rather reminiscent of yours now that I think of it, and—"

For the second time since he'd walked into her office, Kate held up her hand. "My mother, yes, that's her. I get it." What did her mother do, buttonhole every good-looking man she came across and try to steer him directly into her path?

Mother, she silently cried, *you know better.*

Knowing that there would be no peace for her until she knew, Kate had to ask. "What were you doing, talking to my mother?"

"Hiring her actually," Jackson said. "I'm having a small 'get acquainted' party at the bank—I'm the new district manager—and I needed a caterer. Your mother comes very highly recommended. The branch manager had her cater his Christmas party."

Kate had to give her mother that, even though right now, there was a very strong urge to wrap her fingers around her mother's slender neck and just squeeze. Just for a second. Just until she promised never to do this kind of thing again.

When she spoke, restrained anger made Kate's voice sound very formal. "My mother's very good at what she does."

"How about you?" he asked, turning the tables, his eyes pinning her in her place. "Are you very good at what you do?"

She never flinched or looked away. However uncertain she was in her chaotic private life, that was how confident she was in her professional one.

"I am excellent," she assured him. "And I can give you a list of references if you like. Current clients," she added.

Still sitting at her desk, Kate shifted in her chair so she could face her computer. She hit the keyboard, bringing the computer back around from the land of saved watts and slumber. The picture of a beach at sunset faded away and a desktop full of folders popped up. She was about to open one of them when he stopped her.

"Thanks, but don't bother. I like making up my own mind."

She dropped her hand. "And you can do that over lunch." It wasn't a question, just an assumption built on what he'd said a few minutes ago. She did her best to bank down the trace of sarcasm.

He smiled, inclining his head. "Exactly."

If lunch was what he wanted, lunch was what he would get. But not before she had a question of her own answered.

"All right. But before we go, I need to know just what sort of services you'll require."

That really sounded like a loaded question that could be answered in a variety of ways, some of which could get him slapped. Where had that come from? he silently demanded. Granted she was attractive—exceedingly attractive—but that wasn't the reason he was here. What was going on with him?

Maybe, he theorized, he'd been all business for so long, something inside of him was rebelling, trying to break free. Trying to remember what life was all about outside of the pressures of the banking industry.

Or maybe this was his own version of a meltdown. He couldn't honestly say. He *could* say that he had to keep his answer straight and business oriented. Otherwise, there would be repercussions. Serious ones.

"To give you the *Reader's Digest* version, my parents doted on Jonah. He was the firstborn and the golden child. He was—and still can be—very charming and engaging when he wants to be. However, that didn't change the fact that he has a very weak character and my parents eventually had to admit that Jonah had to be saved from himself. So, when they had their will drawn up—they essentially divided the money between Jonah and me—they made sure that his was in the form of a trust fund. Each month a certain amount—generous even by today's standards—would be doled out to Jonah, but the principle would remain intact and in trust until Jonah's thirty-fifth birthday, at which time he would get it all." Jackson paused for a moment, silently wishing that Jonah was the brother he wanted him to be, a brother who didn't need to constantly be reined in or policed. He hated being the bad guy. "Jonah turns thirty-five next month."

It was easy to read between the lines. "And you don't want him inheriting the money."

"No, I don't," Jackson agreed bluntly. "If he gets his

hands on the money, he'll either be dead in a month, or the money'll be gone in six. Or maybe both. If my brother survives, he'll be in debt in seven. It's his nature and although I have bailed him out in the past, his problem keeps mushrooming and eventually, there won't be enough money in the world to cover his debts."

Jackson knew that what he was asking for wasn't easy, nor was it strictly orthodox. Legally, Jonah had every right to expect to finally be united with his inheritance. Jackson was trying to have his parents' wishes and authority usurped by finding a loophole and extending the age limit on the trust. The only reason his parents had picked thirty-five was because they'd honestly believed Jonah would finally get his act together by then.

Surprise, folks. He's still a kid.

He looked at Kate. "Are you up to that, Ms. Manetti, or is it too much of a challenge for your firm?"

Kate raised her chin. "I don't know about my firm, but I enjoy a challenge, Mr. Wainwright."

"Good to hear. All right." On his feet, he rounded the desk and stood beside her chair. "Let's go to lunch."

She'd thought that the matter was settled, despite all his talk about eating. Obviously not. How much more was he going to ask her? Oh well, it *was* lunchtime. She might as well indulge him.

Taking her purse out of the bottom drawer, Kate closed the drawer and rose to her feet. "Am I still auditioning for the part of your lawyer?"

"Yes, you are," he confirmed, deliberately keeping a straight face. But there was a smile in his eyes. "But right now, I'd say you have the inside track on getting the part." She looked at him and it was obvious that she wanted to say something in response. "What?"

Her suspicions had been stirred, but for now, she decided to keep them to herself. "Nothing."

"I require truthfulness at all times."

"All right." She stopped just shy of the door. "Are you really looking for a lawyer?"

"What would I be doing here if I wasn't?"

Infrequent phone calls and contact not withstanding, she knew her mother. Knew how Theresa Manetti thought. Nikki was getting married and she wasn't. Her mother was bent on changing that. Somewhere there was a saint's statue melting because of all the candles that were being lit in front of it. But to ask this man if he'd been sent here to pretend to need her services, all under the guise of meeting and dating her, somehow sounded very conceited. On the chance that she was wrong and he *was* on the level, Kate swallowed her question and forced a smile to her lips.

"You're right," she agreed amiably. "Why would you be here if you didn't need a lawyer?" She glanced at her watch. How did it get to be so late? Especially when it felt as if time was standing still? "If we're going to go to lunch, we'd better get moving."

In his opinion, Theresa Manetti's daughter was moving just fine as it was.

"Your choice," he told her out of the blue. "The restaurant," he explained. "I've been gone a long time and things have changed a lot around Bedford. My favorite restaurant's history, so I leave it up to you to pick one."

"What was your favorite restaurant?" she asked as they walked out of her office.

There was a fond smile on his lips as he said, "Gin-Ling's."

"You like Chinese food?" It was rather a safe deduction.

"I'm rather partial to it, yes."

Well, they had that in common. The next second, she banished the thought from her head. She was *not* going to fall into her mother's trap. "I know a wonderful Chinese restaurant," she told him.

His expression brightened just a shade. "Sounds promising. You can give me the directions when we get to the car."

If nothing else, he thought, holding the door open for her, he was going to get a good meal out of this and perhaps discover a new favorite restaurant.

And if he was lucky, Jackson added silently, he'd wind up getting a very attractive family lawyer to boot.

Things could have been worse.

Chapter Three

Located in the center of an outdoor mall, the China Pearl was a modest-size restaurant that saw more than its fair share of traffic both for lunch and for dinner. There was a bar, small but well stocked, to the right of the entrance and the reservation desk. Four rows of six booths each composed the rest of the floor plan.

After leading them to a booth, the hostess gave them dark green bound menus to peruse and quietly faded back to her post.

Kate pretended to look at the menu. It hadn't changed in over a year. At this point, she knew it by heart. What she didn't know was very much about the man sitting across from her. Was he on the level or the first of an endless line of setups arranged by her mother? A little probing chatter wouldn't be out of order to assess the situation.

"So," she placed the menu on the table in front of her, "are you here in Bedford permanently, or is this just a temporary move until you can straighten things out?"

If it were only that simple, Jackson thought. "Unfortunately, this isn't anything I can put a bandage on," he answered. "I've already tried that. Jonah needs someone in his life on a regular basis, not someone who checks in on him once a week." No matter how many questions he barked into the phone, he thought.

Wainwright seemed to take his responsibility seriously, she thought. Since she'd entered family law, she'd discovered that a lot of people bristled when it came to doing what needed to be done, feeling shackled by "the ties that bind." Was Wainwright just paying lip service in order to make himself look good, or did he really mean what he told her, that he wanted to protect his brother from himself? She supposed it shouldn't really matter to her. Either way, it began to sound as if he really did need a lawyer. Her curiosity was aroused. "That sounds like it can get to be a pretty heavy burden."

Jackson shrugged as he scanned the menu. "It already is. Jonah doesn't like being 'supervised,' he likes being indulged." And that was his parents' fault. Jonah was artistically gifted and, in an attempt to nurture that talent and make it bear fruit, his parents, especially his mother, bent over backward to accommodate Jonah. He loved his brother, but he wasn't about to let him run right over him.

Jackson looked up from the menu. "I'll be honest with you. I've got a feeling that was why Mort suffered his heart attack. The stress of trying to keep my brother in line and out of jail finally got to him."

"Jail?" she asked.

"Disorderly in public," he recited. "Bathing in the fountain in front of city hall at one in the morning—"

"That doesn't sound as if it merited jail."

"Naked," Jackson added.

"Oh. I'd better stock up on blood-pressure medicine, then," Kate quipped. The corners of her mouth curved as she allowed her amusement to surface. "If you don't mind my making an observation, you don't really know how to sell something, do you?"

His eyes held hers. She couldn't quite make up her mind if his were pure blue or if they had a touch of gray in them.

Doesn't matter if they're purple. He's just a client, remember? her inner voice chided.

"I just want you to know up front what you're getting into, Kate," he told her simply. "If you'd rather not have to deal with someone who can make you contemplate justifiable homicide even as he charms the socks off you, I need to know now so I can find someone else to handle this trust-fund restructuring."

"I'm no stranger to contemplating justifiable homicide," she assured him with a smile. "I have a very charming brother of my own."

Their server, a petite young woman in a rich, royal

blue dress with a Mandarin collar and two discreet side slits that stopped just short of the middle of her thigh, brought them a pot of tea and backed away, her silence indicating they could take their time ordering.

Picking up the teapot, Kate filled the two thimble-size cups before them. "Tell me more about Jonah."

Jackson took a breath. Where did he begin? And how did he say this without coming across as bitter? He wasn't bitter, just tired—and losing hope that Jonah would ever come to his senses. "He'll try to charm you into giving him what he wants. If that fails—"

"It will," Kate assured him.

In his experience, women had trouble saying no to Jonah, but he wasn't about to make any assumptions about this new lawyer until he had an opportunity to watch her interact with his brother. "Then he'll try to intimidate you, except that he's not very good at that. Mostly he uses guilt."

"Guilt?"

Jackson nodded. "He wields it like a top-flight surgeon wields a scalpel. He'll make you feel guilty for turning him down. Jonah's very good at manipulating people. He's accumulated a lifetime of experience, working on my parents."

Listening, Kate detected an undercurrent of more than one emotion. His relationship with his brother, she decided, was complicated. "Are you two close?"

Not anymore, Jackson thought. Something else to hold against Jonah. He missed what they'd once had. Missed being proud of his brother instead of drained by him.

He took a sip of tea, letting the warm liquid wind through him before answering. "We were when I was a kid. These days, I'm the bad guy." He laughed shortly. "Jonah's closer to total strangers he hooks up with at clubs than he is to me. There's always someone with him who's his new best friend."

Kate studied Jackson as he spoke, forcing herself to focus on what he said, not the way he looked as he said it. Looks, the crackle of chemistry, none of that mattered anymore, she thought fiercely. It had taken her a long time, but she'd finally learned her lesson. Good-looking men were only hunters and gatherers of women. You couldn't build a stable life with a gatherer.

"You love him a great deal, don't you?" she asked as he paused.

Jackson shrugged, taking another sip. "That has nothing to do with it."

"It's nothing to be embarrassed about," she said matter-of-factly. "If you didn't love your brother, you'd let him get his hands on his share of the inheritance, walk away and go on with your life."

"Maybe I just don't want to be connected to a scandal and if Jonah has free rein to do what he wants with his money, there'll be serious repercussions. I guarantee it. And I'd rather avoid that if I could."

"Understandable," she agreed. "But even a few of our presidents have had to deal with the annoying specter of clueless, classless brothers whose actions kept landing them on page one. They all survived." Kate raised her eyes to his. She considered herself a fairly good judge of character when it came to her clients. She just failed miserably when judging men on a personal level. "You strike me as a man who knows that the people who count will judge him on his own merits."

"Maybe you've forgotten the purpose of this lunch, but it was for me to get to know you, not the other way around."

Amusement curved her mouth. "Things don't always go according to plan."

"No," he agreed, thinking of the life he'd once planned with Rachel. "They certainly don't."

Their server returned, a silent, genial inquiry in her eyes. Kate nodded and ordered first. "I'll have the lobster Cantonese, egg-drop soup and a spring roll."

Inclining her head, the server turned toward Jackson.

He hadn't made his selection yet. Hearing what Kate ordered, he decided to go with that. "That sounds good," he said to the server, surrendering his menu. "Make that two."

The young woman smiled, nodded and retreated with their menus.

Kate folded her hands before her. "All right, what would you like to know?" she asked the moment their server had left.

What you'd look like, waking up beside me in the morning.

He had no idea where that had come from. He did know that he would have felt more comfortable if his lawyer had been less attractive. Or a man. It was hard to keep his mind on business when the sight of her kept ushering in completely unrelated stray thoughts.

"What would you like to tell me?" he asked politely.

She poured more tea into her cup, then raised it to her lips, buying herself some time.

This was an odd way to conduct a first interview, she thought. Wainwright had placed control, at least temporarily, back in her hands. Was that to make her feel comfortable? Or to get her to relax before he sprang his real questions on her?

And then there was that tiny, nagging thought. Her mother had sent him. There was still a possibility, growing smaller now she had to admit, that this was all a setup.

"That if you're looking for a good lawyer, I won't disappoint you." Then, in case he thought she was bragging, Kate gave him a little background information. "My brother and I are third-generation lawyers. My father helped found this firm. *His* father was a criminal lawyer. Grandpa had his own one-man practice," she elaborated. "Most of the time he defended people who, without him, would have had nowhere to turn for proper representation. I'm not afraid of hard work," she continued. "My brother will tell you that arguing's in my blood. If you decided to go with my firm—with me—I'll do my very best to accomplish whatever you ask me to."

The last line hung in the air between them and she prayed he couldn't interpret that the wrong way, because suddenly, they sounded like a sensual promise to her ear. What was wrong with her? She was usually sharper than that.

Taking a breath, she delivered her closing argument. "And if you're afraid that your brother will sweet-talk me into bending the rules for him, don't be. You pay the bills, you get to make the calls," she assured him. "I'm just the instrument that makes whatever you require done come true."

"An instrument, eh?" he repeated. The analogy amused him, but he made no further comment on it. He had a more important question. "Do you really think that you can keep Jonah's trust fund safe?"

"Yes," she said confidently.

"How?"

"It won't be the easiest thing to overhaul," she admitted. "But I think there's a way around it. Your parents initially had the trust fund drawn up because they didn't consider Jonah mature enough to manage his own money, right?"

"That about sums it up," he told her.

"If I can show that Jonah's maturity level hasn't progressed to the level of an average thirty-five-year-old man, the level your parents felt was right to finally allow him to have control over his share of the money, we might be able to push the time limit back, make it more flexible by specifying that certain conditions have to be met. And if they're not met, the present arrangement of giving him a certain amount every month will continue. Indefinitely," she concluded.

"And just how do you intend to accomplish that?" he pressed.

"By compiling reports on your brother's irresponsible behavior—interviewing his friends, any officers who might have been called in because of complaints by his neighbors or who issued tickets for reckless driving, things like that. It gives us a leg to stand on. I can submit the report to a judge and have the trust sustained," she told him. She expected Jackson to express relief. Instead, she saw a frown forming on his lips. "Is something wrong?"

He was thinking of the repercussions of filing this sort of a report. "I don't want him to be publicly humiliated."

"Doesn't have to be publicly," she assured him. "It just has to go to a sympathetic judge." He needed more, she thought. He really *did* care for his brother. "I won't do anything without first running it by you. Fair enough?"

He nodded. "Fair enough." Their server was back. As she divvied up the different plates, placing a small bowl of soup before each of them, the conversation was temporarily tabled. When she left, Jackson said to Kate, "You've got the job."

Kate had already assumed that she had, but she thanked him politely for the confirmation, then went on to tell him, "I'm going to need all the papers from the original trust fund filing as soon as possible."

"I'll have to look for them." He thought for a moment, trying to remember where his copy was. His best bet was to secure the copy that had to still be in Mort's

office. The late family lawyer had to be the most orga-
nized man he'd ever met. "Soon as I get my hands on
them, I'll have a courier bring them to your office. Better
yet, why don't you come by Republic National's corporate offices this Friday after five and I'll hand them
over to you personally?" Because she looked slightly
puzzled at the time he mentioned, Jackson explained,
"That party I'm having your mother cater, it's set for
Friday in our conference room. It's meant to be a kind
of icebreaker to get better acquainted with the people
who'll be working for me. It'll be nice to have someone
there who *doesn't* work for me." He smiled at the
thought.

"Technically speaking," Kate pointed out, "you're
my boss."

He wasn't deterred. "Then, for the evening, we won't
speak technically." His voice softened a little. "I need a
friendly face I can trust to be honest," he said. "It'll
help me relax."

"Wouldn't want you tense," she murmured. *Or me,
either,* she added silently. And she was despite all her
best efforts not to be.

Kate lost more time than she'd intended to. It was a
few minutes after four when she finally got back to her
office. After having lunch with her new client—there
was no way she was giving him back to Kullen after
laying this much groundwork—she had him drive her
back not to the office but to its parking structure.

Once there, she had just enough time to dash to her own car and drive off to the county courthouse. She already had all the papers she needed in order to file for Mrs. Greenfeld's official name change. She'd packed them earlier in a spare briefcase she had locked in the trunk of her car.

The simple task took close to two hours thanks to the fact that the courtroom was packed. Nothing new there. While she entertained the idea of just going home from there, she had too much waiting for her on her desk. With a sigh, she drove back to the Bedford-based firm. With any luck, she'd be able to go home by six.

But probably not.

Sinking into her ergonomically designed leather chair, Kate barely had time to let out a long sigh before Kullen stuck his head in.

A feeling of déjà vu slid over her.

"So, how did it go?" he asked cheerfully, closing the door behind him. He took a couple of steps in, then stopped to study her and see how receptive she was. He wanted to be ready for a quick escape, should the need for that arise. Because he knew his mother had sent this new client to them and had expressly told him to make sure that Kate was the one who took him on as a client.

Kate glared at him. "I shouldn't even talk to you."

He winced. "That bad, huh?"

She shook her head. "No, actually it wasn't bad at all."

"So he was good-looking?"

That caught her up short. Kullen had never met with

Wainwright so he would have no idea what he looked like. "That has nothing to do with it. Why would you even ask that?"

Not wanting to let on that their mother had mentioned that little fact, he glossed over it and shrugged. "You know me, I'm always saying sexist things."

"Did Mom put you up to your vanishing act?"

He almost asked how she knew but managed to catch himself in time. "No, I told you, Sheila accidentally scheduled both appointments at the same time. Thanks to your being such a workaholic, I was able to keep my original appointment."

Kate saw right through that. Her eyes narrowed, pinning her brother in place. "With Allison?"

He would have denied it if he'd thought that it would work. But he knew it was useless. Somehow, Kate *always* knew when he wasn't on the level with her. "Why can't I lie to you?"

Kate laughed, shaking her head. "God knows it's not for lack of trying on your part. But I know you too well. I know all your tells."

"Tells?" he echoed.

"Your nostrils flare when you lie." She frowned, thinking of the woman her brother had just wasted time with. "I thought that by now you would have moved on from that bimbo."

Humor curved his mouth, even as he tried to sound serious. "Have a little respect, you're speaking of the bimbo I love."

She sincerely doubted that her brother had ever been in love. The strongest emotion he'd probably ever experienced was infatuation. "At least for today."

"All any of us have, Katie, is the moment," he deadpanned.

Kate sighed. Maybe she didn't get out these days, but her brother got out *too* much, spreading himself incredibly thin. His time could be so much better spent.

"Honestly, Kullen, I don't know what you see in that woman. I've removed lint from the dryer that's more intelligent than she is."

"I'm not really interested in giving her an IQ test."

He was better than that, Kate silently insisted. She knew if she'd said it out loud, her brother would deny it. "You are impossible, Kullen."

"But happy," he countered with a broad smile. "Very, very happy. You really should try it once in a while, Kate."

She could feel her guard going up. "What? Going out with Allison?"

"No," he said seriously, "being happy. Not every guy out there is a rotten SOB."

No, only the ones I'm attracted to. Kate closed her eyes for a second, gathering strength. "Don't you start sounding like Mom."

"Hey, her heart's in the right place." He started to open the door again.

"Remember that when she suddenly starts working on you."

He paused to look at her over his shoulder. The grin on his face was utterly boyish. Kate could readily see why, at any given time, there were so many women pursuing her brother. He had a face that could stop a heart and fill it full of longing.

"She'd have to catch me first. Besides, you're her pet project for now and given your 'willingness' to cooperate, I'd say Mom is going to be busy for a very long time."

Kate pointed to the door. "Get out of here."

He was on his way out, but he needled her a little more. "Stop scowling, Katie. You know you can't stay mad at me."

"This time around, I intend to give it a real good try," she informed him. But as her brother walked out, she raised her voice and called after him, "Don't forget, you owe me."

He half turned in the doorway. "Say what?"

"I said you owe me."

"My undying love," he replied. "After that, we'll talk."

"You owe me for taking on your client," she said pointedly.

Curiosity got the better of him. "So this was actually on the level? He really does need a lawyer?"

"Oddly enough, yes, he was on the level."

Kullen laughed shortly to himself. "She found a legitimate one to send. Mom's good."

Easy for him to say. "I'll remind you of that when it's your turn."

The wide grin was back. "Never happen."

"Don't underestimate that little woman," Kate warned him, thinking back to the days not all that long ago when her mother was actively lobbying for her to get married. "When she makes up her mind about something, she clamps down harder than a junkyard dog."

"She'll have to corner me first," Kullen crowed just before he closed the door behind him.

Oh, she will, Kullen, Kate silently promised with more than a little confidence. *She will.*

Chapter Four

Kate had every intention of calling her mother and letting her know that she didn't appreciate being manipulated like this. But the phone on her desk rang just as she reached for it. She was wanted in a general meeting. For the time being, anything private had to be pushed to the side. Kate promised herself to make the call to her mother when she got home.

But by the time she got home, all Kate had the strength to do was crawl into bed.

The following day was just as packed, with no letup in sight. And then, somehow, it was Friday and she had her newest client's function to attend.

Looking back, Kate wasn't even sure why she'd agreed

to go. It really wasn't to get those papers she needed to start the extension on the trust because they could have come just as easily—and more efficiently—by courier as she'd first suggested.

Maybe, that annoying little voice in her head speculated, she'd said yes to Jackson's invitation because she was ever so slightly attracted to the man. Be that as it may—and he *was* attractive—she planned to fight that attraction with her very last ounce of strength.

It had taken her a long time to get herself together. She was drained and very tired of the so-called dating game. Tired of putting herself out there emotionally only to have her hopes dashed over and over again by men who didn't turn out to be worth the effort. She'd actually thought that she'd finally hit the mother lode with Matthew. The man was handsome, intelligent, sharp and ambitious. He seemed perfect in every way. Not only that, but there was chemistry. Oh God, there was chemistry, that magic "something" that made her tingle whenever she was near him.

She didn't trust chemistry, not anymore. It had blinded her to things she might have noticed sooner— like the fact that Matthew turned out to have a ten-feet-tall libido.

No, no more chemistry for her. No more men, period. At least, not socially.

To that end, when she'd gotten up this morning, Kate had had every intention to dress the part of a subdued, scholarly professional. That usually made her look years older than she actually was. And that, in turn, would show Mr. Wainwright that theirs was nothing more than strictly a professional relationship.

But somewhere between the shower, the closet and the eyebrow pencil, the rebellious side of her kicked in. The side that liked testing her and pushing her to her limits, no matter what the case. So, rather than pin her hair back or up, the way she did when she was due in court, Kate wore it loose, letting the natural curl take over. Her hair looked like a black storm at sea.

She still chose a suit to wear, but it wasn't one of her more somber ones. This suit was an eye-opening turquoise. The pencil skirt was teasingly shorter than the one she'd worn when she'd had lunch with Jackson. The hem found its place somewhere along her thigh rather than her knee, exposing very shapely legs. The blouse was a satiny shade of cream.

And just before she left, she took a pair of cream-colored strappy heels with her. They were a full inch higher than the ones she usually wore to the office.

All in all, she looked like Hollywood's idea of a lady lawyer in a romantic comedy—and she knew it. What wasn't clear was why she was doing it.

Catching a glimpse of herself in the downstairs dining-room mirror, Kate hesitated. If she wasn't running late this morning, she would have hurried back up the stairs and changed into her usual somber apparel.

Or so she told herself as she dashed out the door.

* * *

"Hey, you look pretty good," Kullen observed as, nine hours later, she passed him in the hall on her way to attend Wainwright's gathering.

Kate stopped for a moment and looked at him. "You sound surprised."

"I am," he admitted. "I forget how good you can look when you're not trying to impress Rothchild with your brains."

He was referring to her father's edict that men didn't believe that a woman could be both attractive and smart. If she wanted to get somewhere in this field, her father had told her that she would have to pick which way she wanted to be perceived. Pretty or intelligent.

Because her father so seldom went out of his way to mentor her in any fashion—that sort of thing he saved for Kullen—she took his words to heart and made her choice. She picked smart and the subdued clothes that went with that.

But because she didn't want to hear any of Kullen's pseudo-intellectual observations, she pretended not to understand. "I'm not even going to try to unscramble that. I'm just going to take my compliment and leave."

"Speaking of which," his eyes swept over her again with even more interest than the first time, "where are you leaving to?"

She wasn't about to surrender information so easily. "Maybe I'm going home."

Kullen shook his head. "Not looking like that you're not. You got a date, Katie?" he asked incredulously.

It had been a long day and her temper had grown shorter by the hour. She had little patience left for Kullen's inquisition. "What, Mom has you spying for her now?"

"Ever think that maybe *I'm* concerned about you?" There wasn't even a glimmer of a smile on his lips.

She knew he cared about her, as she did him. But that didn't mean that he would miss a chance to bedevil her. "Nope. It never occurred to me."

Kullen placed a hand dramatically over his heart. "I'm wounded."

"You'll heal," she assured him. "Don't forget to get your bimbo shots. Prolonged exposure to bimbos causes wounds to fester," she tossed over her shoulder as she turned a corner and came to the bank of elevators.

Behind her, in the distance, she heard the sound of her brother's deep laughter.

Well, at least one of Theresa Manetti's children was happy, Kate thought.

Half an hour later, after crawling through rush-hour traffic, she left her car in the parking structure across the street from the bank. It had taken her thirty minutes to go ten blocks.

The Republic National's building was twelve years old and, at its inception, had been the last word in modern. It still was.

Standing fifteen stories tall, every one of its floors

was filled with offices that were in some way connected with the bank. Impressive by day, with the sun reflecting off each one of its carpet-to-ceiling glass-framed floors, the building was even more impressive at night with the rays of the full moon glinting off its otherwise darkened windows.

The building looked beautiful, but cold, Kate thought, approaching the edifice.

The description echoed in her brain.

Was that how people saw her? She knew without conceit that she was attractive. Knew it in the same way that she knew her eyes were a deep blue. She hadn't done anything to make them blue, they just were. So it was with being attractive. Yes, she spent time in the morning putting on makeup, but it was just a smattering. Nothing earth-shaking or image-changing. She was what she was and she was satisfied with that.

Why was she even thinking about this? she upbraided herself. Her mother, she thought. Her mother had started this by playing matchmaker.

Sorry, Mom, that ship no longer docks here.

She had to walk past a security desk in the lobby before reaching the bank of elevators. Kate paused to sign in. Again she briefly entertained the idea of just turning around and going back out. She could offer some excuse to Wainwright about having something come up at the last minute—it wasn't that much of a stretch, things were *always* coming up.

But at bottom, she knew that would be running and

Anthony Manetti's daughter didn't run. It was as simple—and as complicated—as that.

Besides, Kate silently asked herself as she stepped into the elevator car, what was she afraid of? She knew damn well what happened if she gave in to chemistry, so she wouldn't. There was nothing to be afraid of, she silently insisted.

Her stomach tightened as the floors went by.

The conference room had recently been remodeled. Among other things, the east wall had been taken down, merging it with the other conference room and creating a single room that was twice as large. It was a show of confidence to its employees that they expected better economic times to be just on the horizon.

Aside from the regular conferences, the room could now handily accommodate social gatherings at Christmas and other festive times of the year. It was certainly large enough to hold all the department heads and their people without anyone being forced to literally rub elbows.

All but awash in milling bodies the moment she walked into the conference room, Kate took the opportunity to acclimate herself. Was Jackson really in charge of all these people? He looked almost too young for that sort of responsibility. But then, she supposed that being forced to be his brother's keeper had left him little time for a carefree life.

She scanned the area for his face.

* * *

He saw her the moment she walked in.

Jackson stopped in mid-sentence as the elevator announced its appearance with a distinctive bell. He glanced in its direction each time he heard the bell. Two beats later, his family lawyer, true to her word, entered.

But with a hell of a difference. Even though that was what she was, Jackson found it difficult to think of Kate Manetti as his new family lawyer. She was far too vivacious to be a straitlaced lawyer. Or even a terrific lawyer.

If Jonah saw her, he would do his damndest to try to add the woman to his trophies. Jackson suddenly felt very protective of her.

"Excuse me," he murmured to Ed Wynters, the man he'd been speaking to. He placed his wineglass on the table. "I see someone I need to talk to."

Wynters, the vice president of Equity Loans, turned around to see who the new district manager was referring to. A wide smile flittered over the VP's portly face.

"I'd need to talk to her, too, if I wasn't such a happily married man," he added with just a touch of a sorrowful note lingering on the last three words.

Jackson didn't offer a response. He was already weaving his way toward her.

"You made it," Jackson said when he reached her. Instinctively he sensed that she wouldn't have wanted any undue attention directed her way, which was why he hadn't shouted his greeting from across the room.

Kate turned to the sound of his voice. "I said I would," she reminded him, conveniently omitting mentioning that she'd almost turned around twice while en route. All he needed to know was that she was here, not the indecision that had marked her path.

"Yes," he acknowledged, "I remember. But a great many things can happen between 'yesterday' and 'today' to change that."

That hit a little too close to the truth for her comfort. Wavering and uncertain was not the kind of aura she wanted to project publicly *or* privately.

"Luckily, they didn't." She took a breath and forced a smile to her lips. "So, did you bring the papers with you?"

"Don't tell me you intend to grab and run. Stay a few minutes," he coaxed, slipping a hand lightly to her waist and guiding her in the direction of the buffet table. "Enjoy the food. It's really excellent." He realized he was praising her mother and laughed at himself for forgetting. "But then, you'd already know that, wouldn't you?"

"Yes, I would know that." Her mother was an excellent cook, there was no denying that. The woman's flaws came under the heading of motherhood. Theresa Manetti really needed to learn to butt out unless her opinion was specifically requested.

As she spoke to Jackson, Kate couldn't shake the uneasy feeling that she was being watched. She scanned the room, trying to locate her mother. Because of all the people milling around, getting in the way, it was impossible to see everywhere.

And somewhere in all this, Kate would have bet a year's salary, her mother was lurking. Theresa Manetti made it a rule to be on site for every party she catered in order to make sure that everything went smoothly—and to do damage control if it didn't.

But if her mother knew she was here, Kate suspected that the woman would probably be trying to keep a very low profile.

Come out, come out wherever you are. You can't hide forever, Mother.

Abruptly, Kate realized that her newest client was asking her a question. Forcing a smile to her lips, she turned her attention to him.

"I'm sorry, I thought I saw someone I knew. I didn't. You were saying?"

"Would you like something to drink?" Jackson gestured toward the minibar that had been set up just beyond the buffet table. "The bar looks small, but it has just about anything you might want."

She caught herself sparing a side glance in his direction. The words *I don't know about that* popped up in her head out of nowhere. Recovering, she was just grateful they hadn't emerged on her tongue, as well.

Out loud, she dismissed the offer. "I'm driving."

"Not this minute," Jackson countered.

"No," she agreed, holding her ground like a soldier, more stubborn than brave, "but in a few."

"Stay," he coaxed in a voice that could have just as easily been used for seduction. "I thought of a few more things to ask you."

It was an excuse made out of tissue paper. But, even knowing that, Kate allowed herself to be led to the bar. So what could it hurt to stay awhile? After this, she was going home and nothing pressing awaited her.

"A screwdriver," she told the man behind the bar.

Jackson's eyes slid up from her toes to her face, taking a prolonged route up. She could almost feel him doing it.

"Nothing more exotic?" he asked her.

Why was it suddenly warm in here? Had a few hundred more people been brought in? Or was the oxygen being sucked out? she wondered nervously.

"I don't need anything more exotic," she managed to answer as the heat evaporated the saliva from her mouth. "I like screwdrivers."

"I'll try to remember that," he replied.

Why did that sound like a promise?

The cold glass when the bartender handed it to her felt exceptionally good in her hand.

"Mrs. Manetti, I'm running out of napkins," Eva, a pretty little redhead, declared as she approached the woman who was all but a patron saint in her eyes. Because of Theresa Manetti, she was in a position to accumulate enough money to allow her to pay for her second year of college instead of dropping out.

"There're more in the truck, Eva." Pausing, Theresa fished out her car keys from her pocket. She held them out to the girl. "Here, take Jeffrey with you and go get them. The truck's parked in the basement directly by the elevator."

Eva's smile was tolerant. "I don't need Jeffrey to come with me, Mrs. Manetti. I can get the napkins by myself."

"It's after hours in an office building and you're a very attractive young woman." Theresa patted the girl's cheek with affection. The young were fearless. The not-so-young knew there was an underbelly that wasn't always so nice. "Better safe than sorry, my dear. Humor me. Take Jeffrey with you."

There was affection in Eva's voice as she said, "You worry too much."

Theresa laughed softly. "My daughter tells me that all the time."

"My mother never tells me that," Eva confided. She considered for a moment, then said, "I like you worrying, Mrs. Manetti. I'll take Jeffrey."

"That's my girl."

When Theresa looked back to where she'd first spotted her daughter standing, talking to Jackson, Kate was no longer there. And neither was Jackson. She could only hope that they had slipped away together. The next moment, another one of the servers she'd hired was asking her about one of the trays of appetizers.

Before she knew it, Theresa had lost herself in the dozen and a half details that always arose at a catering function, all of which demanded her attention.

"So what are those questions you wanted to ask me?" Kate prodded. Several minutes had gone by and they had all been immersed in small talk and an undercurrent of

flirtation on Jackson's part. She couldn't help responding to him. In her defense, any woman with a pulse
would have. As long as she didn't allow herself to take
it seriously, she'd be fine.

He smiled into her eyes over his drink. "Are you
always this focused?"

She was caught up in a verbal version of dodgeball,
she thought. Well, two could play that game. "Is that one
of the questions or something that just occurred to you
on the spur of the moment?" she asked.

His gaze made her warmer. She shouldn't have had
a sip of the screwdriver. That didn't help matters any.
"Would there be different answers depending on the
circumstances?"

All right, she'd play along. And then maybe he'd
give her those papers. "I'm here as your lawyer," she
emphasized, "so yes, I try to always be this focused."

"And if I'd asked you to come here not as my lawyer
but as an extremely attractive woman, then would you
be this focused?"

Because the intensity of his gaze had caused her
mouth to go dry, she didn't answer until she took
another sip of her drink. A long one. "But I'm here
to pick up your papers. The ones to enable me to
extend the life of your brother's trust fund, remember? That would make me your lawyer, not your
guest."

"Could you forget about the trust fund for the next
few hours?" he requested. "This is the beginning of the

weekend. There's no need for you to work on anything until Monday morning."

She had to remind herself to breathe. *Not good.*

Clearing her throat, Kate forced the words out. "I like to stay ahead of things," she informed him. "That means sometimes not just burning the midnight oil but the weekend one, too."

His smile found its way to each and every one of her bones, threatening to melt at least half of them. "Well, I'm certainly glad your mother gave me your number and your brother turned out not to be available. I'm obviously getting my money's worth. Speaking of which—"

She'd lost the reference point. "Money?" Kate asked uncertainly.

"No," he laughed. "Your mother." He pointed to the left with his glass. "She's right over there."

Kate turned and saw the woman. Eye contact was definitely established. "So she is."

When Kate made no move either to wave at the woman or walk over to her, Jackson's curiosity was aroused. "Are you two not on speaking terms?"

"She's working. I don't want to break her concentration." And yelling at her mother would definitely break her concentration, Kate added silently.

"So this is why you couldn't lend me the money when I asked you to the other day."

The accusation came from behind them. Jackson and Kate turned around simultaneously, although Jackson didn't really have to. He knew who it was.

"I'm hurt, little brother. You didn't invite me to this little party you're throwing. But you can make amends," the man said magnanimously. His eyes washed over her in a slow, obviously appreciative motion. Kate felt as if her clothes had just been melted away. She resisted the urge to throw her hands up around herself to cover her nakedness. "You can introduce me to this magnificent creature."

Kate instinctively knew this had to be Jonah.

Chapter Five

Tension traveled through Jackson's shoulders, making them rigid. He braced himself for a scene. Jonah knew where he worked, but his brother hadn't known anything about the get-acquainted party that he'd decided to throw. Was he here at this time by accident, or had he turned up with some kind of agenda?

"Jonah, this isn't the time," he told his brother quietly.

"Oh, but this is exactly the time, little brother," Jonah assured him. His eyes never left Kate. "Now, tell me, just who is this lovely creature and how did you get lucky enough to meet her?"

Jackson looked at her as if he was asking her permission to make the introduction under these circumstances.

She inclined her head ever so slightly, intrigued by Jackson's reaction. Just like that, Kate thought, Jackson Wainwright had turned from a sensual man into a protective one. She had to admit she rather liked that quality in a man.

Careful, Kate, don't lose your focus.

Ever so subtly, Jackson guided them to a lesser trafficked corner. "Jonah, this is our new lawyer, Katherine Manetti. Kate, this is Jonah, my older brother."

Jonah took the hand she extended in greeting, slipping it between both of his.

The dark brown eyes momentarily shifted from her face. "I'm always open to making the acquaintance of a beautiful woman, but why do we need a lawyer?" he asked, sparing his brother a glance. "Or are you the one who needs one? Planning on needing a lawyer to defend you from charges of embezzlement, little brother?"

"She'll be taking Mort's place, Jonah."

"Ah, yes." Nodding, Jonah continued holding her hand. "Mortie." Jonah leaned in toward her, dropping his voice as if to share some kind of dark secret with her. "Poor Mortie has gone to the big courtroom in the sky. Or wherever it is that useless, annoying lawyers go." He beamed at her and she had to admit, the man had a very disarming smile. Like his brother. "No offense, lovely lady, but why would we need another of Mortie's kind?" The question was directed to his brother even though he was still watching Kate. "All he ever did was oversee that stupid trust fund like an iron-fisted troll. His time with us would have been up next month anyway. I turn the magic age then, remember, Jackson?"

"I remember," Jackson replied, holding his emotions in check. "That's exactly why we need Kate."

Jonah's mouth curved slyly. "Oh, I can think of a lot of reasons we—at least I—could need Kate here. And that damn constricting trust fund has absolutely nothing to do with it."

"That's enough, Jonah," Jackson ordered.

Jonah hardly paid attention to the warning note in his brother's voice. "No, not by a long shot. I'm just getting started." His eyes all but shone.

"Jonah, I think that it's time for you to—"

Jackson was going to tell his brother to leave, Kate thought. She could see the whole scenario unfolding, the one that she was certain Jackson would have really wanted to avoid. Slipping her hand out of Jonah's, she deftly moved between the two men and deliberately focused her attention on the older of the two.

"Since I'm your lawyer, Jonah, why don't we go somewhere where you can talk more freely and get acquainted?" she suggested.

Jonah grinned like a small boy who'd just trumped his brother. He glanced over Kate's head at Jackson. "Sorry, little brother, looks like the lady prefers charm to intelligence."

She was making a mistake, Jackson thought. She had

no idea what Jonah was like. Or what, once drunk, he was capable of. "Kate, you don't have to—"

Her arm threaded through Jonah's, Kate turned her head toward Jackson. "I always make it a point to know the person I'm representing, Mr. Wainwright," she informed him very formally.

The expression in her eyes told him it was better if he backed off—and that she knew what she was doing.

Logic warred with chivalry. Jackson had been here for only a few weeks. He'd specifically thrown this party to integrate himself with these people and have them see him in the right light. This was *not* the time or place to have any dirty laundry aired. He hoped that she knew what she was doing.

"There's a coffee shop at the end of the block," she continued, talking to Jonah again. "Why don't we go there?"

"My place isn't that far," Jonah told her, his meaning crystal clear.

It'll be a cold day in hell before that happens, Jonah, she silently vowed.

"Yes, but the coffee shop is right here," Kate countered. "Might as well take advantage of that." *Instead of me.*

Jonah let a small sigh escape. "The coffee shop," he repeated with a resigned nod.

Jackson knew what she was doing and he didn't like it. Jonah was his problem. No need for her to have to put up with him, other than to provide the legal muscle.

"Kate—"

"Face it, Jackie, she's made her choice," Jonah crowed.

With that, secure in the way her arm was tucked through his, Jonah led her back to the elevator. It arrived almost the moment he pressed the button.

Kate deliberately slipped her arm out of his as she stepped into the elevator. She had no intention of being sealed to his side a moment longer than was absolutely necessary.

Although she maintained a smile on her lips, she tendered Jonah a warning. "You're not to embarrass him in public like that again, Jonah."

Jonah's grin broadened, and he seemed somewhat impressed. "Whoa, the lady has a bite. I like ladies with spirit."

They reached the ground floor in the blink of an eye. Pausing to sign out, Kate turned to him and asked, "Why do you do that?"

Jonah scribbled his name on the line after hers and then pushed the outer door open for her. "Do what?"

Kate led him to the right. The coffee shop was only a few steps away. Several of the outdoor tables were occupied. But one or two were still free. "Why do you act like a caricature of the drunken black sheep of the family?"

They went inside the shop. Only one person was in front of them.

Jonah shrugged in response to her question. "Maybe because I am."

Giving her order to the man behind the counter, Kate waited until Jonah followed suit before discounting his answer. "There's more to you than that."

"Want to unwrap the layers? I'll stand real still," he promised, doing his best to sound lecherous.

Their coffees were mixed and ready. Jonah paid and they sat down at an outdoor table. She took a sip of the bracing drink.

"Did you know that your brother has a painting of yours in his office?" she asked.

The look on Jonah's face told her he thought she was making it up. He never stopped to ask how she knew that he painted. "No, he doesn't."

"Yes, he does," she countered. "I've seen it. It's the one of the art fair at Laguna Beach," she added in case he still didn't believe her. "You've got a lot of talent, Jonah." She studied him for a moment. "Maybe you're afraid of that talent," she guessed. "Afraid to work at it. If you never push to succeed, you never have to deal with finding out if you can. So instead, you do this. You do things to excess."

He shrugged carelessly, staring down at the coffee container as if he wished he had something stronger to pour into it. "And maybe you're a frustrated pseudo-psychiatrist."

His tone was harsh, but she didn't pull back. Kate saw the retort for what it was, a fearful response. She'd hit a nerve. Jonah was a lost boy who tried to cover up his shortcomings with an abrasive swagger.

"Your brother went through a lot of trouble to move down here so he could keep an eye on you."

Jonah grew defensive. And annoyed. "Nobody asked him to."

"True," she agreed. "But maybe he knows a cry for help when he hears it."

"Nobody cried, either," Jonah informed her tersely. Then he softened, smiling again. "You're right. My brother is a good guy and he has put up with a lot from me."

She got the feeling that Jonah wanted to do better, he just didn't know how. "So why don't you take pity on him and give him a break?"

The grin grew wider. "He expects it. I've got a reputation to maintain. Being a screwup is what I do best."

"You don't mean that," she told him.

He shrugged in a self-deprecating manner. "Oh yes I do."

"It doesn't have to be that way," she said softly.

Not wanting to continue in this venue, Jonah changed the course of the conversation. "Once I get what's coming to me, Jackson doesn't have to hear from me at all if he doesn't want to."

She studied Jonah a moment longer, then asked, "What do you plan to do with the money once the trust is awarded to you?"

There was a full, robust enthusiasm in his voice as he declared, "Enjoy it."

"You mean spend it," Kate interpreted.

He laughed at her attempt to make the situation more significant than it was. "That's one way to do it. Want to come along? I could use some gorgeous eye candy hanging on to my arm while I sail through the high life. It's a lot of money," he confided with a wink. "But then, you probably already know that."

Actually, she didn't know the specifics, not yet. Kate continued studying him as she sipped her ice blend mocha coffee. "What are you going to do once the money's gone?"

The shrug was careless and completely honest in its lack of guile. "That won't happen for a while. I'll worry about it then." A touch of impatience entered Jonah's voice. He didn't like resistance. It didn't make him play harder. It made him give up. "You know, you might not look like him, but you're a lot like Jackson. Worrying about stuff that's in the future. The future's just that, in the future. Who knows, I might be dead before I run out of money."

She thought of what Jackson had said about his brother's penchant for substance abuse and hanging around unsavory characters.

"That might very well be," she agreed. "But you don't want to do that."

"Right now," he said, leaning close, "what I want is to get my toes warmed by a very gorgeous, classy-looking woman," he breathed.

Kate never flinched, treating him like an over enthusiastic puppy. "Tempting as that sounds, you're my client, Jonah. There are rules."

"I'm not," he protested. "Jackson is."

"Actually," she corrected, "you both are." For now, there was no need to tell him any more detail than that.

Jonah sighed. Anything he had to work for to win wasn't worth the effort. "So you're saying no?"

"I'm saying no for ethical reasons." Her smile never wavered.

"Too bad." His disappointment sounded genuine. "We would have had one hell of a night."

It cost her nothing to leave his ego intact. "I'm sure we would have."

Jonah brightened like a man who believed he was getting what he wanted after all. "Well then, why don't we—"

"I'd be disbarred, Jonah," she emphasized. Her coffee finished, she wiped her lips lightly, then stuffed the napkin into the empty container. "Can I call you a cab?" she suggested.

Jonah eyed her quizzically through the fog in his eyes. "Why? Am I going somewhere?"

"To your house."

"But my car—" He pointed vaguely in the direction he'd last left the parking structure. It had moved. Or the earth had. Either way, he realized he was pointing at a jewelry store.

"—will still be there tomorrow." No way was she allowing him to drive himself to the bathroom, much less out on the road. He reeked of alcohol. "You don't want to risk getting a DUI, possibly hurting yourself or someone else, do you?"

His grin was slightly sloppy now. "Why, Katie, you care."

"I looked into your record. Your brother's pulled a lot of strings to keep you from being sent to jail on drunk and disorderly charges."

"Yeah, good ol' Jackie, he always comes through. He deserves better," he confided.

She made no comment. They'd already run this go-around. "One day he's going to run out of strings and you're going to wind up out of luck. My advice is that you quit while you're ahead."

"You're not as much fun as you look," Jonah lamented as he nodded at her words.

Kate laughed shortly. "I've been told that," she admitted. By princes who turned out to be frogs, she thought, reminding herself why she'd sworn off the species.

Seeing a cab let off a fare across the street, Kate whistled loudly and waved her hand to get the man's attention. She succeeded.

Jonah ambled over from their table. "That's pretty impressive," he commented.

"My brother taught me," she told him matter-of-factly, leaving out the part about badgering Kullen for weeks until he finally gave in.

The cab she'd hailed went down to the end of the street and did a U-turn, coming back to them.

"Your ride's here," Kate informed the unsteady Jonah cheerfully as she opened the rear passenger door for him. With a resigned sigh, Jonah came forward and started to get into the cab. "Watch your head," she cautioned, placing her hand over the top of it as he ducked into the taxi.

Once seated, he peered out at her hopefully. "Sure you don't want to come with me?"

She kept her smile in place. "I'm sure." Moving to the driver, she rattled off Jonah's address for the man, something else she'd committed to memory. She looked in on him one last time. His eyes were getting droopy. She'd made the right call.

"Sleep it off, Jonah," she instructed by way of a parting.

"I'd rather sleep with you," he called out the open window as the cab driver sped away.

"Not even in your wildest dreams," Kate murmured, stepping back on the curb.

For a fleeting moment, she thought about going back upstairs to Jackson's party. She still didn't have the papers that she'd come for. But running interference for Jackson and getting Jonah to go home without, accidentally or on purpose, causing a scene had left her drained.

She could always get the papers on Monday, she decided. Kate turned toward the parking structure and started to walk. At least she'd managed to divert a minor disaster and she'd gotten to meet the black sheep—who was more gray than black. What a handful he must have been for Jackson, she mused, feeling more than a little sorry for the younger Wainwright. It spoke well of him to have taken it on.

He doesn't need you to write a testimonial for him. She was going to have to keep her guard up all the time,

Kate schooled herself. Otherwise, she would find herself sliding down a very familiar slope—and she knew how that always ended up.

Entering the parking structure, Kate squared her shoulders. She absolutely hated looking for her vehicle. It was never where she was sure she'd left it. Hunting for it took anywhere from fifteen minutes to an hour.

Tonight was no different.

As she pulled up in the driveway, visions of a hot bubble bath proved too seductively tempting for her to resist. Since she was home earlier than she expected, she would take advantage of that and get some overdue sleep. She'd earned it, she told herself. And then some.

But Kate had no sooner closed the door behind her, locking it, and kicked off her shoes than the doorbell rang.

Surprised, she jumped. Now what? she wondered impatiently.

She wasn't expecting anyone, but Kullen had a habit of dropping by without warning. Although never on a Friday night. For a second, she held her ground, waiting to see if whoever it was went away. The infrequent door-to-door solicitor usually gave up after one try.

Any thoughts of ignoring the doorbell ringer and going upstairs for that bubble bath were torpedoed when the bell rang again. And then again.

So much for her theory. "Okay, okay, I'm coming," Kate called out.

Cautiously, she opened it, the chain she'd hastily secured when she came in still in place. What she saw was a delivery boy standing there with what looked like half the local flower shop's supply of pink roses over-flowing out of a large vase.

"Delivery for Ms. Manetti," the delivery boy told her before she had a chance to ask.

"Just a second." Shutting the door for a moment, Kate unlatched the chain and then reopened the door. As soon as she did, the flowers, all tucked carefully into a slender ivory pearl vase, were thrust into her hands. Stunned, Kate stared at them. No one sent her flowers.

"You're sure these are for me?" she questioned the delivery boy.

He held up his clipboard. "Your name and address matches," he said in a flat voice. "So I'm sure. Sign here, please," he instructed, thrusting the clipboard at her this time. Kate placed the vase down on the side table and quickly wrote her name in the space the delivery boy pointed to. "Thanks," he muttered, adding, "have-a-nice-day" as if it were all a single word to be carefully chewed before uttering.

Shutting the door with her back, Kate looked the vase over, searching for a card. And when she found it, she was no more enlightened than before. Maybe that wasn't quite accurate. It narrowed the playing field down to two.

The card said, "Thank you. J. Wainwright."

She frowned. They were both "J. Wainwright." Was Jonah thanking her for sharing a coffee with him, or was Jackson thanking her for whisking his brother away before he embarrassed both of them?

Closing her eyes, she offered up a quick, silent prayer. "Don't let it be from Jonah." The man might be tempted to follow up his delivery—and what was worse, it would mean that he knew where she lived. She liked having her privacy and *not* having a client turn up on her doorstep at will.

When what she was really hired for came to light, Jonah was not going to be happy. She wouldn't put it past him to camp out on her lawn in an effort to get her to reverse any new changes to the trust fund.

She glanced at the card that came with the flowers. Along with instructions on how to care for the roses was the name and phone number of the florist. First thing tomorrow, she promised herself, she would call and see if she could find out if that was *J* for Jonah or *J* for Jackson.

Until then, there was a bubble bath with her name on it, she thought, smiling to herself. And God, did she ever need it.

Stopping to smell the roses one last time, she went upstairs.

Chapter Six

The longer Kate remained in the bathtub, the harder it was for her to contemplate getting out. Periodically adding hot water to keep the temperature comfortable just increased her reluctance. But she had a feeling that if she didn't force herself to pull the plug and terminate this bath, she was in real danger of falling asleep and just possibly sliding down into the water.

Soaking in the tub had certainly done its job in relaxing her.

That evaporated the moment she thought she heard the doorbell ring again.

Kate had finally gotten out of the bathtub and was reaching for her bathrobe when she heard the doorbell chimes. Ordinarily, she wouldn't have. The radio or the music from her iPod would have blotted it out. Music was part of the winding-down process.

But tonight, because of everything going on in her head and the pace she'd put up with today, all she'd craved was a soothing silence. And because of the silence, she was able to hear someone ringing her doorbell.

Kate sighed. Who had declared her house the new Grand Central Station?

Quickly tugging on the ankle-length aqua-colored robe and knotting the belt at her waist, Kate flew down the carpeted stairs in bare feet.

The top half of her oversize front door was composed of colored beveled glass, which allowed her to make out the outline of the person standing on her front step.

A male person, she judged, given the breadth of the shoulders.

Another delivery? Somehow, she doubted it.

As she made her way to the door, Kate picked up her cell phone from the side table and dropped it into the right-hand pocket of her robe. Just in case she needed to make an emergency call. One of the lessons her father had inadvertently taught her was to be prepared for all contingencies.

Stopping short of the door, she raised her voice and called out, "Who is it?"

"Jackson."

Relieved that it wasn't Jonah popping up on her doorstep, Kate opened the door before she thought the situation through. Before the question, what was he doing here and how did he know where she lived, had a chance to take root.

For a fleeting moment, Kate felt vulnerable. But she banished that with her customary bravado.

"Party end sooner than you thought?" she asked wryly. She held the door open and stepped back so that he could come in.

Party ended the minute you left, Jackson caught himself thinking, but he wasn't about to admit it out loud for a whole host of reasons, the most important of which was not wanting his new family lawyer to think that there was no difference between him and Jonah. *He* was the civilized brother.

Although he wasn't feeling entirely civilized right now, not when he found himself staring at a woman wearing only a bathrobe and who was, more than likely, barefoot up to the neck under it.

The scent of jasmine and vanilla in the air didn't exactly help keep his mind on the straight and narrow.

Subtly taking in a breath, Jackson said, "No, it ended right on schedule. I just wanted to come and thank you in person."

So he did realize that she was running interference when she'd taken Jonah away, she thought, pleased. For a while there, she wasn't sure. But, being a lawyer had taught her to *never* assume anything without having it clearly delineated. So, adding just the right touch of innocence to her voice, Kate asked, "For?"

"For taking Jonah outside before he wound up causing a scene." His mouth curved in a humorless smile. "He has a tendency to get carried away without taking any of the consequences into consideration. I don't exactly relish being embarrassed, intentionally or not."

"Who does?" she countered quietly.

About to say something further, his line of vision drifted over to the vase with its two dozen plump, pink roses.

"Oh, they came." Jackson made no effort to hide the pleasure in his voice. "Nice to know you can still rely on some things."

She followed his gaze. The roses seemed to grow more gorgeous every time she looked at them. "You must have ordered them the second I walked out."

"I did."

She'd left the party just a little after six. That was late in the workday for florists. "I can't believe that you found someone to deliver them at a moment's notice at that time of the evening."

"You'd be surprised what you can get if you offer to pay triple the rate."

My God, she thought, considering the price of roses these days, that must have amounted to practically a small fortune.

"There was no need—" she began to protest.

"There was a need," he contradicted. He liked watching her in action, not to mention that he appreciated her handling Jonah. This was just his way of showing his gratitude.

Kate felt like baiting him just a little, although for the life of her, she wouldn't have been able to explain why.

"What if I was allergic to flowers?" Kate posed, amused.

"You're not."

Her amusement faded ever so slightly. More personal information. "How do you know that?"

"Same way I knew your address. I know things." The look on his face was unreadable. "I like to familiarize myself with the people I—um—" He realized that there was no really graceful way for him to conclude his statement.

"Hire," she supplied with a serene smile. "Don't worry, I'm not offended." What bothered her was that he'd investigated her, but in a way that was his right. And what made him a savvy businessman. "I am very secure in who and what I am. Lawyers are generally hired guns when it comes to corporate types." She looked at him pointedly.

He couldn't begin to visualize her as a "hired gun." However, just wearing boots and a hand-stitched leather holster…

He cleared his throat, stalling for a second as he reined himself in. What the hell was going on with him? "Even family lawyers?"

"Even family lawyers," she assured him, then explained. "In essence, you're hiring me to protect Jonah from himself even if he doesn't like the idea."

He was instantly alert. "You told him?"

"Not yet," she was quick to reassure him. "But when I do, he won't like it." It wasn't much of a guess. Jonah was locked into a heavy-duty romance with money and what it could do for him.

"I'll take care of that—telling him," Jackson clarified in case she wasn't following him. "You shouldn't have to be subjected to his first reaction to the news."

"I can take it, Jackson," she assured him with an amused smile. "I'm a big girl."

There's no disputing that. The top of her robe was parting a little with each breath she took. Jackson forced himself to look into her eyes.

"Did I interrupt something?" He nodded at her robe, still keeping his eyes on her face.

Kate had gotten so involved in the conversation, in having him here, she'd almost forgotten she was wearing next to nothing. She looked down at the robe and saw that it was parting. She tugged it back into place.

"Oh. No. I was just getting out of the tub when you rang the doorbell."

"Unwinding?" After dealing with Jonah for the first time, he could understand the need.

Her shoulders rose just a tad, then fell again. "Something like that."

"Jonah didn't try anything…?" He let his voice trail off.

"Jonah was fine," she quickly assured him, unconsciously placing her hand on his arm. "He was more than a little inebriated. We had coffee at that little shop on the corner and then I put him in a cab. He's going to have to get his car tomorrow," she added before he could bring that up.

"Wallace will get it for him."

The name was unfamiliar to her. "Wallace?"

"Wallace Brubaker. Jonah's all-around assistant. Wallace has been with him since Jonah was a teenager." Humor curved the corners of his mouth. "I'm not sure that Jonah could get dressed in the morning without Wallace."

Kate raised her eyebrows. "Maybe it's about time your brother learned a few basics like that," she suggested. "Might make him more in tune to the real world."

The scent of her bath salts was getting to him. Vanilla and jasmine. He assumed that they were clinging to her skin. Whatever the case, the combined scent was definitely getting under *his* skin. It was a struggle to keep focused when his mind kept drifting to far more stimulating subjects than his brother.

He needed her to get dressed.

"Speaking of which," he said, trying to keep his voice light, "maybe you'd like to do that, too?"

Puzzled, she asked, "Do what?"

"Get dressed," he said, tactfully looking away.

Which made her look down at her robe again. The belt had loosened again, allowing for more movement. Very specific movement. The robe was parting a lot lower than she would have ever intended on her own. One more careless shrug and it was all over.

"Oh." This time the single word was bursting with thinly veiled embarrassment. She tugged the belt tighter, bringing the two halves of the robe closer together. "Maybe I should get dressed," she agreed, attempting a segue.

Jackson nodded, deliberately keeping his eyes focused above her neck. "Good idea. I'll wait down here."

She wondered if he realized that he'd just invited himself to stay, or was he just accustomed to doing that without thought? Even so, she sensed a tension running through him. Somehow, she doubted that this time around the tension had anything to do with the subject of Jonah.

Stopping halfway up the stairs, Kate turned around, unable to resist asking, "Am I making you uncomfortable, Jackson?"

He came to the foot of the stairs and looked up. There was a small smile on his lips that she couldn't begin to fathom. "You have no idea," was all he said to her.

It was enough to warm her. And warn her. She was standing on very thin ice.

Taking a deep breath, Kate promised, "I'll be right back," and went up the rest of the stairs a lot more quickly.

Jackson tried not to notice the way the damp robe clung to her curves as she went.

But he couldn't help himself.

Kate couldn't remember when she'd gotten dressed so fast. The closest was the time she was in college and she'd woken up with only twenty minutes to get dressed and get to her constitutional law final. This time, she made it in less than five.

Part of her hurry was because she didn't want to keep Jackson waiting. And part of it was because some small part of her was afraid that Jackson might rethink the situation, and his gallantry, and decide to come up to "help" her get dressed.

The thought of being naked around the man had her fingers getting in each other's way as heat traveled up and down her body.

When she sailed down the stairs five minutes later, Kate was wearing jeans and a dark blue pullover, its sleeves pushed up on her arms to just below her biceps. She was still barefoot and her hair was secured in a ponytail. The only makeup she'd hastily applied was lipstick. She looked like a freshman in college and nothing like the young woman who had graduated in the top five percent of her class at Stanford.

Jackson was exactly where she'd left him, at the foot of the stairs. Except that he was facing the door rather than looking up.

He turned around when he heard her, about to comment that he'd never known any woman to get dressed as fast as she had, even during an earthquake. But the comment died the moment he looked up at her. A last-minute effort kept his jaw from dropping.

The woman who had come to his rescue at the party had been a gorgeous, sophisticated creature. The one he now stared at had a sweetness to her he hadn't glimpsed at first.

"Where's your big sister?" he asked.

Kate was aware of her appearance. As if she'd just

fallen off a turnip truck. But she wasn't trying to impress this man. She was just trying to be herself and this was how she looked when she wasn't being a lawyer.

"Very funny. Sometimes I like to be casual," she told him.

Maybe she liked being casual, but there was nothing casual about his reaction to her, Jackson thought.

The next moment he reminded himself that this was his lawyer. He wasn't supposed to react to her on anything but a professional level. A casual, teasing flirtation was one thing, but this was something else. Something that he hadn't felt in a very long time. Something that he really didn't welcome.

"Most women over the age of fifteen wouldn't venture out in public without any makeup," he observed.

Yet there she was, fresh-faced and beautiful. She made him nostalgic for simpler times. Times when all he had to concern himself with was his own life and the future was wide open. And the threat of unbelievably gut-wrenching pain was not even a remote reality.

"This isn't public," Kate pointed out. "It's private."

She realized that her words could easily be misconstrued. If it had been Jonah on the receiving end, she was fairly certain he'd attempt to make the most of "private" and she might have even been forced to fight him off right now.

She flushed and murmured, "You know what I mean."

Yes, he knew what she meant. Thank God one of them was grounded. Opening his jacket, Jackson took out the envelope he'd brought with him. The contents of the envelope—as well as wanting to personally thank her—was why he'd actually come here in the first place.

"Before I forget—" he handed the envelope to her "—I thought you might want this."

Accepting the manila envelope, she looked down at it. It was thick and bulky. Kate raised her eyes to his.

"The papers for the original trust fund I take it?" she guessed.

Jackson nodded. "The very same."

She appreciated the effort, but she hadn't wanted him to go out of his way. The man was undoubtedly tired.

"You didn't have to come over with them tonight," Kate told him. Tired, she was in no shape to go over legal papers.

Jackson waved a dismissive hand at her protest. "It was the least I could do after you distracted Jonah for me."

Kate smiled and lifted one slender shoulder in a shrug. "Oh, Jonah's not so bad," she told him.

While he appreciated the fact that she seemed to have identified the *real* Jonah, he needed her to understand that she still had to be careful around Jonah.

"Don't let him know you think that." Jackson was dead serious. He'd seen his older brother go through more than his share of women. Some had actually been decent. Others had been there strictly because of Jonah's money. All had made him accustomed to getting his way. "Otherwise, he'll be pledging his undying love to you within a week."

"Don't worry, that wasn't a personal observation, that was strictly from a lawyer's point of view," she told Jackson, then, to reassure him, she added. "I'm not about to get involved with him, either."

It was only after the word was out that Kate realized her slip. The look on Jackson's face when their eyes met told her that he'd caught it, as well.

"'Either'?" he questioned, his tone indicating interest.

Kate had always prided herself for being good at damage control. Now was no different. She rose to the occasion.

"Meaning I don't get involved with any of my clients, not in that way." This needed more explaining, she could tell. "I can be understanding. I can give you a shoulder to cry on, a hand to hold in trying times, a sympathetic ear to listen to your troubles." And then she delivered the most important part of her statement. "But all my other body parts are strictly mine and not for lending out."

He laughed then, amused, charmed and definitely intrigued. But then, if he was being honest with himself, he'd already been all of those things before he ever reached her doorstep. But he wasn't at liberty to enjoy any of those sensations—because he remembered the other side of the coin and he was not about to open himself up to that—ever again.

"I think I'm going to give your mother a finder's fee for bringing you to my attention." She seemed puzzled and Jackson went on to say, "I have a very strong feeling that this is going to be one hell of an association, Katherine."

The butterflies in her stomach that had suddenly and without warning risen up from their dormant state told her that she shared the same feeling.

In spades.

Which meant trouble.

Chapter Seven

"Can I offer you some coffee?" Kate asked, doing her best to sound nonchalant.

She had a sudden, urgent need to keep busy, to do something with her hands. This unsettling restlessness stirred up inside of her and she wasn't quite sure how to handle it. She hoped that if she just kept busy until it went away, she'd be all right.

Coffee's not what I'd like you to offer me.

The thought streaked across Jackson's mind without preamble, surprising him as much as he reasoned it would have surprised her, had he said the words out loud. But there was no way he could turn the thought into reality. Not with her.

Although he hadn't exactly been a monk, Rachel's death when he was in college had scarred him. The pain he'd gone through, losing her, wasn't something he wanted to endure again. The easiest way to avoid pain was to avoid a real relationship. Which is what he did.

If things looked as if they might, even remotely, be taking a serious turn, he broke it off. It was as simple as that.

And right now, he had the uneasy feeling that what hummed between him and Kate could very easily become serious if he allowed himself to give in to the very primal urges ricocheting inside his body.

Besides, having any personal relationship with this woman might, by its very existence, taint the nature of the trust fund he was trying to have resurrected. At the very least, it would make for a hell of a tabloid story, one Jonah would bring to the news media's attention in an effort to get what he felt was rightfully his.

But despite his resolve, Jackson still couldn't help wondering what Kate's body would feel like, pressed up against his. Not being able to scratch that itch just made him more aware of it.

The corners of Jackson's mouth quirked into a quick, enigmatic smile. "No, but thanks for the offer. I should be going," he explained. "I've already taken up too much of your time."

She didn't see it quite that way. He'd brought over the paperwork she'd requested. That in turn would help her get a jump start on Monday morning.

"Well, don't feel bad about that," she told him. "It's part of the package. You have me on retainer, remember?"

Her reasoning amused him. "Does that mean I was getting charged by the hour when you came by to the office tonight?"

"I haven't quite worked that out yet," Kate told him, an easy smile on her lips. "I was initially coming there for these papers," she pointed out, holding up the envelope he'd just given her. And then her smile reached her eyes. They crinkled. "Don't worry, Jackson. I'm not that mercenary. Consider coming to your party a freebie."

"And subtly drawing Jonah away?"

"More of the same," she answered.

"That would make you quite a bargain," he replied, only half kidding.

"So I've been told."

This time, the pull he felt between them was a little stronger. Jackson decided that he needed to leave before he found another excuse to stay—and did something he wasn't supposed to.

"Well, like I said, I'd better be going." But even as he repeated the trite phrase, reluctance to vacate the premises kept him in place. "Thanks again for getting Jonah to leave."

"Don't mention it." Taking the initiative, Kate turned toward the door, silently ushering him out. To seal the deal, she indicated the envelope and promised, "I'll get back to you on this." Because she knew that he probably wanted a tentative time frame, she added, "Most likely on Tuesday."

Jackson nodded. "Sounds good."

He lingered a split second longer by the door. He couldn't remember ever wanting to kiss a woman as much as he wanted to kiss her. Desperate for a way to label and contain this feeling, he told himself that it had to do with forbidden fruit. He knew he shouldn't kiss her so he wanted to. No big mystery there. He just had to continue resisting until the feeling passed.

"I'll see you soon," he told her.

Go already, she silently pleaded. She didn't know how much longer she could go on, ignoring the crackle of electricity between them. "Yes, you will."

She could feel her resolve cracking into tiny little pieces.

Damn it, Jackson, why aren't you kissing me? I was practically naked in front of you. Didn't that create some sort of reaction from you?

Maybe, instead of a warm bath, she should have just taken a cold shower. If this was Jonah instead of Jackson standing on her threshold, all she would have had to do was allow her glance to linger suggestively. Kate was fairly confident that by now, several sheets would have been incinerated from the heat of the lovemaking that would have ensued.

But she wasn't attracted to Jonah, she was attracted to Jackson. And she was going to pay. Big time. Unless she could do it on her terms.

"Good night," he murmured.

Jackson turned and began to walk away. She started to close the door. Suddenly, he doubled back and thrust his hand in the way, preventing her from completely shutting the door.

"Forget something?" Kate asked, keeping her voice mild even as she felt her heart leap up into her throat.

He needed to have his head examined. He'd almost been in the clear. "Kate…"

Her breath backed up in her lungs. "Yes?" she whispered between dry lips.

He'd started this, he needed to finish it—before she thought she was working for a village idiot. "How much would it complicate things if I kissed you right now?"

Outwardly, she strove for a semblance of calm. She could control this, she silently insisted. This was purely a physical thing, nothing more. "That all depends."

"On?" he prodded.

Just the slightest hint of a smile curved her lips. "On the way you kiss."

Very slowly and carefully, Jackson silently released the breath he'd been holding. "You want to find out?"

She lifted her chin. "I've never turned my back on a challenge."

"Good thing to know," he told her just before he slipped his arms around her and drew Kate closer to him. His mouth came down on hers.

At bottom, Kate would have said that she wasn't expecting the earth to move. Shimmy maybe, but not actually move.

She should have known better.

The kiss did not engulf her. Not at first. Warm, gentle, coaxing, it still managed to open a door to another world. Opened it until she suddenly found herself free-falling through space. There was no longer a threshold, no longer a house. No longer anything but flash and fire and heat—incredible, soul-singeing, all-consuming heat.

Kate gripped his shoulders in order to hang on, afraid of tumbling to the bottom of a five-mile abyss and smashing into a million pieces.

More afraid that the kiss would stop before she had her fill.

Pressing her body against his, she was both sorry that she had gotten dressed and greatly relieved that she had at the same time. Because if she were still in that robe, there wasn't a single doubt in her mind how this kiss would have ended. In her bed, burning up those aforementioned sheets.

The moment his mouth touched Kate's, Jackson realized that he'd known all along what this would be like. Known that this petite, intelligent, animated woman with the killer curves and midnight-black hair had the power to ignite a fire within him at first contact.

He just had to keep it in perspective, that's all. While he could satisfy his curiosity about kissing her, he knew that he definitely could not allow this to progress to its natural conclusion. That would be violating a host of rules, not a single one of which clearly came to mind at the present moment.

Jackson framed her face with his hands, deepening the kiss just one more inch, then terminating the entire experience, albeit reluctantly.

But it was a matter of survival. His.

His mouth tingled as he drew his head back. "I'll be waiting for your call," he told Kate, stepping away from her.

Turning, he quickly walked away—before baser instincts than he'd just displayed made him sweep her up in his arms and make love with her no matter *what* the consequences.

"Uh-huh."

It was the only sound Kate could produce at the moment.

Her strength barely lasted long enough for her to close the door behind his departing back. The second the door met the jamb, she slid down to the floor, her back against the frame, her limbs utterly liquefied. Possibly forever.

Who was *that masked man?*

Talk about a kick, Kate thought.

Wow. Oh wow.

It probably had something to do with her brain being fried, but she couldn't remember *ever* reacting to a man like this. Not even Matthew. He had turned her on, yes, but this was way beyond just physical attraction. Had her new client not left when he had, she would have been in dire danger of just ripping off his clothes and then launching an assault on him until he made love with her.

And wouldn't that look lovely on your review? Get a grip, Kate. You know where this is going to wind up. And *you're not going there again, understand?*

Using the doorknob for support, Kate slowly pulled herself up to her feet. She needed a stiff drink, she decided. Maybe several, so that she wasn't tempted to jump into her car and drive to Jackson's house to end what he had started.

When first Monday and then Tuesday came and went, enough time had passed for her to return to her senses. She was grateful that she hadn't gone with her urges. Something she'd regret.

But that didn't mean that the memory of the toe-curling kiss had faded or even degraded from an A-plus to a B-minus. The spectacular incident was still very much an A-plus, but she would have to be content with keeping it as a fiery memory. Under no circumstance could she allow herself to get carried away, not again. There were definitely times when the "road not taken" was best not taken. Especially when she knew where that road led.

Putting in a full day and then some on Monday and then Tuesday, she was in the office a full hour before she was supposed to be on Wednesday. She was more than two-thirds finished with the rough draft of what Jackson had asked her to do. After Matthew, work became her solution for everything.

This time, it was her way of handling all that charged, unfettered energy racing around inside of her.

In his office, continuing to familiarize himself with the particular, inner workings of this particular district of Republic National and its individual branches, Jackson frowned. He stared at the column of numbers on the Excel spreadsheet currently on his monitor. He'd just been conducting a random check on some of the accounts and he'd accidentally come across an inconsistency.

It was a shortfall, small in the scheme of things but definitely there.

He'd been following the thread now for the last three hours, pulling up screen after screen, the tension inside him growing. Each time he thought he'd just made a mistake, there was that little blip, that tiny grain of sand inside his shoe. In this case, it wasn't sand, it was missing funds. The bank's funds.

Someone was skimming.

Embezzling.

It was an ugly word, an uglier reality. And it had begun at precisely the same time as his transfer to this district had occurred.

Coincidence or deliberate?

At the moment, he couldn't trace the disappearing funds back to their source, but because of the glaring time line, he knew that it could be interpreted to make him look guilty as hell.

Who would set him up? Or was he just being paranoid about this?

Jackson scrubbed his hand over his face, trying to
think, to sort out his scrambled thoughts. He definitely
didn't need this. Dealing with his brother, who seemed
to suspect something, and this attraction to Kate were
bad enough. A possible embezzlement scandal was like
the proverbial last straw.

Except that he couldn't allow it to break him.

Given that, what could he do? Was it one of the other
bank officers, taking advantage of the confusion that his
transfer had temporarily generated? After all, he was re-
placing a district manager, Alan Jefferies, who he'd
heard, had to be "convinced" to take early retirement.

Convinced? Or coerced? And if the latter, why?

Or was the culprit one of the score of tellers this
branch had, deftly removing funds in order to pay off a
gambling debt? God knew he was more than passingly
familiar with that kind of a situation, thanks to Jonah's
latest addiction.

For all he knew, this might even be connected to Jonah
in some fashion. He just didn't have enough information.

Biting off a curse, Jackson felt one hell of a head-
ache coming on.

He didn't hear the phone on his desk ring at first. He
was that consumed by what he was doing. But after the
second time, the ringing registered. Even so, he fleet-
ingly entertained the idea of just ignoring whoever it
was on the other end of the line.

But he didn't have that luxury. Not as a district manager. Stifling several choice, terse words, Jackson yanked the receiver up from its cradle. As he put it against his ear, he barely refrained from snapping out his surname. "Wainwright."

"I have a rough draft of the papers drawn up," said the voice on the other end of the line.

Recognition was swiftly followed by a wave of warmth. Kate.

"So soon?" he asked, surprised. This was Wednesday morning. Despite her promise Friday night, he hadn't really expected to hear from her until at least the end of the week. He knew he wasn't her only client and he didn't think she'd drop everything to do his bidding. Moreover, there were still three weeks left until Jonah's birthday. They had time.

He heard her laugh.

"Hey," Kate said, "when you're good, you're good. Seriously, it turned out to be easier than I anticipated, thanks to Jonah's documented penchant for excess. He virtually made your case for you."

For a brief moment, Jackson thought he could detect a smile in her voice. He visualized one on her lips.

Though he tried not to let it, the image stirred him.

Jackson took a breath. He made a decision. He needed someone to talk to. Someone to brainstorm this problem with. The logical choice would have been one of the bank's lawyers, but he didn't know how far up the chain this embezzlement went, if it was embezzlement.

Despite all the hours he'd logged in at Republic National up north, down here he was essentially "the new guy." New guys had to tread lightly.

And as the new guy, he had only the ultimate clout that the others were willing to cede to him. In this precarious position, he really didn't want to make waves, or inadvertently have suspicion point to him. Especially not until he figured out who was stealing and just how much had been stolen.

"I need to see you," he told her without any kind of preamble.

"Are you asking me as the man who is retaining me, or as…?" She didn't finish, letting him fill in the line as her voice trailed off.

"Is there a third choice?"

"Not that I'm aware of, but I always like to leave myself open to things," she said with an amused laugh.

"I need a friend," he finally told her. She made no response to that. Not a good sign. Still, Jackson heard himself asking, "How soon do you think you can get here?"

If he was asking for the impossible, he might as well know now.

"I'm on my way right now," she told him. He thought he heard the sound of a drawer being closed on the other end. She was reaching for her purse, he guessed.

The next moment, he chastised himself that he was overreacting. This just wasn't like him.

"No," he ordered suddenly.

"I'm not on my way right now?" Kate questioned, puzzled.

"No," he repeated. "Don't come. I'm probably just making too much of this."

She had no idea what "this" was but she did note the consternation in his voice. That meant something was bothering him. Whether he actually needed a lawyer or a friend was moot. He needed her in whatever capacity he chose to place her in. That was good enough for her.

"You don't strike me as an alarmist," she told him. "So, unless there's a major accident involving farm animals on the freeway, I should be there in about twenty minutes."

Jackson tried again. "Look, forget what I said. I don't feel right about making you drop everything and just come running like this."

But he was stating his argument to the dial tone. Kate had already left the office.

Chapter Eight

Kate didn't arrive at his office in the promised twenty minutes. She arrived there in seventeen, slightly breathless because she had walked quickly from the underground parking facility where she'd left her car to the bank of elevators and then even more quickly down his hallway.

The moment he saw her, Jackson rose from his desk and crossed to her with his hand outstretched.

He was grateful she was there, but at the same time, he also felt guilty for making her come. Guilty as well as foolish. There was still the chance that he was making a mountain out of the proverbial mole hill.

But even if he wasn't, this was something he should

be able to handle on his own without outside emotional support.

"I take it there was no accident involving farm animals on the freeway," he said by way of a greeting, recalling the last thing she'd said to him before terminating their phone call.

"As luck would have it, no," she answered amiably.

Kate put down the briefcase she'd brought with her. The newly drawn up trust-fund papers were inside. For the time being, that was placed on the back burner. She parked the Italian leather briefcase next to his desk. Though he was trying to mask it, she could see that Jackson was agitated.

"Now, other than the usual, run-of-the-mill reason," Kate began warmly, "why do you feel that you need a friend?"

Several responses, all entrenched in small talk, rose to his lips, but they faded away. He owed her the truth. "I need to talk something out."

Kate gracefully dropped into the chair in front of his desk, making herself as comfortable as she could under the circumstances. She gave him her full attention. "So talk."

Jackson sat down in his chair, the rigid tension of his body in direct conflict with the small smile on his lips. The smile vanished the moment he spoke. "I think someone at the bank is embezzling."

Kate's eyes widened ever so slightly. The news surprised her. "Isn't that a rather difficult thing to do in this day and age?"

There were security programs safeguarding the bank's depositors and investors. But this wasn't happening online.

"Sometimes the simplest approaches are the best. People expect this sort of thing to be done online, by clever hackers." He waved a hand at the screen on his desk. "There's no sign of anything like that going on."

"Then how do you know that funds are being embezzled?"

"Because there's a shortfall. A little here, a little there," he told her. "Someone is *physically* stealing small amounts at a time." He blew out a frustrated breath. "Whoever it is that's doing it is literally 'skimming' off the top."

This was the digital era. There was no such thing as privacy anymore. "Nothing show up on your surveillance cameras?"

He'd already thought of that. But this whole problem was still very fresh.

"I haven't started checking them yet," he admitted. "The moment I do, it'll give whoever's doing this a heads-up."

He had a point. If there *was* something going on. There was still a chance, albeit a small one, that it might all just be a miscalculation on his part.

"You're sure about this?" Kate pressed. "You *are* new to this position. It's possible that you might have made a basic mistake. You know, carried the hundreds column instead of the tens," she elaborated, only half kidding.

If he had to, he could add large strings of numbers in

his head. A unique feat in the day and age of heavy dependence on the computer and the scientific calculator.

"I've gone over everything five times," he told her. "The end-of-week figures don't tally. Each time, they're off by very little. But they *are* off."

Intrigued, she slid to the edge of her chair. "How much are you talking about?"

He didn't have to refer to his notes. It was all in his head. "At last total, almost ten thousand dollars. I know what you're thinking," he said before she could point the fact out. "That's not much money in the scheme of things. But it still puts the bank in the red by that sum."

He'd guessed wrong. That was definitely *not* what she was about to say. "It might not be much to you or the bank," Kate pointed out. "But it can be a fortune to someone who doesn't have it."

She could remember back when she was much younger, when money for Nikki and her mother was in scarce supply. She vividly remembered the concerned look on not only Maizie's face, but Nikki's, as well. Only people who had money could afford to be blasé about it.

"Okay," she recapped, "so far we've established that you have to check the surveillance camera footage. Have you tried running background checks on your employees?"

"All Republic National Bank employees have background checks done on them before they're hired."

But Kate shook her head. "*Recent* background checks," she emphasized.

As far as he knew, it was only done once. "What are you getting at?"

He was right, Kate thought. Ten thousand wasn't all that much—unless it meant the difference between life and death and there was a bookie or a loan shark involved. "Someone could suddenly be living beyond their means, or is held captive by the same malady as your brother: they're addicted to gambling, to the rush that comes from winning."

He never could understand that. The so-called rush from winning didn't begin to balance out the sick feeling in the pit of a person's stomach that losing huge sums of money had to have generated. Pitting himself against the "house," whatever the house might be, had never held any allure for him.

"I'd need to have the investigation done off the books," he told her.

Kate nodded. "That was my thinking."

He considered the matter for a moment. "That means I can't use the bank's investigators." He looked at her. "Would you know anyone to recommend? Maybe someone your firm uses?" he suggested hopefully.

Kate didn't have to think before answering. "Yes— and no," she answered.

"Come again?"

"I know someone you can use, but it isn't anyone affiliated with my firm. To be honest," she told him, "I think you'd be better off with an entirely private investigator."

The reference brought back memories of far less

complicated days and made him smile. "You mean like Thomas Magnum or Sam Spade?" he asked, naming two popular fictional characters.

"Yes, except real—and female," she qualified.

Jackson looked at her a little uncertainly. "A woman private investigator?"

Some things still took time to change, she thought. This was one of those last frontiers. "Don't look so skeptical, Jackson. Women can ask questions that men can't, and people just chalk it off to idle curiosity, nothing more."

That made sense, he supposed. He didn't care if the investigator was male or female, just thorough—and good. "I want this investigation to be kept strictly confidential. Is this someone you can vouch for?"

That was an easy one to answer. She grinned. "Absolutely. We grew up together. I have complete faith in her. If there's a secret life being led, Jewel is the one to find it for you. If she can't, there's nothing to be found," she assured him with feeling. "I'll give her a call and if she's free, I can bring her around tomorrow."

Now that he'd decided on a course of action, Jackson was anxious to get started. "This afternoon would be better. I want this resolved as quickly as possible."

She didn't blame him. "No one wants this kind of thing to linger," she agreed.

Opening her purse, she took out Jewel's business card. She knew Jewel's personal cell number by heart—

God knew she called it often enough. But Jewel's business phone was another matter. She'd never had to make use of it. Before now.

After tapping out the numbers on her cell-phone keypad, Kate listened to the phone on the other end ring. And ring. Finally, the voice-mail feature kicked in.

A melodic voice told her, "You've reached Parnell Investigations. Sorry, I'm on a case and can't answer your call. Leave your name and number after the beep and I'll get back to you as soon as possible."

Kate waited for the appropriate signal before saying, "Jewel, it's Kate. I've drummed up some business for you. One of my clients has need of your very particular set of talents as soon as possible. Call me when you get this." She snapped the phone closed and dropped it back into her purse. "I'll put her in touch with you the minute she calls," she promised.

That out of the way, Kate took a breath. "Now, do you want to review the papers extending the terms of Jonah's trust fund?" she asked. "I haven't filed the final paperwork yet, but that should just be a simple formality. I just wanted to review things with you in case you've had a change of heart."

"Why would I have a change of heart?" Jackson questioned.

She'd always believed that anything was possible. That was why God had created optimists. "Maybe Jonah suddenly had a life-altering experience and is now capable of being master of his own destiny," she suggested. Admittedly, the suggestion was more tongue-in-cheek than anything else.

"If that *ever* even remotely happened, I'd be calling up your mother to throw another party. A huge one," he emphasized. "No, from where I stand, I'm afraid that is never going to happen."

Meeting Jonah had allowed her to form her own opinion of the man. He'd struck her as harmless, but, unlike his brother, rather shallow. Kate tried to imagine what that had to be like, dealing with someone like Jonah on a regular basis. It must have been very trying for Jackson.

"I guess it's kind of like constantly dealing with Peter Pan," Kate speculated, raising her eyes to his to see if her comparison struck him as being on target.

"Yeah, except that Peter Pan's actions never threatened to bankrupt Tinker Bell or the Lost Boys," Jackson commented.

Kate knew he was serious, but she couldn't help being amused by the reference.

"Good point." Leaning over, she drew the briefcase closer to her and snapped the locks open, then took out the papers that were intended for Jackson's in-depth perusal. "Here." She pushed the pages into Jackson's hands.

Jackson quickly skimmed through the packet, occasionally pausing to reread something. From start to finish, it took Jackson all of five minutes.

Kate watched him, impressed. It had taken longer to

gather the papers together than for him to review them. "Let me guess, you're a speed reader."

Jackson nodded. "In the interests of not being buried under huge stacks of paperwork, I took a course," he admitted.

If she'd read that fast, not a word of it would have stuck. "And you retain everything?" she asked Jackson skeptically.

He had the kind of mind that could call things up at will. Whether it was a face or a passage, he only needed to see it once and it was forever a part of him.

"If you have your doubts, you could quiz me," he offered with a hint of a smile.

The questions she wanted to pose had nothing to do with his skill or any legally binding statements. Her questions would have been far more intimate in nature.

You're slipping again, she chided herself. *You remember what'll happen if you do. Right now, he doesn't seem to have any flaws, but he will. Disappointment's just right around the corner.*

Her mouth quirking in a fast smile, she dismissed the offer.

"Maybe sometime when we both have nothing else getting in the way," she told him. She could see by his expression that he thought that an odd choice of words. That made two of them. But the undercurrent of electricity that was, even now, humming between them would *definitely* get in the way.

She glanced at the packet on the desk before him.

This was what she had to focus on, nothing else. "So, is it satisfactory?"

It was hard to drag his mind back on the topic. Her perfume swirled around him, causing his thoughts to drift toward things that had nothing to do with his work. It took effort to bank down the grin that the images running through his head coaxed to the foreground.

Taking a breath, he nodded at the papers. He had to remember that this was important. Jonah's future depended on it. "Looks great. You're sure that it'll hold up in court?"

She wondered if nerves had prompted him to ask, or if he actually thought that she was capable of doing a slapdash job. "Yes, I'm sure it'll hold up. You're thinking that Jonah's going to contest it?"

If he were a betting man—and he wasn't—this was what was known as a sure thing.

"Damn straight. The last two weeks Jonah's gone out of his way to let me know how much he's really counting on this money. My guess is that he's got most of it, if not all of it, already accounted for and, most likely, spent." This despite the fact that the trust fund came to a considerable amount.

Jackson was instinctively bracing himself for the outraged assault, alternating with expressions of genuine hurt, all of which would come to pass within a few minutes of Jonah's learning that the original trust fund was being resurrected. This despite the fact that, at bottom, his brother had to know that this was all being done with only his best intentions and welfare in mind.

Since Jackson had just given his approval, she needed to move on to the next step.

Kate rose to her feet, tucking the papers back into her briefcase. There was still enough time to get down to Civic Center Drive where the courthouse was located.

"All right," she said pleasantly, "if there isn't anything you want to change or add, I'll go down to the courthouse to file this. In the meantime, I'll be waiting for Jewel's call. I'll let you know the minute I hear from her."

Jackson nodded, telling himself that looking forward to her phone call shouldn't be at the top of his list of priorities. But even a man completely dedicated to his career had to look forward to something outside the box.

"Fair enough."

Kate began to leave, then stopped. She put her own interpretation to the expression on his face. "Don't worry, Jackson," she assured him. "We'll get whoever's behind all this." Even if Jewel wasn't her friend, she wouldn't have felt any hesitation in assuring him, "Jewel *is* very good at ferreting things out."

He had no doubt of this. Unfortunately, he couldn't offer her the same courtesy. He had a feeling that she might not appreciate the fact that, for one fleeting second, he'd let his mind indulge in a torrid fantasy of her.

"I was just thinking about Jonah," he told her. As he spoke, he switched gears. The rest was easy, because his mind *had* gone in this direction earlier. "Wishing things were different."

This had to be really difficult for Jackson, Kate thought. She knew how she'd feel if there was a schism between Kullen and her. Hurt, devastated and angry. She'd come out of her corner swinging, furious that he would allow something as cold as money come between them.

"Maybe he'll surprise you and still come around," she said encouragingly. "Your brother could be one of those late bloomers. You know the type. Just as you give up on them, they suddenly become mature and responsible in the second half of their lives."

Even though he desperately wanted that to be true, Jackson knew better.

There was a smile in his eyes as he asked, "And do you believe in the Easter Bunny, too?"

There wasn't a second's hesitation on her part. "With all my heart," she told him with the kind of conviction that swayed juries and convinced reluctant participants in civil suits to come around.

Her enthusiasm gave him an iota of hope. The light in her eyes warmed him.

He asked before he could think better of it. "Kate, are you busy tonight?"

When she wasn't in the office burning midnight oil, her evenings were pretty solitary these days. But evenings at home were few and far between. "Well, I'm going to be trying to get hold of Jewel again once I file these papers."

Damn it, why was her pulse jumping around so much. He wasn't asking her out. And even if he did, she really couldn't accept. Lines would wind up getting blurred.

Would? she mocked herself.

Out loud, Kate asked, "Why? What did you have in mind?"

He watched her face as he told her, "Dinner."

"Dinner's always good," she said noncommittally, her mind racing, drawing up a chart of pros and cons. She tried to add weight to the pros even as she knew she should be doing it to the opposite side.

His eyes on hers, Jackson half asked, half suggested, "Have it with me?"

"A working dinner?" It was a straw, but she grasped it. Inclining her head after what was supposed to appear to be a debate, she said, "Sure, why not?"

He didn't want to talk business tonight, at least, he didn't want to *plan* to talk business tonight. "I was thinking more along the lines of—"

Kate cut him short. In order to alleviate her conscience, she had to put the situation in a certain light. "A working dinner." It wasn't a question, it was a statement.

He knew better than to press the point. She'd obviously worded it the way she had for a reason. Whatever it took to get some time alone with her, he was on board.

"A working dinner it is," he echoed. "I'll pick you up—"

Again she contradicted him. "I'll meet you there," she told him. It would be safer that way, less tempting for her to go home with him and *really* sample those lips she'd been looking at so intently.

"We'll meet at the restaurant," he agreed without missing a beat. Then his curiosity got the better of him. "Any particular reason it has to be that way?"

"You're a new client," she reminded him. "Appearances are important."

He wasn't all that into appearances, but he could understand how she might be. Was she worried about the way things looked to the senior members of the firm she worked for, or was she concerned about the way the people who worked for him would perceive things?

"I suppose you're right. Would you like to know which restaurant?" he asked, amused.

"Might make it easier," she allowed, a smile shining in her eyes.

He mentioned the name of a restaurant that prided itself on its variety of meat and potatoes dishes, Swift's. It had been around since way before he'd moved up to San Francisco. In his estimation, it might be interesting to find out if the food there was still as good as he remembered.

"Swift's," she repeated, nodding. Again, she lingered. "And you know, my offer still stands."

He found the reference a little unclear. "What offer's that?"

"I can review the key points of the new trust fund with Jonah." There was a reason for her suggestions. "He might not rage at a woman."

Jackson laughed shortly. "No, ordinarily he wouldn't.

However, since you're also the lawyer who put all this in motion, he just might make an exception."

She wasn't intimidated. She'd been in the middle of battles between outraged family members and survived. "Still, if you find it hard to tell him, that's what I'm here for."

Oh, he could think of a lot of other uses for her that had nothing to do with sensitive older brothers who felt betrayed.

Rousing himself, Jackson said, "I'll see you at six. Unless you hear from your friend earlier."

She nodded. "Six," she repeated, then echoed, "Unless I hear from Jewel."

And with that, Kate forced herself to cross the threshold and finally leave—before she came up with another reason to stay.

Chapter Nine

"If this is a working dinner, exactly what is it that you think you're working?"

The question was directed from Kate to Kate, or at least to the image she saw reflected in her wardrobe door mirror.

The bed behind her looked as if it was sagging under the growing weight of clothes in her hunt for the perfect outfit. So far, she'd found fault with each one she'd tried on.

What she was currently reviewing with a super-critical eye would have never found its way into the work place—unless "work" involved squiring upscale clients who had a large wad of disposable cash to waste by investing it in a single evening's "entertainment." High priced, but still a lady of the evening.

"You don't want Wainwright getting the wrong idea," she told the reflection sternly as she began to snake the outfit she had on down her hips. When it hit the floor, she picked it up and flung the garment onto the pile accumulating on the bed.

Standing in sky-blue lingerie, Kate frowned. At this rate, she would either have to cancel dinner, falling back on the age-old cliché that she had nothing to wear, or she would resort to something her mother used to refer to as a "party dress." The term dated back to when she was eight years old.

"Of course, you could always wrap yourself up in cellophane," she quipped. "Or go naked."

Her palms were damp, she realized. This was ridiculous.

Why was she so nervous? Kate upbraided herself. This wasn't a date, this was just a meeting with a client that happened to take place over cutlery and selected cuts of beef, nothing more. That he happened to be gorgeous, well, that wasn't her fault. That was just an extraneous fact.

Determined to regroup, Kate sank down onto the only tiny corner of her queen-size bed that wasn't littered with discarded clothing.

She knew damn well what was at the bottom of all this. While professionally she had a sharp legal mind coupled with keen instincts, the instincts she had in her private life left a little to be desired.

Who was she kidding? They left a great deal to be desired. A great deal, she emphasized. The same woman who could succinctly read a jury, an opposing counsel and the most poker-faced of judges suddenly had the in-depth instincts of a pet rock when it came to reading a man in her private life. And she had the scars to prove it.

That was the only explanation for not picking up any of Matt's warning signs. Matthew McBain, a dashing, top-flight criminal lawyer who had single-handedly turned sleeping around into an art form. There'd been whispers about his extracurricular activities and, though it hadn't been easy for him, Kullen had come right out and told her what Matt was up to. But she, Pearl Pure-heart, had refused to believe it.

Until the evidence became so overwhelming and damning that only a first-class fool would have denied it. Her heart all but constricting in her chest, she gave in to the inevitable and had handed Matt his walking papers. Rumor had it that he'd found another warm bed before the day was out.

Matt always had a way of bouncing back, she thought cynically. While she didn't bounce so well. After Matt, she had finally admitted that her penchant for picking good-looking scoundrels had to go. The only way she could do that was to turn her back on dating.

It had been a very long time since she'd entertained the idea of socializing. Pretending to be tough as nails and utterly invulnerable, Kate might have fooled others, but, bravado aside, she couldn't fool herself.

And right now, despite everything she vowed to the contrary about this being a professional meeting over dinner, she was scared. Scared of being a fool again. Of leading with something other than her brain and suffering the consequences for it.

Why was she doing this to herself? she silently demanded of the image in the mirror.

"You're not entering a relationship, you're entering a restaurant to have dinner, that's it. End of story," she said out loud, underscoring her agitation. "You're the one making a big deal out of it. Nobody else is even noticing. Now get dressed and get the hell out of here," she ordered tersely.

The woman in the mirror didn't look convinced.

With a sigh, Kate shifted so that she could review— for a second time—the haphazard piles of clothing on the bed. Hopefully, she could find something halfway suitable that didn't require an intimate rendezvous with an iron, something she was less than apt at wielding.

Just as Kate located an outfit that, upon closer re-evaluation, she decided merited a passing grade, she heard her cell phone ring. The sound came from somewhere on the bed—muffled because it was obviously buried beneath layers of fabric.

"Oh God," she muttered. Kate began to toss clothes onto the floor in an effort to find the phone before it stopped ringing.

Maybe it was Jackson, calling to cancel. That would probably be for the best, she told herself. There was no chance of making a tactical error at dinner if there was no dinner.

But even as she pretended that she welcomed this possible turn of events, she felt the tips of each of her fingers turning cold.

There was just no winning.

Just as the song that comprised her ringtone ended, she finally located the phone. Flipping it open, she cried, "Hello, Jackson?" without bothering to glance at the name currently highlighted within the caller-ID screen.

"No, it's Jewel," the melodic voice on the other end of the call said. Her next words carried more than a little interest in them as she asked, "Who's this Jackson?"

"A client." Well, that was the truth, Kate silently said.

"A client, huh?" She knew that tone. Kate grimaced as she reacted to the probing sound. "What else is he, Kate?"

She was in no mood to be probed, even by one of her two best friends. Her guard automatically went up. "What do you mean?" she asked warily.

She could hear the smile in Jewel's voice. "Just that I can't seem to recall you ever being breathless about a 'client' before."

"I was just trying to locate my cell phone before you hung up. It was buried in a pile of—" No, she thought, mentioning the clothes would be a huge mistake. "Never mind." She dismissed the subject. "I'm glad you called me."

"So am I," she said heartily. The next words out of

her mouth told Kate that she wasn't about to back away. "Spill it, Kate."

"Spill what?" she asked, trying to sound innocent. Even to her own ear, it sounded forced. The vote was in. If she'd opted to be an actress when it came time to choose a career, she would have starved to death.

"Come off it, Kate," Jewel told her. "I make my living tailing unfaithful spouses. I've got keen powers of observation—and I know when someone's lying."

"Well, I think you and your 'keen powers of observation' need a little tune-up because you're definitely misfiring." She steered the conversation in another direction. "Anyway, I called you for a reason. I've got a client who needs some discreet investigating done."

Jewel sighed, weary. "Male or female?"

Kate thought of the people she'd seen at Jackson's party. She assumed he would want all of them looked into. "Both."

"Both?" Jewel repeated incredulously. "I think you just lost me." She tried her hand at filling in the blanks. "Your client's married and swings the other way, too?"

In a moment of sudden clarity, Kate went from being confused to realizing what Jewel had to be thinking. "No!" she cried sharply. "He doesn't want to have a spouse tailed. He doesn't have a spouse."

Since most of her surveillance work involved cheating spouses, Jewel was puzzled. "He doesn't?"

"No. He wants to have his tellers' recent dealings looked into." The silence on the other end told Kate that she needed to start at the beginning. "He's a district manager at Republic National Bank and he wants to make sure that no one in one of the branches he oversees has anything out of the ordinary going on." And then she illustrated what she meant. "Large deposits out of the blue, sudden lavish spending sprees, things like that." And then she cinched the deal. She put it in the form of a challenge. Jewel was every bit as competitive as she was. "Are you up to it?"

"An honest-to-goodness investigation that doesn't involve using a telephoto lens to take pictures of sweaty people stealing an hour's worth of passion in a seedy motel? Up to it? Kate, I think I'm going to cry."

Kate laughed. Jewel always had a flair for the dramatic. "I take it that means that you're available?"

"You bet I am," Jewel answered with enthusiasm. "Even if I wasn't available I'd be available. This'll be a breath of fresh air compared to what I've been doing." She savored the thought for half a beat before getting down to the pertinent questions. "What, where, when, who and how?"

"My client can answer the questions better than I can. I'll put you in touch with him," she promised before giving Jewel some of the more basic information. "His name's Jackson Wainwright—"

"Jackson Wainwright." Jewel rolled the name off her tongue, as if sampling it for familiar tastes. "Didn't I just read something in the local paper about him getting into it with a cop over creating a disturbance in public?"

"That's his brother Jonah and a whole other story. Jackson's the good brother. He just transferred down here from the bank's home office in San Francisco to keep tabs on his big brother before Jonah winds up hurting himself—and possibly someone else to boot."

"And where does investigating his employees come in?" Jewel asked. "Or does he want me to keep tabs on his brother, too?"

"No. Wainwright thinks someone's embezzling from one of his branches. He needs his employees' files reviewed, cross-referenced and all that good stuff you know how to do so well."

"Flattery will get you everywhere—and even if it didn't, taking on something new made your argument for you. Tell Wainwright that when I meet with him, I'd like him to give me a list of all the employees' names and social security numbers. That way I can get started right away."

"Sounds good to me," Kate told her. "So when can I set up a meeting? I think he's really anxious to get this thing started."

Jewel didn't even have to think about it. "Anytime he's free. My schedule's flexible. This less-than-sterling husband I've been tailing has already given me enough material to allow his wife to take him to the cleaners twice over. The guy's involved in a threesome even as we speak. I can have this all wrapped up by tonight."

Kate heard her friend sigh again, a little more deeply this time. She knew exactly what Jewel was thinking.

That this kind of thing, being paid to spy on cheating spouses, was beneath her. Jewel only took on these assignments to pay the bills while she waited for something better to come along. Who knew? Maybe this would somehow lead to her doing something else, something more interesting, more challenging and most important of all, something that didn't have her coming home wanting to take two showers to wash the stench of infidelity off her skin.

"Wonderful," Kate declared, knowing that if anyone could get information, it was Jewel. She was tenacious and, just as important, she had access to all sorts of people who could help her. "I'll let Wainwright know at dinner tonight."

The moment the words were out, Kate knew she'd slipped up.

"Dinner, huh?" The two words burst at the seams with all sorts of implications.

"It's a working dinner," Kate was quick to emphasize. But the damage, she knew, was done.

"Uh-huh."

"No, really," Kate insisted. She wanted Jewel to believe her. "I'm reworking the terms of a trust fund for his brother. It's about to expire and Wainwright thought that—"

"You don't have to explain to me, Kate," Jewel assured her. "I'm already in your corner. I'm your friend, remember?"

"And if you want to stay that way and know what's

good for you, you'll find a way to get rid of that smug, I-can-see-through-you tone in your voice."

"Yes, ma'am," Jewel teased. "Consider it done." She heard Jewel laugh, then clear her throat in a futile attempt to cover up the sound. "Call me as soon as you have a date."

The request took Kate completely by surprise. "What?"

"For me to meet Wainwright," Jewel clarified. And then she couldn't resist asking, "Why? What did you think I meant?" she pressed innocently.

Kate glanced at her watch. Oh God, she was going to be late. She was never late. Larger butterflies replaced the mid-size ones already circling in her stomach.

"I've got to go," she announced just before she flipped her phone closed. She had exactly five minutes to find something suitable to wear. Or cancel.

"You look terrific," Jackson said with unabashed appreciation, rising in his chair as the server brought Kate over to his table. He'd begun to think that she had changed her mind at the last minute and opted out. The wait, he now thought as his eyes swept over her, had been well worth it. She wore one of those little black dresses and it accentuated all the right places. His new family lawyer had quite a figure on her.

The compliment made her cheeks warm. She was grateful that the lighting was dim. "Thank you. I was running late so I really didn't get a chance to be very selective. This is just something I grabbed out of the closet and threw on."

He doubted the process had been that hurried. She looked far too good for that. But he saw no reason not to play along. "Haste looks good on you," he told her. "You should do it more often."

Something in his voice tipped her off. Kate's eyes narrowed as she studied his face. "You know I'm lying, don't you?"

"Lying's a bit harsh," he observed. And then he grinned. "But no woman I have ever known just 'throws' clothes on. Young or old, appearance matters to them. Although, I have to admit, if anyone could get away with the rushed, I-don't-give-a-damn look, it's you."

Kate toyed with the edges of her menu. "Thank you—I think."

"It was meant as a compliment," Jackson assured her. And then he sat back in his seat. "So, do you want to order first, or would you rather show me something you have tucked away in your clutch purse that'll qualify this as a 'working' dinner and make you feel better about being here like this?"

Ordinarily, she would have taken offense. But he'd said it so guilelessly that she found herself charmed instead.

"I don't have anything to show you," she admitted. "But I can tell you something instead."

"Okay," he said gamely, resting his hands on the edge of his side of the table. "What?"

"Jewel got back to me." There was no sign of recognition on Jackson's face when she said the name. "My friend who's a private investigator," she clarified.

"Oh, right," he said, remembering. "When can she meet with me?"

"She would be able to clear some time for you this coming Monday in the afternoon if that works for you."

Taking out his smartphone, Jackson opened it and consulted the feature that kept track of his schedule. It was one of the state of the art models that surrendered its information at a touch. He still had to flip through several screens before he found what he was looking for.

Nodding to himself, he flipped the phone closed and returned it to his jacket pocket. "Monday afternoon works out fine for me." He raised his eyes to her. "Say around two?"

"Two," she repeated with a nod. "I'll let Jewel know."

"All right," Jackson said with a nod. "Now that that piece of business is out of the way and we can officially refer to this as a 'working dinner,' what would you like to have for the eating portion of this dinner?" he asked her as he opened his menu.

You, on a plate, garnished with parsley.

Stunned, Kate blinked. The thought had come out of nowhere, ambushing her. Maybe it *had* been too long between men.

Better yet, she decided the next moment, she needed to get back to the gym again. If she exercised for an hour after a full day at work, she would definitely be too tired for these kinds of thoughts. And as an added bonus, if she followed this course of action, she mused, her body would be toned, as well.

Kate slanted a glance at her client. One perfectly shaped eyebrow arched. Clearly, Jackson was waiting for her to make her selection.

"How's the prime rib here?" she asked, glancing at the menu's second page.

"Excellent. Actually, to the best of my recollection, you can't go wrong ordering anything here."

That was good enough for her. Kate closed her menu and placed it on the outer edge of the table. "Then I guess I've made my choice. I like my meat rare."

Their eyes met and held for a moment. The smile on his lips told her that he took her words to mean something else entirely.

Maybe, subconsciously they did, she thought as her icy fingertips made an encore appearance. Right now, she was relieved that Jackson didn't have a reason to take hold of her hand.

Very subtly, she dropped one hand to her lap and then moved it ever so slowly until it was beneath her thigh. She had to warm her hands up somehow and aside from rubbing them against each other as if she meant to start a fire by magic, this was the only way.

Unless she got something hot to wrap her hands around to warm them.

She saw the server approach, ready to take their orders. "Ready to order?" the young woman asked.

"Coffee," Kate declared. "Could you bring me some coffee, please? Oh, and I'd like the prime-rib dinner." She went on to describe the way she wanted it prepared.

When she finished, Jackson repeated, "Coffee?" Usually that was ordered after the meal, not before. "Planning on pulling an all-nighter?" he asked.

She didn't need coffee for that, she thought, casting another glance in his direction. She was already way past being wired enough to remain up all night.

But she couldn't just leave his question hanging there, so she murmured, "You never know."

Chapter Ten

The meal was every bit as good as it had promised to be, more than living up to the restaurant's five-star reputation. The only thing that was better, in Kate's estimation, was the conversation.

When the server returned to clear away their dishes and ask about their choice for dessert, Kate shook her head. "I'd have to wear it, not eat it," she told the young woman.

The latter's eyes shifted to Jackson. "I'm pretty full, too," he told the server, then took a second glance at the back of the menu. The description he was reading more than sold itself. "Although this ice-cream dish sounds really good." Putting down the menu, he appealed to Kate. "Split it with me?"

The mere thought of eating another bite of anything almost made her sides ache. "I really don't think there's any room left in my stomach for even a breath, much less any kind of food."

"There's always room for ice cream," Jackson assured her cheerfully.

"I think you have your commercials mixed-up. That's Jell-O," she told him."

Jackson stood his ground. "Ice cream melts, Jell-O doesn't, at least not as quickly." He leaned over and took her hand in his. "C'mon, Kate," he coaxed. "Be adventurous."

She raised a skeptical eyebrow. "You consider eating ice cream adventurous?"

"In your case, yes," he teased. "You've got to start someplace."

Kate sighed, pushing the menu toward the server. Capitulating, she gave Jackson her terms. "All right, but you eat most of it."

"That's not really the idea behind 'splitting,' but all right." He looked at the server. "One order of Brandy Snowdrift and two spoons."

The woman nodded, tucked the menus under her arm, piled one empty plate on the other, then picked them up and gracefully withdrew.

"She'd better come back quick," Kate commented. "I can feel the food expanding in my stomach, taking up the last of any available space." Humor glinted in her eyes.

He liked talking to her. Liked enjoying simple

things with her. "You don't generally eat dinner, do you?" he guessed.

A good deal of the time, she couldn't get to the gym, or even have time for a brisk walk. She watched her weight by regarding food as fuel, not falling into the trap of thinking of it as a support system.

"My quota's usually about two meals, broken up and scattered throughout the day."

She had a very nice shape, but "really thin" was only a whisper away. "If you weighed any less, you'd probably have to carry rocks in your pockets when our winds kick up around here." The Santa Anas could be fierce at times, pushing SUVs from one lane to another, uprooting trees. How did someone as slender as Kate manage in weather like that?

A moment later, Jackson caught a movement out of the corner of his eye. Turning, he saw the server returning to their table. "Ah, it seems that if you wish for it, it will come," he told Kate.

Kate was about to ask him what he was talking about when the server unobtrusively placed a small pearl-white dish on the table. It was piled high with brandy-soaked French Vanilla ice cream, sumptuously smothered with whipped cream.

Kate's blue eyes widened. "I don't care how much this slides down, it's all got to pool together somewhere."

"I'll take the first spoonful," Jackson volunteered, adding, "It's a dirty job, but someone's got to do it." Slipping the spoonful between his lips, he closed his eyes for a moment, *really* enjoying the taste. Opening his eyes again, he told her, "This is even better than their prime rib."

As far as she was concerned, the two appealed to completely different taste buds. "I find that hard to believe."

"Okay, Doubting Thomasina." Jackson inserted the spoon into the mountain of ice cream, filling it. "See for yourself."

Holding the ice cream laden spoon aloft, he coaxed it to her lips.

The protest that she could feed herself faded away. A surge of heat made its appearance, encompassing her body. After a second, she opened her lips and let Jackson slip the spoon in.

Was it just her, or did that feel insanely sensual? Like something hot and yet cool at the same time had slid up and down her spine.

Was sliding up and down her spine.

"More?" he asked in possibly the sexiest voice she'd ever heard. Her heart was hammering practically loud enough to drown him out.

"More," she murmured, nodding.

Jackson fed her another spoonful, then brought one more to his own lips, his eyes never leaving hers. The temperature in the restaurant went up at least another fifteen degrees.

Possibly more.

She wasn't completely aware of things after that. What seemed like a huge bubble slipped over the two of them, sealing off everything beyond the table. Leaving just the two of them, one slowly depleting dish of ice cream and a single spoon doing double duty.

There was something hopelessly sexy about sharing not just the same desert, but the same spoon, Kate couldn't help thinking. Her entire body tingled with each spoonful.

By the time the ice cream was gone, so was she. Or at least it felt that way.

The server returned then and asked something that sounded like, "Would there be anything more?"

God, he hoped so, Jackson thought. Deceptively simple to the casual eye, the act of eating this ice cream with Kate had electrified him.

The server continued waiting for instructions. Jackson shook his head and handed her his credit card, all without looking away from Kate's face. The moment he heard the server retreat, he asked, "Would you like to come over for a nightcap?"

Her head was already spinning, and that had to be from the residual brandy vapors. While she knew how to handle her liquor, just this once, she wasn't going to take a chance. Someone had changed the ground rules on her when she wasn't looking.

"Right now, for whatever reason, I seem to be intoxicated. I don't think I should have anything more potent than what I've just had."

The beverage didn't matter. The company did. "Coffee, then," he suggested quietly. "Orange juice, diet soda. Whatever quenches your thirst."

It wasn't any of the above that would quench her thirst, Kate thought. It would be the man who was offering them.

Not a good idea.

This was where she begged off, saying something witty—or at the very least, coherent—as she turned him down. "All right," wasn't part of a refusal, and yet, those were the only words that found their way to her all but parched lips.

The server returned with the credit-card receipt. Jackson quickly signed it, then dug into his pocket and placed a large bill on top of the signed receipt. It was the woman's tip, one she wouldn't have to wait around until the slips were cashed at the end of the day—or longer.

"Wow," the girl exclaimed, picking up the bill. All pretense at being poised dropped instantly. "Thanks, mister."

In his position, he didn't get to see the effects a little more money had on people's lives.

"Don't mention it," he told her with a genial smile.

Was this for her benefit, or was he actually this generous? Kate couldn't help wondering.

"Do you always toss money at people?" she asked him once the woman had left.

"Only when the service is good."

Rising, Jackson came around behind her chair and helped her on with her lacey shawl. His fingers skimmed her bare shoulders, whether by accident or design, Kate didn't know. Either way, she was certain that the result would have been the same: giant butterflies dive-bombing into each other as the temperature of her skin rose again.

The cool night breeze hit her the moment they walked out. It was more than welcomed. For form's sake, Kate wrapped the shawl around herself a little tighter. She waited for common sense to materialize along with the bracing breeze.

It didn't.

She took the few steps down to level ground. Maybe second thoughts could mount a defense.

"My car…" Her voice trailed off as she looked at the vehicle, parked to the rear of the lot.

"I can have one of my people come and get it for you."

She looked at him as his words sank in. "You have people?"

"On occasion," he allowed. He wasn't the type who enjoyed being waited on hand and foot. But there was no denying that Rosa was a far superior cook than he could ever be. Or that Elsa could clean rings around him. And for that, he paid them handsomely. "Or I can drive you back here later. Or tomorrow," he amended. Jackson watched her expression. "The choice is yours."

Well, at least he wasn't one to push his advantage. And the advantage was certainly his to push. She wasn't exactly feeling like a bastion of strength at the moment. But she didn't want to seem dependent on him for anything. That included transportation. "I guess I can have a cab bring me back here later."

"There's a host of possibilities," Jackson agreed.

Their eyes held for a very long moment. "Yes," she replied, "I suppose that there are."

Lacing his hand through hers, Jackson gently guided her over to where his vehicle was parked. It was closer than hers, a pristine silver sports model from the Mercedes line. A convertible, currently its top was up. Kate appreciated sleek lines.

"Nice car," she told him as they approached it.

Jackson unlocked the passenger door for her and held it open. "I've always had a weakness for beautiful things," he confessed with a smile.

Again, his eyes met hers.

The man was smooth, Kate thought. Very smooth. And these were just lines, nothing more. Handsome men had lines. But for the small space of time while they hovered in the air between them, she allowed herself to believe those lines.

"This is where you live?" Kate cried incredulously, her mouth all but falling open as they approached his current address. "It looks like something out of Mansions R Us." From where she stood, the building appeared to go on forever. "When do the tours go through? Or are they over for the day?"

The gates parted to admit them as Jackson punched out a code on his remote. "It's not that big," he protested with a laugh.

The driveway was bigger than the house where she'd grown up. "Not compared to a small country, no," she agreed, "but I think Rhode Island could certainly get lost in here."

Rather than house it in the two-storied, ten-car garage, he decided to park his vehicle in the driveway.

Getting out, he rounded the trunk and reached Kate's side just as she opened her door. "I guess it doesn't seem that big to me because I grew up here. This is my parents' house."

Swinging her legs out, Kate took the hand that he offered. There was such a thing as carrying independence too far and she had always liked chivalry.

Given that bit of information, that it was his parents' house, she looked at the building with a slightly different viewpoint. "Does that mean that your brother lives here?" she asked, curious.

He silently blessed his parents for their foresight. "My parents bought Jonah his own place about fourteen years ago." They walked up to the front door and he punched in another set of numbers on the keypad in order to disarm the security code for ninety seconds. "Mother didn't approve of his lifestyle and she knew there was nothing she could do to change him."

"Out of sight, out of mind?" Kate guessed.

Jackson's grim smile told her she was right. "You do what you have to do in order to make it through the day." With that, he opened the door for her and allowed Kate to walk in first.

It was like entering a completely different world. She dealt with wealthy clients all the time and she and her family were far from poor themselves, but this was a step above that. More accurately, several steps above that.

"So you live here alone?" she asked. The very foyer was larger than her first apartment had been. "Do you have to drop breadcrumbs to find your way back to the front door every morning?"

"Haven't had to do that for a while," Jackson responded with as straight a face as he could muster. Taking her hand, he nodded toward the rest of the house. "It doesn't bite," he promised.

Maybe, but the big question is, do you? she silently wondered.

Each step she took just made the house seem bigger to her. It was even larger on the inside than it had promised to be from the outside. "If you speak up, does your voice echo in here?"

"A little," he allowed. His eyes crinkled slightly in fond remembrance. "As a kid, I used to pretend this," he indicated the foyer, "was the gateway to another kingdom. Over there," he pointed to the left where the hall turned a corner, "was where the evil dragon lived. I used to have to slay him every afternoon if I wanted to make it up to my room."

She could visualize him fighting the fiery dragon. Knowing that he had the same kind of fantasies as any little boy made him seem more accessible to her. And just that much more appealing. "An eternally regenerating dragon. Must have been a big challenge for a small boy. How old were you?"

"Thirty. No, I'm kidding," he said quickly when she stared at him. "I was around eight." He grinned and the years seemed to fall away from him like layers of exfoliated skin. "I've never told anyone that before," he confessed.

"Afraid they'd think you were a little off?" she guessed, trying to maintain a light tone. In reality, she was very touched that he'd included her in this stroll through his young life—if, of course, he wasn't just making it all up as he went along. She tried to remind herself that the rich, as the old book title declared, were "different from you and me." Did that include the way they felt about people?

"Something like that," Jackson affirmed. He guided her to the entertainment center, the well lit one, not the one that looked like a mini movie theater. "My mother's imagination only ran toward suspecting my father of having affairs with different women. My father's imagination was taken up by coming up with excuses he could give my mother explaining why he was gone so much. They weren't all that good," he confided. "An eight-year-old kid could see right through them, let alone a highly intelligent woman who had graduated from Wellesley."

She caught her lower lip between her teeth, torn between feeling sorry for Jackson and wanting to just gloss over this because she instinctively knew he wouldn't welcome pity. "Doesn't exactly sound like people whose lives would have made glowing episodes for a family-channel drama."

He nodded. "More like something you'd find on one of the darker cable channels," he agreed.

Jackson knew that his jaded view of marriage and his desire to keep things light in any relationship had their roots in what he'd witnessed as a boy. That compounded with the way he'd felt when Rachel was killed were largely responsible for his no-strings-attached, seemingly carefree bachelor life.

Kate was still taking in her surroundings with no small awe. "And these 'people' you mentioned before, the housekeeper and the cook, are they here now?" Even if they were, she doubted she would be able to see them. This place had so many square feet to it, a person could easily meander around for days without encountering another soul.

Jackson shook his head. "No, they're off for the night. They don't live on the premises."

She looked around again, as if to reassure herself of the privacy. "Then we're alone in this huge place?"

"Completely." His grin was teasing as he drew a little closer to her. "Afraid?"

She wasn't about to lie to him. "Maybe just a little." Kate wasn't talking about the house, she was talking about the two of them. More accurately, about herself and the very strong attraction she felt for Jackson. Chemistry had always been her undoing.

Silent for a moment, he read between her lines. "I can take you back to Swift's parking lot," he offered kindly.

That was when he cinched his argument. Kate turned around to face him.

"Don't you dare," she warned, her purse sliding from her fingertips. The next second she wrapped her arms around his neck. And then, before she could rein herself in, her lips were on his, igniting the smoldering embers that existed between them.

The flash was inevitable. And immediate.

The second their lips met, Kate knew she wasn't going home tonight. Knew that she had been too long without engaging in physical contact with a man, too long without the feel of strong arms around her, sealing her to someone.

Sealing her away from viable thoughts.

All she had to do was remember that this wasn't serious. This was just for pleasure.

Her body began to vibrate inside, sending out shock-waves even as she felt the kiss deepening.

But if she felt that she could exercise any measure of control over the situation by being the one to initiate the first move, she had thought wrong. Because the second she kissed him, she found herself free-falling through time and space and spinning completely out of control, all at the same time.

It was as if someone had deliberately put a match to her face, to her skin and her body. The very essence of what made her who and what she was, was blazing hot—and only getting hotter.

It was crazy and she knew it. This was what she'd been

waiting for her whole life: a man who could effortlessly make her take leave of her senses and spin so far out of control that she was actually in another galaxy. Or at the very least, in a parallel universe.

She wanted to go fast, to grab everything she could and savor it before the moment was gone. Matt—the man she'd stupidly believed she was going to spend the rest of her life with—had made love as if the very house was burning down and he had to attain his pleasure and flee before it was too late. His goal was to climax, then relax, enjoying the sedativelike effect of an afterglow. Matt claimed it calmed him more than an after-dinner drink. Putting her on some kind of equal footing as popular wines, whisky and vodka.

So it was with great surprise that she heard Jackson softly whisper into her hair, "Slow down, Kate. What's your hurry? We have all night."

His very breath danced along her scalp. It only helped to fuel the fire she felt in her belly.

Chapter Eleven

His words ringing in her ears, Kate drew her head back and looked at Jackson. "All night?" she repeated uncertainly.

Was he presuming too much? Jackson backtracked a little. "Unless you have to be somewhere else," he qualified.

Here, Kate thought, the unsettling effect of his lightly skimming hands along her body almost negating her ability to form any lengthy coherent thoughts. *I have to be right here.*

"No," she literally breathed the word out. "I don't have to be anywhere else."

The smile bloomed on his lips at the same time that it slipped into his eyes.

"Good," he murmured.

It felt as if the second half of the word touched her throat a half a beat before his lips did. And there was lightning. Lighting that continued striking in the very same place, over and over again. Making her pulse race and her body prime itself for what she fervently prayed was to come.

Jackson went on taking his time, postponing his own final attainment of rapture to pleasure himself in Kate's reaction. Undressing her an inch at a time, he excited himself even as he watched the very same thing happening to her.

It was a tango and he led her through all the steps carefully, patiently and with barely harnessed control. Kate made him want to abandon it all and just take her to the highest pinnacle, especially when he found his breath growing shorter and shorter, his blood rushing in his veins.

But Jackson was determined to draw this out, for her if not for him. He had an underlying suspicion that whoever had come before him hadn't fully appreciated the woman that Kate was. Had, instead, just regarded her as an interchangeable partner. Someone to be on the receiving end of his largess.

For an unguarded second, he felt angry for her. But anger had no real part in this dance. It was all about pleasure.

The way she responded to his touch, to his slow, deliberate exploration of the curves of her body, to his lips tracing the varied tantalizing tastes of her skin, awakened something inside of him, despite his best efforts to keep it simple. He wanted to try harder to bring her teasingly to the very peaks, drawing back a little so that her own appreciation could be relished to the fullest capacity by them both.

Jackson reveled in her reaction, savoring more, anticipating the next steps beyond his normal scope of involvement. This one was special.

It was like her first time, only much, much better. Her experience wasn't all that plentiful, the men she'd known hardly numbering beyond a handful, but everything she'd ever experienced paled in comparison to what her body enjoyed right at this very moment.

Young, vital, active and energetic, Kate could still hardly catch her breath. The depth and breadth of the sensations that Jackson introduced her to, the ones that he brought out in her body that she, heretofore, had never known existed, were beyond description.

All she knew was that she'd never felt anything this wondrous before.

Don't get carried away.

She heard the little voice in her head, but she didn't obey.

Just as she didn't think that her body could sustain one more burst of raw ecstasy, she felt Jackson provocatively drawing his body up along hers until their interlocking parts were aligned.

Lacing his fingers with hers, pivoting on his elbows,

Jackson looked down into her face, a smile on his own. The very next moment, he was slipping into her, making them one.

The hypnotic expression in his eyes captured her soul. She couldn't have looked away if her life depended on it. And then he began to move. At first slowly, achingly, tantalizingly slow, and then she felt his hips moving against hers, the tempo growing faster and faster. Just the way his tongue had earlier when he'd anointed her and made her climax the first time.

What little breath she had left caught in her throat as Kate hurried to keep up, hurried to reflect the heat he gave off. If she was going to burn up, then so was he.

The need inside of her was almost overwhelming, taking her by storm.

Kate tightened her arms around him, sealing every part of her glistening body to his. The vague thought occurred to her that the heat generated would fuse them together permanently. If this was the end—and how could her heart ever go back to beating normally after this—it was all right with her. What a wonderful way to go.

When the final crest was conquered, Kate dispensed the last of her breath in a huge, satisfied sigh, weakly sinking back into the cushions of the oversize sofa. Her heart continued hammering.

The last of the swirling sensations faded and Jackson's grip around her body loosened ever so slightly. But he didn't withdraw his arms, didn't retreat. He didn't want to. He wanted to hold her to him. Wanted to feel the reassuring beat of her heart against his.

A sense of awe slipped over him. The world hadn't disintegrated despite the fact that these feelings that had been slamming through him were very new to him. Something had happened here. Logically, he needed time to assess. To regroup. And yet…

And yet the desire to do it again gathered strength, albeit not as swiftly as he would have wanted. That didn't change the fact that he *did* just want to hold her. Possibly for the rest of the night, or the rest of his life, whichever came first.

Kate raised her head slightly in order to look him squarely in the face.

He couldn't read her expression.

"Something wrong?" he asked. Had he hurt her? Was she upset? Lovemaking with a new partner was a little like walking across a tightrope. Exhilarating, but exceedingly tricky.

"No, I just wanted to see if you fell asleep." She'd come to expect that as a norm. And he still had his arms around her. If he hadn't fallen asleep, why were they still around her?

Jackson laughed quietly. He was far too wired, despite the exhaustion, to fall asleep any time in the near future.

"Not likely," he told her. And then her question echoed in his brain, generating questions of its own. "Why? Did the last guy you were with fall asleep?" He could see the answer in her eyes. This woman had awakened every fiber of his body. How could her last partner have fallen asleep on her? "Was he narcoleptic?"

"No. Just typical," she replied. "At least, I thought that was typical until just now."

Jackson threaded his fingers through her hair, gently pulling them through in order to caress her cheek. "Any complaints?"

For a second, she thought he meant about her past lovers and she was ready to give him a resounding "yes," but then she understood the focus of his question.

"About this? No. God, no," she said with feeling. She couldn't stop smiling. "On a scale of one to ten, you're fifteen."

He laughed, charmed by her and also, admittedly, a bit bemused. He wasn't sure whether just to enjoy his reaction to her or be worried by it. "I wasn't looking for a rating."

"I know," she answered. "That's what made it so good."

Jackson tried to piece things together. He drew himself up on his elbow, studying her expression. "That last guy, he asked you to rate him?" he asked in disbelief.

"Not in so many words, but…" Her voice drifted off, letting him make his own assumptions.

He drew her to him again. "Well, no offense, but whoever that last clown was, all I can say is that you're damn well better off without him."

Her eyes smiled as she reined in a desire to run her hands along his chest, his face, his body just for the feel of him.

Don't let yourself get carried away. You won't be disappointed if you don't get carried away.

"I know," she said aloud.

The sigh that escaped as she said the two words was pregnant with meaning. "You want to talk about it?" Jackson asked her. "I'm pretty good at listening."

"You probably are," she agreed. "Don't take this the wrong way, but this is just a little bit weird, talking about Matt while I'm lying here, naked, next to you."

Jackson didn't say anything. Instead, he tugged down the crocheted, cream-colored throw and gently covered her with it.

"There," he pronounced, tucking the edge around her. "You're as respectable as a pious grandmother on her way to daily mass." His smile was encouraging. "You can talk now if you want to."

Kate laughed and shook her head at the description. "Not quite that respectable."

"You can still talk," he urged, his voice low, coaxing.

"No point in talking," she answered. "I just wasted thirteen months on someone who turned out not to be worth ten minutes of my time. Why should I bother wasting any more?"

That meant the man in her past was either a cheat, or he had refused to commit. Possibly both since the two were by no means mutually exclusive. Jackson went with the first. "He cheated."

She noticed that Jackson didn't ask, he stated. Since he had, Kate saw no point in framing a denial. "Yes, he did. The worst part of it was it seemed like everyone else knew he was cheating—except for me." She pressed her lips together. Without realizing it, she moved even closer into Jackson as she relived the awakening moment. "Until I caught him."

Jackson winced in sympathy. "You threw him out, I hope."

"That would have been awkward," she confessed. "It was his house. I was the one who walked out. Ran, actually."

He kissed the top of her head. "The effect's the same."

Jackson probably didn't realize how sweet he was, she thought. He didn't have to be like this. She'd already gone to bed with him. Hell, it had been pretty much her idea.

"Yeah," she agreed. "Total devastation."

"I could see why he would be."

"No, I meant—" Kate raised her head to get a better look at his face. "Do you practice these lines, or do they just come to you when you need them?"

Jackson answered her question with an observation. "You're very suspicious."

"I'm sorry if I offended you, Jackson, but the fact is, if you get burned playing with matches, you start to view matches in a whole different light," she told him grimly.

"Matches can also be very useful," he pointed out, his voice low, sensuously seductive as he began to lightly and slowly strum his fingers along the slope of her body. "Once struck, they can give light to the shadows and chase away the dark. They can light a fire that in turn can cook your food, make your coffee, sterilize medical instruments…"

She held up her hands. "Cease. Desist," she requested. "I get it." And then she laughed. "How is it you wound up becoming a banker? With that tongue of yours, you could undoubtedly sell refrigerators to the Eskimos."

Jackson shook his head. "Too hard to lug around the inventory," he deadpanned.

She began to laugh, then stopped. Kate could feel her blood stirring again. Could feel the longing whispering along the perimeter of her senses, asking for an encore. Begging for it, really. Her eyes began to flutter shut. Not from fatigue but from the need to focus completely on the mushrooming source of her desire.

"I really wish you'd stop doing that," she told him with effort.

He was surprised by the intensity of his desire for her. Almost more than the first time.

"Not that I'm not prepared to do—or stop doing— anything you ask, but you do seem to be enjoying it. Exactly why do you want me to stop?" he asked.

Her breath was growing short again. This man had the most incredible effect on her, she thought. "Because I'm finding it difficult to keep my mind on what I'm saying."

His smile was positively wicked. "Why? Where's your mind going?"

She tried to draw in a long breath. It didn't work. And there went her pulse again, breaking records. "You know where my mind's going."

He ran his hand along her cheek, watching as her pupils grew as swiftly as sunflowers. "Tell me," he coaxed, his breath feathering along her skin, making a chill shimmy up and down her spine.

Any second now, she was going to jump on him if he didn't retreat. "You're making me want to make love with you again."

A mischievous grin curved the corners of his mouth. Just for a fleeting moment, she thought she saw something in his eyes. But it was gone before she could identify it.

"Done." Jackson slipped his hand underneath the throw.

The second he touched her, she was his for the taking—and glad of it. Signs of his wanting her were quite evident. Kate's eyes widened as she looked at him in surprise. "You can do that?"

Amusement wove its way through his response. "I'm not quite sure I know what you mean by 'that,'" he confessed.

Embarrassed, she made the best of it. "Make love more than once."

Jackson didn't answer her immediately. That was because he was processing the full extent of her words and her amazement. And then it all sank in.

"Oh, honey," he told her, wondering just what kind of Neanderthals she'd previously stumbled across, "you've been with the wrong men."

With one snap of his wrist, the crocheted throw was history, thrown back over the rear of the sofa. She wasn't going to be needing it, Jackson reasoned. He was the one who would be keeping her warm. He fully intended to show Kate just how much and how long he could continue to do "that" for a second time.

"Well, it's about time."

It was all Kate could do to swallow the scream that came barreling up her throat to her lips. Up until a second ago, she'd been trying to enter her office without calling any attention to herself and thus to the fact that she was coming in a full hour later than she was supposed to.

The greeting told her that she hadn't succeeded.

Swinging around, a fabricated excuse at the ready, Kate saw that the greeting had come from her brother who had made himself at home on the sofa in her office. For some reason, he was waiting for her. Why?

She realized that the palm of her hand was spread out protectively over her chest. Self-conscious, she dropped it.

"Look, I know I'm late, but that's no excuse for you to give me a heart attack," she accused. Forgoing her usual routine, she dropped her purse to the floor and sank down into her chair. She must have slept all of about twelve minutes last night and she was beat. She hadn't felt like this since college.

"Your late, less than dramatic entrance wasn't what I was referring to by saying it's about time," Kullen told her. "I'm assuming, since you look as if you literally ran into your clothes in order to get here before noon, that you finally hooked up with someone. *That's* what I thought was about time," he explained. The grin on his lips threatened to take over his entire face and then some. "Good for you, Katie."

She gritted her teeth at the nickname, but let that go for now. She believed in picking her battles and this one wasn't it.

"That's what you're basing your assumption on?" she asked incredulously, hoping that a display of enough bravado would make him back away. "That I look as if I dressed fast?"

"That," he allowed, "and the fact that I swung by your place last night and you weren't home. In case you're interested, it was after eleven."

"Eleven o'clock?" she echoed. "What if I was asleep?"

Kullen eyed her, his meaning crystal clear as he asked, "Were you?"

She should have remembered who she was dealing with. The Playboy of the Western World. Kate rolled her eyes. "This isn't the time or place to discuss our private lives."

"Evasion." Satisfied, Kullen nodded. "I have my answer."

She didn't like him reading her like a book. A woman was entitled to have secrets. "You do not," Kate insisted.

"Sure I do." He laughed. "If it was no, you would have said so. Instead, you evaded. Point made, case closed."

He wanted to play it this way, fine. "No," Kate declared, crossing her arms before her chest.

"Too late," Kullen crowed. "I fed you your line. Doesn't count." He was on the edge of his seat now, his hands clutching the armrests. There was glee in his eyes as he asked, "Do I know him?"

"You may not know anyone in a couple of minutes," she threatened. "Don't forget, I was the one Uncle Charlie told all his war stories to and taught how to sneak up on a man and silently render him dead."

Kullen did not seem the least bit intimidated. Rising, he made his way to the door.

"Spunky," he pronounced, nodding his head as he gave her one last look over. "Must have been one hell of a night. Good for you," he repeated just before closing the door behind him.

And just in time to avoid the box of tissues she threw at him. They hit the door and fell to the ground with a thud.

The moment her brother was gone, a wide grin spread out over Kate's lips. Bits and pieces of last night came back to her.

It had been one *hell* of a night, weaving its way into the early morning and taking her—and Jackson—with it.

George Bernard Shaw's fictitious Eliza Doolittle, once she found herself the subject of the famous musical, might have wanted to "dance all night" but as for her, Kate far more preferred the seductive dancing between the sheets that she and Jackson enjoyed into the wee hours of the morning and beyond.

Kate found that no matter how hard she tried to look serious, she just couldn't stop smiling. After a beat, she surrendered herself to the feeling.

Chapter Twelve

"Oh honey, where did you find him, is he taken and can I have him?"

The words emerged like rapid-fire gunshots from Jewel's mouth as she spoke to Kate on her cell phone. She made the call the moment her two-o'clock appointment with Jackson Wainwright was over and she was back in her car.

On her way back to the office from the courthouse where she'd been for the last two hours, taking a deposition, Kate pulled over to the side of the road outside a residential area the moment she heard her phone ring. She was certain it was Jewel and she wanted to hear what her friend had to say, not the least of which was her opinion of Jackson.

Kate addressed Jewel's questions in order. "He's one of Kullen's overflows. Not that I know of. And you'll have to ask Jackson that."

Although she had known Jewel all of her life and had shared almost everything with her and Nikki, Kate wasn't about to mention the fact that she had slept with the man. At least not for a while. Since both Nikki and Jewel were well aware of her last boyfriend debacle, she knew Jewel would attach undue importance to Jackson.

Suppressing a sigh, Kate did her best to sound businesslike. "Do you think you can help him?" she pressed, wanting to get Jewel to focus on something else other than Jackson's looks and availability.

Jewel had the kind of instincts that made her a natural for her chosen career.

"Shouldn't be a problem," she assured Kate. "He gave me the names of all the employees at the branch in question. In this handy-dandy age of the so-called privacy act, all the information is out there in cyberspace, waiting to be plucked. Finding out if one of those people is living beyond their means, or is suddenly writing big checks that need covering shouldn't be much of a challenge."

And then Kate could hear the smile creeping into Jewel's voice. "The bigger question is, can you get Kullen to send some 'overflow' in my direction? Kate?" Jewel queried when there was no response. "You still there?"

She didn't answer Jewel immediately because she

was weighing the pros and cons of her next move. "Yes, I'm still here." Oh, hell, Jewel would find out sooner or later—knowing Jewel, it would be sooner. "Look, you might as well know that my mother had a hand in sending Jackson to Kullen."

"Why would she have sent him to Kullen?" Jewel asked, confused.

"Actually," Kate clarified, "it was a mix-up. My mother, obviously a frustrated Mata Hari with no available outlet and no country to spy for, steered Jackson to my firm and told him to ask for K. Manetti."

Now it made sense. "And they connected him with Kullen."

"Exactly."

"So how did you get him?"

"You know my mother, she's never been very good at being patient—"

Jewel commiserated. "Gives her a lot in common with my mother."

"Anyway, from what I've pieced together, Mother must have called Kullen to ask if I'd gotten any new clients. When she found out that he was about to see Jackson, she undoubtedly ordered him to pass the man to me."

She heard Jewel laugh. "Gotta say that's better than getting a gift certificate to one of the stores in the mall."

For a private investigator, Jewel was certainly missing the obvious. "Jewel, she's meddling."

"She's a mother," Jewel pointed out. "It's what they

do. At least this one's a hunk—" And then she came to a skidding halt. "Wait a minute, then he is taken."

That was one hell of a conclusion Jewel had just jumped to. More importantly, she didn't want Jewel even to hint at that assumption the next time she spoke to Jackson.

"Not by me," Kate said with emphasis.

If she'd hoped that Jewel would drop the subject, she should have known better. "You said that a little too fast, Kate. *Is* something going on between you two?"

Kate evaded the question. "He's a client, Jewel. He needed a trust fund reinstituted."

The chuckle she heard on the other end of the line told her that Jewel wasn't about to be diverted. "Did you reinstitute anything else for him?"

"What does that even mean?" Kate wanted to know.

Jewel sighed. "If I have to explain that to you, Manetti, I guess the answer's no."

She did *not* want to continue in this vein. "Just get him the answers he needs."

"Did you ever consider that maybe the answer he needs is the word *yes?*" Jewel asked.

Dear God, Jewel was worse than her mother, Kate thought. "This conversation is getting too convoluted for me. I've got to go." Kate terminated the call before Jewel could say another thing.

Kate sat on the side of the road for a moment longer, frowning as she stared off into space. She'd spent quite possibly the best night of her entire life with the most incredible lover she'd ever encountered. Even so, she was afraid to let her thoughts go any further. Love was the easiest word in the world to say. Meaning it, well, that was a completely different matter.

Kate knew she couldn't allow her thoughts to drift into unchaperoned corners. She was afraid of the disappointment that she'd encountered time and time again. She had no desire to go that route again.

If she just kept everything in perspective, it'd be all right. *She'd* be all right, Kate silently insisted.

Meanwhile, she had work to do and a set of papers to deliver to Jackson.

The thought of seeing Jackson made her work faster.

Jackson was quiet for a long time as he read through the papers that he had already familiarized himself with when she'd brought them to him in rough-draft form. Everything seemed pretty ironclad.

Jonah wasn't going to be happy. That was a given. But at least his brother would be taken care of and he wouldn't wind up penniless—which was where he'd be, sooner than later, if he were allowed to spend his money unchecked. This trust fund was a way to rein him in—and keep him solvent.

Jackson put the papers down and raised his eyes to look at Kate. She hadn't been out of his thoughts for a single moment since she'd left his place two days ago. Two days and the longing for her had grown more intense, not less. He was unnerved because it made him feel so alive.

Remember Rachel and what that did to you.

He was in big trouble, he concluded. So why did he feel like smiling all the time?

"Perfect," he told Kate.

"I'm glad you're happy with it. Everything is as we'd discussed."

He wasn't talking about the documents. He was talking about her. But that was something, he knew, that was better left unexplained. Instead, he turned his attention to something else that had been on his mind.

"I'm thinking of having a will drawn up."

"A will?" she asked. Was he being responsible, or was there something more to this? Had he seen a doctor lately who had given him unwanted news?

"I know it sounds gruesome," Jackson continued, "talking about a will, but if anything happens to me, I don't want my money tied up in some incredibly lengthy legal battle."

She should have realized, Kate told herself, relieved. Jackson was just being Jackson, thinking ahead. "Understandable—and for the record, it's not gruesome," she told him. "It's very clear-sighted of you. A lot of people put off having a will drawn up because they think that once they do, it's like sending out an open invitation to God to be smitten."

The corners of his mouth curved as he looked at her. "Oh, I think I'm already that."

Kate felt a blush heating her cheeks and creeping up her neck. She struggled to bank it down.

"I'm using the word in the biblical sense," she told him.

The smile turned into an almost boyish grin. "Wasn't that what we were doing the other night, getting to know each other in the biblical sense?"

She didn't stand a fighting chance against the blush. Veins of heat shot up all through her body now. And all because he'd stood up and walked around behind her, brushing up against her.

"You're making it very hard for me to concentrate and keep my mind on business, Jackson."

Hearing that pleased him. "Good, then you're not tired of me yet."

He *had* to be kidding, she thought. The man had a mouth like sin and a positively wicked technique. If they lived to be a thousand, she knew *she* wouldn't be the one to ever grow tired of him. It would be the reverse, something she didn't want to think about even though it was inevitable. And sooner rather than later. She'd been through it enough to have that point driven home. Drop-dead gorgeous men liked to make the rounds.

Kate took a deep breath to steady her shredding nerves. She was a professional, a lawyer. Time to act like one.

"I take it you'll want the will to emulate the terms of the trust fund." And then she elaborated what she meant. "Your brother doesn't get the principle, just a monthly allowance."

Jackson nodded. That was it exactly. "You read my mind."

She laughed softly. "Not exactly a superhuman feat in this case."

"What about now?" he asked, threading his arms around her waist and gently pressing a kiss to the side of her neck.

A squadron of goose bumps suddenly let loose all along her body. "Now you're making me want to do something that'll get me in trouble," she breathed. "We're working," she reminded him. She was being paid an hourly rate to be his lawyer, not his lover, although right at this moment, she would have gladly opted for the latter over the former.

"I don't call this work."

The feel of his warm breath along her neck made her crazy. God, but he made her want to rip off her clothes—and his.

Kate let out a shaky breath, fighting to keep from melting, from having her eyes drift closed. "Jackson…"

"I want to see you tonight," he told her, turning her around to face him. "Someone gave me tickets to that new musical that's previewing here before going to Broadway. How do you feel about people bursting into song in the middle of a conversation?"

Funny he should mention that, she thought. It was something that she felt like doing herself right now. "I happen to like musicals," she told him in as calm a voice as she could muster.

He seemed pleased. "Good, then it's a date. I'll pick you up at five-thirty."

That seemed rather early. Most plays began at around seven-thirty or eight. "Five-thirty?"

He nodded. "It's at the Ahmanson Theater in L.A. The play starts at seven-thirty, but if I remember correctly, L.A. traffic is like an all-out miniature preview of what hell is like."

She nodded. If anything, that was an understatement. "It's gotten worse."

"I can't make it any earlier than five-thirty," he told her, glancing at the schedule on his desk calendar. "I've got a meeting at three that can't be postponed. It's going to be touch and go as it is."

Although she liked the idea of seeing a play with him, in the final analysis, it really didn't matter. Kate would have been equally happy stuck in traffic with him.

But even to hint at something like that, she was certain, would make the man not just back away but run for the hills as fast as he could possibly manage. She would enjoy this while it lasted.

Kate glanced at her watch. She'd already lingered longer than she should have. "I have to get going."

"So do I." He paused for a moment, looking at her. "Would it be out of order if a client kissed his lawyer goodbye?"

The correct answer was yes. She knew that. Basic client-lawyer relations 101. But "yes" wasn't the answer she gave him. "It wouldn't be out of order, just not customary."

"A rebel, beautiful *and* intelligent. Terrific combination," he told her just before he kissed her.

She could have easily sunk into the kiss. Easily lost

herself as well as all track of time. But that, she knew, would lead to other things and they were, after all, in his office. Any minute, someone could knock and want to come in. How fast could he get dressed? she couldn't help wondering before she dismissed the whole thought as grossly unprofessional.

"I'll see you tonight," she murmured as she broke away.

Walking out, she began to count the minutes until five-thirty.

"Jonah, I can't just give you that kind of money." Jackson hated arguing with his brother. He and Kate were on their way out to dinner and he'd just stopped at his house to drop off the report that her friend had compiled for him.

Jonah had rung the doorbell just as they were about to leave again. Kate had exchanged a few words with his brother, who responded in single syllable answers, and then excused herself to give them privacy.

The moment she was out of the room, Jonah had pounced, asking him for close to fifty thousand dollars. Now.

Jonah glared now, his resentment swiftly becoming a viable entity. "You wouldn't have to if you and your lawyer girlfriend hadn't blindsided me and somehow stuck my money back into the trust fund. It's *my* money," he insisted.

They had already been through this two weeks ago, when Jackson had told his brother that he wouldn't be coming into the money he'd anticipated on his birthday.

Jonah had gone pale, then alternated between shouting and pleading, all to no avail. Running out steam, feeling wounded, he'd finally stormed out.

This visit had started out a little more civil, but it wasn't about to stay that way.

"I did it for your own good," Jackson insisted wearily.

Jonah glared at him. "Is that what you're going to say at the funeral? That you did it for my own good?" he shouted. "Don't you get it?" he demanded, vacillating between anger and fear. "I owe these guys big-time. And trust me, these are not the kind of guys you go around stiffing."

"Then why did you go into debt to them?" Jackson wanted to know.

"I wasn't planning on owing them money," Jonah cried. "I was planning on winning." Desperate, he tried to approach the problem from another angle. "Look, you're one of the guys in charge of that big bank you work for, aren't you?"

Jackson eyed his brother with mounting disbelief. "I can't just take the money to cover your debts."

"Not 'take,'" Jonah coaxed, *"borrow."* He flashed the same brilliant smile that had so often won over their mother.

It was wasted on Jackson. "Oh, and how are you planning on paying it back?"

The smile faded a little, giving in to the desperation in his eyes. "I'm good for it."

God but he felt tired, Jackson thought. All he wanted

to do was go out and eat with Kate, steal a little time alone, not fight the same losing battle over and over again with his brother.

"Jonah, you're not even good for coffee. Just how do you think you can pay back the kind of money you're asking me for?"

"I'm working on it," Jonah snapped defensively.

"Now there's a novel concept—work," Jackson noted sarcastically. "You could try working at a job for a change."

"Look, man, it's not my fault I'm blocked. The inspiration just won't come. I'm trying to loosen up," he insisted. "That's why I'm gambling. Gambling relaxes me."

"Oh, really?" Jackson shot back. "Well, you certainly don't look very relaxed to me."

"That's because you're giving me grief," Jonah retorted. "You stole my money, now you don't have the decency to float me a loan."

"There's no such thing as a loan to you, Jonah. This is me you're talking to. Jackson. The brother who's 'loaned' you a hell of a lot of money over the years. It's like pitching money into a black hole. Well, it's over. I'm not going to do it anymore," Jackson declared with finality. It wasn't a threat, it was a statement.

When all else failed, Jonah resorted to his old stand-by. Guilt. "Well, if these guys catch up with me, I guess all of your troubles'll be solved, won't they?" he prophesized.

Kate couldn't take it anymore. She'd been in the other room, politely waiting for the two brothers to hash things out. But their voices, especially Jonah's, carried and she could hear everything. The more she listened to the exchange, the more difficult it was for her to remain silent. This was escalating quickly. She had to say something before she exploded.

When she finally walked back into the living room, the conversation was so heated, neither brother even noticed her. Clearing her throat, Kate raised her voice. "Excuse me."

The expression on Jackson's face appeared strained as he turned in her direction. He was very nearly at the end of his rope. "Not now, Kate."

There was no way she was going to be swept away. "Yes, now."

A cynical smile twisted Jonah's mouth. "Is this where I get the benefit of your wisdom, too?"

Kate moved forward, putting herself between the two brothers as she faced Jonah. "Well, you certainly need to get someone's because apparently you don't have any of your own right now. If Jackson covers this latest debt of yours, what are you going to do?"

"Drop to my knees and worship you?" It ended in a question, as if he wanted to see if he'd guessed the response she was after.

"Wrong," she said flatly. "You're going to take the money to pay off the debt—"

Jonah looked at her as if she was mentally feeble. "Well, yeah, sure—"

Kate held up her hand to stop him from saying

anything more. "Let me finish. You're going to pay off the debt, *then* you're going into rehab."

His immediate reaction was anger. "I don't have a drug problem anymore."

"No, you have a gambling problem now," Jackson said, joining forces with Kate. "You just substitute one addiction for another."

"You are going to get yourself under control," Kate continued as if there'd been no interruption from either of them. "And you're going to paint again."

"You think I haven't tried to paint?" Jonah said, obviously offended.

"Yes, I think you haven't tried to paint," Kate replied calmly. "But you're going to. Okay, to review and continue, Jackson pays off your debt, you go into rehab, get yourself straightened out, join Gamblers Anonymous when you get out and every single day, you are going to work at getting your gift back. No excuses," she underscored.

Jackson looked at Kate with renewed appreciation and not a little admiration.

"And if I refuse to go to rehab?" Jonah challenged belligerently.

This time, it was Jackson who fielded the challenge. "I won't give you the money."

Jonah turned on him. "You'd let me get killed?" he asked hotly.

"I hope it won't come to that," Jackson said in a calmer voice than he'd used earlier. It belied the inner turmoil he actually felt. "I'm hoping that somewhere in there is still a piece of the brother I used to idolize."

Stumped, his back to the wall, Jonah shoved his hands into his pockets. His eyes shifted from Jackson to Kate and back again. "There's no other way?"

Kate shook her head. "No other way." Her voice was firm.

Jonah let out a shaky breath. "I guess I have no choice, then." He raised his eyes and glanced at Kate. "I've done this before, you know. Gone to rehab. This is the end result," he told her bitterly, indicating himself.

"This time it'll stick," Kate said with conviction.

Jonah laughed shortly. "You're some kind of cock-eyed optimist, aren't you?"

"Part-time," she allowed.

Jackson looked at his brother. "I liked the other women you dated better. They were bimbos who didn't interfere."

"I'm the family lawyer," Kate reminded him. "It's my job to see that things run smoothly for you."

Jonah sighed. "I could bully Mortie," he said with a degree of nostalgia.

A hint of a smile played along her lips. "I'm not Mortie."

"Yeah, I know." Shoulders slumped, Jonah gave in. "Okay, we'll give your way a try."

Kate smiled. "Glad to hear it."

Jackson said nothing, but she felt his approval as he slipped his arm around her waist. She assumed that wasn't something that he'd ever done with Mortie.

Chapter Thirteen

Jackson leaned against the door he had just closed and watched Kate for a long moment.

"Do you have any idea how incredibly sexy you look to me right now?" he asked. Jonah had just left, a check in his pocket. That had been Kate's doing, as had Jonah's promise to enter rehab. If his brother reneged, the check would immediately be rendered null and void.

The woman was definitely a ray of sunshine in his life—in both their lives, Jackson silently amended. He was beginning to forget what life was like without her.

"No, actually, I don't." And then Kate smiled that inviting smile of hers. "But I'm hoping that you'll tell me."

He crossed to her, a wicked smile on his lips. "Better yet, I can show you."

"Better yet, you can show me," she agreed, her smile entering her eyes.

Jackson laced his fingers through hers and then began to gently guide her toward the stairs. "You know, I never would have thought that a bossy woman could turn me on." He glanced over his shoulder and winked at her. "I was wrong."

Kate glanced over *her* shoulder toward the front door. "Aren't we going in the wrong direction?" she asked more seriously.

He stopped for a moment. "You want to make love in the driveway?" he teased.

"No," Kate laughed, "but didn't you say you had reservations for dinner at The Belle of the Mississippi?" The exceedingly popular restaurant was usually heavily booked.

"I did. I do, but I can get new ones," he assured her. He was coaxing her up the stairs, taking one step at a time because he was going up backward in order to face her. "I know people."

"And if these 'people' you know say, 'Sorry, Jack, we're all booked up'?" she teased.

"First of all, nobody calls me Jack. And second—" Jackson lifted his shoulders in a careless, *que sera sera* gesture. "Worse comes to worst, there are leftovers in the refrigerator. Rosa made a pot roast yesterday," he told her.

"I *love* pot roast." Kate said it with such feeling he suspected that she wasn't really referring to the pot roast.

Jackson could understand her hesitation in making a real declaration about her feelings. He felt that way himself. He had feelings for her. He *knew* he had feelings for her. The hesitation occurred when it came to giving *voice* to those feelings. This was hard for him. He'd been in this place before and it had all blown up on him. He needed to go slow. Make certain that it was what it was and not something that would pass. Until he was sure, the less said, the better.

Or, what if he said it to her, told her he cared about her, and she only echoed the words back out of pity, or because it was too awkward not to?

Or, worse yet, what if she *didn't* echo the words? What if there was only silence hanging between them like some huge, unmanageable, blazing albatross?

"Yeah, me, too," he told her. "I love roast beef, too."

And for now, that would have to do. Until, at the very least, he had some kind of indication from her that it was all right to give voice to his feelings because she felt the same way.

The moment he drew Kate up to the landing, Jackson began undressing her. She'd thought that he would wait until they got into his bedroom. It thrilled her that she was wrong.

Laughing as he slid the zipper down her back, she twisted out of range. "What are you doing?"

"Utilizing my time efficiently," he told her with a straight face.

The next moment, he swept her up into his arms and pressed his lips to hers, ending any further discussion, relevant or otherwise.

"You're sure?"

Sitting at his desk several weeks later, Jackson looked at the report Jewel had just brought to him. Kate was in the office, as well, but for the moment, he was only aware of the ambivalent feelings racing through him.

How was this possible? The person behind the missing funds was the last person he would have suspected.

That was why it was possible. Because the thief looks so innocent.

"I'm sure," Jewel assured him.

Technically, her work had been concluded when she finished compiling the financial scan of the branch tellers' accounts and their current spending histories. But, being Jewel, she had gotten engrossed in the problem and gone the extra mile.

More accurately, the extra *several* miles. She'd continued conducting the investigation to satisfy her own curiosity because she'd come across suspicious dealings that had piqued her interest. And she had been right.

Jackson glanced up at her after reading the second page. "It says here that Elena Ortiz was turned down by

Lincoln Mutual for her request for a loan of fifteen thousand dollars."

Jewel nodded and summarized the rest of her report. "Elena goes to this fast-food restaurant on the corner of Alton and Jeffrey every Friday at one o'clock. She gets a soda and sits down at one of the tables. In a few minutes, this man with the blackest hair I've ever seen joins her. They exchange a few words, then they exchange an envelope. She passes it to him," Jewel added before he could ask. "And then she gets up and leaves. She never finishes her soda."

Jackson gave voice to the first thing that came to his mind. "Blackmail?"

Jewel nodded. She glanced in Kate's direction before saying, "That would be my guess. I tailed him and copied down his license. The car's a rental. According to the rental agent, he always rents a different car on Fridays and he always pays cash."

"Didn't he have to show them his driver's license before he got the car?" Kate asked.

"He did and they had a copy on file. I flirted my way into getting a copy of my own." She looked at Jackson as she reached into her purse. "Want to see it?"

Jackson was already putting his hand out. "Absolutely." Jewel pulled the sheet out of her purse and gave it to him. Jackson read the name out loud. "Diego de la Vega."

Kate recognized the name instantly and frowned. "Looks like we're hunting Zorro." When Jackson looked at her, puzzled, she elaborated, "That was Zorro's Clark

Kent name. His secret identity," she explained, then sighed, frustrated. "Looks like this guy has a sense of humor."

"Maybe," Jackson allowed, his face grim. How far did this extend? Or was it just a two-character drama? "But I don't. Not when it has to do with stealing from the bank." He looked up at Jewel as he opened the middle drawer of his desk. "You've done a great job, Jewel. I really appreciate it." Taking out his personal checkbook, Jackson wrote down the fee they'd agreed on plus a bonus for her extra time and work. Finished, he tore the check out of his book and held it out to her. "Why don't you give me a few of your cards? I'll hand them out to people who might find themselves in need of a good private investigator with initiative."

"I'd appreciate that," Jewel told him, taking several cards out of her purse. They did an exchange, he taking the cards and she the check. When she glanced at the sum, she stopped. "You wrote it for too much."

"No," he contradicted, "I wrote it for the right amount." He smiled broadly at her. Because of her, he had his thief. The bank was safe again. "Thank you."

"Thank *you*," Jewel emphasized. Crossing to the door, she stopped for a second and looked at Kate. "I'll call you," she promised. The next moment, she was gone.

Kate nodded in response, but her mind wasn't on Jewel. It was on Jackson's teller and what was about to happen next. Her empathy instantly went out to the petite woman she'd met at the catered party Jackson had thrown. It felt like a million years ago now.

"Talk to her, Jackson," she urged.

His expression darkened ever so slightly. "Oh, I fully intend to."

She caught his tone instantly. "No, *talk* to her," she emphasized. "Find out what's going on. Give her a chance to explain," she implored.

He shifted to face her and she saw the contained anger. She knew him. Jackson felt responsible. He was in charge and anything that went wrong was on him. "I'll tell you what's going on. She's stealing."

"But there's probably a reason."

He shook his head, shutting her out. "Not my problem."

He began to walk toward the door and she put herself in his path.

"Technically," Kate underscored. "But this isn't just a bank teller," she insisted. "This is a *person*. Someone who doesn't look as if she'd steal unless it was a last resort."

His expression was impassive. "And you can tell all this by looking at her?"

She heard the unavoidable touch of sarcasm in his voice, but told herself not to take it personally. He was just upset.

"I have good instincts, at least in some areas," she amended, thinking of her penchant to be attracted to the wrong men until now—she hoped. "Call Elena in," she urged. "Talk to her." And then she thought of a better idea. "Or let me talk to her."

"Can't do that," he told her flatly. "You're my lawyer, not the bank's."

He had a point, but she wasn't giving up. "Then let me at least sit in."

What possible justification did she have for that? "As what, my conscience?"

Kate inclined her head. "If you wish." But she did have a better negotiating chip to play. "Think of it this way—if she decides to shout 'harassment,' I can be your witness to the contrary."

That at least was a valid argument, although he had a feeling that wasn't why Kate wanted to be there. She could temper him if need be. Did she believe he was going to roast the girl on a spit? "You won't give up, will you? Are you always this tenacious?"

"It's my job," she told him with a small smile. "Speaking of which, how's Jonah coming along?"

For the first time in a long time, Jackson felt he had reason to entertain a little hope. "He's scheduled to come out of rehab this weekend. I'm picking him up and having him stay with me for a while." He wanted to be there in case Jonah began to backslide. The moment he framed the thought, Jackson realized that he had used the words "in case," not "when." It felt good. "I'm trying not to be too optimistic, but he sounds really good," he confided.

"Be optimistic," Kate encouraged. "Show Jonah that you're rooting for him to succeed."

"Isn't that putting too much pressure on him? Jonah doesn't do well under pressure."

Kate naturally gravitated to the positive side. "Better that than his feeling that you're just waiting for him to mess up."

Jackson thought it over for a moment. "Maybe you're right," he allowed.

"Of course I'm right," Kate assured him cheerfully. "I'm your lawyer." She glanced toward the door and envisioned the tellers on the other side. "Now call Elena in."

Jackson put his hand on the doorknob, his mouth set grimly. Kate was glad he was letting her stay. She had a feeling she might be needed for moral support if nothing else.

Elena Ortiz was barely five feet tall and looked as if the only way she could come close to weighing a hundred pounds was if she had a friend stand on the scale with her. Her shoulder-length blue-black hair was as straight as a razor and she wore it up, as if to appear older than her twenty-two years.

Her brown eyes were huge as she walked into Jackson's office. She seemed fragile, as if she was ready to break in two at any moment.

"You wanted to see me, Mr. Wainwright?" she asked in a small voice.

"Yes, I did, Elena." Jackson gesture to the chair in front of his desk. "Please, sit down." He turned toward Kate and made the introduction. "This is my lawyer, Kate Manetti."

"Your lawyer?" Elena echoed nervously. She extended her hand to Kate only after the latter had put hers out first.

"I asked to sit in," Kate explained, instinctively knowing that the young woman would immediately think the worst and become frightened. Kate couldn't help feeling sorry for her. As if to confirm her suspicions, Elena's hand was icy cold when she shook it.

Jackson began his interview quietly. "Elena, are you happy here?"

Kate noted that a smattering of relief filtered into the young woman's eyes. Poor thing obviously thought this was an evaluation. Or at least she was praying for that.

"Oh yes, very happy," Elena responded with enthusiasm.

Jackson nodded and immediately got down to the heart of the matter. "Then if you are so happy here, why are you stealing from the bank?"

Elena's eyes widened and her face paled visibly. She looked as if she would pass out at any second.

"What? No, no, I'm not stealing," she cried. Distress vibrated in every syllable.

"There's no point in denying it, Elena," he said calmly. "I've had you followed." Her distress mounted prodigiously, every thought reflected in her face. "Who is the man you give envelopes to every Friday?"

Instead of answering, Elena covered her face with her hands and began to cry.

Kate couldn't maintain her silence. "If you tell us, we can help you," she interjected. She exchanged a glance with Jackson. He didn't seem all that pleased with her light touch. But she sincerely felt that coaxing instead of threatening would work best with the frightened young teller. "Elena, you have to talk to us."

After a beat, Elena raised her head. Tears streamed down her face. "If I don't give him the money, he will kill her."

"Kill who?" Jackson instantly demanded.

"My sister. Lupe." Every word seemed an effort for her. Sobs wove themselves through every breath she took. "I told her to wait. *Begged* her to wait. I said that I would send for her when I had the money." Her eyes shifted to Kate, appealing to her maternal instincts. "But she is seventeen and impatient." Elena pressed her lips together before going on. "She paid this organization to bring her into California."

"A coyote?" Kate guessed. Coyotes were cold-blooded men who charged a great deal of money to guide desperate people across the border in the dead of night. A good many never completed the journey. The desert was strewn with the bodies of former coyote clients.

But Elena shook her head. "No, he is part of some organization," she insisted. "They smuggle things." Then, to illustrate what she meant, she said, "Drugs, people. Prostitutes," she added in a lower, more horrified voice. It was obvious that this last term held special meaning for her. "That is my sister's choice. If I cannot pay them, she can let them kill her or become a prostitute. Either way, she is dead," Elena told them grimly.

"How much did they ask for?" Jackson asked. He had a tally of how much had gone missing over the last two months, ever since he'd taken over. He wanted to see if it matched what Elena was going to say.

"Fifteen thousand dollars. Fifteen thousand more," she corrected. "Lupe already gave them five thousand. I don't know where she got that money from," Elena confessed, despair vibrating in her voice. She was a woman on the verge of a breakdown, not knowing where to turn, what to do and needing to remain strong. It was obviously tearing her apart.

She raised her eyes to Jackson, pleaded. "I did not want to do this, Mr. Wainwright. I did not want to steal from the bank. I have always been a good person. But I have no money. I tried to borrow it, but I could not get a loan and she is my only sister—" Her voice broke as more sobs burst from her throat.

Unable to keep her distance any longer, Kate rose and came over to the young girl. She put her arms around Elena and held her.

"We'll get your sister back safe," she promised, stroking Elena's head. "And don't worry about the money. It will be put back."

"I will go to jail?" she asked fearfully, clearly hoping against hope that the answer would be no.

Kate didn't intend to add to the young woman's anguish right now. Elena was going through enough as it was. Kate could easily see how fragile her state of mind was.

"Something can be worked out." The moment she made the promise, she could feel Jackson looking at her. She'd succeeded in making him angry. That wasn't her intention, but she had a conscience to follow. A conscience that wanted to alleviate suffering, not inflict it.

"Right now," Kate continued, "we need to find a way to get your sister back and put this Diego de la Vega and his little organization out of business."

"I would be so grateful," Elena cried.

"Elena, would you mind returning to your station?" Jackson politely requested. "I need to have a few words with my lawyer."

Elena was instantly on her feet. "Yes, of course, Mr. Wainwright. And thank you, thank you both!" she cried with feeling.

The moment the door was closed, Jackson turned to Kate. She held up her hand before he could say anything. "I know what you're going to say."

"No," he contradicted, "I don't think you do." He wasn't angry about her usurping his position, or even that she'd made assumptions about what he was going to do. Right now, it was Kate's safety that troubled him. She was the type to sail into the eye of the storm, not away from it. "This isn't some episode from *Law & Order,* Kate," he told her. "These men think nothing of killing people. You can't deal with them. You can't try to reason with them. It's too dangerous."

Kate let out a huge sigh. "And I just got my cape out of the cleaners, too," she lamented mournfully. And then her expression instantly lightened. "Of course I know that these are dangerous men. All the more reason to get them off the street and into custody. I doubt that

Elena's sister is the first person they've held hostage for the purposes of extortion. And she's probably not the only one right now, either. But don't worry, I'm not about to go riding into their camp on a white horse.

"I do, however, know a few of the people working at the Immigration and Customs Enforcement department. After Elena pays this vermin the rest of the fifteen thousand and gets her sister back intact, the ICE agents will come charging in and arrest these bastards. Everything will be aboveboard and nice and legal." His expression told her he was far from convinced. Was he worried about her, or worried about the bank's reputation? That thought bothered her, but she couldn't tell. "Are you angry because I told her she wasn't going to jail?"

"That's not our decision to make," he told her.

"Sure it is. Because it's up to you to decide whether or not to call the police in about the embezzlement. You could say that it was just a record keeping error. A glitch in the software. That happens more times than you could believe."

"In other words, lie and cover up the theft." He set his mouth firmly.

"In other words, give someone a second chance," Kate corrected. "Elena was caught between the proverbial rock and hard place, Jackson. What if it was your sister those slime bags had? What if it was you who didn't have any money to save her?"

"I would have found another way."

She shrugged. "You're smarter."

"Now you're trying to flatter me into sweeping this under the rug?"

She smiled up at him brightly, the soul of innocence. "Is it working?"

"Call your friends at ICE. They're going to be in position to take this guy down the next time Elena has an envelope for him."

Mentally crossing her fingers, Kate took out her cell phone to make the call. But not before she kissed Jackson. Long and hard.

"What was that for?" he asked, recovering.

"Call it a retainer—for later," she told him with a wink as she began to tap out the phone number she needed on her cell phone.

Chapter Fourteen

The moment Jackson gave her the go-ahead sign, Kate did just that.

She lost no time in getting in contact with Agent Howard Brady. She'd gone to school with Howard, who had majored in languages, and had been friends with his wife, Shelly, before the two had ever gotten married. After college, they'd kept in touch via newsy Christmas cards, which was how she'd initially discovered that Howard now held down a fairly responsible position at ICE.

Meeting with Howard for lunch, Kate carefully sounded him out. She constructed a so-called hypothetical scenario in order to ask him what the department's stand was on Elena's situation. She knew, less than halfway through her narrative, that Howard was aware that the situation wasn't really hypothetical, but he played along anyway and heard her out.

With some cajoling, she finally managed to obtain a pledge of leniency from him. She had him put it in writing. They used the back of a napkin. When the "pledge" was safely in her purse, Kate gave him the rest of the details. She told Howard that as far as she could ascertain, the man holding Elena's sister hostage was either the head of an illegal human smuggling ring, or at the very least, one of the ring's main components.

"I can get him on a platter for you," she promised enthusiastically. "But only after he gives up where her sister's being held. If you grab him up before that, the girl is certain to be killed by one of his henchmen."

Howard was silent for a moment as he ate. "And this banking district manager, Wainwright," he finally said, "he can back up your story?"

"Every last syllable."

Finished, Howard pushed away his plate. "Okay, you have a deal."

Elena looked fearful when she was introduced to Howard, and even more so when Howard informed her that she would have to be wired for her next meeting with her sister's kidnapper. But with no other recourse open to her, she finally agreed. There was no other way to rescue Lupe.

Kate wanted to go with Elena for the last meet, but she

knew that if they deviated from the set formula, the man would turn and run and then Lupe would be lost to them.

"I will be fine," Elena told her, her voice quaking. Squaring her slim shoulders, she went into the fast-food restaurant alone.

A few minutes later, unable to just sit and wait, Kate entered, as well. She mingled with the customers who, at that time of day, were a cross section of blue- and white-collar workers, all intent on grabbing a quick, inexpensive bite for lunch.

The plan was that since this was the last payment, Elena told the former coyote that she had the envelope hidden in a safe place. She would give him the location once she was taken to where her sister was being kept hostage.

Grumbling, the trafficker cursed her several times over, then finally agreed to her terms. He told her that he would bring her to her sister.

And then his eyes drew together malevolently as he added, "But if you are lying about the money, it will be the last lie you ever tell—and the last breath your sister will ever take." With that, he grabbed Elena by the arm, yanked her out of her seat and roughly guided her out of the establishment.

Kate's heart had almost stopped when she glimpsed the look on the man's face as he passed her. Counting to five, she followed them outside, pretending to walk to her car.

Instead, she hurried over to a van with the logo of a local utility company slapped on its side. Howard and his partner were maintaining surveillance from inside the vehicle.

Glancing over to make sure that she wasn't being observed, Kate knocked once and got in. Howard's partner was already starting up the van.

"Let's go," Kate cried.

Howard looked at her, stunned. "You're a civilian. We can't take you with us," he protested.

"Think again," she'd retorted. "I'm responsible for that girl being in this position. You can't let her out of your sight and I'm not getting out. Now go!" Kate ordered.

Muttering words in a language she didn't understand, Howard tapped his partner on the shoulder. They were on the road a moment later.

In the end, it all turned out better than they could have hoped for, Kate thought, relieved beyond words. For a while there, the outcome had been touch and go. Once or twice, she'd come very close to jumping out of her skin. But when the smoke cleared, figuratively and otherwise, Howard and his partner had an impressive bust on their hands. Almost thirty girls had been rescued from a very grim fate. Best of all, Elena was reunited with her sister. It was a tearful reunion.

Because Kate as well as Howard had pulled a certain amount of strings, Lupe was going to be allowed to remain in the country in exchange for her testimony against the people who had smuggled her across the border. In addition, Elena would testify about the blackmail. There was no doubt that the traffickers were going away for a very long time.

Kate caught herself singing as she drove back to Jackson's office. Things couldn't have gone better, she thought happily. Jackson had wanted to come with them, but there was a scheduled meeting he couldn't postpone. She was now going to his office to fill him in.

At first, she didn't think anything was wrong. His meeting over, Jackson listened to her narrative attentively. He was a little quieter than she'd become accustomed to, but he did have a great deal to take in.

His expression darkened noticeably when she came to the part about getting into the ICE van and going with the agents as they followed Elena and the trafficker.

He hadn't heard her right. She couldn't be saying what he thought she was saying. The woman was smarter than that. "You did what?" Jackson demanded.

She was so wrapped up in her narrative that, for a moment, Kate didn't understand what it was that Jackson asked. Or why he sounded so angry. In the time they'd been together, she'd never seen that expression on his face before.

"I'm afraid I don't—" Kate didn't get a chance to finish.

"But you *did,* that's just it." Didn't she understand the kind of risk she'd taken? A completely *unnecessary* risk. The woman could have been killed.

A cold chill went down his spine, reminiscent of what he'd experienced when he'd learned about Rachel being run over in the crosswalk. Damn it, he couldn't go through this again, couldn't stand having his gut ripped out again.

"You're not supposed to go running down the street after human traffickers, especially the kind who would just as soon kill you as look at you."

Kate resented his tone. Resented, too, that he made her sound like some kind of empty-headed nitwit. "I didn't go 'running down the street' after him," she corrected tersely, "I was in a car."

One wrong move and she could have become just another memory. What the hell was wrong with her? And what the hell was wrong with him, opening himself up to unspeakable pain again?

"Like that's supposed to make a difference?" he snapped. "You shouldn't have done it. You should leave things like that up to the professionals."

Maybe the man still didn't know what made her tick, Kate thought. Maybe she didn't mean enough to Jackson for him to understand the kind of person she was.

Was he going to be another prince who turned out to be a frog? Had she been right all along, to be afraid that he'd be like all the rest? Oh God, her heart began to hurt.

Damn it, Mom, I told you this was going to happen. Why couldn't you just have left things alone? Why did you have to bring him into my life?

"I don't do standing on the sidelines too well," she ground out.

"Maybe you should learn." If anything had happened to her, he wouldn't have been able to live with himself. Wouldn't have been able to recover. If not for him, there was no way she would have gotten involved in this.

"Standing on the sidelines is your calling, not mine." The accusation came out before she could stop it.

Jackson's eyes narrowed. "What's that supposed to mean?"

She was *not* about to explain something he already knew. "I think it's self-explanatory." Her voice was cool in sharp contrast to the anger she was feeling.

He wasn't in the mood for games. It was all he could do to keep from shouting. "If it was, I wouldn't be asking, would I?"

Kate blew out an angry breath. Maybe he *was* that dense. "How long have we been seeing each other?"

Jackson felt as if he'd just been dropped in the middle of the forest in the dark—blindfolded. He knew the answer—almost seven weeks—but it had no bearing on her reckless act. "What the hell does that have anything to do with what we're talking about?"

Oh God, it was worse than she thought. He was completely oblivious, wasn't he? Or, more likely, he didn't care. How, after all she'd been through, could she have willingly walked into the same situation again? Even idiots learned from their mistakes.

"Everything," she retorted. "Where do you get off, telling me what I can and can't do?"

"I'm the guy you've been sleeping with." *The guy*

who loves you too much to survive having anything happen to you. He'd been right to try to protect himself. This wasn't going to work.

She was right. He *didn't* care. He just wanted to control her. No matter how much she wanted him to love her as she was, it wouldn't change anything. She was an idiot for ever putting her guard down. An idiot for loving him. It was final. Another prince had turned out to be a frog.

"Is that all that you are?" she challenged.

This whole conversation was getting convoluted and ridiculous. If he had to explain things to her, maybe there was nothing to explain, at least, not as far as she was concerned.

Exasperated, he cried, "What do you want from me?"

"Apparently more than you can give." She grabbed her purse and pushed the strap on her shoulder. "I have to go." She didn't wait for him to say anything. Instead, she crossed straight to the door. "I told Elena and her sister I'd be right back. I just thought you'd want to hear what happened."

"Kate—"

But she didn't stop, didn't turn around. Reaching the door, Kate marched out without another word. It took all she had not to slam the door in her wake. That would have been childish. It would have felt good, but it would have been childish. And the pain she felt didn't belong to a child.

She forced herself not to run, but it didn't matter.

Jackson didn't come after her, didn't call out. Didn't make any attempt at all to bring her back.

The pain in her heart grew more intense as she went on walking.

Jackson stared at the door that Kate had just closed in her wake. He was angry and utterly at a loss as to what had just taken place here. Until she'd walked in, he'd spent the entire morning feeling as if his whole life was being precariously balanced on the edge of a razor-sharp saber. More than once he'd upbraided himself for letting Kate go along with the agents and Elena for the last exchange. So many things could have happened to her. The last half hour before Kate arrived in his office, his head had been filled with recriminations as he cursed himself for not stopping her. Or, since she was determined to go, for not going with her, meeting or no meeting. But he had been needed here and in a moment of weakness, he'd kept his protest to himself.

But there were so many variables that went into comprising the scenario, so many things that could have gone horribly wrong. Even now, it made him sick to his stomach just to contemplate them.

Because the thought of losing Kate was too awful to think about. It was Rachel all over again. He'd barely survived that. He couldn't, *wouldn't* go through that again.

Even so, he could feel himself wavering. Jackson was torn between going after her to tell her everything that was in his heart—and just pulling back and cutting his losses. Reclaiming himself before he was hopelessly and forever lost.

The decision was taken out of his hands the next moment as his phone rang. Picking up the receiver, he heard the bank's vice president on the other end. His presence was needed at the Aliso Viejo branch.

His private life was being temporarily preempted by his professional one.

"I'll be right there," he promised.

Maybe this was for the best. Maybe he'd just been saved.

Kate did her best to remain in perpetual motion. She kept busy by helping Elena and Lupe square things away, smoothing out every possible feather that had been ruffled. She called in every favor she could to insure that the sisters would not ultimately be deported. In the interim, she worked with each to insure that their testimony against the traffickers went smoothly.

Even though he hadn't tried to contact her since she'd walked out of his office, Jackson was a man of his word. Kate was confident that Elena would not be charged with embezzlement. Kate believed her when Elena tearfully swore she would be grateful for the rest of her life.

"Just don't get into any more trouble," Kate warned affectionately. "And if you need anything at all, be sure to come to me." She'd pressed one of her business cards into Elena's hand. Elena held it against her heart as she waved goodbye when Kate drove off.

With that settled, Kate tried to fill every waking moment with work. She volunteered to pick up the slack at the firm, coming in early, staying late and helping the other lawyers put together briefs.

But eventually, she had to go home.

Home to an emptiness that slashed at her as painfully as any knife making contact with her skin.

She put the TV on the minute she walked in the door and kept it on until she left for work the following morning in an attempt to slay the silence.

She couldn't sleep, couldn't really eat.

This was ten times worse than when she'd fallen for Matt, she thought. She didn't know she could hurt this much. There was no place she could go to hide from the pain.

Jackson's sudden reversal of behavior had come without warning. Up until then, there hadn't been so much as a hint of this other side of him. All along, he'd been perfect. His sense of responsibility to his brother, his way of operating at work, the displays of charity, all of it shouted of a man who was decent and kind and good. Granted she'd gradually grown more and more concerned when he hadn't said anything about his feelings for her, but she'd tried to be patient, because everything good was worth waiting for.

But she'd gone on waiting. If he did have any deep feelings for her, he kept them to himself.

It was Jackson's presumption that he could order her around without verbalizing the least sort of affection for her that finally set her off.

Damn it, she thought, staring at the ceiling in her bedroom, watching shadows ebb and flow, when was she going to learn? Hadn't she been the one to profess that she was tired of kissing princes only to discover that they were actually frogs? How many times did that have to happen before she finally got the message?

The message that not everyone was meant to wind up with someone for life? Her lot fell in with that number, not with the starry-eyed, happily-ever-after crowd. The sooner she accepted that, the better.

Kate buried her face in her pillow and cried.

She'd been like this for two weeks now, feeling tears gather in her eyes for the third time that night as she wandered about her house like a ghost, unable to find a place for herself. She'd rebuffed all her mother's attempts to get in contact with her, claiming she was incredibly busy. She was *not* about to talk to her mother about Jackson and that was all her mother was interested in discussing.

If she didn't get more than ten minutes' worth of sleep soon, Kate thought miserably, she was going to fall apart.

Maybe she needed a prescription for sleeping pills. She really didn't want to have to go that route, but if she kept up like this, she was going to wind up driving up the wrong freeway ramp or something equally as disastrous. The idea of hurting someone else by accident chilled her heart.

First thing tomorrow, she decided, she was going to call her doctor and—

Was that the doorbell?

Finding herself in the kitchen, Kate stopped and listened. That *was* the doorbell.

She glanced at the clock on her microwave. It was almost eleven. Who'd be calling her no—

Oh God, no. Not now. She shut her eyes, searching desperately for strength. It was her mother, she just knew it. Since she couldn't get her on the phone, her mother had come in person.

Go away, Mom.

The doorbell rang again, longer this time. And then again for a fourth time. Kate sighed. She knew her mother. The woman was quiet but as tenacious as a pit bull when she wanted to be. Her mother would be leaning on that doorbell all night until she opened the door.

"All right, all right, I'm coming," Kate shouted as she made her way to the living room. "Did it ever occur to you that I might be sleeping?" she demanded, looking through the peephole.

"Were you?"

The voice on the other side of the door was a great deal deeper than her mother's. And with good reason. It wasn't her mother.

It was Jackson.

"Your mother sent over chicken soup," he announced, holding a container aloft so that she could see it through the peephole.

That got her to open the door. "You went to see my mother?" Kate demanded incredulously. He didn't bother calling her, but he was socializing with her mother?

"Since you didn't come with an instruction manual, I needed to talk to someone wiser than me because I needed help." He offered her the container. "She thinks you can use this."

Taking the container, Kate put it aside on the hall table. "Help you what?" she asked, vacillating between wanting to throw her arms around him and wanting to strangle him. The internal tug of war caused her to remain where she was.

"Can I come in?" he asked.

Kate sighed, opening the door wider. "Sure," she said with no emotion. "Come in." She shut the door, struggling to ignore the fact that her heart had just launched into double time. "Help you what?" she repeated.

God, but he had missed her, Jackson thought. Missed the sight of her, the scent of her. He hadn't lied. At a loss, he'd sought out her mother to enlist her help as to how to get the woman he loved back. Because he'd made a huge mistake, thinking he could just shut down and walk away. It was too late for that. He loved her and he wanted her in his life. Five minutes, five years, five decades, it didn't matter, he'd take what he could get.

Right now, he wanted to touch her, to hold her, but this needed to be resolved first. "Help to find a way to apologize."

"Do you have any idea what you're apologizing for?" *He's here, don't put him through the Spanish Inquisition.* God, that was her mother's voice in her head. She'd officially gone over the edge.

The corners of his mouth curved just a little. "For pushing you away because I was afraid of how I'd feel, losing you."

"Maybe it's because I haven't had any sleep, but that doesn't make any sense," she told him.

"Yes, that's why I went to your mother. Because I can't do this."

She *really* wasn't following him. "Do what?"

"Face another day without you in it."

Oh God. She wasn't going to melt, she chastised. Not yet, not until she heard him tell her what she needed to hear. "That's a good start. Go on," she encouraged.

"I don't have a speech—"

"I wasn't asking for one," she told him softly, then gave him a small hint. "I was asking you to tell me what you were feeling."

That was easy enough. The hollowness was killing him. "Empty. Lost. Lonely."

"And?" she coaxed.

"And if you don't come back, I don't know what I'm liable to do."

"Because?"

Frustration momentarily got the better of him, but Theresa had counseled him to be honest. To let his heart do the talking. So he did. "When you told me that you'd gone with those agents, all I could think of was that I could have lost you just like that, in the blink of an eye. That would have killed me." He took a breath. "I really, really miss you, Kate."

"And?" she coaxed.

Jackson blew out a breath. "And I love you?"

She pressed her lips together to hold back a grin. "Is that a question?"

"It's anything you want it to be," he said in exasperation. "But no, it's not a question. No matter what you feel, I love you." He took a breath. "That's not the easiest phrase for me to say, Kate," he admitted.

"Yes, I know." She looked at him for a long moment. He'd "shown her his." It was time she did the same. "And as for what I feel—" She closed her eyes, seeking courage. Wondering if she was going to regret this. But love *did* take courage. And maybe, just maybe, a prince frog was really a frog prince after all. "I love you."

His arms went around her immediately, but she put her hands against his chest, holding him back. There were more questions she needed to resolve. "Do you really mean it, or are you just saying it because you think that's what I want to hear?"

"Yes. And yes. Yes, I really mean it and yes, I said it because I thought that was what you wanted to hear."

"Otherwise you wouldn't say it?" she questioned.

He feathered his fingers through her hair. He'd *really* missed touching her. "I was raised to believe that actions spoke louder than words."

"It's a toss up," she acknowledged. "Actions are good, but so are words."

He wanted to prove his point. "That guy you were engaged to, did he say he loved you?"

"Yes," she admitted reluctantly. "He did."

"And did he? Did he love you? Did he love you the way you deserved to be loved?" Jackson pressed, then answered his own question. "I don't think so because, if he did, he wouldn't have cheated on you."

Okay, he had a point, but that still didn't mean she didn't want to hear Jackson tell her he loved her. A woman needed words. "Look, maybe—"

"Me," Jackson went on doggedly, "I will never cheat on you. Because it's wrong to cheat on the mother of your children."

Kate held up her hand. "Hold it. How did I go from being the person you couldn't say 'I love you' to to the mother of your children?" she asked.

"Gradually, I hope." His eyes smiled into hers. "I want us to have a couple of years together first before we become a family."

Had he just glossed over a marriage proposal? "Aren't you taking a lot for granted here?"

"Nope, not a thing." Jackson paused to take out a small black velvet box from his pocket. He'd shown it to her mother first, to prove that he was serious before he took her into his confidence and asked for help. Opening the box, he offered the heart-shaped diamond to her. "Katherine Colleen Manetti, will you make me—

and your mother—the two happiest people on the face of the earth?"

"And how can I do that?" Kate found she could hardly squeeze out the words. Her throat had all but closed on her.

"Tell me you'll marry me."

She took a deep breath in an attempt to steady her pulse. "Not bad," she murmured. "Still needs work, but you're getting there."

His eyes held hers. "Does that mean yes?"

She let him put the ring on her finger, then wove her arms around his neck. Tonight, she thought, she was going to sleep like a baby. Eventually.

"What do you think?" she countered.

His arms closed around her. "I think if I don't kiss you, I'm going to explode."

"Can't have—"

His mouth came down on hers and she didn't get a chance to get to the last word. But it was okay. Some things were just understood between two people who loved each other.

* * * * *

A sneaky peek at next month...

Cherish™

ROMANCE TO MELT THE HEART EVERY TIME

My wish list for next month's titles...

In stores from 19th August 2011:

❑ Once Upon a Time in Tarrula – Jennie Adams

& To Wed a Rancher – Myrna Mackenzie

❑ Little Cowgirl Needs a Mum – Patricia Thayer

& Once Upon a Proposal – Allison Leigh

❑ Through the Sheriff's Eyes – Janice Kay Johnson

In stores from 2nd September 2011:

❑ McFarlane's Perfect Bride – Christine Rimmer

& Taming the Montana Millionaire – Teresa Southwick

❑ From Daredevil to Devoted Daddy – Barbara McMahon

Available at WHSmith, Tesco, Asda, Eason, Amazon and Apple

Just can't wait?

0811/23

MILLS & BOON
Book Club
2 Free Books!

Get your free books now at
www.millsandboon.co.uk/freebookoffer

Or fill in the form below and post it back to us

THE MILLS & BOON® BOOK CLUB™—HERE'S HOW IT WORKS: Accepting your free books places you under no obligation to buy anything. You may keep the books and return the despatch note marked 'Cancel'. If we do not hear from you, about a month later we'll send you 5 brand-new stories from the Cherish™ series, including two 2-in-1 books priced at £5.30 each, and a single book priced at £3.30. There is no extra charge for post and packaging. You may cancel at any time, otherwise we will send you 5 stories a month which you may purchase or return to us—the choice is yours. *Terms and prices subject to change without notice. Offer valid in UK only. Applicants must be 18 or over. Offer expires 28th February 2012. **For full terms and conditions, please go to www.millsandboon.co.uk/termsandconditions**

Mrs/Miss/Ms/Mr (please circle)
_____

First Name
_____

Surname
_____

Address
_____

_____
                                          Postcode
_____

E-mail
_____

Send this completed page to: Mills & Boon Book Club, Free Book Offer, FREEPOST NAT 10298, Richmond, Surrey, TW9 1BR

Find out more at
www.millsandboon.co.uk/freebookoffer

Visit us Online

0611/S1ZEE

The World of Mills & Boon®

There's a Mills & Boon® series that's perfect for you. We publish ten series and with new titles every month, you never have to wait long for your favourite to come along.

Blaze® Scorching hot, sexy reads

By Request Relive the romance with the best of the best

Cherish™ Romance to melt the heart every time

Desire™ Passionate and dramatic love stories

Visit us Online Browse our books before you buy online at **www.millsandboon.co.uk**